THE HARP

BRIANA SASSO

For all those who help make our world a better place

In Loving Memory

Mr. and Mrs. Joseph and Laura Feraco

Author's Note

The world is not a perfect place, and I am not a perfect person. We are all human, and humans make mistakes. We sometimes make poor choices, driven by selfish desires. We put ourselves and our loved ones first, and for this we cannot fault one another. However, our society is crumbling, and those crumbs may individually be the size of a grain of sand, but remember that those grains of sand are combined to make the glass at which we throw stones, both literally and figuratively. We have to do better. We have to be better. We have to support one another in these difficult and challenging times.

It is not easy, and it does not happen all at once. But I challenge each one of you to rekindle the camaraderie that we have lost as a nation. Get to know your neighbors again. Stand up for those who are being put down, but in a positive way. Violence and anger are not solutions to any problem. We have to stop fueling the fire of hatred and wrong-doing. Instead, channel that energy into making positive changes through acts of kindness.

What we stand to gain in peaceful unity is great, but the devastation that we will feel as a *human* race will be much greater if we continue on this destructive path.

Be kind to one another.

-B

The wise woman builds her house,
but with her own hands the foolish one tears hers down.
Proverbs 14:11

Learn from yesterday,
live for today,
hope for tomorrow.
Albert Einstein

Everything that I thought I knew about my life, about the world around me, was inaccurate. Not truly an outright lie, but also not the outright truth.

I couldn't have predicted that at sixteen my life would completely change, for better or for worse. That challenging everything I knew wasn't an act of rebellion, but a natural and inevitably necessary reaction. That the cliché, "Things are not always as they seem," would prove more true to life than I could have ever imagined. My entire life was to be upended and I wasn't ready. But are we ever really ready for the responsibilities that come with entering adulthood?

I've always thought the expression "being raised" was peculiar for describing the aging of children. Because the truth is, are we really being elevated? Are we really attaining new heights beyond the obvious physical growth? When we reach adulthood, every thought we ever had and every piece of knowledge we held about life is utterly shattered and destroyed. We learn that princesses are not saved by handsome princes every day and that money does not magically appear in your pockets. Relationships are no longer sown over bicycles and freeze-pops. Problems cannot be solved with Band-aids and snuggling. It is no one's cruel choice to cut these illusions off at the knees. Sooner or later, it just simply cannot be avoided.

Truly, I don't see why anyone would choose to be raised if there was a choice. I would have preferred to stay all skinned knees and early bedtimes. I'd rather the monsters that I thought were under my bed rather than the human monsters that are all too real.

No, it definitely should not be called raised.

I've tried to think of what it *should* be called, but I can never really put my finger on it. Being prepared? Now that would never work either because no one can claim to be prepared for what you learn when you come of age. Being forced into adulthood? No, that wouldn't really do either since it will happen without external encouragement. There's simply nothing that fits to describe the experience of growing up.

Maybe our families are just gardeners. They water and feed us and keep us safe from predators as long as they can, and when we're fully grown, they put their hands up in surrender and slowly back away, hoping for the best. Hoping that we will bask in the sun and become fruitful, that a deep frost will not shorten our season.

Or maybe they should call it being awakened, because truly life is as if a dream during childhood. We are pleasantly lulled through our days and then suddenly we are jolted awake, disoriented and confused, and we wake up crying and sweating and calling for our mothers, except this time no one comes running.

Yes, that's exactly what it was like for me during my awakening.

My life had changed so quickly. There were so many burning questions that I wanted to ask, and I didn't know who to trust. It was like a giant tower of blocks were crashing down all around me, every step that I took more dangerous than the last.

I didn't understand any of it at first, even when I thought that I did. The world was no longer simple, no longer straightforward or clear cut. I had to decide for myself instead of someone else deciding for me. I was terrified of making the wrong decisions and making a mess of everything. It wasn't just me who would be affected but the entire world, and that's a hefty burden to carry when you've just been awakened.

When I look back on my life and think about the decisions that I have made, I wonder what the present would be like if I had chosen differently. All of the "what ifs" careen through my mind like intergalactic ships racing past each other faster than the speed of light. I still question whether I did the right thing, whether humankind was better or worse off because of me. Given the chance, would I go back and change it all?

It is a daily mental struggle that I face, given that I *could* change it all if I chose.

But I'm stopped by the fear that the outcome could be far worse. I know what the present looks like now because I'm living it. I don't know what the present would look like if I had made different decisions. And who am I to decide, to change everyone's lives, when they may be perfectly happy the way that they are now?

So I fight the urge. I convince myself that I have done what I was destined to do; no more and no less. This is the path that my story was meant to follow as the Harp.

I woke up to the vibration of my bed, my signal that it was time to end my slumber. My eyes popped open automatically. I'd never been one to struggle with coming out of a state of sleep. I did not yawn or stretch or throw the covers over my head. Instead, I sat up and swung my legs over the side of the bed. Then I stood up and walked over to the control panel on the wall of my sleeping quarters.

I briefly pondered what color to wear that day and then selected blue. While I waited, I could hear the familiar clicks and shuffling of the selections being made behind the wall where all of my clothing, shoes, and accessories were stored. I picked at my nail until a barely audible *beep* signaled that my clothes were ready to be chosen.

I pushed the smooth, white button of the shirt drawer. It opened, displaying three options for tops and the underclothes that matched. I removed a white button-down with light blue polka-dots and a white tank top and bra. Then the drawer closed and I could hear the rejected choices being sorted back into their rightful places.

I continued on like that with the other drawers, selecting pants, shoes, and accessories to match the shirt I'd selected. When I had considered my options and made selections, all of the other pieces got returned to their places as well, and the control panel thanked me and then fell silent.

I got dressed quickly after this and moved on to the bathroom to complete my morning routine. After using the toilet I sat down on another seat, and another control panel appeared before my eyes, a hologram this time. That morning I was feeling simple, so I selected a high bun from the hairstyles menu and light makeup from the cosmetic menu. Then I lied down with my neck on the raised rest and gathered my hair above me. I felt around for the start key, closed my eyes, and pushed it.

In a matter of three minutes, my hair and makeup were done for me. The combs on mechanical arms smoothed my hair quickly and gathered it into a high ponytail, securing it into a bun within seconds. The touch was so light that I could barely feel the brushes sweep across my face and eyelids, the expert arms having memorized the contours of my face long ago. When all was said and done, an ever-so-light *ping* sounded and my head and face were released, free to sit up again.

There was never any room for error as the modules had been so perfected, but out of habit I momentarily appraised myself in the mirror to be sure.

Approving as always, I walked down the hall to the eating quarters where my mother and father were already dressed smartly for the day.

"Good morning," my parents greeted me in unison. Every morning they somehow managed to say it at exactly the same moment.

"Good morning," I said. "You both look nice today. It's a shame you have to cover up with lab coats."

My parents were both physicists. They wore white coats as soon as they stepped into the research sector, so I never could understand why they bothered to get so dressed up every day. No one would notice if they wore comfortable clothes.

"Oh, if I was so worried about fashion I would be working in the design sector! You know me. Brains, not beauty," replied my mother ironically, because she was actually extremely beautiful, with her shiny blond hair and flawless skin. It was strange how ageless she seemed compared to other adults in the community whom I had watched grow visibly older.

My father pointed at my mother and made a funny face.

"Crazy," he said.

He on the other hand, was not the most attractive man. His face was pockmarked with scars (which I had never asked about) and his nose was a little crooked, as if he had been in some sort of fight, which I could guarantee, if you knew my father, could not be true.

Our eating quarters consisted of a large wooden table surrounded by high-backed chairs. While everyone else had sleek, unmarred furniture, my parents preferred what they called "rustic" items. The chairs were horribly uncomfortable and the table, being virtually unfinished, was nicked and scratched from wear and tear.

On the wall was yet another control panel, and I scrolled through my breakfast options. I selected a vegetable omelet, extra cheese, with a glass of grape juice. There was a whizzing and whirring within the walls as the meal was prepared. A message appeared on the screen informing me that we were out of grape juice, and it would be an extra moment while more was fetched through the tube, which carried ingredients from the communal pantry to our individual homes.

By the time the omelet had cooked, another message had appeared stating that the grape juice had arrived. A compartment slid open revealing a chilled, freshly poured glass of purple liquid, and another unveiled a steaming omelet with cheese melted all over. A fork and butter knife lie neatly on a napkin next to my plate, and a straw was in my glass, as our system knew that I always drank with one.

A warning on the screen told me to beware the heat of the omelet. This always made me laugh. If I was old enough to read, I knew that an omelet was hot. If I wasn't old enough to read, the warning did me no good. It seemed rather pointless.

I took my plate and glass to the table and sat down to eat. The meal, as always, was cooked to perfection and I enjoyed every morsel.

My parents sat with cups of coffee for only a second longer, having already consumed their breakfast in pill form. They had long ago decided that time was not to be wasted chewing and swallowing when all the sustenance and nutrients needed could be consumed in one tiny pill.

"Woops! Time to go, Barnum!" my mother said to my father as she looked down at her wristwatch.

"Okay, Boss Mildred," he replied.

My parents had this thing where when one used his/her first name, the other always responded the same way. When my father was the one replying, he always did it with a wink and a twinkle in his eye. He could make any situation seem like he was playing a secret game.

I covered my mouth with my hand and said goodbye to them through a mouthful of food. Then my mother blew me a kiss, my father mimicking her, and they both rushed through the door. The heavy metal door closed with a *click* much more quietly than you would have expected.

After I finished eating, I selected the "clean" option on the panel and a compartment opened for me to put my dirty dishes back in. Then I walked back down the hallway to the bathroom to polish my teeth.

I removed the delicate tool from its sanitation station and dipped it into the white solution, which both cleaned and whitened teeth at the same time. I touch the tip to the surface of my front tooth and pressed the 'on' button. Tiny arms that look like windshield wipers swipe around in nanoseconds to get the job done, and then I move on and repeat the process for every surface of every tooth. This was always the longest part of my morning because I made sure that I got in every crevice. My mother always rolled her eyes at me when she was home to see me do it.

"See you next week," she would joke.

After I inspected my teeth in the mirror and decided they were acceptably clean, I checked the time. It was exactly eight in the morning, which meant it was time to start walking to school.

Secondary Academy, for students my age, was located in the west wing of the academic sector, which was the furthest section from my home. I guessed that when they designed the place, they decided it would be easier for younger kids to walk less, so the Primary Academy was closer to the general walkway.

I grabbed my bag of schoolbooks and shut the door behind me. I stepped out onto the common balcony, which ran the entire length of the whole Compound and connected us all together. It was exposed to the open air normally, but that day it was covered to ensure that we could walk freely without getting wet in the rain. I stopped and looked out across the enormous courtyard. I always liked to take in the sights of people rushing to and fro before starting my walk to school.

The Compound was silver and hexagon shaped, and each side of the building was a half mile long. There were different sectors for living quarters, working quarters, medical quarters, and academic quarters. The courtyard was where we did any outdoor activity; as it was so large, we had sports arenas, entertainment halls, and gardens. Everything we needed was located within the Compound, and there was no need to ever venture outside of it. I wasn't even sure what *was* outside of the Compound. My entire life had been spent there and I had never had a reason to want to leave.

I knew that the Compound was heavily guarded, but from what was always a question. Beyond the hexagon was a larger hexagon of a concrete wall with mounted soldiers and weapons at all times. We were told that it was just a precautionary measure, and since I had never actually seen a soldier use a weapon, I didn't question it. That's just the way the Compound was and we accepted it because we never had a reason not to. We were to be protected, just in case.

I let myself enjoy the couple minutes of people-watching, and then I had to continue on to class so that I would not be late… again.

I was smart, but not very studious. My lessons were natural to me. I wouldn't call my memory photogenic, but I had a fascinating ability to recall information that I had seen or heard only once. This allowed me to excel in my classes, but I never did more than I had to do. Many times I could see the irritation on my professors' faces due to my lack of motivation, and once one of them had even approached me on the subject.

"Eloise," Professor Stanton had said, "you demonstrate remarkable ability and potential. I fear, however, that you do *not* possess the necessary drive to rise above as someone of your status. You will be lost among the rest unless you start desiring true achievement."

Someone of my status.

Since my parents were physicists, in our community it was automatically assumed that I would also become a respected and admired member of society. In the Compound, scientists were revered for their work. I supposed it was because our lifestyle and all its conveniences were thanks to them. We depended on the constant flow of information, the new weekly findings, to sustain our way of life.

I respected that, but what Stanton had said was true. I didn't have the drive to become my parents. I wasn't sure who I was or who I wanted to be, and I didn't want to be pushed to be something that might not be a good fit. Maybe I would be better off in the art sector of the Compound. While they were not well-respected, they seemed like a happy enough bunch.

While I wasn't submissive, I also wasn't disrespectful. You couldn't call me a slacker and I didn't get in trouble for my shortcomings. I thanked the professor for her concern and said that I would consider her wise words.

I wasn't lying. I would consider it. I would just consider all of my other options, too.

Lost in my reverie about that conversation, I wandered through the hallways on auto-pilot, and I was at the door of my first class before I had even realized I had traveled that far.

I pressed my hand up against what looked like a metal grid next to the door. As if by illusion, the mesh turned to a jelly-like substance and enveloped my hand, identifying me using my fingerprints and the lines on my palm. I checked into each class this way every single day so that my attendance could be taken. This also made sure that no one was admitted into the room that shouldn't have been.

A soft *ping* alerted me that the identification process was over. A picture of my unsmiling face appeared on the panel above the metal grid, and underneath my picture was my full name and a timestamp of my arrival that morning. There was no sneaking by under the radar if you were late.

With a sound like a suction being released, a solid metal door slid open, revealing the entrance to my classroom. I stepped through and then the door shut behind me once again with the same vacuum-like noise.

It seemed as if I had arrived just in time, and I walked over to my personal desk. There were only six other students in my class. The Compound's philosophy was that only select people had the mental capacity to carry out certain lines of work. We were selected based on our level of intelligence at a young age and then placed into academies. Secondary Academy was the only school in the Compound that allowed us to carry on with general studies in the teenage years before specializing. Most of the others began to learn their specific trade at the age of thirteen, so as to best be trained to do their identified jobs. Those of us who attended Secondary would specialize later on, as it was deemed necessary for us to learn each subject more deeply for the more highly qualified positions that we would eventually take on.

Now that I was in my sixteenth year, I would finish my general studies and begin my specialization the following semester, which would depend on not only lengthy tests, but also the recommendation of professors. I had seen others who were older than me struggle with the choice that was often made *for* them. It was pretty rare that a student would refuse his or her selection, but when someone did, the news traveled quickly.

When I was ten, there was a boy with caramel-colored skin and a handsome face that I fawned over every time he walked by. When his results came in, he was chosen to work in the communications sector, which ensured that departments shared information with one another, and they were also responsible for dealing with the correspondence between Compound Senators. Believing that this was not the right placement for him, the boy went up in front of the Council and debated, arguing that he should continue his studies in the medical sector. Apparently his uncle had a friend on the Council and the boy won his case. He went on to become an antidote developer, which was a person who studied past and present illnesses and researched to find cures. Though there was some skepticism at first, he had proved his worthiness.

Not all who defied the system were that lucky. There was once a girl who completely lost it when she culminated her Secondary only to be told that she actually belonged in the retail sector, and not at the management level. She attacked a Council member and was incarcerated for her actions. I never was actually sure what became of her.

There were others who sometimes went up against the Council who I never saw again. It was possible that they were located somewhere in the Compound where I simply did not run into them, but the rumor was that they had been exiled.

Though I suppose that I should have been more nervous about the upcoming decision, I figured that I would be placed in the same category as my famous parents. It was probably assumed that I had only inherited their genius and would succeed in the same field. Given the chance, I probably would have done whatever the Council told me to do.

I took a seat at my desk, pushing thoughts of the Decision out of my mind.

"Just in time, yet again," whispered my friend, Althea, at the desk next to me. She was a pretty girl with a rounded body and dark skin that I envied. It always looked flawless and alive. I literally paled in comparison with my blanched skin.

"You know me. Life on the edge," I replied and winked at her.

I took a set of keys out of my bag and unlocked my desk. I removed my school laptop, and while I waited for it to turn on, I took out my history textbook and opened it to our current chapter. It was my favorite class, which made it difficult to have at the beginning of the day, as I had nothing to look forward to the rest of the time. I was enthralled with the events of the past, all the crime and horror that people had once inflicted on one another. It was hard for me to understand. Why did it take so long for humans to figure out how to live in peace?

We continued our lecture on the Holocaust, a bizarre period in history when one single man was able to persecute and murder millions while the world stood by for a few years until they finally decided to stop him. I couldn't fathom how anyone could be so weak as to be controlled by one person, to stand by and watch – or even participate! – in the wrongful death of innocent people. I was so glad that I lived in a world where everyone was content, a world without war and suffering. A world where all had their needs met; no one went without.

Professor Hunter always ended our classes with a controversial discussion, which almost always caused me to leave with high blood pressure. I loved a good debate, but I was too passionate about my thoughts and beliefs, and I couldn't help but get somewhat emotional as I pled my case.

In particular, there was a boy named Epstein who would purposely argue every single thing I said, just to get me going. And I fell for it every time, unable to give in or ignore him.

Today, Professor Hunter raised a question that at first seemed unrelated and was difficult to answer.

"Today," he began slowly in his husky voice, "I want you to think about what kind of person you are. Think about why you make the decisions you make. Then I want you to answer the following question. Are you better than others your age in the Compound?"

It was really a very uncomfortable question to answer. We knew that we had been chosen for Secondary for that very reason. We were better than our peers academically. But who wants to answer that question and sound like a jerk by saying yes?

There was silence, and as Professor Hunter scanned the room, you could see the other six pairs of eyes dart in the opposite direction or down at their desks.

His eyes fell on me.

"What about you, Miss Carlisle? Are you better than the others?"

Crap, I thought to myself. I paused for a moment, holding his gaze before I answered.

"Well, um..." I started weakly. My classmates were all looking at me now that they were safe for the moment, waiting for my response. "I guess that depends on what you mean by better."

When in doubt, answer a question with a question. I had learned this strategy very young.

"Very interesting point," Hunter responded. " 'Better' *is* a very vague word open to interpretation. Very well, then. Are you better than anyone at anything?"

I paused again, tapping my finger lightly on the desk.

"I suppose I probably am. And I'm sure there are lots of people who are better at something than me. For example, I am probably better at responding to a professor's question unexpectedly than some others. Others are probably better at having the courage to zip-line across the Compound than I would be."

Hunter chuckled. "Those are some...interesting examples. And you're probably very right about your assumptions. However I want us to think about the word 'better' now in relation to a person as a whole being. Are you a better human being than someone else? Is your life more valuable than another person's in the Compound?"

He posed the question to the entire class again. This time Epstein was quick to respond.

"That's easy to answer. Yes, I am better than someone else in this Compound, and yes, I am more valuable."

Epstein sat back and crossed his arms with a satisfied look on his face.

"Well aren't you confident," I retorted. Sometimes things just fell out of my mouth without thinking.

"Do you care to elaborate on your thoughts, Mr. Sturm?" Professor Hunter asked.

"Sure. The reality of life is that some of us are built to last. And what I mean by that is that some of us are stronger and smarter than others. That's why we're even in this class, right? We were smarter than others. Being smarter means that we have more talents and abilities, which means that we can do more for our community. We can do things that our peers can't. We can invent things and make changes that the smaller minds of our peers cannot even fathom. Since we can do all of this, we are more valuable to our community. It's simple."

"Being smarter does not always mean you are a better person," Althea said pointedly as she looked directly at Epstein.

"Both excellent points," said Hunter. "Both raise to question what makes a person *better*? What exactly is it that makes us valuable to others? Is it others who get to determine our value, or can we determine our value ourselves?"

"I think that you determine your own value. You decide if you are going to let someone else walk all over you, or if you are going to stand up for yourself and make yourself a force to be reckoned with. Only the individual can truly be in control of one's own destiny. If I choose not to allow others to make me feel worthless, then I create my own value," I said.

"Ah," Hunter nodded.

"Try as hard as you might, just because you value yourself does not mean that you can force others to value you. Take the Holocaust for example. Plenty of those who died felt as though they were valuable, but because they were weak and powerless they actually had no value," Epstein responded.

"Had no value?" I said bewildered. "How can you suggest that any human life has no value? There were bakers and grocers and farmers who were murdered who had once helped feed people. Doctors and dentists who helped fix people's ailments.

Are you telling me that these people had no value, that they were just wasting space and deserved to be eliminated?"

"I'm telling you that they were unnecessary. There will always be someone else to take the weaker person's place when he or she is gone. People in power, people like me, will always have more value because the stronger person, the better person, will always be ahead," Epstein said.

"People like you?" Althea spun around. "Oh, he did not just suggest—"

"Okay! Unfortunately time's up for now," Professor Hunter interrupted. "But this is a perfect transition into tonight's assignment."

For homework, we were assigned to write a philosophical essay about the reasons why people made the choices that they had made, whether they were for or against the war, and how that may have influenced the present way of life at the Compound. Class was over and I moved on, pressing my hand into the mesh at the next classroom door where I would have to endure the snarky and self-absorbed Epstein for yet another hour. And then four more hours after that.

During the lunch hour, I walked with Althea to the Camelot Café, a castle-themed coffee shop in the courtyard that was our favorite. Hoping to get some work done while I ate, I had brought my laptop along. While I wasn't an overachiever, I liked to get my assignments over with so that I would have the afternoon to myself.

I ordered a blueberry muffin and a frozen cappuccino, and then Althea and I sat in a corner booth. She began to ramble and complain about Epstein as I opened up my laptop again.

An alert appeared in the corner of my screen notifying me that I had a video message. It was from my mother. She sometimes would send me these messages in the middle of the school day, informing me about some new and exciting theory that she had come up with, or sometimes she would ask me something silly, like if I could see gray hairs in her eyebrows.

Generally speaking, the Compound connection was never interrupted. Downloads and uploads were instantaneous and glitches are rare. I clicked on the message and the video downloaded on my screen. I pressed play, but the picture was oddly fuzzy and disconnected. I had never seen such a poor connection before.

I could somewhat make out my mother's face in the jumbled mess of squares when they sometimes connected to form a coherent picture.

"Eloise.......tell you before.....sorry......in the lab......after school.....I love you," was all I was able to understand as the video jumped around making her voice sound robotic, and then my mother's face disappeared from the screen altogether.

"Huh," I said to Althea. "That was weird."

"Yeah, I've never seen that before," she agreed and bit into her croissant.

I shrugged. "Maybe she wanted me to stop by the lab after school."

We finished our lunch and then attended the rest of our classes for the day. I had a difficult time concentrating as I kept trying to figure out what my mother's message meant. Was she just telling me that she had forgotten a meeting and would be staying late in the lab, or did she want me to actually go to the lab after school? It wasn't the usual kind of message that she would leave me.

By the end of the day, the nagging feeling remained and I decided to stop by my parents' lab to check and make sure that they didn't need me. It was on the way home anyway, and if they were just going to be late coming home then I would find out in person.

I said goodbye to Althea, promising to update her later, and then I walked to the scientific sector, which was located on the northwest hall of the top floor.

Normally there was a secretary sitting at a desk outside the main door to the sector, but she wasn't there, so I pressed my hand into the scanner to gain access. Obviously not everyone had access to this department, but because my parents were who they were (and I assumed the Council's prediction of my career path) I had been given clearance to come and go as I pleased.

The scientific sector was, generally speaking, a very sterile and quiet environment in the first place. Most of the doors you walked by had small windows, and you could observe scientists hunched over a microscope, computer, or Petri dish, working silently and alone. Some doors did not have windows, and I assumed that was where people were working on more secretive, or perhaps disturbing, projects. I shuddered at the thought. There were very few people who were privy to the type of work that went on in the labs, and not even I – as Mildred and Barnum Carlisle's daughter- was included in that elite list. My parents were open about their own lives, but it was strictly forbidden to discuss the nature of their colleagues' work.

I walked down the hallway towards my parents' lab. As I got closer, I noticed that many of the rooms were empty. This was a little odd, but not altogether abnormal. I assumed that maybe there was a meeting after all, and that that was where everyone was. I almost turned back around, presuming I would not find my parents. But I wanted to be sure since I was already there, and I wasn't entirely in a rush to get started on the hours of homework that I had to complete.

I had to press my hand into the scanner once again to gain access to my parents' private lab. I never did ask many questions about their work, but whatever it was that they specifically did required the highest level of clearance. Very few people were qualified to be admitted.

My identification was accepted and the door *whooshed* open and then sealed behind me again.

At first glance, the lab appeared orderly yet empty with no sign of my parents. Bookshelves lined the walls filled with books that did not interest me. I began to think about spending years working in a place like this, in privacy and isolation. I mean, sure, my parents had each other when they were working. But most people in the scientific sector led very solitary lives, married to their work. That wasn't how I pictured spending the rest of my life. In fact, it made me feel claustrophobic – trapped – to think about the possibility.

I readjusted my bag on my shoulder and walked further into the lab, just to make sure there was no one there.

"Mom? Dad?" I called.

No response.

Must be that meeting, I said to myself and turned back around to leave.

At that moment, someone came rushing through the lab door from the hallway.

"Woo, you sure are hard to find! So glad you're here. Come on let's go," said the stranger as he raced past me to the other side of the room.

"Who the hell are you?" I asked as I studied his features. He was clean-shaven and had a roundness to his face that made him still look boyish even though he was clearly a few years older than me. His sandy-brown hair was pushed up in the front in a way that suggested he didn't purposely spike it, rather like he had just rolled out of bed.

"There's no time for that. Didn't you get your mother's message?" he asked.

"I got *a* message, but I could barely even tell it was my mother because it was so messed up. She didn't mention anything about a strange man barging in on me," I replied.

He grabbed me by the arm and urged me forward a few steps.

"We have to get you out of here," he said.

"Whoa, whoa, whoa," I said as I pulled back. "I have no idea who you are and I'm not going *anywhere* with you. I'll wait right here for my mother to get out of her meeting."

"What meeting?! Your mother has been indicted along with your father. They could be dead by now for all I know. They told me to get you out of here safely before it was too late, and that's what I'm going to do!"

Then he grabbed me by the upper part of my arm again and half-dragged me.

"What are you talking about? Indicted? Dead? You're crazy. My parents are two of the most celebrated citizens in the Compound. Get off me!" I shouted and fought against his strong grip. I stumbled backwards towards the door, trying to remember where the secret emergency button was located.

The stranger pressed a finger in his ear and spoke.

"Eloise is being a bit difficult," he said to someone who was clearly not in the room.

He paused and then started again. "With all due respect, we are out of time. I'm trying to convince her, but she is not cooperating..."

While he was distracted by the conversation, I inched myself backwards. If I couldn't find the button, I could at least try to make a run for it.

Think! I commanded myself. I had spent so much time in the lab growing up that I should have known every square inch of it. My parents had even purposely trained me for all emergencies, right down to how to wash a chemical spill off of skin, so much so that my reaction to this situation should have been automatic.

"Gee, I don't know, should I sit her down and have some tea?" the stranger said sarcastically into the air.

He was clearly very involved with his argument. I wasn't an athlete or anything, but I could be pretty fast for a short burst of time. I tried to quickly calculate in my mind the number of steps to the door and how long it would take me to exit based on my approximate speed. As I was getting lost in the numbers in my head and he was carrying on his conversation, it hit me.

The emergency button was located on the underside of my mother's desk. It was done this way purposely, so that it was neither blindingly obvious nor would it be impossible to get to in an emergency situation.

I walked in a manner that I thought was casual towards her desk. I hoped I looked natural. I didn't know much about the handsome stranger, but I didn't want to move too fast or too slow and alarm him. He didn't seem to want to hurt me, but then again he was trying to tell me that my parents had been arrested, so I couldn't be confident that he was mentally stable.

"Fine, I'll do what needs to be done. Do I have your word that there will be no consequences?" he asked, and then he nodded to whoever was on the other line and the exchange seemed to end.

I had just reached my mother's desk when his attention focused back on me. I leaned up against it, facing him, and tried to, what I hoped was nonchalantly, run my hand on the underside of the desk.

"Listen," he said. "Name's Beckett. You can call me Beck, if you like. There are a lot of things you don't know about, and I don't have time to explain them all right now. All you need to know is that you're in danger, and I'm trying to help you. I'm here on your parents' orders to keep you safe. You need to trust me, and we need to go. Now."

"Well, I would trust you, except my parents have never done anything wrong in their entire lives," I kept fumbling around under the desk.

"What are you doing?" he asked.

"What are you talking about?" I answered as my fingers brushed over the button and I pressed it.

The bright work lights shut off and only emergency lights were left on, dimming the general light in the room drastically. Red emergency lights were flashing (which I didn't even know existed) and a blaring siren sounded.

"Damnit," I said through gritted teeth. I thought it would be a silent alarm.

"Oh, man!" said Beckett with a look of horror. "What did you just do?! Now we're really out of time!"

This time he swooped over and wrapped both of his arms around me in a bear hug. Then he picked me up and carried me over towards the window. He put me down gently and grabbed a lab chair, smashing it through one of the large panes of glass. It shattered outwardly and fresh air rushed into the room.

"You're mad," I said, gaping in fearsome awe.

I turned to run full speed towards the door, but he grabbed me and spun me around to face him. He held me firmly on the sides of my arms and looked directly into my eyes. There was an intense, pleading look on his face that was so desperate I almost trusted him.

"Eloise, please. Your parents were not just physicists. You're right that they're very important to the Compound, but not in the way you think. There's more to your world than you know, more dangerous things that your parents were secretly fighting against. They've been found out and now it isn't safe here for you. They're going to come for you next. You've got to come with me now. It's the only way."

Beckett, whoever he was, was begging me. He hadn't hurt me, my parents were actually missing at the moment, and he seemed sincere. My instincts were fighting with one another.

Half of me wanted to scream and kick at him to let me go, while the other half lay all her trust in him, believed him to the very core. Part of me irrationally thought of the prospective adventure as a destiny being fulfilled after spending my life going through the motions. Maybe it was my only chance to be something other than my parents reincarnated.

I could hear a helicopter in the distance getting closer, its propellers beating against the air.

"This doesn't make any sense!" I shouted against the rising noise.

"I know it doesn't make any sense right now!" he shouted back. "I promise I'll explain later, all of it, but right now we have to go!"

"How do I know I can trust you?"

"You can't know. You just have to follow your gut."

I stared at him for a silent moment as the helicopter hovered right outside the window. Clearly it was there to whisk us away. As I saw it, I had two options. I could stay there and possible be perfectly safe, or perfectly unsafe. Or I could go off on this new adventure with this strange, good-looking man who I'd never met before, and possibly be safe, or possible be unsafe.

There was no definite answer. I didn't know which choice was the right choice, if there was a right choice. I found myself wishing that at any moment my mother would come waltzing through the door and ask what was going on. I wished that someone would choose for me. But that wasn't going to happen.

My skin grew warm under Beckett's fingers, which were still clamped firmly on my arms. It seemed like he was giving me a choice, but it also seemed like he would go against my wishes if I didn't cooperate. The notion of a choice was merely a nicety.

I breathed out a heavy breath. Adventure was tempting. Maybe I would finally get to see what lie beyond the Compound, if anything.

"Okay, fine," I yelled, throwing caution to the wind.

Beckett's mouth turned upward into a bright smile that illuminated his face and made him more handsome, and he let go of my arms. He turned towards the broken window and gestured to the helicopter.

"Bring it closer!" he said into his mouthpiece again.

It was at that moment that I noticed that Beckett was armed. He was wearing a waistband with several different weapons that I couldn't identify attached to it. It looked like a criminal's utility belt. Not that I actually knew what a criminal was at the time outside of what I had read in the history textbook.

The helicopter hovered as closely to the building as it could without striking the propellers against the side. I could feel my face contort into confusion as I observed. It was way too far for us to be able to reach it.

"You're going to have to trust me, Eloise, okay?" his voice strained against the hammering of the propellers. "This is going to look scary, but you're going to be just fine. I'm going to get myself hooked up, and then I'm going to come back for you. Understand?"

I nodded.

At that moment, someone slung a two-foot wide plank across the open air, connecting the helicopter to the ledge of the window. My stomach lurched as Beckett took a first tentative step onto it, testing the strength and placement before allowing his full weight onto it. It seemed impossible for the helicopter to hover steadily in place long enough for him to cross.

"I'll be right back," he looked back and said to me, and then he continued across the plank.

Just as Beckett made it halfway across the board, I could sense a disruption behind me. I turned around to look back into the lab and saw Professor Hunter sprinting across the room. It startled me and I feared for Beckett who wobbled on the plank as he noticed.

"Damnit!" I heard him yell as he steadied himself.

I ignored Professor Hunter's presence for the moment, watching Beckett to make sure that he made it across. I realized that my nails were digging into my palm out of nervousness, and I wondered how I could be so worried for someone that I didn't even know, someone I wasn't even sure that I could trust.

When I saw that he had made it safely to the other side, I turned back around to face the professor.

"Eloise, quick!" said Hunter. "He can't get to you now. Come this way and I can help you. The others are on their way."

"Stay back!" I warned him.

"Stay back? Eloise, what are you doing? You know me. This isn't safe. You can't trust these people. There are things that you don't understand. If you come with me I can help you. I can explain it all."

"God," I whispered to myself as I dragged a hand across my face.

Everyone was saying the same things, but it was clear that they were not on the same side of... of... whatever it was they were opposed to. On one hand, I had known Professor Hunter virtually my entire life. He had only been my teacher for the past couple of years, but I had grown up in the Compound where he had always been a familiar face. I trusted him on a normal day. I liked him.

I looked back at Beckett who was crossing the plank, coming towards the opening of the window again. He was now wearing a harness which was attached to the helicopter, and there was a second attached to him that I assumed was meant for me.

"Eloise, you're running out of time," Professor Hunter said urgently as he glanced at Beckett. "Come this way. I'll get you out of here."

"You're right. What am I thinking?" I said with sudden clarity. "I don't even know this guy."

My courage for the adventure suddenly faded and was replaced by a fear of the unknown. I turned back towards Professor Hunter and safety, prepared to run for the door, but Beckett was too fast for me.

I felt something slip suddenly around my waist. I saw Beckett's hands make quick work of securing me to him and he pulled me backwards towards him.

I felt my face drain of color, already regretting the original choice that I had made to trust this stranger.

"Let me go!" I yelled and my elbows flew backwards, slamming into Beckett's abdomen.

Professor Hunter grabbed onto my arm and struggled to pull me towards him as Beckett began to struggle towards the helicopter.

"Eloise, come on!" Beckett yelled in my ear. "He is part of the enemy!"

We stood on the ledge of the window, and I screamed. I clung to Professor Hunter with all my might, clawing at his arms as Beckett pulled me.

"You're going to make me do everything the hard way, aren't you?" I heard him say.

I could feel motion behind me as Beckett fumbled around for something at the same time that I saw armed guards burst through the lab door.

"There they are!" I saw a uniformed man point towards us and shout.

Then I saw Beckett's arm swing out in front of me holding a gun. He pulled the trigger and I saw two streams of light fly out and strike Professor Hunter in the chest. The professor's grip on me fell slack and he tumbled over onto the floor.

"No!" I screamed in a panic, my body flying into a frenzy trying to escape the harness.

The armed guards were halfway across the room, weapons raised, when Beckett jumped backwards out of the window. We were free-falling in the air for about three seconds before the rope connected to our harnesses pulled taut and my surroundings went black as I passed out.

*   *   *

When I awoke I was lying on the floor, my head propped up so that my chin was touching my chest. I tried to move to readjust myself, but my neck was stiff and my arms felt too heavy to lift. When I fully came to my senses, I realized that my arms were actually tied down, giving me a limited range of motion.

My head seemed a bit fuzzy like it was the time I woke up from anesthesia when I had my appendix removed as a kid, and my tongue felt dry and foreign in my mouth. It took me that time I spent assessing myself to realize where I was, or rather where I wasn't, and I began to panic all over again.

Though I hadn't received any career-specific training, I tried to remember the basic information I had learned in our senior seminar about all of the different occupations. I tried to steady my breath as I attempted to recall the simulations I had watched that the military sector had developed. They always showed us possibilities of the most dangerous situations, with the intent that any spineless candidates would be eliminated by professors before they were selected for a sector.

One video simulation had actually portrayed someone in a situation quite similar to my own. The person had been kidnapped by insurgents, tied with his hands behind his back on a chair, and blindfolded in a dark room. My class watched as the person, trained by the Compound, was able to escape the situation and save himself. Incidentally, I had no desire to become a part of the military sector and could not remember what tactics the soldier had used.

Feeling slightly dizzy, I sighed and slumped back down, staring at the ceiling sulkily. To my knowledge, there was no possible way to free myself. My arms had some freedom to move, but they had been purposely limited to not be able to reach one another. I thought I might have been able to wriggle one hand through and use it to untie the other, but whoever had restrained me had thought of this possibility as well and made sure that the rope was incapable of moving that far. I also had some martial arts training as every child was required to study as a member of the Compound. I had always wondered what the purpose was because I had never come into contact a situation where it would be necessary. Now I unfortunately understood, but my skills would be of no use until I was free.

Resigning myself to the fact that I had no current plan of escape, I began to take in my surroundings. I was on the floor. To my left there was a booth with a table, and next to that a sink with a few cabinets above and below. Further down on my side of the wall it looked like there were a couple of large, boxy looking objects and a couple more cabinets. It was all very odd, but I got the sense that it had a homey feel rather than a place where people would be tortured and killed.

Suddenly, I also realized that the room I was in was moving as whatever I was in hit a bump, and I was jolted off the floor for a second. It definitely was not the small helicopter that I had seen hovering outside the Compound window, so we probably were not in the air. Something must be moving across the land?

What do these people want with me? I thought to myself.

I thought about what the stranger, Beckett, had said to me about getting orders from my parents to take me. It just didn't make any damn sense. I had never spent a single day without my parents, and they told me everything there was to know about their jobs, about their lives. We had no secrets from each other. What could possibly have been going on that I wouldn't know about? What could Mildred and Barnum possibly have done to get themselves in trouble with the Compound?

My captors had to be lying to me. That was the only feasible answer. So what was the real reason they had taken me out of all the people in the Compound?

I didn't know what the outside world was like, but I could only assume that it was pretty desperate if they were willing to risk their lives kidnapping two renowned physicists' daughter. And from the Compound at that. They must have had absolutely no idea who they were messing with. Our military sector had to be the best trained force in the world. Then again I was ignorant about the rest of the world – I hardly even knew that other people existed at all – so maybe they weren't.

I let out a growl of frustration. It didn't seem like these people meant me any harm. Maybe they were just looking for money or supplies in exchange for my safe return. But then again, if they were so desperate, how would they have been able to afford a helicopter to fly me away from the Compound? And speaking of, how in the world did they manage to get past the security surrounding us and then back out again? Something wasn't adding up.

Behind me, I heard a door open and shut. I craned my neck backwards to see who had entered the room.

"Well, well. Little Miss Sunshine is awake again," Beckett said, standing with his hands on his hips.

He walked to the front side of me with an amused look on his face and waited for me to speak.

"I would get up and shake your hand, but someone has *tied me down*," I said through clenched teeth.

"Well if you hadn't been so busy trying to kick my ass I wouldn't have had to do that," he replied, crossing his arms in front of him.

Beckett still had a stupid grin on his face like he knew about some joke that I wasn't aware of, and it angered me even more that he could be so laid back about the whole situation, like taking a teenage girl captive was a joke.

"Are you really enjoying being a criminal that much? Because I don't think there's anything funny about this," I spat.

His smile faded and he dropped his arms, sighing as he sat down on the booth. Then he rested his forearms on his thighs, bent his head, and ran his fingers through his thick hair.

When he looked back up at me, he clasped his hands and rested his pointer fingers on his pouty lips and paused before speaking again.

Getting a closer, longer look at him, I determined that he must be around eighteen or nineteen years old, and the sad expression on his beautiful face strangely made me want to comfort him. It seemed like he was truly concerned or worried.

"No, Eloise, I am not enjoying this at all. You've made this very difficult for me," he finally said.

Any sympathy I had for him washed out of me like water through a drainpipe.

"*I'm* making this difficult for *you*?" I said incredulously. "Oh, I'm sorry. Did you expect your kidnap victim to be more pleasant? Please excuse my poor behavior."

"Kidnap victim? I saved you! Why can't you understand that?"

"Well, gee, maybe it's because you haven't explained *anything* to me!"

"I was going to, Eloise, but you attacked me on the helicopter, and then you tried to bash my head in on that cabinet over there, so it was a little difficult to get a word in," he said, clearly frustrated.

I noticed the bandage on his forehead then. And the way my name rolled so naturally off of his tongue, as if he had known me for years.

"I don't know what you're talking about." I was the one attempting to cross my arms now, and I looked away from him, staring at the wall.

"You passed out in the harness, and when you woke up in the helicopter you freaked out and started going Kung-Fu on me. I restrained you myself until we landed. When we got off the 'copter, you walked off of it like a normal person and I thought everything was fine. Then we got on the RV and you started swinging at me again. We had to sedate you and tie you down so you wouldn't be a danger to yourself or anyone else. You didn't even give me a chance."

"I don't remember *any* of that. One lie after another," I shook my head.

"I'm not lying," Beckett said more patiently now. "The sedative we gave you was pretty heavy duty, and considering the duress you've been through, your mind is probably trying to protect you."

I looked at him with what I hoped was an apologetic expression.

"I'm sorry. Listen, I have this really bad itch on my nose and I can't reach. You think you can get it for me?" I said in my sweetest voice.

Beckett seemed to relax a little and smiled at me, as if he was relieved that I finally appeared to be coming around. He leaned towards me and reached to scratch my nose. Before he even saw it coming, I pulled my knee in towards me and then kicked outwardly, connecting with his nose.

"Aw, come on, El!" he said in a muffled voice as he clutched the center of his face. "Jesus! I'm just trying to help you. Damnit!"

I could see blood oozing through his fingers, and I sat back with a satisfied smirk.

"I guess you're *still* not ready to get the whole story. Next time I try, I'll wear full body armor," he said angrily, and then he stalked back out of the room the way he had come.

My satisfaction with injuring my captor didn't last very long as I quickly grew lonely. While my parents worked long hours and I could always find peaceful quiet at home, I wasn't used to being so alone. Living in the Compound, all I had to do was walk out of my door and look out over the courtyard to feel connected to other people. Wherever I was now, I was very alone.

As time passed, my stomach began to grumble and I was starting to feel the urge to pee. I began to wonder when Beckett would come back, or if he would even come back at all. Maybe I shouldn't have acted on impulse. Maybe I should have been more cooperative and thought first before pushing away my only current resource.

I blew a piece of hair out of my eye and it landed back on the side of my face, tickling. This time I really did have an itch and there was nothing that I could do about it. *Karma*, I thought to myself. I inched my shoulder up to the spot and used it to rub the itch away.

I didn't know how long I had been asleep, so I had no idea how much time had passed since I had left my parents' lab. I could only assume that it was dark outside and some time at night. Heavy shades were drawn on the few small windows that I could see, and the lights were on in the room I was in, so it could have well been daylight, but I thought I would see some semblance of sun shining against the shades if it was there.

Stubbornness kept me quiet. I didn't have much patience for the unknown, and my foot began to bounce out of anxiousness. I wanted to know who had taken me, where I was, where I was going, and why, but I didn't want to seem eager, didn't want to seem too quick to believe what they told me. As boring as my Ancient Philosophy class had been, if it taught me anything it taught me to not be afraid to question.

I tried to play all the scenarios out in my mind as I sat in frustration on the floor. Perhaps my parents had developed some strange mutation that was running loose in the Compound eating people, or maybe they had simply refused to follow the orders of the Council. Though our community was a well-oiled machine, I could assume that dissent would be met with severe consequences.

Something just wasn't adding up. My parents had always been law-abiding citizens who contributed to society. They were held in high esteem for their work and were invited to every gala or event that was held in the Compound. Their work was important. Though as I thought about it, everyone's work seemed important. Everyone had a specific role to fill in order for the Compound to function, and everyone did so without complaint. We all needed each other in order to survive. If my parents had done something wrong, it had to be an accident. I couldn't imagine them jeopardizing their lives over something small.

Finally, I couldn't take sitting there by myself anymore. I had to give in to use the bathroom at least. I probably could have gone much longer without eating; I could control what I put in, but I couldn't control what was to come out.

"Beckett!" I called as loudly and friendly as I could.

There was no response, and I hadn't even heard any movement in all the time that had passed besides the occasionally bump of whatever it was that was moving.

"Beckett!" I called again.

Still nothing.

I was angry with myself, then, for so many things. For having trusted Beckett in the first place; I should have run in the opposite direction right away when I saw a strange man in my parents' lab- and for then kicking him in the face, causing him to leave me alone. For being a part of the reason that my history teacher had been shot- I still didn't even know if he was alive. For not knowing what the hell was going on in my own parents' lives or work. For not being able to get myself out of the situation.

I began to stamp my feet in anger like a child over it all. It was the only thing that I could do to alleviate my feelings at the moment. I guess I could have screamed my head off, but no one seemed to be able to hear me anyways.

In the middle of having my tantrum, the door behind me opened again and in walked Beckett with gobs of white stuffed in his nose.

I laughed in spite of the fact that I was being held hostage by the stranger in front of me.

"You've got a little something hanging out of your nose," I said, smiling.

"That would be a little bit of cotton to stop the bleeding. Thanks for that by the way," he said. He sounded funny, too, due to his nose being blocked and I laughed again.

"I'm glad you find my pain so amusing," Beckett said again, not sounding the least bit glad.

He stood with his arms crossed again, leaning against the counter and looking at me as if I were a misbehaved toddler. Though he was clearly irritated, he exuded the patience that I lacked. It seemed as if he would wait an eternity for me to be agreeable and listen to what he had to say.

"Mmm, sorry about that," I responded, probably not sounding the least bit sorry. I had a difficult time hiding my emotions. Clearly. "I really need to go to the bathroom. And I'm starting to get hungry."

"That sucks."

"What do you mean, 'that sucks'? Aren't you going to let me go to the bathroom or feed me, or is this exactly what I thought in the beginning? When does the torture begin?"

Beckett sighed and massaged his chin with one hand. "Well, you see, I'd love to help you out with that, but I really can't afford to get any more banged up. If you weren't so damn aggressive, we would've had you fed and watered already."

Watered? What am I, a plant?

"Not much I can really do about that now," I said.

"That's true. So I'll go on and get you a bucket to use for the bathroom, and then I'll go get you something to eat while you do your business. I promise I'll knock before I come back in."

A horrified look spread across my face.

"A bucket? I can barely even lift myself off of the floor! That's disgusting!"

Beckett shrugged and a smirk played at the edges of his mouth.

"That's the best solution I have for you right now, sweetheart, since you can't behave."

"I'll behave. Just let me use a real bathroom, for God's sake!"

"Well now, how am I supposed to know I can trust you, Miss Eloise?"

I stole a line from him. "You can't know. You just have to follow your gut."

Beckett laughed and shook his finger at me. "Oh, I see what you just did right there. Clever girl still. They were right."

"Who's 'they'?" I asked.

"Never mind that," Beckett said. "I'm gonna trust you now, like you sort of did me. But I swear, one wrong move and I drug you up again and make you sleep it off. No funny business."

Then he took a blade out of his back pocket and swiftly cut the bindings that were tying me down to the floor before I could even get alarmed at the sight of a weapon. Offering me his hand, he pulled me up off of the floor so fast that I almost crashed into him.

Our faces were only a couple of inches apart, and I was very aware of Beckett's hand on my back, steadying me. I could smell the mint of his breath and some sort of cologne clinging to his plain, black t-shirt.

"No more funny business," I agreed.

It turned out that the bathroom was not much of a room at all. After Beckett had untied me, he led me a foot past the cabinets I had been staring at to a door. When I opened it, I saw that it was just big enough for the little toilet, sink, and a rather skinny person. Small spaces tended to make me claustrophobic, and had I been alone I would have left the door open, but Beckett was not moving from right outside the door, presumably to prevent any escape I might plan. So, I reluctantly shut the door and did my business as quickly as possible.

When I emerged from the bathroom, I released a breath that I had unintentionally been holding in. Beckett, waiting as I had predicted, laughed at the sight of me, his crinkling eyes spreading into creases as if by habit.

"What's the matter, El? Can't do two things at once?" he teased.

"I don't like small spaces," I said defensively. I didn't like anyone to think I was weak, especially not him. "And why do you keep calling me that, like you know me?"

I knew it wasn't difficult to guess my nickname, but it was too familiar coming out of a stranger's mouth.

"Because I want you to feel like – to know that – I'm your friend, not your enemy. It just comes natural," he shrugged.

There were a series of comments that ran through my mind, none of them friendly, but I didn't want to end up alone and tied down again, so instead I didn't even respond. If he could play games, so could I. I could pretend to be friendly, having a secret agenda all the while, and I would wait to make my move when the time was right.

We locked eyes for a moment as I hashed all this out in my head, and when I was done with my thinking, I realized that Beckett might have thought my gaze meant something else.

I cleared my throat to break the uncomfortable silence and looked away.

"I'm still hungry," I said.

Right," Beckett responded and gestured forward. He wasn't going to risk turning his back to me at any point now. So much for trust.

He walked a few steps over to one of the big boxy things against the wall I had shared and opened a door. I felt a rush of cold air and saw food stored on the inside. I was pretty impressed. I hadn't even seen Beckett push any buttons to make an order. How did it know? Maybe the Compound was not the best and the brightest after all.

My curiosity got the best of me.

"How did you do that?" I asked.

Beckett had been leaning over into the cold cabinet, looking at its contents. He straightened up at my question.

"How did I do what?"

"Make the food appear. Where's the control panel? I didn't see you push any buttons to order."

He burst out in laughter straight away. I felt momentarily unintelligent, thinking that I had missed something and it had been obvious. Not used to not being the smartest person in the room, I felt my cheeks get hot in embarrassment. Confusion was a sore and alien feeling, and I didn't enjoy it.

"Oh, man," Beckett finally said in between laughter. "I forgot how clueless you are about the rest of the world."

"I'm not – I'm very intelligent. Do you have any idea what I scored on my aptitude tests? There was a reason I am in Secondary, I –" I stammered indignantly until he cut me off.

"Whoa, whoa, whoa, my little fire-cracker. I believe you, okay? We know how smart you are, no need to go kung-fu on me again," he said, and then seeing my frustration and embarrassment with him laughing at my expense, he softened. "Listen, all I meant was that you have lived a very different life than the rest of us. There are a lot of new things that you're going to have to learn and get used to. And I can help you as long as you're willing to work with me."

You have lived a very different life than the rest of us.

Who was "the rest of us"? From what I could remember, I didn't ever see Beckett in the Compound. Even if he was a few years older, I surely would have seen him or heard of his assignment to either the workforce or Secondary. Though we were a large community, news generally traveled quickly. And why would I have to learn and get used to things? How long would it be before I would be able to go home again and get back to my life?

The thought that maybe Beckett intended that I never return almost triggered my panic mode, but I had to stay calm and level headed until I knew exactly what was going on. I had to play it smart, be patient.

"Okay," I finally said.

This boy sure does have a lot of the patience that I seek, I thought to myself. No matter how long it took me to think about everything that was going on and have debates in my head, he was always waiting without complaint.

"So what is this thing then?" I asked.

"This," Beckett said, tapping the thing on the front of the top door, "is what we call a refrigerator. It's where we store some foods so that they don't get rotten."

"What's 'rotten'?"

Beckett ran a hand through his mop of hair. I assumed he was realizing just how much he would have to explain to me.

"You're used to pushing a few buttons and then the food magically appears, right?" he asked.

"Well, it's not magic. There's actually a lot of science behind the fact that –" I stopped myself as Beckett raised his eyebrows at me. He wasn't looking for a scientific explanation. "Yes."

"Right. And you don't get to see what goes on behind the scenes, where all the food is prepared for you so that you don't have to do it yourself. Out here, you go to a store and purchase the individual items to make a meal, and then you have to go back home and prepare it yourself before you can eat. It takes a lot more time than the push of a button, but a lot of folks get some satisfaction out of it."

He paused, making sure that I didn't have any other questions. Then he shut the refrigerator door and continued his speech.

"The refrigerator door needs to stay shut so that it keeps the food on the inside cold. When the food stays cold, it stays fresh for a longer period of time before it's unsafe to eat. This over here "- he pointed to the smaller boxy looking thing with all the knobs and buttons – "is called a stove. We use it to make foods that have to be cooked first before you can eat them, like meat, eggs, or even cake. On the top is where you can put pans to boil water or fry an egg, and the door opens to put things that need to bake on high heat for a longer period of time. Any pots or pans that have been on the stove or in the oven are very hot, so you can't handle them with your bare hands. That's why you use this. It's called an oven mitt and protects your hands from hot items."

He held up what looked like a large glove. I noticed how his enthusiasm seemed to increase as he was explaining to me.

"You like to cook, don't you?" I asked.

"Yes, actually. I'm pretty good at it, too. Maybe sometime I'll cook you a real meal. But for right now, we're pretty limited with the food we have since we are on the go."

"I think you're probably good at teaching people things," I stated another observation. I amused myself with the fact that I was sizing Beckett up like I was preparing for an experiment, ever the scientist-in-training, even if I didn't want to be.

"Correct. I'm quite good at that, too. In fact, my job is typically to train people in whatever area I am asked. That's why I was selected for this mission. Plus they thought my startling good looks would make you swoon," he winked at me.

"You wish," I rolled my eyes at him.

Beckett returned to the refrigerator and surveyed the few options again. I watched him, deciding for sure that he was a stunning creature. I wasn't sure if it would altogether help me believe in whatever these people were trying to tell me, but it certainly didn't hurt.

"Well, how about peanut butter and jelly?" he asked.

"Sure," I said.

Beckett took out a jar of grape jelly from the refrigerator and a jar of peanut butter from one of the cabinets. A half loaf of bread was already on the counter. As he busied himself making a quick sandwich, I couldn't help but imagine a little man like him bustling about inside my walls at home, preparing all of the food that I ate. He finished and put my sandwich on a paper plate, which I had also never seen before. My meals always arrived on ceramic.

"How about something to drink?" he asked as he placed my plate on the table.

"Just water would be fine, thank you."

"Ooh, she has manners," Beckett joked.

"Trust me, I never cease to amaze."

"I believe it," he responded, and then he stared at me for an unreasonably long time, as if he was sizing me up for an experiment, too. Then he reached into the refrigerator once more and pulled out a bottle of water.

I sat down in the red booth at the table and started eating. I was so hungry that I only paused to think about eating food from strange people after I had swallowed my first bite. It was unreasonable, really, to even think about it. If Beckett had meant me any harm, he wouldn't be sitting here explaining refrigerators and ovens to me over a sandwich. Unless of course these were a sadistic people who liked to watch their victims suffer.

I shook the thought from my mind and concentrated instead on filling my stomach. Beckett sat down across from me with his own sandwich and bottle of water.

"So, who are these people that you keep referring to? The 'they' that you speak of," I said.

"It's really a long story, El. There is so much to tell you. Trust me, we've really gotta just take it one piece at a time. I don't want to overwhelm you or scare you. Let's just worry about the refrigerator kinda stuff for now, huh?"

"I think you underestimate me. I just want to know why I've been ripped out of my home all of a sudden. If I can handle that, I think I can handle what you have to tell me."

"Oh, I don't doubt that you can," he replied and scratched his head. "I'm just honestly not really sure where to begin."

"I thought you were supposed to be good at this."

Beckett laughed. "Yeah, that's true. I guess maybe I'm overanalyzing a little bit because I want to impress you."

He took a bite of his sandwich and stared at me, measuring my reaction.

I narrowed my eyes at him playfully, "Nice try, but I'm not buying what you're selling that easily."

Beckett smirked again and shook his head. I wondered how many girls he had won over with his charm and familiarity. He probably went into this mission thinking that I would just be another sixteen year old girl who would take one look at him and do whatever he said.

You have met your match, Beckett, I thought to myself.

Just as we were each enjoying our moment of silence, probably trying to figure each other out, I felt a jolt and my paper plate slid a few inches on the table.

A man walked into the room just then. I wasn't even thinking about the fact that anyone else might be with us, wherever we were. He was tall with tanned skin and curly, jet black hair. An eye patch covered his right eye and there were tattoos up and down his arms. He looked formidable, like he walked straight out of a children's tale about pirates.

"We're here," he said in a gruff, scratchy voice and walked back out of the room.

"That's Mad-Eye. Can you figure out how he got his nickname?" Beckett asked.

"What happened to him?"

"Eloise, that's a story for another day, too. He looks a bit scary, but I promise he's a big teddy bear," he said and then he stood up, offering me his hand. "My lady?"

I wasn't sure what to make of my surroundings when I stepped out of the vehicle we had been traveling in. It looked like a large car - it was the first I had ever seen in person as there was no need for them at home – but it didn't really make sense since there was so much furniture inside. I was pretty sure that wasn't standard.

"Um, Beckett," I said. "What is this?"

"This old beauty," he said as he tapped the metal side, "is an RV. It stands for recreational vehicle. Used to be mostly for families to travel, but now we use it for different purposes. Let's a bunch of people be able to travel at once for long distances in comfort."

I nodded.

Used to being regarded for my high intelligence, it was difficult to get used to the idea that there was still so much for me to learn, particularly out here in this new world that I didn't even realize really existed. It was terrifying and frustrating, yet exciting and interesting at the same time. I was probably the only person from the Compound who would know all of this new information. When I returned, I would be even more valuable to our community due to my insight. Maybe they'd even create a new job for me and I wouldn't have to become a physicist- like an ambassador to the outside or something.

The RV wasn't the only odd thing about this new place. In front of me stood a gigantic brick building about two city blocks long and six stories high. I couldn't tell how wide it stretched from where I was standing, but it seemed to me as if it was big enough to house a large number of people. An idea came to me.

"Beckett, is this your Compound? Are there other Compounds that exist?" I asked excitedly. Maybe there were entire communities like the one I came from!

He laughed in a friendly way.

"No, Eloise, it's not our Compound. There are no other Compounds except for the one you came from. Thankfully," he said.

I tried to hide my scowl by turning away and facing down the street. Beckett was always putting my home down, acting is if it were a place of evil instead of a place of harmony. What was it that he had against the Compound? Maybe he didn't have any idea just how easy life was there. Or perhaps he was jealous.

As I looked down the long, paved street, I saw various buildings of other shapes and sizes lined up beside one another. There was nothing beautiful or pristine about them. In fact, everything looked rather old and dilapidated. There were pieces of trash here and there on the street and strange writings on some of the walls. They reminded me of cave drawings that I had seen in my history text, though I doubted that they held the same historical importance.

Beckett tapped me on the shoulder, breaking me from my thoughts.

"Come on. I want to show you inside."

I followed him, though reluctantly. Part of me still wanted to lash out, to get aboard the RV and take off back to the Compound. Though I didn't know how to drive. Or where the hell home was. But I reminded myself that I had to behave until I understood what was going on. I had to be rational, or at least outwardly *act* rational. Even if these conditions weren't ideal and I was surrounded by strangers, at least I was able to move freely. No good would come of being restricted again.

We walked in through the main door into a lobby that reminded me of a much, much smaller version of the courtyard. There were a few couches and plants surrounding a glass coffee table in the center. There were a few other tables for two spread throughout the open area. Opposite of where I was standing there were French doors that led to what looked like some sort of library. To the left, through a double archway, it looked like there was a pool table and another seating area near a fireplace.

I was a bit surprised by the inside after seeing the outside. I expected to walk into a place that was worn down and dirty, and instead it seemed to be orderly and quite nice.

"We put this together to make it feel like home and bring people together. No one really uses this area that much, though. It's really kind of a shame," Beckett said.

"Why doesn't anyone use it?" I asked.

Beckett scratched his head and pulled back one side of his mouth. "I don't really know, to be honest. I guess we just don't have the time."

He's not telling me something. The thought crossed my mind involuntarily and I hated that I felt a constant mistrust. Perhaps it was a defense mechanism, but it was going to be exhausting to constantly be on guard.

"There's more to see," he said as he gestured for me to follow.

We walked down a hallway to the right.

"Stairs or elevator?" Beckett asked.

"Ah, stairs actually. I feel a bit cramped from our ride," I said.

A few more paces down the hall we stopped at a white door, which Beckett opened. It led to the stairway. We climbed two flights of stairs and then came to another door, which had been painted purple. I followed him through it into another hallway that was lined with bricks painted purple on the left side with the windows.

"What's with the purple?" I asked.

Beckett threw his hands in the air. "When we moved in here we color-coded each floor. Consider it an interior design choice gone bad."

The hallway seemed to stretch the length of the building, and on the right side there were doors equally spaced apart. Though Beckett didn't specifically state it, I assumed they were apartments where people lived. I guess he figured I knew as much.

"Where is everyone?" I asked. I was used to seeing at least *some* people bustling about no matter what time of day it was. Everyone here couldn't possibly be on the same exact schedule.

"Busy, working somewhere mostly. I'm sure there are folks home, but they typically don't hang out in the hallway," he winked at me.

We continued walking down the purple hallway, and then Beckett showed me the other floors, all looking exactly the same except for the color of the stairway door and the bricks on the window-side. It reminded me of the Compound, in a way, except the building seemed to be far smaller. I assumed that this must be only one of many spaces for living quarters. This couldn't possibly be the entire population of people who lived on the outside. Could it?

When we finally got to the top floor, which was painted a calming blue, Beckett stopped in front of one of the doors.

"And this is home sweet home," he announced.

"This is where you live?" I asked the obvious.

"Yeah, this is it. And this is where you'll be staying for the time being. We don't really have any extra places right now, so...." he trailed off.

I didn't know that I was entirely comfortable with the idea of staying in the apartment of a strange man, but I assumed that they wanted to make sure I didn't escape. I could only hope there was a separate bedroom with a door I could lock.

Beckett opened the door and let us in.

"It's not much, but..." he said. He actually seemed a little uncharacteristically sheepish.

There was a small kitchen area with what I now knew was a refrigerator and an oven. There were wooden cabinets for storage and a few odd things on the counter that I assumed would have something to do with the preparation of food. There was, however, a steel square looking thing the height of the counter that I was unfamiliar with. I pointed at it questioningly.

"Oh, right. That's a dishwasher. After you eat, you can put your plate and glass and everything in it, and it will clean it for you."

I was somewhat impressed. In the Compound we probably had them, too. We just never saw what happened behind the walls.

Continuing to appraise the space, I saw that beyond the kitchen there was a large couch that faced a television. There were two doors which I assumed led to a bedroom and bathroom. I helped myself to the knowledge and opened the doors. I was right.

All of the spaces were pretty small and the furniture was very simple. There were no decorations hanging on the walls or personal mementos anywhere, but it was clean and neat. I had never been in the apartment of a single man, but I assumed that this was probably exceptional. I wondered if he had cleaned up in anticipation of my arrival or if it was always like this.

"It's nice," I said simply.

"Are you always so polite, Eloise?" Beckett asked with a smile playing on his lips.

I knew he was mocking me. I could read his emotions by his body language already. When his mouth was itching to turn into a smile, I knew that he was teasing me. When his hands were running through his hair or they were hanging casually in his back pockets, he was at ease. I knew that crossed arms meant he was feeling authoritative and was in no mood to be joked around with or messed with. Scratching the back of his head meant that he was uncomfortable or confused, that he didn't have an answer to give at the ready.

"I think you already know the answer to that, but I don't know what you mean in this instance," I replied flatly.

"Well, you're uncomfortable right now," he said.

"How do you figure?"

Beckett walked towards me slowly.

"I've been watching your eyes move around the room, taking everything in. You're stiff. Your arms are straight down by your sides and your hands are clenched. You have an alerted look on your face, like you're waiting for something to pop out at you. I can see that mind spinning, calculating and measuring every item in the room, making judgments out of what you see."

So he had been studying me as closely as I had been studying him. Since he had been crossing the room the entire time he was talking, he now stood directly in front of me. His proximity had my entire body on full alert. The logical part of my brain was screaming at me to be aware of a dangerous situation, but the emotional part of me could only focus on the lulling tone of his voice and the way that he looked at me with sincerity in his eyes. I felt like I was on autopilot, temporarily mesmerized by his nearness.

What was wrong with me? I had never so much as looked at a male in the Compound, never mind to be so mindlessly taken with one. Maybe it was *because* Beckett was dangerous and new. Maybe it was just a reflex of teenage hormones that had been bottled up and escaping all at once. Whatever was happening, I altogether didn't feel myself, but in that moment I liked it, the electric feeling of the world around you blurring outside of that one person.

Beckett gently placed his hands on either side of my face. While it surprised even myself, I didn't try to hurt him.

"You need to relax a little. Know that you're safe here."

Then he leaned in towards my face and I thought he was going to kiss me. In a split second there were a million thoughts crashing through my mind. *This is wrong, this is wrong, I like it, what's going to happen, oh my god, push him away, I've never kissed anyone before, he is so good looking, what is wrong with you.*

And then he didn't kiss me. He whispered in my ear, "I have one more thing to show you," and then backed away.

Something in me suddenly snapped, and I realized that my heart was beating faster than normal and I had been holding my breath. A wave of anger rushed over me- at myself for letting a stupid boy have such a hold over me and at him for knowing exactly what he was doing. He was proving a point. Beckett knew just how to get me to let my guard down, and he wanted me to know it, too.

"Well, you're right," I stammered. "I am uncomfortable. Now."

Beckett reached the door to the hallway and then looked over his shoulder and smiled at me arrogantly. "No you weren't."

Then he walked out into the hallway and expected me to follow him wherever it was he was going. I breathed out through my nose angrily and crossed my arms. Stubbornly, I wanted to do the opposite of what Beckett wanted me to do, to get back at him. But I also knew that that would be exactly what he would expect of me, to prove yet again that I was a mere child instead of a strong-willed adult. Weighing these thoughts, I ended up in the hallway to try to prove that I wasn't predictable.

"Where are we going?" I asked, leaving any emotion out of my voice and trying to show him that I was unaffected.

"Up," he said.

Beckett and I walked to yet another staircase. I was getting sick of them at this point, having walked up so many.

This one was not color-coded. It was dusty and dirty from what I assumed was a lack of use. I couldn't imagine that too many people made a habit of climbing up onto the roof.

We emerged from the staircase and Beckett walked over to the edge. There was a waist-high wall that made it seem more secure, so I stood next to him and looked out over the landscape.

Having lived my entire life in the Compound, I didn't know anything besides what lurked inside the six walls. We did have green areas for recreation, but it was nothing compared to what I was setting my eyes upon at that moment. There was such a mixture of sights. Trees and buildings alike lined my vision no matter which direction I looked in. In the distance I could see a mountain in one direction, a body of water in another direction, a cluster of tall buildings in another, and finally a sea of green in the last.

No matter where I looked, I didn't see any walls. Nothing was being fenced in or kept out. Everything seemed to just coexist. While some structures looked more well-kept than others, there didn't seem to be chaos on the streets. I had spent my entire life thinking that the outside was either a barren wasteland or in a constant state of war. Having been educated as the Compound's elite, I thought that I had more knowledge than anyone, but the truth was that I knew nothing.

I felt foolish for having believed that the Compound had been the only civilized group of people on the planet. How silly it seemed now. I had seen maps of the world before, but I don't think I understood just how vast a place the earth was. I still probably didn't know even at that point, but it was the first time that I began to question my way of life. In an instant, everything that I was used to, everything that I had been taught and told, felt like a black mark. Like a lie.

"It's beautiful," I finally said as the wind blew my hair around.

"I'm not sure I know too many people who would agree, but I'm glad you think so," Beckett replied with a smile.

Beckett continued standing there with me for a long time, looking out over all the sights that he was used to seeing, that never-yielding patience always on display.

I couldn't find the right words. There were too many questions racing through my mind. I couldn't even put together one coherent thought before my brain moved on to a new one. It was a lot to take in, this newfound freedom. If Beckett had hoped to achieve a state of confusion in me, he had succeeded. How could I not question everything when I had spent my entire life hidden away? What was the reason? What was the Compound trying to protect us from? I felt cheated.

"So you don't have any walls," I said after another long pause.

"No walls. Except the ones in the buildings that hold up the roofs."

After getting over the initial shock of such a wide open space, I could see the people moving about. Cars driving through the streets, a mother pushing a carriage. Life existed here just like it did in the Compound, except people here seemed free to do what they wished. I had thought my life was full of choices, but everything had actually been decided for me. I had been an obedient cog in a machine without even realizing it.

"Everyone's so....free," I said.

Beckett paused for a while before answering. "No. Everyone's not so free."

I looked at him leaning on one elbow with a serious look on his face.

"Eloise, I want you to understand that there is not a single place on this planet that is perfect. The Compound has its problems, the Open has its problems. There is no winner here."

I rubbed at my eyes and sighed. If he wasn't trying to show me what I had been missing and prove that this world was better, what point *was* he trying to make?

"Beckett, you are the most infuriating person I have ever met."

He laughed. "That wouldn't be the first time I've heard that."

"I'm serious. You take me from my home, tie me up and drug me. Then you bring me here and show me all the things that I didn't even know existed, and then you tell me that it's not any better than where you took me from? What is the point of all of this? What kind of game are you trying to play? I just want an explanation."

"I am explaining it to you."

An exasperated sound escaped my lips and I pushed Beckett in frustration.

"Whoa, now, let's not start that again. Shoulda brought my bodyguard," Beckett said with his hands up in surrender.

I gave him a look that said I wasn't in the mood for his playfulness.

"Look," he said, "there is a lot more to this than you can see here just in this moment. And it isn't possible for me to tell you everything at once. You have to take one piece at a time and then put it all together for it to make sense. You need patience, El."

He was pleading with me through his eyes, even if he words sounded commanding.

"Can you at least tell me why you brought me up to this roof? What part of the puzzle is this supposed to be?"

"Truthfully? I knew that just seeing the world in a different way would get you to start questioning the way you had seen it before. You're not someone who can be convinced of things so easily. I can't push you to do it or make you do it. You believe in things best by discovering them on your own. When you look out on this city with fresh eyes, you *do* see beauty. You *do* see harmony and peace and togetherness. That's not something that I could tell you. It's something that you have to experience yourself, untainted by people who have seen it a thousand times and know differently. Being able to see the positive side of things helps you better understand the negative later on without being so biased. I want you to form your own opinions."

I had no other response than to nod at him. He was right about me. It didn't matter what Beckett *told* me. I had to see things for myself to believe them, which was funny because my instinct was the opposite of the way that I had been brought up. In the Compound, you believed what they told you because you didn't know to question it. What would be the point? We were safe there and we wanted for nothing. There was nothing to complain about when you were blissfully ignorant of whatever it was I was going to learn.

I had a sudden ache for my parents then. It had been probably close to forty hours since I had last seen them- the longest period of time I had ever gone. I wondered where they were and if they were safe. If they were alive, even.

Beckett stayed with me on the rooftop as long as I needed, without interruption. I looked out over the city, observing its movement and thinking about everything that had changed, while being thoroughly aware that Beckett was spending his time studying me.

When I finally had enough and my brain was pulsating from having thought too much, I turned to Beckett.

"Okay," I said, and we both walked toward the stairway and back into the building.

The events of the past twenty-four hours had worn me out. It felt like I hadn't slept in days, when in reality I had slept the entire time Beckett had knocked me out. My body ached as much as my mind. I kept rolling my shoulders to try and get the stiffness out of my back. I wished that my mind had an off button, because as tired as I felt, I wasn't sure I could ever sleep with all that I had tumbling around inside my head.

When Beckett and I climbed back down from the roof, he led me to his apartment. I wasn't sure if he had planned it that way, to only give me that one piece of information at the time, or if he noticed that I needed rest and obliged.

I was scared of letting my guard down. I was still in a strange place with strange people, and though they seemed to wish me no harm, I had no idea what their real purpose was in taking me from my home. Could I really allow myself to close my eyes and leave myself in the most vulnerable position possible? Then again, I wouldn't have the strength or enough of their trust to try and escape unless I got some rest. It would at least be nice for everyone else to be sleeping at the same time as me. Maybe then I would feel more confident that no one would try anything while I was out.

Beckett opened his door using a key, something that I hadn't seen him do before.

"So you do try to keep each other out," I pointed out.

"Huh?" Beckett questioned. I pointed to his hand. "Oh, right, the key. It's a safety precaution. Not everyone has a place to sleep indoors at night or the same belongings. You have to work for what you have."

Everyone works for what they have, I thought to myself. No one was just handed anything in the Compound either. You had to play your role in society in order to have a place in the living quarters. I wanted to ask him to explain exactly what he meant, but I didn't feel like launching into another long conversation with roundabout answers at the moment. So I let it go and made a mental note to myself to revisit the topic later.

"You look like you could use a nap," said Beckett.

"You should probably work on your choice of words when talking to a girl," I replied.

He laughed. "Honesty is my thing."

Okay, I get it, I thought to myself. He was going to keep trying to prove it to me at every turn.

When I didn't respond back, Beckett said, "You've got three options. The couch, the floor, or my bed."

My face felt warm, and I wasn't sure if it was because of embarrassment at the thought of sleeping in a man's bed or anger that he was limiting me and telling me what to do.

"Quite frankly, none of those choices sound very pleasant," I said.

He crossed his arms. "Sorry, princess, that's all you've got."

So much for that charm.

"Well, I'd prefer the bed then. As long as I can lock you out of the room. You really should have invested in a two-bedroom apartment."

I didn't care if I sounded like a spoiled brat. Coming from the Compound, that's probably what Beckett already thought of me anyway.

"Didn't anticipate the need. Bed's yours for the duration of your stay. I'll take the couch."

It was amazing to me how Beckett could be playful and relaxed one minute and so stone-faced and business-like the next. Maybe he wasn't as simple to decode as I thought.

"Thank you," I uttered reluctantly. Then I walked into his bedroom and shut and locked the door behind me.

Though the room was simple and there were not very many places to hide things, I had the urge to snoop, to look through the stranger's belongings and learn more about him. The best way to keep yourself safe is to know as much as you can about the enemy. I had learned as much in studying history. Now I was faced with the task of applying this knowledge to real life.

It seemed too quiet for me to start rifling through things at the moment. All I needed was for Beckett to hear me. It wouldn't serve me well for him to know I wanted to know more about him. I decided I would have to wait until later when he was asleep, or maybe if he left me alone when he thought that I was asleep. Getting intel was a mission that would be delicate.

Tentatively, I kicked off my shoes and sat on the edge of his bed. For some reason I had expected the bed to be firm and uncomfortable, but it was actually soft and marshmallowy like my own. I ran my hand over the fabric of the plain, dusty-blue blanket. It was soft, but thin- nothing like the plush luxury that I was used to. It felt intrusive and too intimate to get under the covers, so I lie down on top of the blanket on my side with my legs curled up.

My original intention was to feign sleep until I was presented with an opportunity to search through the closet and drawers, but my eyelids betrayed me. I fell asleep so quickly that I didn't even remember doing it.

* * *

When my eyes fluttered open, I saw that there was still light peaking through the window. Either I had slept for a very short or a very long amount of time. Yawning, I sat up and rubbed at my eyes, gunk and makeup alike leaving a trail on my hand. Strangely enough, I still didn't get that disoriented feeling that you expect to have when you wake up in a strange place. Looking back on it, I wondered if I always had some underlying disassociation with the only home I had ever known. Like there was an unrest that was always there that I didn't notice until someone forced me to.

Swinging my legs over the side of the bed, I shoved my shoes back onto my feet and tiptoed towards to door to listen for movement. I sighed angrily as I heard Beckett fiddling with something in the kitchen. No way I could start searching for answers with him around.

I opened the door and a wave of good smells smacked me in the face. My stomach instantly rumbled, recognizing the aromas as something it wanted. My brain, on the other hand, reminded me again that I should be more cautious about things I ingest from strangers.

Beckett was busy standing over the stove singing while preparing something that smelled like what I thought was bacon. He hadn't heard me come out of the bedroom. That survival instinct kicked in again, and my first thought was to grab something heavy, smash it over his unsuspecting head, and make a run for it. For a split second, I weighed it in my mind with some serious consideration. But the truth was that I still had no idea where I was in relation to the Compound or how to survive out there in unknown territory. So instead, I opted to make my presence known.

I did a mixture of clearing my throat and coughing, which was supposed to sound casual but actually came out awkwardly obvious that I was looking for attention.

Beckett spun around wielding an instrument that had a handle with a flat, square piece on the end.

"Good morning, little miss sunshine," he said with flair. He was back in his over-the-top charm mode. "You must be well-rested after that twelve hour nap, huh?"

He winked at me and went back to the eggs and bacon sizzling on the stove. There was a small popping noise and he reached over with one hand to remove toast from a small appliance on the counter, his other hand never abandoning the other food.

I stayed silent while I watched him move expertly around the kitchen.

"See I'm already learning more about you," Beckett said. "You're not a morning person. Coming out of the bedroom all grumpy and quiet. I, on the other hand, bounce out of bed in the morning. Well, I guess in this case I bounced off the couch, but regardless it's another beautiful day in paradise."

Beckett's peppy optimism bewildered me. Nothing about his life seemed like a cause for celebration, but he made breakfast seem like a special occasion rather than a daily activity. He hummed along as he began to transfer food onto plates, and then he brought them to the kitchen table and sat down.

"Hope you're hungry," he said and ate his own food without hesitation.

I stood in place for a moment, debating through my stubbornness whether or not I was going to sit down and eat the meal that he prepared for me. The opinion that prevailed, however, was that going on a hunger strike would do no good for me when I finally needed it to get out of this place, so I sat down.

On my plate there were two fried eggs, four slices of bacon, two slices of toast, and a hash brown patty. One thing I could not deny was that the items not only smelled delicious but looked it, too. We ate in silence. Bite after bite, I shoveled the food into my mouth until my plate looked as if it had been licked clean. Beckett had some talent as a cook.

"I'm sorry the food was so terrible. Looks like you hated it," Beckett teased again.

"You're hilarious," I responded, gulping down the rest of the apple juice that he had poured into a glass for me. "And for your information, I am a morning person."

Beckett clasped both hands to the side of his face in an exaggerated gesture.

"You do speak still!"

"This funny-guy routine is going to get real old, real fast," I grumbled back.

He sighed. "Okay, Eloise, I get it. You just don't like me right now. Well, we have a lot to do today, so get ready and be at the door in fifteen minutes."

I guess showering is over-rated here.

"Actually, I was busy observing you. Talking is a distraction," I said. "I'd love to get ready for the day, but unfortunately I was ripped from my home where everything I own is. So, sorry, but I think I'll have to pass."

Beckett flipped the switch to all-business. "There is a bag with fresh clothes and everything else you girls supposedly need in a bag on the bathroom floor. You don't get to pass on anything."

"And where did those come from?" I asked.

"Friend of ours did a little shopping for you. Thirteen minutes."

I walked into the bathroom and saw a large duffel bag sitting on the floor. It took up a good portion of space since the bathroom was not all that large, so I carried it into the bedroom and dumped its contents on the bed. Out spilled several outfits, shampoo, conditioner, body wash, a razor, toothbrush, deodorant, and some other random small tubes that I assumed were makeup.

It was in that moment that I realized I had never actually done my own hair or makeup before, and it seemed to me as though life here was not managed by control panels because I hadn't seen one anywhere. Slight panic overcame me. Though I was not as bad as some, I still had the vanity of a teenage girl, and I was petrified of what I would look like without any makeup on or with my hair a mess in public. In the Compound, the way that you presented yourself very much reflected your status and self-respect.

I stepped back out into the kitchen. Beckett was sitting on the couch in the living room, waiting for me to be done.

When he saw me, he popped up out of his seat. "You're a fast one! Good, let's go," he said and began walking towards the door.

"Wait!" I called. My face felt pale enough and I thought I looked the right amount of bedraggled to convince Beckett that I couldn't go. "I'm not feeling so well."

Beckett crossed his arms and looked at me as if I were a naughty child. He spoke to me that way, too. "Now Eloise, we are not going to keep playing this game. If you want to understand everything, then you have to trust and follow me whenever I say to. Let's go and stop wasting time."

"I'm not joking. I'm really not feeling well."

"I'd believe you expect you look fine to me. And you just woofed down that breakfast like your life depended on it."

"Look fine? I do not look fine. Maybe it was your breakfast that made me feel sick!" I snapped.

Beckett paused for a moment, appearing deep in thought, before answering me.

"That's what this is about," he finally said.

"What's what it's about?" I answered, totally aware of how stupid my question sounded.

"You're worried about the way you look."

I swallowed, unable to submit to anything he said, no matter how accurate. "That's not it. That has nothing to do with anything."

He raised his eyebrows at me. "Eloise."

Beckett really had the father figure down when that was the act he wanted to put on. He could stand there with his arms crossed, staring at me for hours and wouldn't budge. I knew that

I wasn't going to win, no matter what I tried to use as an excuse. In the future, though, I would always try even though I knew it was a losing battle.

"Fine," I said avoiding eye contact. "I don't know how to do my own hair. Or my makeup."

I felt my cheeks get red. It must sound so silly to him, the poor little rich girl from the Compound couldn't even take care of her own body. I was embarrassed to admit it, even more so than I was embarrassed to lack the vocabulary to live in this new world. That was the first time I had ever lacked the two things that I had been taught were most important to have: an education and skills.

Beckett didn't laugh like I expected him to. Instead, he nodded and headed for the door again.

"Where are you going? I said I'm not going out there," I stammered.

"I'll be right back," he said and then disappeared out the door.

I flopped down on the couch with my elbows on my knees.

When Beckett came back, he wasn't alone. Trailing right behind him there was a pretty girl about my age with long, straight brown hair. She was dressed fashionably and wore a bandana tied up on the top of her head as a headband. The girl looked cute and perky, things that I utterly was not.

"Hi!" she said as she pushed past Beckett. "I'm Rose. Beckett tells me you may need a little assistance."

Rose's smiling face was so welcoming that I couldn't ignore her outstretched hand. I shook it and smiled shyly back at her.

"A girl from the Compound," she said. "I've always wondered what the world of beauty was like there. Tell me about it!" Her enthusiasm and interest seemed genuine. Considering how well put-together she looked, I supposed it wasn't at all surprising. She would be a beauty queen no matter where she lived. Here, the Compound, or another universe. Rose was just *that* girl.

"Umm, well..." I began nervously. I had the instinct to feel superior to these people, yet for some reason I was intimidated. I searched my depths for some confidence and stammered forward. "Life is a lot...simpler. In the Compound, I mean. You, um, have to do a lot less for yourself. Like I've never cooked before because the kitchen does it on its own. And there's this menu where you can select your hairstyle and makeup in the bathroom, and then you lay down and it gets done for you. Oh, and my closet. It's sort of all computerized, too. You just push a few buttons and then you have some options..."

I stopped there, unsure if that was the information she was looking for, if it was too much or too little. For the first time in my life, the Compound seemed like a fictional place removed from reality. I felt like a spoiled brat who didn't know anything of importance. Sure, I had had my education and I had extensive knowledge on a lot of different subjects, but when I realized that there were so many little things that I was ignorant of, I felt like I had actually been living under a rock.

But Rose wasn't condescending. She didn't sneer at me or roll her eyes.

"Wow! Imagine that. I would kill for a life like that," she said, and then she and Beckett exchanged a knowing look about what she had said. "I didn't mean *actually* kill, Beckett. It's just an expression."

That was weird, I thought to myself.

"Beckett, I think your little plans are going to have to wait. We need a girls' day," said Rose.

"Rose, we really don't have the time—"

"You're going to have to make the time. She *needs* this," she insisted, her eyes boring into him. "There's always tomorrow."

As much as I couldn't win battles against Beckett, it seemed like Beckett knew he couldn't win against Rose. Personally, I thought he gave in way more easily than I had learned was characteristic of him.

"Okay, you're the boss," he said. Then he squeezed Rose's hand with a smile. "See you gals later."

The image of Beckett's hand on Rose's kept flashing through my mind. Was I missing something? Was Rose his girlfriend? Was she the one who had gone shopping for me? Beckett had not confirmed either idea, but it seemed like it would make sense. That would be why Rose could get Beckett to change his mind and not me. I wasn't special. I was just a girl that he had been sent to "rescue" from the Compound. He had come out of duty, not anything else. I was angry with myself- for even caring if Beckett had a girlfriend, for ever perhaps thinking that maybe there could be something more there with him…

"You ready to get started?" Rose asked brightly, snapping me out of my thoughts.

"Uh, sure," I said in what I hoped was a friendly way.

Rose reached for my hair and I instinctively pulled my head back. A little look of hurt crossed her face.

"Sorry, I just, um, haven't had the chance to shower. So my hair probably feels really disgusting."

"Oh!" Rose said, regaining her brightness. "Of course Beckett wouldn't think of these things." I could almost taste the familiarity and love rolling off of her tongue when she said his name. "Did you shower like normal in the Compound? Like, yourself?"

"Uh yeah, believe it or not," I said with a little laugh. "That's one thing they actually taught us to do."

"Okay, well how about you take a shower and then we can get started on teaching you how to be a girl out here in the Open?"

The Open. I let the words dance around in my mind. Yeah, that was a good way to describe a place where you could live without walls and guns fencing you in.

"Sure, I'll be out in a few," I said and smiled at Rose.

There was something about her that made me feel an instant sense of trust. Though I was still struggling with the fact that I had been virtually kidnapped, each passing moment in this new place made me feel more at ease, more unquestioning than I should have been given the circumstances. I still didn't know where I was exactly or what had happened to my parents, but I did know that I was missing part of the story no matter where I was, and I didn't want to be kept in the dark anymore. Whatever it was that I didn't know about the place that I called home, I desperately wanted to understand.

Showering, at least, was as it had always been. I turned the water on to a stiflingly hot temperature, closed my eyes, and let the water cascade over my body. I took the moment to appreciate the simple, relaxing pleasure of being clean.

I surveyed the supplies that Rose had brought. They looked different than what I was used to. I squeezed a dollop of shampoo into my palm and gathered my hair up onto the top of my head, massaging it onto my scalp. The scent of strawberries reached my nose. My shampoo in the Compound had always smelled of mint. I wondered if this fruity aroma was standard in the Open, or if there were more choices than home even when it came to shampoo too. I assumed that I answered my own question when the conditioner smelled of lavender and vanilla.

It was silly, but I felt small surge of anger over the scents of my bathing necessities. I had lived my entire life unaware that every facet of my day had already been chosen for me. Every aspect of my life had been out of my control as I remained blissfully ignorant. There was no such thing as variety outside of the options in my closet, and even then I was only given three that were preselected. Why had I never noticed that I never really had any free will?

As I turned the water off and towel dried my dripping hair, I became more attuned to the idea that I could believe in the people in the Open. Maybe they really had rescued me. Maybe I had actually spent my youth as a captive and now I was free. Excitement coursed through me and I started regretting that I wouldn't spend the day learning and exploring with Beckett. Hurrying to dress myself in the clothes that Rose had chosen for me, I hoped that if I let Rose quickly teach me, I would be able to get to extract other information afterwards.

"Pretty fast for a girl," Rose smiled as I walked back into the living space. She was sprawled across the couch comfortably; as comfortably as if she had spent a lot of time there before. I shook off a little flare of annoyance that confusingly passed through my mind at the thought of Rose spending alone time with Beckett.

"Should we get started?" she asked.

I almost let it fly out of my mouth that the sooner we were done the better, but I realized in enough time that it would come across as rude and crass. Rose didn't know I was keen to learn more about her home, and I wasn't going to share that fact with anyone just yet. Keeping the strangers unawares would keep them on their toes. It wouldn't do to have the entire Open knowing that they already had me right where they wanted me. So instead, I just smiled and nodded.

Rose sat up and opened a table top mirror, gestured for me to sit down beside her, and then studied my face. I felt so awkward with someone gawking at me all undone. Normally only my parents saw me without my makeup and hair done, and even that was only on occasion. A sting pinched at my heart thinking of them, and I felt selfish that I was sitting there learning how to pretty myself when I should be on some sort of brave crusade to find them.

"Well, I guess we ought to start with your hair," Rose finally said. She reached into a bag she had on the coffee table and pulled out a rectangular plastic tool with a lot of teeth. "This is a comb. You should have one in the bag I put together for you."

The seriousness of the lesson seemed so ridiculous that we both burst out laughing. Most girls in the Open probably learned these things from their mothers when they were five years old, and here I was at sixteen getting a lecture about how to untangle my hair. Ridiculous, actually, was probably the kindest word you could use to describe the situation. I couldn't imagine that Rose could wear so much patience with a smile. It must have been a virtue in the Open.

"You take this and you work through the tangles starting at the bottom of your hair. Then you keep working a little higher up at a time until all of the knots are out from your root to the ends. When that section is done, you keep moving to all of the other sections of your hair until everything's all smooth."

My face must have shown that her words were foreign to me. I was a hands-on learner. Listening to her directions did nothing to help.

"Here," she said. "I'll show you."

Rose took the comb and mock-demonstrated how to work the tool through her hair. It of course didn't snag once, her impossibly smooth and shiny hair too perfect for snarls. I wondered if anyone could achieve that in the Open or if it was just another trait of a lucky beauty queen.

With some difficulty, I eventually combed through my entire head of hair. Judging from the amount of hair that I had seen escape from my comb, I wondered how much of it was still actually attached to my head. I picked up a clump that had fallen onto my lap.

"Is this normal?" I asked, slightly panicked.

Rose giggled. "Yes, yes. You've probably just never seen it before, but every time you comb your hair some loose pieces come out. Considering the journey you've had and the last time you washed your hair, a little more than usual probably came out. The more days that pass or the more you put your hair through, the more that you'll see pull free. Nothing to worry about, I promise."

I breathed a sigh of relief. All I needed right now was to be suddenly bald on top of everything else.

"Okay, now what do you want to do with your hair?" asked Rose.

"Uh, well, I like to have it out of my face usually," I answered.

"Ponytail? Regular braid? Side braid? French braid? Braided braids? Bun?"

The onslaught of options made her seem like a live version of my control panel in the bathroom in the Compound, except this time having so many choices left me feeling exasperated. Selecting a button and having it done for me was one thing. Having to do it myself was another.

"What's the easiest?" I asked sheepishly.

"Ah, good point. We probably should start you simple. Let's work on a pony- every girl's staple."

She spent what seemed like the next several hours patiently teaching me how to gather up my hair, smooth out the bumps, and wrestle the mass into an elastic. By the time my repeated attempts had resulted in something that seemed to resemble an acceptable ponytail, my hair felt dry and my arms were aching from spending so much time raised.

"Great!" Rose complimented me. "Now let's do makeup!"

I tried to imagine what it would be like to be genuinely excited about this process, but I just couldn't see it. So much time and effort spent to do what took me three minutes of lying down in the past.

"Rose, I'm really just a simple girl," I said. "I appreciate all that you're doing, but this is all sort of overwhelming right now."

"Oh my gosh, of course!" she exclaimed holding a hand to her chest with an apologetic look. "I'm so sorry. I just get carried away."

She smiled sweetly at me and I felt bad for not letting her issue the full extent of her efforts. Rose was seemingly so authentic in everything that she did that I felt myself wanting to cheer *her* up.

"Can we just stick to the basics?" I suggested.

Her eyes lit up again as she nodded.

Holding her chin in her hand, Rose examined me again.

"Eloise, you actually have a really naturally pretty face, so you don't need too much. Your skin has a nice even tone, so we can skip the foundation and tinted creams. How about if we just do something simple with your eyes and lips?"

I blushed at the compliment. I had never looked at myself and thought that I was extremely ugly, but I had always had a professional makeup artist in my bathroom at my beck and call. It was a totally different story to have a real-live human being look at your naked face and tell you you were pretty.

"Sure, thanks, that sounds good," I stammered.

Rose taught me how to drag the black eyeliner above the lashes of my top lid evenly, how to put on some simple daytime eye-shadow and apply mascara. She took out a small tube and glossed my lips. Luckily, this process only took a mere five minutes. I felt much more confident about the simple steps of applying makeup than the ordeal that was attacking my hair.

"What do you think?" Rose asked, holding up the mirror.

"Perfect," I breathed in satisfaction at seeing a face in the mirror that I recognized. The makeup was close to what I normally chose, even if my hair was still somewhat messy and off-kilter looking.

Rose put the mirror down and turned towards me. "So what do you think? Pretty painless right?"

I sighed. "Being a girl is so much work."

Most people in the Open probably would've resented my comment and sneered at the "poor" Compound girl who had never had to lift a finger in her life, but not Rose. She just laughed at me in a kind way.

"You're right, but it gets easier."

It was awkwardly silent then. Not having my hair or makeup to fuss over left us without a reason to have a conversation.

Searching for something to talk about, or at least to have something to do, I looked around the open space of the apartment and my eyes fell on the time. It was already two in the afternoon. How was that possible? Project Turn-Eloise-Into-a-Girl had taken even longer than I thought.

"Time flies when you're having fun, huh?" I muttered.

As if on cue, the door to the apartment opened and in walked Beckett.

"Hello, ladies," he said with a lazy smile as he shut the door. "Glad to see you could turn our friend Eloise into something presentable. This morning...yeesh."

I glared at him and he laughed.

"Take it easy, killer. I'm only teasing you," he winked at me.

Rose stood up and walked over to Beckett with her hands on her hips.

"Be nice," she said.

"You're telling me?!" he said pointing to himself. "I'm always nice. I'm the *epitome* of nice." He grabbed her roughly to his side and gave her a silly, sloppy kiss on the top of the head.

Jealousy waved through me as I turned away, not wanting to invade their intimate moment. It sure felt much more specific to Beckett this time than it did to just not generally having anyone to act that way towards me. I tried to shake it off, but it just made me feel more lonely.

"Is it okay if I take Eloise on a field trip now?" I heard Beckett ask.

"I suppose I'll share," said Rose.

I heard footsteps and then Rose was in front of the couch smiling at me again. I stood up and she enveloped me in an unexpected hug.

"Thanks for the help, Rose. I really appreciate it," I said.

"Oh, no problem!" she beamed. "There's much more fun to come. You still have a lot to learn!"

We said goodbye and then Beckett and I were alone again.

"You ready?" he said.

"I guess," I said sulkily, still harboring the envy of Rose and Beckett's interactions.

"Cheer up, buttercup," Beckett said as he held the door open for me.

I started walking down the hallway of his floor. Beckett quickly caught up and I felt his arm sling across my shoulders. A rush of tingly electricity moved through my body. I felt embarrassed by the excitement for a half a second, and then all I could concentrate on was his nearness. I tried to remind myself that Beckett acted this casual and friendly with everyone, but I couldn't help enjoying the moment.

"So I hope you aren't opposed to a little exercise," Beckett said and then looked down at my feet. "Oh good, you have on sneakers. Probably should've checked that before you walked out."

"Do I have a choice if I am?" I asked.

"No, not really."

I hoped that his idea of exercise was similar to the kind I was used to, which was minimal. Sure, we had plenty of opportunities for activity in the Compound, but I had no idea if that translated the same in the Open. So far everything else had been different; who knew if he would have me fighting lions like a gladiator or something.

When we got to the parking lot, I expected that we would be heading towards the RV we had arrived in, but instead Beckett led us to a regular four-door car. I had never actually been in a car before. Only saw them in history texts or in movies that we were shown. Once again, my ignorance was highlighted by what should have been a simple daily task. I didn't know how the vehicle worked, let alone the fact that I couldn't drive one.

I reached for what looked like a handle on the front door of the passenger side and pulled, and it popped open with a creak.

Beckett watched me and laughed as I examined the interior before hesitantly sitting inside.

"I keep forgetting just how many things you aren't used to," he said. "It won't bite."

"Yeah, thanks," I said with irritation, pulling the door shut roughly.

"Easy, Eloise. This isn't the sturdiest car. It might just fall apart."

I felt alarmed for all of two seconds before I noticed the devilish grin on Beckett's face. His constant teasing and playboy mannerisms should have been unbearable, but instead it somehow made me feel special to be under his scrutiny.

While we drove Beckett talked a lot, trying to explain to me the basic workings of the car. I learned that to turn it on, you put the key into the ignition and turned until you heard the roar of the engine. There was a stick-like thing in between our seats that he moved around to go backwards or forwards. It looked like there were other options too, but we didn't get into those. The two pedals on the floor under Beckett's feet were basically for stopping and going. It all seemed relatively simple.

"Piece of cake," I said when he was done with his little oral lesson.

"You think so, do you?" Beckett asked.

"Yeah. All you have to do is turn it on, step on the gas, and turn the wheel. It's not exactly complicated."

"Okay, Miss Eloise. How about you try it then?"

I blanched at the thought of being behind the wheel of something that could potentially kill someone, most notably myself, but I couldn't let it show in front of Beckett now that I had claimed it was simple. I was almost sure he could see the fleeting look of indecision that must've crossed my face, but I recovered quickly and tried to play it cool.

"Let's do it," I said staring straight ahead with a ridiculous flick of my hair. Attitude was not my thing when I was trying hard for it.

Beckett just smiled and continued driving in silence. We left the crowded city and ended up on a long, two-lane road lined with trees. After a time, he pulled off the road into an opening you would have missed if you didn't already know it was there. At the entrance, there was a huge, intricate rod-iron frame with the actual gate missing. I had never seen anything like it, the metal spiraling up in curls and leaves into the sky. I assumed the gate was missing because these people didn't believe in keeping people locked in anywhere.

The car stopped a little ways through the gate. There were paved roads that connected throughout the area in front of me. In between I could see that there were rows of mostly rectangular shaped cement slabs sticking up out of the ground. It looked like some sort of amphitheater, which was weird since America didn't have that kind of history. Surely Beckett would explain.

In the distance, the paved road led up a steep hill that prevented me from seeing beyond.

Beckett moved the little stick thing in the middle and the car parked. He unbuckled his seat belt, got out of the car, and walked over to my side.

Pulling on the handle, he said, "Your turn, princess. Show me your skills."

I swallowed hard, but kept a defiant look on my face. When I sat in the driver's seat, I tried to mimic the position that I had seen Beckett take, but my feet didn't reach the pedals. Internally, I was in a battle between my pride and the fact that I needed to ask for help in order to even try and prove that I could drive the thing.

Luckily Beckett spoke first. "Now the first thing you want to do when you get in the car as a driver is adjust the seat and mirrors so that you are comfortable and can see. If you reach down with your left hand, you'll feel some buttons that you can press or move to change the seat. Then move this mirror up here –it's called a rearview mirror – to make sure you can see behind you. You want to move the side mirrors with the little arrows on the side there until you can see what's behind you to the left and the right."

I quickly fiddled with the buttons and then tilted the mirror to match my height.

"All set?" Beckett asked. I nodded. I really wasn't sure, but I wasn't going to admit it.

"So now I want you to press down on the left pedal with your right foot, which is the only foot you'll use to drive. You always have to step on the break before you can shift the car into gear. Now take hold of the stick shift and move it down into the D-position for drive."

I swallowed hard again and followed his directions. The more time I spent with Beckett, the better I could understand why he was chosen for this mission with me. He might be a sly jokester the rest of the time, but when it came down to business, he was equally as serious. And patient, always patient.

"Here comes the fun part," he smiled, a little bit of mischief creeping back onto his face. "When you're ready, move your foot to the right pedal and press down lightly. The harder you press, the faster the car will go and we don't have a whole lot of room for that. When you get to one of the turn-offs, one of these side roads here, you can turn the wheel right or left. That's really all I can say for now. You have to learn by doing."

Both hands white-knuckled on the wheel, I slid my foot over to the gas and tapped it. We jerked forward about a foot. Beckett laughed.

"You have to keep your foot on the gas the whole time you want to move."

I tried again, putting gentle pressure on the pedal. We crept forward slowly but steadily, and I gained confidence with each passing foot. I put a little more pressure on the pedal and the car gained a little speed, continuing forward. It was as easy as I had thought.

"Can't go straight forever. Take one of these turns," Beckett directed.

I stepped on the brake a little more dramatically than necessary and we lurched forward again.

"You don't have to slam on the brakes unless there is something in front of you that you are trying to avoid hitting," he smirked. "It's just a gradual pressure. You'll get the feel for it."

We idled in the middle of the road. I was scared to make a turn. The cement slabs seemed so close to the road that I was sure to take one of them out on accident.

"Would you like some help?" Beckett asked.

"A little guidance for my first turn would be helpful," I said coolly. I couldn't admit to the fact that I needed to rely upon him for help. Too much ego.

Beckett leaned over the middle console – that's what he said it was called – and reached one arm around my shoulders. He placed his left hand over my left and his right over my right, and that electric feeling returned, pulsing through my veins as naturally as my blood.

It was a little cramped and uncomfortable, the way we were sitting, but I sure wasn't going to complain about the warmth I could feel from his skin being on mine.

"I'm going to help you turn the wheel, but you still have to be in control of stepping on the gas. Remember, light and steady. And if I say to step on the brake, step lightly then too. I don't want to go through the windshield today."

I wanted to turn and give him a look, but his face was so close to mine that there wasn't enough room without my lips touching his. While I wouldn't have exactly minded, this didn't seem like the right moment to "accidentally" kiss him. First of all, I had never been kissed before, and secondly, my generally impossible attitude did not lend itself towards the soft and fuzzy.

I was conscious of the fact, but I hadn't worked past it yet at that point in my life.

"Okay, take your foot off of the gas. We're on flat ground, so we won't move too much," he said as the car rolled slightly forward. "When you're taking a turn, you still need a little gas to give the car enough momentum, but when you're going at higher speeds you usually step on the brake a little bit so that you don't tip over when you turn. Because we're going slow, I want you to actually give it a little gas and I'll help you turn the wheel."

At that moment, I could barely concentrate on anything besides the fact that Beckett's voice was virtually whispering softly right in my ear. I could feel his breath on my neck and smell the cologne on his shirt. He could have told me to floor the gas and slam into a tree and I would have done it, I was so caught up in the nearness of him.

I swallowed and followed his directions. Beckett's hands guided my own and we completed my first turn. Disappointment took the place of his warmth when he backed away.

"Good! Now let's drive up to the next turn and you try it on your own," he said, his voice free of any sarcasm.

Again and again, I wove the car through the connected roads and practiced taking turns. After a while, the car did start to feel like a natural extension of my body. I loosened up a little and used a little more speed. When we had sort of gotten back to the exact location we started, I was facing that steep hill ahead, and I was curious about what was beyond it.

Figuring I was ready to show off a little bit, I stepped hard on the gas, not quite flooring it but giving it enough to make the tires screech.

"What're you doing?" Beckett asked.

I looked at him sidelong and smiled. "Just taking you for a little spin to see what's on the other side of this hill here."

"Eloise, that's really not a good—"

"Oh, ease off, Beckett. I won't make you go through the windshield," I teased.

When we began to climb the hill, though, I realized that wasn't quite Beckett's worry. Suddenly there was a man in the middle of the road. I slammed on the brakes and Beckett cursed.

"What the hell, Eloise!" he shouted.

"Did you... Did you just see that?" I sputtered.

"What, my life flashing before my eyes? Yeah, I saw it perfectly!"

"No. There was a...a man in the middle of the road. He had on a top hat and he was there, just back there!" I looked back behind the car and expected to see a crumpled figure on the ground, but there was nothing.

Beckett seemed to instantly calm down. "Oh, no. No there was nothing there, El. Don't worry about it. Probably just a shadow because the car was moving faster and you aren't used to it."

While Beckett was multi-faceted, it wasn't like him to jump from one emotional extreme to the next quite that quickly, at least not that I'd seen. I made a mental note of how odd the whole situation was and then brought us to the top of the hill. I slowed it to a stop and tried to take in the sight before me. Beckett was silent again and the car's engine murmured. It seemed too loud for the peaceful place, so I turned it off and got out of the car.

On this side of the hill, the land sloped back down and then up and down again in waves as far as the eye could see. In every direction I looked, I could see all of these cement slabs continuing to stick up in rows out of the ground. Even out on the horizon it looked like an endless sea of gray dots. My theory of an amphitheater seemed completely unlikely.

What was this place?

At my side, Beckett wasn't saying a word, which was strange. There was no sign of his cockiness or sarcasm. Even his stance wasn't as casual as usual. His hands were stuffed into his pockets, but somehow it made him look stiff and uncomfortable.

I tried to lighten the mood and cover up the fact that I wasn't sure what we were looking at. "This is the biggest amphitheater I've ever seen."

"What?" Beckett asked and looked at me.

"You know, an ancient outdoor arena. All the seats. The little gray markers all look like seat backs."

Beckett smiled sadly. "Well, it's a place of rest, but no, it's not an amphitheater."

Something about the way he said it made me feel suddenly cold. The hair stood up on my arms and I hugged them to myself.

"Beckett," I said quietly. "What is this place?"

"It's a cemetery, Eloise. It's where we lay our dead to rest."

It took me a moment to process what he was saying.

"So the gray stones..." I started.

"Each one is for a person who has passed on," Becket responded quietly.

I covered my mouth with my hand, sickened at the sight that had seemed so peaceful only a moment before.

"Oh my god," I said. "There are so many. Beckett, there are so many of them. There are so many dead people, Beckett, why? Why are there so many? Why are there so many dead people?"

I was hysterical and repeating myself, tears starting to spill from my eyes. I didn't know why I reacted that way so suddenly. Maybe I was subconsciously wondering if my parents were now a part of that number. Or maybe it was the fact that I wasn't used to death. I knew people didn't live forever, but it wasn't at the center of attention in the Compound. It happened quietly and out of sight, like it was an embarrassing event instead of a right of passage.

Beckett grabbed me into a fierce hug, my face pressed against his shoulder. He stroked my hair and tried to comfort me.

"Shh, shh, shh. It's okay, El, it's okay. Don't you worry about them. Shhh....," and on and on until I quieted and stopped the unreasonable shaking.

When I was finally calm, Beckett leaned back so that I was facing him with his arms still wrapped around me.

"It's okay, okay?" he said gently.

I nodded, suddenly conscious of the mascara that was probably leaking down my face. I swiped at my cheeks, attempting to make it better, but probably making it worse. There was a half a second when I thought it looked like Beckett wanted to kiss me, but maybe it was just the yearning in my imagination or my emotional instability. And it was definitely still the wrong moment for it to happen.

"Let's go," said Beckett. "I think that's enough excitement for one day."

We got back into the car, Beckett driving this time. He backed up into one of the side roads and turned around so that we could leave. As we passed back through the beautiful rod-iron gate, I looked back behind us at those solemn grave markers. I shuddered again to think of why they were all there.

When I was facing forward, I thought I caught another glimpse of the man in the top hat. But when I spun around quickly there was nothing there.

"What's the matter?" Beckett asked looking back over his shoulder.

"Nothing. I thought I saw something, but it was nothing," I dismissed it, shaking my head.

Beckett gave me a strangely concerned look and then covered my hand with his and squeezed.

When we got back to the apartment, I felt totally and utterly drained. Rose was nowhere to be found. I assumed that she had gone back to wherever it was that she lived. I told Beckett that I couldn't keep my eyes open and went in the bedroom for a nap.

A couple of hours later, I woke up to the noise of a gentle knock on the door.

"Mmm?" I called unwilling to lift my head from the pillow.

The door creaked open and Beckett poked his head in the crack. Suddenly conscious of my sleepy appearance I sat up quickly in bed, wiped the sleep from my eyes, and ran a hand through my hair. I hoped it wasn't too obvious that I cared what I looked like in front of him.

"How was your nap?" he asked in a whisper.

"It was good," I whispered back. "But I'm not sleeping anymore, so I don't know why you're talking so quietly."

"Oh, right," Beckett replied, uncharacteristically timid and polite.

I raised my eyebrow at him. He'd better have a good reason for waking me. I was a beast without sleep.

He cleared his throat. "Bunch of us are getting together for dinner for one of the guys' birthdays. Thought it might be a good opportunity for you to get to know everyone."

"Um... yeah. That's cool, I guess."

As if I probably had much choice.

"Alright, then we have to get moving soon. Be ready in, say, fifteen minutes?"

"Sure," I said.

Beckett paused awkwardly for a moment as if there was something else he wanted to say. But then he finally took his head out from the crack of the door and backed out, shutting it behind him.

I shook my head and sighed. Boys could be so weird. One minute Beckett was a criminal, the next he was acting like an older brother, and the next he was flirting and batting his eyes at me. I couldn't figure him out. I tried not to get my hopes up for any one scenario. After all, he was still the enemy as far as I really knew. Somehow, though, I kept easily forgetting that detail.

I was used to being put together all the time because it was always done for me. When I looked at myself in the mirror that day, I saw an overgrown little girl looking back at me. The results of the simple lessons Rose had given me had seemed just fine at the time, but now that I was going out somewhere, I felt ragged and immature. The ponytail that sat at the back of my skull seemed lank and boring, and I felt like I looked like a boy when you couldn't see my hair head-on. Frustrated, I took the elastic out and shook my hair loose. It had some body from being up all day, but I knew that once gravity took effect it would be awkwardly flat with a bump across the middle from the pony. Considering I didn't really know what else to do with it, I didn't have any other options.

I wiped the smudged eyeliner out from under my eyes. A minute later, there were red marks because my skin was sensitive, and they left me looking like I had been crying. I hoped they would fade quickly. Reaching into the kit that Rose had given me,

I pulled out the eyeliner and mascara and tried to reapply it so it would look fresh. What *really* happened was that I somehow made myself look worse. I didn't get the eyeliner on in a straight line, and the mascara left clumps all over my eyelashes. I was hopeless at being a girl when left to my own devices.

I contemplated washing it all off and starting over, but I didn't want to keep Beckett waiting since there would be other people waiting for us somewhere out there in the Open. Instead, I tried to even out the eyeliner a little with my finger and pull a couple clumps off of my lashes. The result wasn't much better, but I could only laugh at myself. Why did I care so much what I looked like in front of these people? First of all, I didn't know them. And second of all, I was basically their prisoner! First impressions had already passed, and being the victim, I could only come out on top.

"Whatever," I muttered to my reflection.

When I came out of the bathroom I was grateful that Beckett didn't make any snide remarks, or I probably would've refused to go. Maybe he was just being polite, or maybe there was some trend already out there unbeknownst to me that made being a hot mess look cool.

By the time he exited the bathroom, Beckett had that movie-star-but-I'm-not-even-trying look to him again. It made me feel doubly immature and embarrassed to have to walk in by his side. I caught myself subconsciously tugging at my clothes and wishing I had my closet from home. There was nothing technically *wrong* with what Rose had chosen for me. Jeans and a short-sleeve shirt were utterly normal for a teenager. But not for me. I was used to choices and trends and the outfit lacked any kind of style or flare.

I began to wonder whether the Open had the luxury of such selections, but then I remembered that Rose was extremely fashionable. She was the one who had chosen my clothes, so maybe she wanted me to pale in comparison to her. Maybe she didn't want her precious Beckett to look at anyone else. The flash of jealousy made me angry with myself for thinking that Rose could be a friend, but then it passed as quickly as it came. It would be too hard to act that nice. I was just self-conscious and oversensitive. I needed to get a handle on my emotions or I would only make things worse for myself.

"You ready?" Beckett asked.

I dropped my head and looked at him. "I think *I* should be asking *you* that question."

He smiled a one-hundred watt smile and sighed. "It's not easy being this handsome, you know."

"Get over yourself before I throw up," I said and pushed past him towards the door.

"There's the sweet, tender Eloise we know and love."

Beckett couldn't see me roll my eyes at him, but the action felt so natural, as if I had been doing it all of my life. The banter was already so familiar, far more familiar than it should have been considering the circumstances. I should still be on my guard, fighting to escape at every chance that I got. I knew how to drive a car, so technically I had a way out besides on foot. I didn't know which direction to go in, but I could get out of the clutches of Beckett and his people and just try to make a run for it back to the Compound. Surely there would be someone along the way who would be able to direct me.

These thoughts swam through my mind as I walked down the stairs with Beckett, but I didn't have it in me to run away. The experiences I had had so far (besides the actual kidnapping) had all been positive. I didn't feel there was any danger to me, and I actually liked the people that I had met so far. I had a feeling that the Compound Council would frown on my actions and wonder if I even had belonged there, but I couldn't help enjoying the freedom that the Open had to offer, even if it was fleeting. Especially if it was fleeting. For once in my life, there wasn't someone or something secretly guiding my every move. I didn't know before that I was so controlled, but now I did. And every fiber of my being thought that it was wrong. How could I go back to something so confining before seeing everything else that the world had to offer?

Beckett had been rambling away the entire time I was lost in my head. When I finally returned my attention to him, it was too late to even try to pretend like I had been remotely listening to what he was saying.

"...but don't worry, he means nothing by it," he finished and looked at me for my response.

When I gave him an expressionless look, he automatically knew I had no idea what he was talking about. At least I knew that I would never be a good poker player.

"You didn't hear a word I said, did you?" he asked.

I shook my head. "No, sorry."

He actually looked a little disappointed, like a child that had been showing off a new trick and realized his parents weren't even looking, though he covered it well.

"Oh, well. Guess now you'll have to figure out who's nice and who isn't on your own," he said devilishly.

Beckett must have been filling me in on the other dinner guests. It probably would have been helpful for me to hear beforehand, but I wasn't going to ask him to repeat himself. He obviously had already put a lot of flair and effort into it the first time to be so abashed by the fact that he hadn't had my attention.

The two of us got into the car – Beckett in the driver's seat. He obviously wasn't impressed enough with my driving skills to chance taking me on the open road with other cars and pedestrians. That was fine by me. It was too nerve-racking to have so much to think about at once anyways, and even I could admit that I'd be too distracted to be trusted.

We drove through the city streets until we got to the main road that we had been on earlier that day. This time, though, we didn't drive quite as far. Beckett pulled into yet another drive that was hard to see. I sure hadn't noticed it the last time we were out.

There was a long lane leading to what seemed like nothing from my original vantage point. It was dirt and gravely, so we had to take it slow or the bumps would make our heads touch the roof of the car. As we drove further, a building rose on the horizon. When we got close enough, I could see that it was a gigantic white mansion. A square shaped arrangement of columns supported what looked like an upper deck in the front, and each end was capped with a circular structure, almost like parapets you would see on a castle. Tall windows lined both the first and second floors, and I could imagine all the natural light that must flood in the rooms on a sunny day. It looked like something straight out of a movie that took place somewhere called Beverly Hills.

"Who do you know that lives here?" I asked incredulously when we parked alongside several other cars in the circle surrounding a fountain out front. The house was nowhere near as large as the Compound, but it was still pretty impressive for a single residence.

I was suddenly feeling even more self-conscious about being so poorly dressed for a night with what I thought must be the echelon of high society in the Open.

Beckett laughed. "Well, this used to be someone's house back in the day, but now we just call it Headquarters."

"Headquarters for what?" I blurted out.

He wagged his finger at me playfully as he led me towards the door. "Ah, ah, ah. Guess you should have been listening, Miss Eloise."

The inside of the massive house was just as remarkable, if not more, as the outside. The main foyer when we walked in was this huge, open space with a grand staircase in the center. Two wide sets of velvet lined stairs curled in towards each other until they met at the landing on the second story. From that point there was a long hallway that stretched on in either direction further than I could see. An enormous chandelier hung in the center of the room, illuminating the paintings on the walls. Truthfully, I was much more interested in exploring the architecture and layout of the house than I was in meeting human beings, but Beckett didn't give me an option.

He nodded at a man standing by a door on the left dressed all in black whom I hadn't noticed before. He held himself in a very rigid position with his hands crossed in front of him. I could only assume he was some sort of soldier or guard. It made me wonder who or what needed guarding.

Beckett grabbed my wrist and tugged me along like an errant child. Annoyance was my first reaction, and I almost jerked my arm away, but then I focused on the feeling of his warm fingertips on my skin and followed willingly. It was strange how even though I had grown up in a loving home, when Beckett touched me it felt like I had never known the closeness of another human being. The way my mom would hug me or the way my dad put his arm around my shoulders felt almost cold in comparison. I swallowed and tried not to well up at the thought of my parents, whom I felt guilty for hardly thinking of since I had left.

We walked through a sitting room with stiff-looking furniture that was meant for looking elegant and not for providing very much comfort. The fireplace was lit, which I found odd as it was not cold out at all. I caught a glimpse of myself in an ornate, bronze-framed mirror and noticed that my cheeks were flushed. My nervousness was inevitably worn on my face, and I instinctively went to wipe it away as if it were rouge. I didn't want to appear a weak child in front of whoever it was I was going to meet. I wanted to appear pleasant and cooperative, yet let the other strangers know that I wasn't so easily figured out.

Beckett and I continued on through the next room, which appeared to be a study or drawing room. I wasn't well versed in specificity of the names of rooms. The Compound didn't necessitate many differences.

It was again a spacious area, with high ceilings and floor to ceiling windows on one side. The other walls of the room were lined with books, and I fantasized about sitting in one of the great leather chairs by the fireplace, reading for hours on end until I had read every book there. There was also a great, long counter with tall chairs lining one side and a variety of bottles lined up behind it. Different shaped glasses hung upside down from some sort of organizing system above the counter.

"It's called a bar", Beckett said, clearly having noticed my staring. I was suddenly aware of the fact that he had stopped, allowing me time to take everything in. "A gathering place for people to drink alcohol and socialize. Do you know what alcohol is?"

He was smirking at me like he knew a secret that I didn't.

"Yes, thank you, I know what it is. I've been drinking red wine with dinner since I was twelve," I responded hotly. It shocked me the way the words came out. I didn't remember ever being so angry in all my life, but with Beckett it was like he was always pushing a button.

It was true, though, about the alcohol. Mostly I had learned in school that it was a vice that destroyed people, and that variety and over-consumption was something that most people couldn't handle. As a result, the control panel in the kitchen would only pour you one glass per person once per day to avoid any unruly behavior. There were limits in the Compound. Of course there were, as I reflected back on it. Just another way our lives were being controlled without us really acknowledging it. Why had I never questioned the way that people drank so freely in the movies we watched or the literature we read? I guess it all seemed so distant and foreign at the time, a fantasy world.

Beckett had made a smart decision by not responding. He had learned enough about me to know when enough was enough, when it was the right time to tease and when it was the wrong time. He was smarter than I thought someone in the Open could be.

I looked back at him and he took it as a sign that I was ready to move on. His hand was no longer on my wrist; instead he led and assumed I would follow. And I did, though I was disappointed that my aggravation had pushed him away. I didn't really like the person that I had become lately.

Double doors opened up into a dining room fit for royalty. The long rectangular room was off-white with gold trimmings. The columns built right into the wall and the Oriental rug adorning the floor made me feel as if my sneakers were not worthy of being in the room. The gold table had elaborately carved legs and was so long it had to seat about thirty guests. The high-backed chairs were also regal-looking with their red, velvet cushions. Another chandelier hung above the center of the table, this time lit by real candles. My mind played movies of kings and queens that I had studied in European history class. It was all so beautiful.

I could get used to this, I thought to myself.

At that moment, I could have sworn I saw a familiar-looking woman sitting in a chair at the end of the table out of the corner of my eye. But when I looked again, there was no one there. My imagination was playing tricks on me, the fantasy in my mind attempting to come to life.

"Don't worry, we'll be back," Beckett said giving me a strange look, breaking me out of my reverie.

I followed him through another set of massive double doors into a more modernized kitchen. It was like stepping over the threshold into another world, never mind another room. The two rooms being side by side almost seemed an impossibility, the old world meeting the new.

The kitchen was probably the size of my entire apartment in the Compound. The tile floor was the color of ash and cut in the shapes of diamonds. Cabinets sprawled around a center island and were equally as ornate as the table and chairs in the dining room. Zebra-print rugs lie on the floor in between the cabinets and the island. I almost laughed, they seemed so out of place in the otherwise classically decorated house.

Tall, black chairs with lions carved into the arms lined one side of the marble countertop, providing plenty of options for places to sit. The appliances were silver and shiny, and appeared to never have been used. On one side of the room there was another grand table and set of chairs, though not quite as big as the other in the dining room. Arches lined two sides of the room, and in between them were glass cabinets holding fine China and glassware that also looked untouched.

As we walked towards the arches, I could see that the kitchen opened up into what appeared to be a ballroom. There was an assortment of leather chairs that lined the perimeter of the room, a fireplace at either end, and several chandeliers hanging from the ceiling. A sprawling red carpet lie over a hardwood floor. Again I felt as though I could see ladies in grand dresses twirling through the room with dapper gentlemen in tuxedos. But the vision disappeared with a blink, and instead I saw people dressed like me scattered throughout the room.

I was relieved that everyone else appeared to be dressed just as casual, and as much as everyone looked out place in the extensive house, we looked ordinary amongst one another.

I must've let out an unintentional sigh of relief because Beckett said, "See, I told you there was nothing to worry about."

"No you didn't!" I protested. I had never even actually admitted to him that I was worried about the way I looked.

He gave me a knowing look. *How on earth could he read me so easily?*

Beckett caught someone's eye across the room. "Ah, there's the birthday boy!"

I turned around to face the direction in which he was yelling much more loudly than he normally spoke. A Greek god came sauntering toward us. I blinked again, thinking I must be seeing things, but he remained there in my vision, getting ever closer.

The man had blond hair that curled tightly to his head and evergreen eyes. Perfectly manicured eyebrows and long lashes framed them. He had a strong, chiseled jawbone that made him look like a sculpture in the foyer had come to life.

Beckett and the stranger embraced in a manly hug, clapping each other on the back.

"Thank you, kind sir," the stranger smiled at Beckett, and then he turned and looked at me. I felt like a silly little girl, ready to melt onto the floor as we made eye contact. "And who might this be?"

"This is Eloise," Beckett answered for me as I stood there with a deer-in-headlights look.

"Pleasure to meet you, Eloise," he said as he bent over with an arm behind his back and kissed my hand in a manner as old-fashioned as the house. "I'm Alastair, but you can just call me Al."

"Nice to meet you too, Al," I managed.

"I understand you've been liberated from the Compound," Alistair said.

Beckett shot him a don't-go-there look, but Alistair didn't seem to notice. Or maybe he just didn't care.

"Yes, that's right," I answered. Beckett gave me a puzzled look, and I surprised even myself that my words were so agreeable. Had it been Beckett that said that, I would have jumped down his throat reminding him that he kidnapped me.

"So tell me, what was it like there? None of us have ever been on the inside, except for old Beckett here, I guess. Is it as awful as it sounds? So many rules, so many restrictions. What do you think about having lived in ignorance for so long, now that you're out?" Alistair asked nonchalantly.

I didn't really know how to answer the question. Again, it didn't anger me. I just felt so flustered in Alistair's presence that I couldn't find the words. "Well, I, um…"

I began to fumble around for something to say, but Beckett butt in before I even had a chance to embarrass myself.

"I don't really think this is the appropriate time for that kind of conversation, Al," Beckett said firmly, but friendly.

"There isn't really ever an appropriate time, Beck, but these are things we need to know. The more we know, the faster we can act. She is the only key we have right now. I just wanted to know a few things is all. You don't mind, Eloise, do you?" Alistair asked again.

Beckett stepped in front of me immediately. He wasn't a large guy, but he was taller than me, and enough so that I couldn't see Alistair anymore.

"I said not now," Beckett said quietly, all the friendliness gone out of his voice. Part of me wanted to tell him off for deciding what conversations I could have and when I could have them. But the other part of me enjoyed the fact that he was protective of me.

They appeared to stare each other down for a few seconds, though I couldn't see either one of their faces. I could almost taste the tension between the two of them, the sense of friendship upon their greeting dissipated. I looked around the room, wondering if anyone else had noticed the disagreement, but everyone else was busy in their own conversations.

"Okay, Beckett," Alistair said finally. If it wasn't for my assumption that he was absolute perfection, I might have assumed there was a little menace in his surrender.

Alistair sidestepped Beckett and spoke to me again. "Perhaps we can chat another time, Eloise?"

I just nodded and smiled, unable to find my voice as I tried to comprehend what just happened between Beckett and the guest of honor. Alistair walked away and Beckett turned around to face me.

"Sorry about that," he said as he stared after Al. His tone was softer with me, but he was clearly still distracted and agitated.

"What was that all about?" I asked.

"Nothing," he said through gritted teeth.

"It wasn't nothing, Beckett. What was he talking about, me being the key? Why was he so interested in the Compound? Why didn't you want me talking to him?"

"Eloise, please."

My frustration returned quickly. "Don't do that. Don't treat me like a child."

Beckett ran a hand over his face. "I'm not treating you like a child, Eloise. There is just a lot to learn, and that's not what tonight is about. Tonight is about having some fun without worrying about everything else. One piece of the puzzle at a time."

The anger that had begun bubbling up inside of me again subsided. Beckett seemed unwavering in his answer. Though I was impatient to know what the two men were talking about, and as much as I didn't like being left in the dark, I wouldn't press the matter that night.

Just then, the lights dimmed and someone put on dance music.

Like the flip of a switch, Beckett's face lit up in a smile. "What do you say, El?" He held out his hands to me and gestured with his head towards the dance floor.

Song after song, Beckett spun me around and made a fool of himself. He was a good dancer, but he would go into these exaggerated moves just to entertain me too. It took me a while to loosen up, but eventually I was copying what he was doing, not caring what I looked like. Eventually Rose joined in and introduced me to her friends who also joined us on the dance floor. Beckett even had everyone else copying his dance steps for a couple of songs. At the end, everyone was breathless from laughing so hard.

I had never felt so free. My hair flew wildly around me as I shook my head to the beat, my arms flailing at my sides like they were barely attached to my body. I was a sweaty mess, and my stomach hurt and lungs burned from all the laughing and movement, but I felt as alive as I ever had. Surrounded by these people who didn't judge me, who didn't expect me to be proper and act a certain way, I felt like I could do anything. It was amazing how much stronger I felt when there were no expectations. The adrenaline rush the party had given me made me feel like I could take on the world. Fun was not forbidden in the Compound, but there was something different about knowing that I could dance my way right out of the door and not run into a wall.

When we stopped for pizza and cake, I was ravenous. I ate four slices of pepperoni and a piece of cake loaded with frosting, which I gulped down with what seemed like a gallon of water. Beckett leaned down into his cake to take a bite and purposely got frosting on his nose. I laughed deeply at the ridiculous look on his face.

"What?" he said cross-eyed. "Is there something wrong with my face?"

"You mean more than usual?" I said, bursting into a fit of giggles at my own joke.

"Oh, is that so?" Beckett said, laughing too. "Well, I think you have something on your face too." He reached forward with his thumb as if to wipe something off my face, but instead I felt a new frosting smear that wasn't there before.

"What?" I said, trying to cross my eyes. "Is there something wrong with my face?"

"You mean more than usual?" he bantered back. I pushed his shoulder playfully as we both laughed.

"If we weren't somewhere so fancy, you'd be totally covered in cake right now," I said.

"We could always go outside," Beckett joked.

I smiled and narrowed my eyes at him as I wiped the frosting off my face with a napkin. The lights flickered and then the room went completely dark. A second later, colored lights flew around the room, lighting it up just enough so that you could move without bumping into anyone. I jumped up and threw my plate and napkin in the trash.

"Come on!" I called to Beckett.

The fun continued for a couple more hours. I had cooled down while we ate, but it didn't take long for me to get sweaty again. It was probably the most exercise my body had ever seen. When I took breaks in between dances, I mingled with the crowd. Fueled by sugar and newfound courage, I found myself talking to these strangers with ease that I had never known. Conversation came so fluently that I wouldn't have recognized myself if I was on the outside looking in. When the night finally ended, I was actually disappointed to go. The lights turned back on and people began to say their goodbyes. From the looks of it though, the conversations were not going to be short ones. Apparently no one else was ready to leave either.

"I'm just going to go to the bathroom before we go," Beckett said and then walked off into the crowd.

Normally, I would've felt awkward and uncomfortable being left amongst a group of people I hardly new. But that night had left me feeling confident and bold as I stood alone.

"Hey, Eloise!" called a voice behind me. I turned around and saw that it was Alistair. "Did you have a good time tonight?"

"Oh, yes, thank you. It was great!" I answered, no longer shy. "Happy birthday, by the way. I'm sorry for being rude and not saying it earlier."

"Aw, no worries. Sorry I didn't get to chat much with you. I can make up for it now though. Want to take a walk through the garden?"

"Oh, I don't know. It's getting late. Plus, Beckett will be looking for me. We were about to leave."

"There are plenty of lights out there, so you can still appreciate its beauty at night. And Beckett looks like he might be a while."

Across the room, I saw that Beckett was engaged in a conversation with a group of people. It appeared that he hadn't even made it out of the room to go to the bathroom yet. If he was going to be a while, there was no sense in standing there by myself. He *was*, after all, always encouraging me to take advantage of all the Open had to offer.

"Sure, why not?" I said brightly as I turned backed towards Alistair.

He beamed back at me and took me by the hand, leading me out a set of French doors onto a patio. A cobblestone path led off into a row of hedges. We walked down the path, which eventually opened up into a courtyard with a fountain in the middle. Beyond I could see rows of varieties of flowers that I had never seen before.

"Wow," I said in awe. "This is gorgeous! Who takes care of it all?" We had gardens in the Compound, both for food production and for meditation, but they didn't quite compare to what I was seeing.

"We all take turns maintaining the grounds," Alistair responded. "Let's sit."

We sat on the edge of the fountain, which itself was backlit just enough to not disrupt the moonlight reflecting off of the water.

"So how do you like life so far in the Open?" he asked as he dragged his slender fingers lazily through the pool.

"It's certainly different," I said. "It's a lot more....open." I laughed freely at my own joke again, aware that I felt as comfortable as I did with Beckett.

Alistair smiled at me. "I'm sure it is."

His eye contact didn't make me uncomfortable anymore. I swung my legs up and wrapped my arms around my knees.

"So, what is this place? Beckett said it was Headquarters, but I wasn't listening when he told me what that means exactly." The words came out coy and casual, though I didn't really purposely intend them to.

"I don't listen much when he talks either," Alistair smirked at me conspiratorially. "It's where the Alliance meets to discuss strategy. Whenever we have a mission, we get together to discuss the plans. Most recently we met to discuss retrieving you from the Compound."

"And what's the Alliance?"

He paused before he answered me, as if pondering why I didn't know anything. "The Alliance was a group that was formed after the chaos of the United States' collapse. Each sector decided upon their own course of action, their own way of dealing with picking up the pieces. The Alliance was a loosely formed group of people who were like-minded and interested in preserving the way of life experienced in happier days. Over the last hundred years, the goals of the Alliance have changed with the times as necessary. That's how we came upon rescuing you."

I wrinkled my eyebrows at him. What he was saying seemed very vague and didn't make much sense. I knew that there had once been a united nation call the United States, and that it had collapsed after a series of events, but whatever he was saying about sectors and like-minded people went right over my head.

Alistair was apparently not a very observant person because he kept talking as if I was following what he said.

"When we finally gathered enough information from those who were shunned or released from the Compound, we had learned enough about time travel to take action. We've come a long way since everything came to pass in our history, but we know that we can set things right. So after making contact within the Compound, we knew enough to get you out. We were able to bypass the security systems and get the helicopter in there. It was really a piece of cake looking back on it. The Compound thinks they have it all figured out," he sneered and shook his head.

He shook his head and smirked. I was more lost the more he talked, but the sugar and exhilaration of the night left me confident and daring. I was fueled by an unfamiliar self-awareness.

My chin rested on my knees, I tilted my head to the side flirtatiously. "Seems like a lot to go through for a sixteen year old girl."

Who am I? I thought to myself. It was as if someone else's words had left my mouth, and my body language was not my own.

"Oh, believe me, it was," Alistair said as he leaned towards me. "But I think maybe it was worth it."

He spoke so close to my face that I could feel his breath on my lips. There was a split second where I thought he would kiss me, or that I was brave enough to make the first move. The thrill of the attention of a perfect stranger and the lack of rules in this new world gave me the audacity to behave in a way that I never had before. I closed my eyes and almost felt his lips on mine when I heard a rustling in the hedges and feet padding down the path.

"ALISTAIR!" Beckett shouted.

I jumped, startled, and lost my balance. My reflexes were quick enough that I caught myself from being completely submerged in the fountain, leaving only my arm and sleeve sopping wet. I stood up and backed away a couple of steps, and the courage drained out of me as quickly as the drips of water fell from my arm.

Even through the shadowy darkness, I could see from the expression on his face that Beckett was fuming with anger. His chest heaved in and out and his fists were clenched as his side. It was the first time that Beckett actually looked intimidating, and I glanced nervously from Beckett back to Alistair.

"What do you think you're doing?" Beckett growled.

Alistair was seemingly unaffected by the steam coming from Beckett's ears. He didn't even bother to stand up. In fact, he was leaning back casually on his hands and grinning devilishly. "Just having a friendly conversation with a pretty lady."

Alistair's entire demeanor seemed to taunt Beckett, to encourage a fight. Beckett was still too composed even through his anger, though, to be persuaded.

"Let's go, Eloise," he said through gritted teeth.

For once, I wasn't going to argue and began walking toward the hedges.

"Hope to see you again soon, Eloise. Maybe even without your overprotective guard dog," Alistair called after me and wiggled his fingers, still grinning mischievously.

Beckett took a couple of meaningful steps toward Alistair, but I threw myself into his path and stood in front of him, my hands pressed against his chest. He looked over my head towards Alistair, clearly boiling over to get a piece of him, but instead he grunted and turned quickly on his heel and stormed away.

I followed him slowly, but took one last glance back to Al. His elbows rested on his knees and he winked at me, still grinning. I couldn't help wondering what would have happened if Beckett hadn't run onto the scene when he did.

I hurried after Beckett. He walked around the house straight to the car, not bothering to go inside to say goodbye to anyone else. I could see Rose still there through the window, and I wondered why he didn't offer to bring her home. They sure were an odd couple.

We got into the car and drove in silence for a while. It was uncomfortably quiet, as I was so used to Beckett chattering on.

"I'm sorry," I finally said quietly.

He glanced at me and then looked back at the road. "It's not your fault. I shouldn't have left you alone."

That's all he offered, and then the car fell silent again. I bit my lip and looked out the window into the darkness.

"Was someone a little jealous?" I tried to playfully lighten the mood, nudging him with my elbow. He was silent for a moment before he answered.

"Yeah, Eloise, that's part of it. But that's not all of it," he responded, still staring straight ahead at the road.

"You were jealous? I was only kidding," I said incredulously. "What about Rose?"

Beckett looked bashful momentarily, and then confused. "Rose? What does Rose have to do with anything?"

"You've got to be the worst boyfriend on the planet. Or is it a common practice in the Open to have an open relationship as well?" I retorted.

Beckett looked at me and then burst into laughter.

"What's so funny?" Now I was the one who was irritated. How could he be so callous?

"Rose is my sister, Eloise."

Now I was the one looking bashful. It all actually made sense. Rose was helpful and friendly, but they had never actually done anything to confirm my suspicions. They had a close relationship and they were playful, but I had confused their interactions for something other than what it was. It also made sense as to why Beckett barely paid any attention to Rose all night and had left her behind.

"Oh," I mumbled.

The uncomfortable silence turned simply awkward, but Beckett at least seemed to have cooled down a little. The lack of conversation left me the opportunity to think about what Beckett had said. He had been jealous when he saw me with Alistair. What did that really mean? This new life was endlessly confusing.

I didn't really know what else to say after that, so the car ride home continued on in stillness. I could only assume that Beckett felt the same way because he didn't fill the void with his usual banter.

When we got back to the apartment, Beckett parked the car in the lot. Everyone else must have been long asleep because there wasn't any movement to be seen. Beckett's hand was reaching for the door when I saw a shadow move on the other side of the lot.

"Stop!" I whispered.

His hand froze in place. "What's the matter? What did you see?"

I stared out into the darkness, my eyes darting in between the cars to look for the person I had seen. But there was nothing.

"I don't know. I thought I saw something," I said.

Beckett suddenly seemed on high alert. "Don't move. I'll come around to your side of the car."

Quickly, he opened and shut his door and jogged around the front of the car to my side. He opened my door and gestured for me to get out, all the while scanning our surroundings. Then Beckett shut the door and locked it.

"Hurry," was all he said as he grabbed my hand and ran with me to the door. He didn't settle down even when he closed and locked the apartment door. "Stand here."

Beckett pointed towards the middle of the kitchen. I followed his direction, and he did a quick sweep of the apartment.

When he was done, his shoulders didn't seem quite as rigid.

"What are you looking for?" I questioned.

"What did Alistair say to you?" he countered back.

I decided it wasn't time to press my side of the conversation since things seemed so urgent.

"Nothing really. He was blabbering on about the Alliance and how the United States had collapsed. He mentioned that the Alliance got information from people from the Compound and that's why you had to rescue me."

I wasn't sure if I had missed anything since I hadn't really understood anything that Alistair had said, but I thought I summed it up pretty well.

"That's it? That's all he said?" Beckett asked.

"Yeah, I think so. What did all of it mean? What was he talking about?"

"Look, Eloise, it's late. We can start discussing all of this in the morning, I promise. I told you I would tell you a little bit at a time, but right now is really not the time. I'm tired. You must be tired. We both need rest."

I crossed my arms. "What I'm tired of is you always brushing me off. I want to know what's going on."

"In the morning," he said dismissively and walked into the bathroom to brush his teeth.

"Maybe I'll just go back and ask Alistair. At least he seems to want to give me answers," I said, knowingly stoking the fire.

Beckett dropped the toothpaste back into the drawer and then looked up at me. His eyes showed that my words stung. "If that's what you want to do, Eloise. Go for it. Go ask Alistair and get your answers. He might tell you what you want to hear, charm you. But he won't be able to keep you safe."

He spoke flatly and then closed the door, shutting me out. I swallowed my mixed feelings of guilt and anger. I sat on the bed until Beckett was done in the bathroom, and then I went and prepared myself for sleep.

When I snuggled down under the covers, I listened for the quiet sounds of Beckett's breathing on the couch as he slept, but I heard nothing. Each of us was awake, lost in our own hurt and confusion, the magic of the night of dancing erased.

The next morning, I awoke to silence. I rolled over and checked the clock. It was nine. Either Beckett really had been tired and was still sleeping, or he was able to move with impossible stealth.

I gave myself a quick once-over in the mirror above the dresser, not really caring about my appearance in front of Beckett anymore. I tried to leave the room just as silently to catch him off guard before he knew I was up. Turning the doorknob as slowly as possible, I swung the door open noiselessly towards me, then paused to listen.

I couldn't see Beckett from where I was standing, nor could I hear him. Stepping into the living space, I breathed out a breath of frustration upon seeing that I appeared to be alone. A blanket was left crumpled on the couch and there was no sign of life in the apartment. I thought it strange that Beckett would leave me alone, and I probably should have been on alert, but I wasn't, which would prove to be a mistake.

At the moment, though, there was no danger. I noticed a folded piece of paper on the table with my name on the front.

Eloise

Had to run out for a bit. Stay in apartment. Be back at eleven sharp.

-B

That was it. As usual, there was no further information to explain, and it was messily scrawled as if he had been in a hurry. This made me wonder what was so urgent that Beckett had been willing to leave me unattended. He barely let me go to the bathroom alone.

After getting dressed, I sat on the couch and looked around. I still wasn't used to being alone. In the Compound, I had the freedom to go where I pleased, but I was usually with my parents, in class, or studying with friends. Since I had been in the Open, I hadn't been allowed time to myself, not truly. Now that I had it, I wasn't really sure what to do with myself.

Sitting next to me was Beckett's blanket. I picked it up and brought it to my nose, breathing in his scent. I sighed and went through the events of the previous night in my head. Beckett and Rose were actually only brother and sister. There was this group of people that got together called the Alliance, and they went on seemingly significant missions that I knew nothing about. Beckett and Alistair had some weird history that I also knew nothing about, but there was definitely some bad blood involved. Beckett had feelings for me? Or at least that's what it seemed like based on his comment about being jealous.

I buried my nose in the blanket, trying to process everything that I had learned. It was odd how a smell that was so new was now so familiar and reminded me of home, especially when home was who knows where. I felt a tugging in the pit of my stomach, reminding me that I had left everything that I knew behind and didn't seem to care. I couldn't explain why, but it felt right to be in the Open, like I belonged. And if this would be home now, I needed to know more about it.

Against Beckett's overbearing advice, I decided to leave the apartment in search of answers on my own. If I was going to create a life here, or if I ever wanted to find my way back to the Compound, I needed to be able to navigate the Open by myself. I would just try to be back before eleven and Beckett would never know that I had even gone.

I half expected there to be someone posted outside the apartment door keeping watch in case I tried to leave, but I found no one. I still tried to walk quietly in case I might accidentally grab the attention of one of the neighbors. I didn't know exactly how many people were in on the reason I was taken from the Compound, so I didn't want to risk any conversations. I made it downstairs to the lobby unnoticed. As it was a work-day for most people, it was almost empty. There was one older woman with a severe looking gray bob sitting stiffly in an armchair, reading a book with a boring-looking cover. Something about her was familiar, but I couldn't place it. Before the woman could look up and make eye contact, I tucked my head downwards, kept my eyes on the floor, and made for the exit.

I stepped outside into the sun and looked around. *Now what?*

Looking left and right up the street that the apartment was on, I tried to decide which direction to explore first. To the right, there was a line of what looked like had been businesses at one point, some possibly still open and functioning, some definitely not. To the left, there was an intersection where the street crossed another perfectly perpendicularly. If I continued directly left, there was a series of brick buildings. Across the intersection, a slope led up to somewhere. I couldn't see past what Beckett had explained to me as what was once a highway, a quicker route for a lot of cars to get from one point to a destination. It was hard to imagine that being necessary with the streets as quiet as they were now. If I walked toward the other half of the intersecting street, there appeared to be more abandoned brick buildings and a set of railroad tracks in the distance.

All of my options seemed rather dismal, but I chose to turn right towards the businesses. As I walked, I tried to observe as much of my surroundings as I could. Across the street in the parking lot, most of the spaces were empty from people being at work or just simply not owning cars. I didn't hear a lot of traffic in the time I was there, so I assumed that meant there weren't many vehicles moving. Above the parking lot, facing the highway, there was a billboard advertising a bank. Most of it had peeled away, destroyed by the weather or other offenses. But there was still the bank logo and one line of text towards the bottom.

Pay your college loans off by 2025!, it boasted.

I scoffed at the date. This world had remained untouched for over a hundred years. I had understood that from my studies, but while life in the Compound had gone on, the Open was still living half in the past. The year stuck out to me, and I tried to remember if that was the exact year that civilization had ended. It didn't seem quite right. There had to be some historical significance to it though, because as smart as I was, dates were really not my thing.

I shook it off and kept walking. There was too much more to see to waste my time on a silly billboard.

The sidewalk was uneven all over the place. In spots it looked like someone had tried to patch it up, but they had done such a shoddy job at it that I feared I would trip and smash my face on the ground. So I decided to walk in the street instead. It wasn't like I had to worry about any cars running me over.

As I walked past the first few buildings, I noticed that the first floors were all wooden on the bottom, while the floors above were all brick. I thought it odd to put the materials with heavier weight on top, but what did I know. I kept walking until two buildings down I came to a lower level that was completely glass.

Oh, I thought to myself. I looked around, embarrassed, like anyone who was walking by would know that what I had been thinking a moment ago had lacked any sense. The other lower levels must have been glass at one point also. I wondered if they were covered up because they had been converted to homes and people wanted more privacy, or if they had suffered a more tragic fate.

I must have looked terribly confused, alone, or dimwitted standing there on the street staring at boarded up windows, because when I turned back around there was a man waving at me wildly from inside the shop, with a wide smile plastered across his face. We made eye contact and he began walking towards the door enthusiastically.

When he opened it, a little bell clanged noisily against the door. The man had tightly curled, brown hair that verged on manic on top of his head. His thick glasses were slightly askew, but in an almost endearing way instead of sloppy. I was tempted to walk away, but for one, I had been cursed with good manners, and for another, I don't think I had ever met another human being who looked so excited to see me.

"Hi!" he exclaimed, wondrously. "I'm Eddie. You're new here."

The man was behaving so ridiculously that I had to stifle a laugh. There was a child-like gleam in his eye that prevented me from doing so, but it wasn't easy.

"Yes, yes I'm....new," I replied. "I'm Eloise."

"The best people always have names that begin with an E!" he answered happily, beaming.

At this point, I was unsure of what else to say. He was still standing there, holding the door open with one arm while he talked, looking at me with that ludicrous grin.

"This is an interesting shop you've got here," I said with all the politeness I could muster.

Looking past Eddie, I couldn't ascertain a rhyme or reason to the items that I saw stocked on the shelves. It seemed to be a mish-mosh of everything under the sun. I could see a plaid armchair towards the back of the store with a metal floor lamp standing next to it, there were books and toothbrushes and jars of nails on the shelves, and magazine racks and shoe boxes by the register. What it looked like was a giant mess waiting to be brought to the dump.

"Oh, thank you!" exclaimed Eddie with pride, taking my compliment to heart. "Won't you come in and take a look around? It will give us a chance to talk more!"

Good lord, I cringed inside. *What did I get myself into?*

I looked down at the watch on my wrist. This little detour was really going to cut into my exploring time, but if I spared no more than five minutes then I should still have a reasonable amount left over.

"Sure," I said hesitantly but pleasantly and followed him into the store.

"So where'd you come from?" Eddie asked with genuine curiosity. "The Manor? The Field? The Mines? The Forest? The Hive?"

He fired off the names of what I assumed were locations at me in rapid succession.

I looked at him quizzically. I wasn't sure if there was one answer better than the other. Eddie seemed so innocent and welcoming, but I didn't know what the consensus was in the general public. Was it better to be from one of those places than the Compound? After all, he hadn't even named it as an option.

Based on my initial analysis of Eddie, I decided on telling him the truth.

"The Compound?" I said, tentative of his response.

"Oh, my," Eddie said much more softly. I recoiled slightly on the inside. "I've never met anyone from there before. What an honor!"

At that moment, I knew that Eddie was a friend and not a foe. And it wasn't just because he had paid me a compliment when he barely knew me. I wasn't that egotistic. But he had said it with a reverence that was sincere. Eddie seemed so gentle and indisputably authentic that you had no choice but to like him instantly.

"What's the Compound?" he asked, smiling blankly.

The happiness of being accepted by someone in the Open dwindled slightly when it became clear to me that Eddie had no idea what the Compound was, and probably would have responded the same way no matter where I said I was from. I smiled at him, and then changed the subject, not wanting the attention on myself.

"Thank you, Eddie. How about you show me what you have going on here in the store?"

His expression immediately transformed from awed back to animated and he led me through the makeshift aisles. You had to watch your step so that you didn't trip on a squeak toy or accidentally knock over pots and pans. In some places there was barely any room to walk at all and you had to tip toe. My first impression had actually been mostly accurate. There was no specific purpose identified at first glance. Or second. Or third.

When the tour had ended, I glanced at my watch. It had been twelve minutes. I had to go.

"Eddie, thank you so much for showing me around, but I really have got to get going."

His face crumpled slightly. "But I still have so many questions to ask you! What is life like in the Compound? Is everyone brilliant? How many times do you eat a day? Do you have any stores like this there? Can you run from one end of the Compound to the other in less than five minutes? How many people are there? How far away is it? Could I come visit?"

I was sure he could develop an endless list of questions that I could go on answering for the rest of my life, and they were so bizarre that I couldn't help but to laugh aloud. Then I immediately felt guilty, knowing that the Compound would never allow for someone like Eddie to step foot inside. They did not admire kindness, only your contribution to the community. They would view Eddie as an overgrown, lack-witted child with no value. I thought back to the last conversation we had had in history class, realizing I was getting a hands-on experience that would only make the Compound version of an answer to the question more sickening.

"I'll come back another time and we can chat," I glanced around me quickly for a reason to return. "After all, I need to come back to buy... this mirror."

It was a hand mirror and looked old, very old. The face of the mirror was oval, and the frame and handle was intricately carved in ivory.

"Well, why don't you just get it now?" Eddie asked.

That's a bit rude. Maybe the kindness is a front to get you to buy something, I thought.

"I don't have any money with me right now," I responded a bit tartly.

Eddie began to laugh hysterically.

"Is everyone in the Compound that funny?" he asked. "You don't need any money. It's all yours. Take it!"

"What do you mean, I don't need any money?"

"You don't have to pay for anything in this store. You just take what you want," he replied grinning.

"But Eddie, how do you get paid? Aren't you afraid people will steal from you? What happens if there's nothing left?" Even as the words left my lips, I knew it was nearly impossible with all the junk that was packed in the four walls.

"Paid? What good is money? Oh, I get paid in favors. If I ever need anything in return, I'll just ask. No one needs to steal because everything is free. You come in, take a look around, and if you see something you like, you take it. Wha-la! No stealing possible. And there will always be something left. I go searching for new treasures when the shop is closed."

I thought about this interesting concept. *A store where everything is free.*

I supposed it made sense. If you have everything that you need in life, what purpose does money serve? And if you don't have to pay for anything, there is no need to be sneaky or violent like I had read about. The only part that didn't make sense to me was the favors. Eddie might be reliable, but was everyone else as trustworthy? What would happen when Eddie really needed help? I hoped that his customers would do their part.

"That is very interesting, Eddie. Are all the shops like that in the Open?"

"No, no! Don't be silly. Just mine!"

I sighed. Poor Eddie probably got taken advantage of all the time, but he seemed happy enough, so I supposed there really was no harm done.

"Thank you again. I will take this mirror because it really is a treasure. And if you ever need anything, Eddie, don't hesitate to ask. I have to get going now, but I will come back again to chat," I promised.

If Eddie was still disappointed, I couldn't tell from the way his face was lit up.

"Okay, Eloise. Bye!" And he dismissed me just like that, turning back to whatever it was that he was doing before I came in. What an odd fellow. As I walked out of the door, the bell clanged again and I could hear Eddie humming a happy tune to himself.

I continued on in the direction I had been originally headed, past Eddie's storefront and another that had been abandoned. On the corner of the next street was an empty lot strewn with car parts and litter. The grass was waist-high in places.

These people sure don't care anything for appearances.

I wondered why nothing had been done with all the emptiness. There seemed to be so much waste, so much that could be made anew. It seemed to me that a true fresh start would really need to be a fresh start all around. Cleaning the place up a bit might help change things for the better. Then again, maybe the people who lived in this community, the ones whose ancestors had survived the turmoil of the past, didn't ever want to forget where they had come from. Maybe leaving things the way they were was their attempt to memorialize their history.

The next storefront depicted more of my idealized version of sprucing things up. As I approached, I could see that the windows sparkled in a way that said they must have been cleaned recently and often, and there was a big, yellow awning as bright as the sun stretching across the front. It certainly caught your eye as you walked by it, and I made the mistake of looking in the window as I did.

I probably should have learned my lesson from the last time. I should have just minded my own business and kept on going. But my curiosity always got the best of me. After all, that was the whole point of my little trip anyway, wasn't it?

At first, all I could appreciate was the fact that this store actually appeared to have a purpose and was organized. There was a variety of light fixtures: floor lamps, electric sconces, elaborate chandeliers, ceiling fans, table lamps, lawn posts, strand lights. You name it, it was there. They were all crammed in, but it at least looked like there were actual aisles that you could browse without taking your life in your hands.

Then I noticed the man towards the back of the store.

"Oh, no. You've got to be kidding me," I said to myself aloud. Squinting, I observed the man and realized it was *not* in fact Eddie who had somehow caught up with me in a second location, which was my first thought when I saw the way he was behaving, but a new stranger.

I should have pretended that the glare of the sun on the window prevented me from seeing him. All I needed was to waste another half-hour befriending another eccentric individual. But he was waving his arms above his head frantically and gesturing for me to come in. The look on his face was of pure terror. His eyes were wide on his face and his mouth was twisted into a painful expression.

There was a brief moment where I was battling with a moral decision. In many instances, I felt as if I could defend myself, but I wasn't confident that I would be able to protect someone else in danger. What if it was something serious? I wasn't even supposed to have left the apartment. Beckett would never know if something happened to me. From my vantage point, I couldn't see any possible danger. The Open didn't seem like a very violent place so far. It would have been pretty counterproductive to recreate the history that had destroyed a once great nation. For all I knew, this guy could be like Eddie and be freaking out over not being able to decide which lamp was his favorite.

I sighed and rolled my eyes at myself as I turned the knob to let myself in.

I only took a few steps, wanting to remain close to the exit just in case.

"Are you okay, sir?" I called.

He had stopped waving his arms, but had the same pained look on his face. There were undeniable sweat stains under the armpits of his dingy cobalt button-down, and now that I examined his expression more closely, he appeared to be extremely nervous rather than frightened for his life.

The man let out an unintelligible noise that was a mixture of a gargle and a gulp.

"Hello, Eloise."

I jumped. The greeting hadn't come from the man who was still frozen in place, arms raised. It had sounded from directly behind me. The hair on my arms stood up and a tingle ran through my body. There were very few people here who knew my name, and this was not a voice that I recognized. That could only mean one thing.

Quickly, I scanned the store in front of me and assessed my surroundings. There could have been a door at the back, but I couldn't see one from where I was standing, and I didn't want to take the risk of checking only to be disappointed. That meant the only way out was the way I had come, and it sounded like that wasn't currently an option.

Slowly, I turned around to face whoever it was. I took one step backwards as I did so, putting more space in between myself and the stranger from the Compound.

It was the woman from the lobby of the apartment building, the one with the bob who I had recognized but couldn't place. It all made sense now. She looked familiar because I had known her my whole life from a distance. The woman was a member of the Council, part of the governing staff that the rest of the Compound hardly ever saw.

You can go home now, a voice in my head exclaimed. But something wasn't right. My instinct told me to escape, to get as far away from this woman as possible. My heart hammered in my chest as I tried to devise a plan to flee.

"You look surprised to see me, and not all that *pleasantly* surprised either, which in turn surprises me," the woman purred as she rubbed her fingertips and stared at me. "Perhaps, child, you don't know who I am."

Everything about her was sleek, from the hair, to the clothes she wore, to the way she spoke as if her words were butter. She emanated over-confidence and superiority.

"I'm Eleanora, Eleanora Blake."

She brought her hands together like she was praying at the bottom of her face, her longest fingertips just grazing her bottom lip, and studied me. Eleanora's look was almost one of pity, like she was trying to choose her words carefully for someone inferior who was too stupid to understand her.

Then she spread her hands apart broadly, palms up, and said simply, "I've come to bring you home."

I stared back at her dumbly, surely solidifying her pre-assessment of me. She was probably thinking that I wasn't smart enough to be in the Compound in the first place, and wondering why she had come to retrieve me.

When Eleanora realized I wasn't speaking or moving or throwing myself at her feet in thanks, she dropped her hands to her sides. The fake smile she had been displaying for my benefit remained firmly in place.

"I know this must be a troubling time for you," she continued, words dripping smoothly from her mouth like honey. "I can understand how this could all be very... confusing. But surely you are eager to get back to see your parents. Why don't we go on home and chat about it?"

My parents.

The little girl inside me perked up at their mention, and I almost agreed to go with her at the thought of seeing them again, of having them reassure me that all was well and the world hadn't changed one bit, that it had all been an unpleasant experience that we could forget.

A flicker of interest must have crossed my face because Eleanora squinted slightly and cocked her head to the side slightly.

"Ah, yes, your parents. They are alive and well, as I'm sure you've been told the opposite."

It was then that I realized my chest was heaving in and out, that I had been breathing heavily without realizing it. My hands were clenched at my side and my palms felt sweaty.

You need to calm down, I told myself. Eleanora could read my emotions plainly on my face. That wouldn't work to my advantage.

Had this encounter happened a few days ago, when the RV was carrying me to the Open or when we had first arrived at the apartment, there never would have been a hesitation. But doubt remained now. Who was I supposed to trust? The people who I had known all my life, or the people I had known for a few days? My instinct was still telling me that something wasn't right. There was a reason that all of this had happened. There had to be, otherwise why would the Alliance go through all of the trouble?

Trying to make it look like I was shifting my weight, I took another slight step backwards towards an end-cap with shelves.

"Why should I trust you?" I finally asked, my voice now sure and steady.

The corner of her mouth twitched, almost revealing the annoyance Eleanora felt about my hesitance. She might formulate her plays based on keen observation, but she wasn't alone.

"That's a silly question though, isn't it?" she recovered, still smiling generically. "The Compound is your home, dear. It's where you belong. It's all you know. Why wouldn't you trust me? I'm like family. I'm only looking out for your best interests. It isn't safe here. Let's get a move on so that your life can get back to normal, the way it's always been. You do want to see your parents don't you?"

My heart ached. I felt guilty. But Eleanora knew that. She knew that if for no other reason, I would go home for my parents. I yearned for them, but if they were able to, they would have come to get me themselves. There was no way there would be a rescue mission that they wouldn't be a part of, so I knew she had to be lying. I didn't know what was worse: not going home if they really were alright, or the possibility that they had been harmed. Or killed even.

I pushed the morbid thought out of my mind. As far as I knew, the Compound's mission statement had nothing to do with murdering physicists. If anything, they were imprisoned. I had to trust my gut and hope that someday my parents would understand if I ever got the chance to explain it to them.

I hunched my shoulders and dropped my head, trying to look like a distraught teenager and willing fake tears to come. Drama never was my best class.

"Yes, I want to see them very much," I whispered in an attempt to sound overcome with emotion, in an attempt to distract her from noticing my hand reaching behind me to secure a hold on a metal lamp. "Everything has just been so difficult, so overwhelming. I had to be sure that you are who you say you are."

My face was still parallel to the ground. I didn't want to risk showing my true emotions before it was time.

"There, there, Eloise," Eleanora said, her voice lacking actual comfort. "I understand, darling. Everything will be just fine as soon as we return."

"Everything will be just fine," I responded. "When I get to see my parents again, I'll be overjoyed. But, you see, that won't be anytime soon. Because if my parents *were* just fine, they'd be here."

My head snapped up and I hoped the look on my face was as ferocious as I felt. At the same time, my arm swung out from behind me and the base of the lamp came crashing down on Eleanora's head. In one swift movement, I jumped over her crumpled body and burst through the door.

I had ten seconds – maybe less - to decide where to run. If I went back towards the apartment, they would probably anticipate that if they had been prepared for the possibility of me being uncooperative. There was no way that someone as high-ranking as Eleanora was here on her own. As I turned to run in the direction opposite the apartment, I saw her slowly get to her feet, holding her head.

Growing up in the Compound, there had been plenty of opportunity for exercise and athletics, but I was never a star in that area either. I would be able to run for a little while, but unless a miracle happened I would soon get short of breath.

"GET HER!" I heard Eleanora snarl.

Crap. That confirmed she was not alone. I hoped the pursuers were not very fast. The chances of that were slim to none, so I had to find somewhere to hide that I wouldn't be found instead. And quickly.

Coming up ahead, I spotted a side street on the right. I sprinted towards it, knowing that I had to stay in the general vicinity of the apartment or I'd never be able to find my way back. When I turned the corner, I was already in need of a break. That not being an option, I pushed myself further. My lungs were stinging and my throat was burning already. I turned right on another side street, figuring it would lead me closer to the apartment. Maybe I could even make it back there in a roundabout way. I continued straight, running past a street that led back to the main road, hoping that no one could see me from there.

My mind was distracted by my brain telling my legs to keep moving and my lungs to keep pumping oxygen. I realized too late that I was surrounded by brick buildings and running into a dead end. There was no direct way through to the apartment. Knowing that running backwards could only lead me towards Eleanora and her cronies, I ran towards a door I saw on the left. Crossing my fingers that it wasn't barred shut, I slowly pulled the handle. Miraculously, it opened with a sound. I glanced hastily behind me and saw no one, so I ducked inside undetected.

Pausing to catch my breath and for my eyes to adjust to the darkness, I hunched over with my hands on my knees and squinted. The bottom floor was empty as far as I could see. There would be nowhere to hide if anyone chose this door to look for me. As much as I wanted to sit down on the cement floor and rest, I didn't waste any time. If someone was following me, they would be close.

It didn't take me long to find the stairs, and I tried to climb them as quietly as possible so as to not attract unwanted attention. Who knew how many of the glass windows had been broken and what noise could be heard from the outside. Wanting to put a little extra distance between myself and my assailants, I climbed two stories up. Unlike the lobby, the third floor was full of abandoned machines. There were rows of clunky looking metal contraptions with levers and knobs on the sides. Conveyor belts were covered in an inch of dust, untouched for generations. The place must have been a factory at a point in time, but its days of mass production had been numbered long ago.

I walked down the aisle in between two rows of machines to the very end where a beast of an apparatus stood. It was as good a place as any to hide for now, so I slumped to the floor behind it, closed my eyes, and tried to slow my breathing to its normal pace.

While I rested, I thought about what Eleanora represented. Lies. Distrust. Secrets. Though I never felt truly at ease in the

Compound, always feeling an outsider on the inside, it was *home*. It was the place where all my memories lived, where the only bonds I had created still were. I wondered what I had missed in classes since I had been gone, if I would be allowed to continue my advanced coursework or if I would be dismissed into regular classes...if I returned. I cringed at the thought of where my parents were and if they were worried about me. Gritting my teeth, I tried to convince myself that they were safe. Imprisoned in our apartment, maybe. Unless I intended to go back right away, it would do me no good to wallow.

The abandoned factory was silent. All I could hear was my own breathing as it steadied. Had anyone followed me, they would have had to be inhumanly quiet, my sense of hearing at its strongest with my eyes closed. Assuming it was safe, I opened them.

For a moment, all was still.

My eyes readjusted to the darkness again, and I turned around to scan the room for movement, still crouched on the floor behind the giant machine. Holding my breath, I waited a few more moments before I made any movement. I noticed an old soda can lying on its side nearby. I tossed it across the room and ducked, listening to the clangs as it bounced across the floor. Had anyone been close, there surely would have been movement towards that sound. Exhaling, I stood up.

Out of the corner of my eye, something moved soundlessly in my peripheral vision. I stifled a scream and stumbled a couple of steps backward. Before I had a chance to run, I looked back in that direction and there was nothing there. I shook my head, attributing my mistake to my nerves, and tried to convince my heart to leap back out of my stomach.

But when I turned again, I wasn't alone. There was a man standing at one of the machines and he didn't seem to notice that I was there at all. My first instinct was to dart back to my hiding place, but every time I moved the man became more blurry. He faded in and out in black and white, like an old movie but where the pixels weren't quite aligned. When I stood still again, he would become more clear as if he were standing right before me, true as day. I couldn't really tell what he was doing, but it would have been impossible for him to be so silent. There should have been some sound as he adjusted settings or mounted a piece of metal upon the conveyor belt. But there was nothing.

My eyes had to be playing tricks on me, the stress of the chase making me daydream and see things that weren't there. I squeezed my eyes shut and shook my head, willing the man to be gone when I opened them again. But when I blinked them back open, there wasn't just one man standing there, but two. And then three. And then six. The whole factory room filled with people busy at work, going about their jobs as if I wasn't there, fading in out of clarity. The room even became suddenly lighter, the dust no longer lying in sheets across the machines. Then there was noise, real noise, filling the room with chatter and the hum of clanking machinery. The factory was alive and in its prime.

"This can't be real," I whispered to myself. Just a moment ago, it had been a forsaken, abandoned heap of brick, full of dust and litter. I had been alone in the dark. What was happening?

Suddenly, I felt the urge to get out of there. I was going crazy. The Open was doing something to me and I had to get back to the Compound. It wasn't right out here. I was getting sick. They brought me here to mess with my brain.

All the pieces of the puzzle were clicking together in my mind, or so I thought at that moment. It was a conspiracy. This was the reason they had taken me, to make me insane. But that didn't really make any sense either, did it? What could be gained by altering my mind and making me go crazy?

My eyes then had only a laser-like focus on the exit. I began to move towards it, but every step made the entire room shift, making me feel nauseous and dizzy. I stopped, closed my eyes to regain control, and then opened them and took a few more steps. The room reeled again. The people blurred, the noise level shifted in and out from a whisper to silence to the chatter. Deciding that the only way to get out of this nightmare was to get out of the building, I started to run for the exit. I pushed past the people who didn't know I was there, but I didn't get four yards from where I had started when the whole room began to swim and I lost my balance. I tripped. I didn't know if there was actually something to trip over, or if it was just because the floor didn't seem flat anymore.

Suddenly, there was chaos in the room. The there-but-not-there people were yelling to each other and there was a scurrying that suggested they were frightened. Then a deafening alarm began to blow and there were red lights flashing high above on the wall that I hadn't noticed before. The picture before my eyes now wouldn't stay put for longer than two seconds even though I wasn't moving. The room spun, then tilted from side to side, then it would be still for a moment. All the while, the light would change back and forth from darkness, as if the room were arguing with itself over how to be. My ears stung from the noise flitting between silence, normal chatter, and the blaring alarm. Suddenly, I was choking on actual smoke. Was it a fire alarm that was going off? Had smoke inhalation caused me to lose a grip on reality? No, it couldn't be. There was nothing there just a moment before. What could have possibly started a fire?

I couldn't take anymore. I just wanted it to stop.

Putting my hands firmly over my ears, I pinched my eyes shut as tightly as I could. I began to shake my head vigorously and rock back and forth, screaming for it to stop. I could still hear sounds coming in and out, so I knew it wasn't over. I debated on trying to crawl to the exit, but I didn't even know if it was straight ahead of me anymore or if I had stumbled sideways as I was running.

Through my panicked screaming, I could hear what sounded like an underwater yelling. The first thought that came to my mind was that someone was drowning. I was going to open my eyes and suddenly I would be underwater and it would be me gasping for air and yelling for help. This made me scream all the louder, until I realized that it sounded like the gargling person was yelling my name over and over.

Finally, the sound became clear. "Eloise! Eloise! Can you hear me? Eloise, open your eyes! It's me, Eloise! It's Beckett. It's okay. Eloise!"

At first, I didn't trust that he was real. Slowly, I released the death grip I had on my ears and pulled my hands away from my head.

"That's right, Eloise. It's okay. It's okay now," the voice coaxed me gently.

I blinked my eyes open and realized I was in the darkness again with Beckett standing over me. The people and the alarm and the shifting room were gone. The factory floor looked as it had before, empty and neglected.

My entire body was shaking. There were tears leaking from my eyes that I hadn't known I'd cried, and I was covered in a cold sweat. I let out a noise that sounded like a combination between a sob and a gasp.

"Shhh, shhh, shhh," Beckett tried to comfort me as he lowered himself onto the floor beside me. "It's okay, El. You're safe, you're safe."

His voice was barely audible as he held me and stroked my hair.

We sat there like that in silence for what seemed like a long time until I had cried all I could cry, the members of the Compound long forgotten. When I had calmed down and my breathing steadied, Beckett lifted his head off of mine.

"Let's get you home, Eloise," he said, still as gentle as if he were trying to soothe a baby. "Let's get you home and then we can talk about everything. Everything."

He kept a protective arm around me the whole walk home. I couldn't help but notice the nervous look on his face, or the fact that he seemed so alert, like trouble was still not far away. Earlier that day, I had been full of determination to know. I wasn't so sure I wanted to anymore.

An hour later, I sat curled on the sofa wrapped in a blanket, sipping a cup of tea so slowly that it was mostly full and cold. I hadn't said a word and neither had Beckett. I stared ahead vacantly, still trying to melt the voices out of my head.

I was crazy. Something was wrong with me, severely wrong, and it didn't seem like I could control it. I never should have left the Compound. Ever since I had been in the Open I had been seeing things that weren't there. The man in the top hat, whispers of shadows out of the corners of my eyes. Today's full-fledged hallucination. They had to take me back. Surely I was no use to anyone if I was insane.

Or maybe that was it? Maybe they would extract us from the safety of the Compound, one by one, and then take it over for themselves. Maybe there was something in the air out here that wasn't safe, and they wanted to switch places with us to escape it. But then again, no one else around me seemed to be experiencing the things I was. None of it made any damn sense.

I could feel Beckett staring at me from across the room, like if he took his eyes off of me for one second I would disappear again. I had the feeling that my tight leash had gotten even tighter after my little stint on my own. Now he would never trust me to be alone. I really was a prisoner.

I turned toward him. Beckett sat there looking at me pensively, deep concern etched into the perfect structure of his face. He was more reasonable than I had first imagined. Maybe now he would see that I didn't belong here. Maybe he would respond positively to my plight and take me home.

"I need to go back," I croaked, my voice hoarse from all of the screaming I had done.

"What?" Beckett asked, bewildered.

"You have to take me home."

"Eloise...that's not going to happen."

So much for reasonable.

The anger I had experienced after the helicopter ride flared through me again; Beckett was the enemy once more. He had no right to take me from home and no right to keep me from going back. It didn't matter what it would take. I was going home.

I stood up, put the mug on the table, and let the blanket slide off my shoulders onto the couch. Without another word, I walked towards the door. I had no idea where home was, but it was worth stumbling about the earth aimlessly than it was to stay there.

At first I thought that he was going to let me go because I didn't hear him move, but a second later he had my wrist firmly in his grasp. I yanked it away. He grabbed it again, this time hard enough to hurt.

"Let go of me," I spat and tried to squirm out of his hold.

"I can't do that," he replied calmly.

"Beckett, don't make you hurt you again," I tried to give him fair warning.

"Only you leaving would do that."

I channeled my self-defense training and played on his emotions. I let me body become less tense, let my facial expression appear to be moved by what he said. I looked him gently for a moment, seeming to have surrendered, and when it seemed like he had fallen for my feint, I attacked. His grip had loosened on my wrist, so in one swift movement I pulled away and moved to jab him sharply in the throat slightly to the right of his Adam's apple. I wanted to maim him, not kill him. But this time it was as if Beckett anticipated my move, like he had been playing me as much as I was playing him. This infuriated me, his feelings towards me all being an act. We struggled there three feet from the door, wrestling like children, neither of us really wanting to cause damage to the other. Finally, I managed to trip him and he fell backwards. I lunged for the door and managed to open it about three inches before it slammed shut. Beckett spun me around and slammed me against the door. One hand was at my neck, and the other acted like a bar across my body, holding my arms down. His body pinned the lower half of mine so that I couldn't move my legs.

This is it, I thought. *He's finally going to do it.*

I stared him in the eyes as we both stood there, breathing heavily. If he was going to kill me, he was going to have to watch my defiant eyes while he did it.

But then he slowly released his hold on me, his hands sliding gently to the sides of my arms, his forehead resting against mine. I swallowed hard, trying to weigh the chances I would have if I slugged him right at that moment, my chest rising and falling like a tide of emotion, trying to catch my breath.

"Stop," he whispered finally. "Just stop."

"Let go of me," I said through gritted teeth.

"Are you going to go sit back down?"

I didn't answer. The truth was, probably not. I would probably try and make a run for it again, he would try to stop me again, and then someone would actually get hurt. Because I wasn't going to take orders anymore. Not from the Compound. Not from Beckett. Not from anyone.

Beckett sighed. Then without notice, he swiped his foot across the back of my knees causing them to buckle and scooped me up. Before I could protest much, he carried me to the sofa and propped me on it. I crossed my arms and glared at him like a sullen child.

"You can pout all you want," he said in his assertive voice, "but that isn't going to change the fact that you are not going back to the Compound."

"Why do you care so much? Here I am going literally crazy, and you still want to keep me here as your prisoner. Is this some sick, twisted way of having fun to you people? Watch the poor, sheltered girl try to survive the poison air in the Open? I want to go home where my life is, where it's safe for me! Where people actually care if I live or die! I don't care about this place and I don't care about you or anyone else who wants me here," I yelled at him.

A wounded look crossed his face, and I almost felt bad, but then he lit into me with a rage of his own. He started pacing in front of me and shaking his head.

"Safe, Eloise? You think you were *safe* where you were? *That* is where you would have been prisoner. Those people don't *care* about you. You're just an object to them. They just want to use you. That's not your home, this is your home! *I'm* your home!" he shouted back.

I was confused and I didn't know how to respond, so I just said, "You don't know what you're talking about!"

"Oh, I don't know what I'm talking about, of course not. You're always so damn stubborn, every single time. Man, am I tired of doing this. You have no idea, no idea! Better with age....they don't know what they're talking about....," he yelled at first, but then left off muttering to himself unintelligibly.

Beckett looked furious as he ranted like a mad man; his hands were in fists in his hair as if he was planning on ripping it out. I was beginning to think I wasn't the only one who was going insane. I didn't know who was angrier: me or him. I stood up and started walking towards him as I spoke.

"If I'm so much damn trouble, then just let me go *home*. No one's forcing you to keep me here. Certainly not me! If I'm such a problem, then why are you going through so much to make sure I stay? Huh? Explain that to me!"

Beckett grunted and shook his head at me, exasperated.

I poked him in the chest. "Oh, *now* you have nothing to say?"

I pushed him. "Why are you keeping me here? Huh? Why can't you just bring me back where I belong, and we can both go on pretending like this all never happened? Why can't you just let me go, Mr. Know-it-all? Just get rid of me and never think of me again?"

I pushed him again. "Huh? WHY? Why n—"

"BECAUSE I LOVE YOU!" the words came tumbling out of him like a dam had broken inside. "Because I'm in love with you. I always have been and I always will be. And I will always find you no matter how many times we do this, and I will always bring you home. I will keep saving you until you don't need saving anymore."

For a second, I stood there dumbfounded, shocked into silence. Then I shook my head and started to back away from him.

"No," I said, wavering. "You don't even know me. You don't know what you're talking about. You've gone crazy too, and you're trying to make me crazy. I'm getting out of here, I have to get out of here."

I watched him carefully as if he would start behaving more erratically, suddenly feeling that my life was more in danger in that moment than it had been at any point in time since my kidnapping. Then Beckett was all cool composure again just as quickly as he had lost it. We were like the elements, the two of us. Nature needed the two of us to exist, but at the same time we kept emotionally snuffing each other out.

"No, Eloise, you're not. I'm sorry. I said too much too soon. You need to sit back down and let me explain. I'll tell you everything now. It's time."

I was torn. Part of me wanted to bolt for the door, but the other part of me wanted so desperately to know what he wanted to tell me. If I left now, I would never know. If I stayed, he would tell me what he had to tell me, and then I could take off in the middle of the night if I wanted to. Not knowing which decision was best, I stayed rooted where I was.

"Eloise, just sit down, for God's sake. It will all make sense if you just listen to what I have to say. Or at least it'll make as much sense as it has ever made to me."

I pursed my lips and weighed my options again. If I tried to leave now, chances are I would never even make it out of the door. Beckett knew I was a flight risk and he would be ready to stop me. If I cooperated, I might have a better chance of sneaking out later. So I went and sat down again.

Beckett exhaled in relief. "This is going to take a while. Do you want something to eat?"

He made us some grilled cheese sandwiches and a salad. We ate in silence, though my mind was never quiet. When we were done eating, Beckett still sat without saying a word.

"Well?" I finally said.

"Are you ready?" he asked.

Elbow on his knee, Beckett pinched the bridge of his nose and exhaled deeply. He looked like he was struggling for the right words, still hesitant to share his knowledge with me. I tried to be patient even though what I really wanted to do was throw a tantrum.

Finally he looked at me and asked, "How much do you know about the United States?"

I raised an eyebrow at him. What could a history lesson have to do with the fact that I was seeing things like a crazy person? "I don't know. Enough?"

"Care to elaborate?"

I sighed. "Once upon a time, a large mass of land was called the United States. It consisted of a bunch of broken up pieces of land that had different names and were united under one government. Disaster struck, the United States was no more, and that's how the Compound became what it is."

Beckett leaned back with his hands behind his head smiling, looking like his relaxed self again.

"What are you smiling about?" I asked.

"You were annoyed to have to answer my question, so sure of yourself, and then you give me this garbage abbreviated version of history. Is that what they teach you all in the Compound? They tell you so little that they can still call it the truth?"

My cheeks burned red. I was of the brightest students in the Compound, and he was insulting my intelligence. "I'll have you know that the Compound is full of people who would make you look like a drooling imbecile."

"Alright, alright. I can see your sunshiny self shining through on that one so I won't push any more buttons. But you need to know that the Compound educated you on the information they wanted you to know, and that education consisted of the very bare minimum of the events that occurred. You have to trust that I'm telling you the truth now and listen to what I have to say without criticizing at every damn turn. Understood?"

I wanted to roll my eyes and tell him how smug he was, but instead I just nodded my assent.

"Understood... as long as you stop insulting me at every chance you get."

"Good, agreed," he said. "Now I'm not really sure where to begin here, but I'm going to do the best I can. If I talk in circles you'll just have to keep up. Considering you're the brightest of the brightest, I know I have no worries."

"Didn't you just agree to not taunt me?" I replied.

He smiled that charming smile of his, but then he was all business.

"The United States was as you just described it. Fifty different states of fifty different names and locations, all full of different kinds of people. Nearly the entire population had been immigrants at one time or another, the only native people having been mostly eradicated centuries before. There were so many cultures, beliefs, and traditions that there was no unified system of anything. It was a country full of people learning how to coexist, and they weren't very good at it.

You see, the country had a long history of hate and violence. They were always mixed up in one war or another, whether it was foreign or domestic. It was a war that founded the country. Bunch of people came over from Europe, unhappy with the way things were there, and decided they were going to claim this big old hunk of land for themselves. When that was all said and done, they started bringing over Africans to use as their slaves. Because now that they had their own freedom, why not inflict far worse suffering on another group of people? That there situation nearly divided the country in half, and they fought another war to decide to abolish slavery.

But they didn't stop there, oh no. As time passed on, the population grew and each group tormented the next that chose to immigrate. There was World War I and World War II. Guess you can't really blame the United States for those wars in general, but they always had to get involved even when it was none of their business. Sent over their boys to die in wars that they never should have been fussing about in the first place. And when that wasn't good enough, they continued on with their battle of racism at home, still hating on people who had a different color skin.

That battle really never was solved, but it was put at peace for a while so that the U.S. could fight the Vietnam and Korean wars. Then there was the Cold War which wasn't so much violent as it was egoistic. After that, there was unrest in the Middle East and the United States spent a course of about four decades in and out of war with different countries there. All the while the soldiers were battling overseas, the condition of peace in their own country was unstable at best. Eventually the United States swallowed itself whole."

Beckett's history lesson was more detailed than what I had learned, but it didn't really present any ideas that were new. His story was consistent with everything I already knew. It wasn't like the Compound had hid anything from us.

"Sounds pretty much like what I already knew," I said. I didn't mean to sound like a know-it-all, but I knew that's how it came across to Beckett. I tried to apologize and recover myself by asking a question. "What I don't understand is, if the United States was always a series of waves of violence, what happened in the end that was so different?"

Graciously, Beckett did not point out my earlier comment and just continued on with his lesson. He paused first, as if lost deep in his memory.

"Eloise, it was a time when there was little sense, when people lost their humanity. Human nature is both complex and simple at the same time. We have basic needs, such as eating, sleeping, drinking and breathing. And then we have basic urges, like going to the bathroom, finding a mate, and protecting family bonds. But a human's primal instinct will always be to resort to violence when faced with a struggle. From the beginning of time, people have asserted themselves by means of force. It's deeply rooted in our core whether we want it to be or not. Over time, humans just seemed to go a bit backwards rather than forwards."

"But why?" I asked. "It doesn't make any sense. Any logical person knows that you learn from the mistakes that are made and you don't repeat them, so as to avoid the consequences that were faced before. How is it possible that such an enormous group of people could just ….just do it all over again?"

I was frustrated with these people who I never knew. They must have been outright animals to keep senselessly murdering each other. I was secretly thankful that things had turned out the way that they did. It reassured my thought that the Compound was doing something right. There was no violence there. We only moved forward now.

Beckett shook his head sorrowfully. "There are a lot of circumstances that contributed to it, El. First of all, the United States was a people-pleaser on the outside. The government put on the front that it was a country of welcoming to all who sought shelter, that it was a continuously rising power…the safest and sagest country in the world. In short, the United States was arrogant. They stuck their nose in the affairs of every other country on the planet, when all the while their own people were slowly slipping into a state of disrepair."

He paused again to gather his thoughts, and for once I waited patiently, rapt with the history of a country I had never known.

"From the beginning of time, there have been rich people and there have been poor people. But the United States was known for celebrating the middle class. The middle class was neither rich nor poor, and for a good long while they existed right there in the middle. It meant that they had to work, but they could comfortably afford all of the things that life required and desired. At a point in time, only the father had to work while the mother stayed home and took care of the household and family. They owned cars, paid the bills, and took domestic family vacations. This is what the American dream was founded on- the idea that everyone could achieve this happy little life. Over time the middle class household required two people working to run, and eventually, the middle class almost disappeared. Life become so expensive that there was the largest gap ever seen in history between rich and poor, with most people falling into the poverty category. This left people disgruntled and unhappy. No matter how hard they worked, they never had enough money. Their kids were growing up being cared for by strangers and learning no manners as a result. They were producing generations of unruly children who grew to be unruly adults.

But that was only one reason for the downward spiral. On top of the financial problems, there were the government problems. It all began with the Civil Rights movement. Now don't get me wrong, the Civil Rights movement was one of the most courageous, necessary events in the course of the United States' history. It guaranteed, or was supposed to guarantee, that people of all races were given equal opportunities and rights. That was a good thing. But born of this act of good was the idea that citizens of the United States had an unlimited amount of rights. From that point in history forward, people could sue and make waves for every little thing that they felt entitled to have.

The middle class became resentful of one government program in particular. You see, the government had years before put into place a system of financial benefit that aimed to help people who were struggling, who couldn't make ends meet. It was free money, basically, and free housing. I look at it as a series of unlimited discounts. The point of this system had initially been to help people for a short period of time so that they could get back on their feet and make their own way. And not all people who were a part of this system were playing it. But it got to the point where people mistrusted everyone who needed financial assistance so much that they all got lumped in together. And in many cases, people who actually needed and wanted help only temporarily were waitlisted for it, while perfectly capable people continued to milk the system for all it was worth year after year. It was disgustingly flawed and created an even wider divide between the classes."

Beckett shook his ahead again, this time looking truly disgusted about what he was saying. He was so passionate about his speech that you almost thought he had been there.

"Ahem," he cleared his throat and looked mildly embarrassed. "Sorry, I'm getting off track there a little bit. What was the point I was trying to make? Oh yeah, the sense of general entitlement. That was only one example, people not feeling the need to work for what they had. But then you had people of the middle class and upper class who were just as bad. The schools were a disaster. In the early twentieth century, the teachers were in the charge of the classroom and what they said was law. By the end of the twentieth century, the parents and students were running the schools. People had been given so many rights that it was nearly impossible to get children to behave. Parents made excuses for everything that went on, and the administration said their hands were tied. They were bewildered and just told teachers to deal with it. So the schools became jungles, and there was no real learning taking place half of the time. Meanwhile we

– the United States – were supposed to be in competition with the rest of the world academically.

It became a nightmare, only worsening with time. Generations of half-educated, entitled, lawless children grew into adults. These adults felt like the laws only applied to them when it benefited them. People rioted in the streets when the law *was* upheld, looting stores and setting fire to cars. They were destroying their own homes and neighborhoods. Violence erupted between rich and poor, between black and white again. It became so chaotic that there was no possible way to control the people. The government had allowed people to 'speak their minds' for so long, that it was very difficult to turn back."

I tried to picture the scenes in my mind, of people running wildly in the streets behaving uncivilized. I couldn't understand it. It made no sense to me that people would act this way. I had grown up in a world where it was unfathomable that the rules would not be followed. In the Compound it was so easy to just follow the rules that you wouldn't think of *not* following them. What could stand to be benefited from lawlessness?

"These people don't even sound human," was all I could manage.

"No, they sure don't," Beckett said, looking at me strangely. He began again slowly, "They don't sound human at all. History is one long series of unfortunate events. We never learned from our mistakes."

He was staring at me while he said it, studying me. Beckett spoke slowly as if he wanted to relay a secret message to me, as if the words were somehow more important than anything else he had told me. But I didn't understand anything beyond what he had spoken plainly. Maybe he just wanted to make sure I knew what the world had been before this point. I didn't think I could ever really understand something that I hadn't experienced.

"What happened, in the end? What was the breaking point?" I asked.

"Not much beyond what I just told you. People continued to act of their own accord. Violence increased to the point where no division of law enforcement, the police, the FBI, the CIA, the military... none of them could stop the violence. There was too much going on, too many people taking advantage of the weak, of the nonviolent. It was every man for himself. The evil outweighed the good at that point, and people had to decide: fight or flight. The people who fought either gained power in their own right and led a group of people against intruders or perished trying. The people who chose to take flight were either killed or disappeared into the wilderness somewhere and hid until it eventually calmed down. Some never reappeared. They replayed history basically. They went back to a time of savagery, where your survival depended on your warrior skills. People simply destroyed each other. Some states held out longer than others, like the states with a lower population. But eventually the violence bled -literally and figurativel- to every part of the country. And the great United States was no more than a tangled battlefield."

"That's awful," I said. "How many thousands of people were affected?"

Beckett snorted. "Thousands? Try hundreds of millions."

I was stunned. The Compound couldn't have had more than a few thousand residents, and the Open didn't seem too densely populated. I was good enough at math to know that what

I had witnessed, and the number he had given me didn't match up with the amount of people that I had seen.

"Where is everyone?" I asked, closing my eyes. I feared I already knew the answer.

"Dead, Eloise," Beckett said gently. "Mostly, anyway. The population has recovered somewhat in the last hundred years, but it will take a long time to get back to anywhere near what it was."

I felt sick to my stomach.

"Are there more? Or are the Open and the Compound all that's left?"

"There are more. After the bloodshed ended, people decided what community they wanted to belong to. There's a community out west, the Hive, that is based on a militaristic regimen. Very routine-oriented. Then there's the Manor. They decided to go old school and run a feudal system. The Hippies haven't changed much since the beginning of time- they're all peace, love, and happiness and live mostly out in the Field area. The Forest tribe is still full of fear of history repeating itself. They stay mostly hidden. The Mine is underground. There are pockets of smaller groups all over the place, Nomads who either refuse to be a part of an organized group, or who also fear violence still too much to stay in one place. Then there's the Open, and the Compound, which of course isn't really an option for most people."

I ignored his comment about the Compound since he seemed so prejudiced against it. But it seemed like all of the other communities had a specific purpose, or design.

"What is the premise behind the Open?" I inquired.

Beckett smiled a proud smile. "Ah, there's the beauty of it. Just its name of course. It's open. Open to whoever wants to be here as long as they're peaceful. We're sort of the embodiment of what the United States could have been, should have been. We embrace all of the good parts: the sense of community, the law and order, the American dream. The Open keeps it all alive."

"And it has worked out for you? There's no violence, no crime?"

"I won't say that there is no violence and no crime. It's just kept at a minimum. No one is forced to be here. They're here by choice. If this lifestyle doesn't appeal to them, they can go out and seek a community that does. For the most part, yeah, it works."

"Well what happens when someone doesn't listen? What do you do with people who don't obey the rules?"

He looked at me with a hard expression.

"There are punishments for all crimes, some more severe than others. We don't make excuses for anyone. Everyone here knows the expectation. If you break a rule, you pay the consequence. That's what went wrong with the United States. There were too many bleeding hearts, too much sympathy for people who had 'tough lives'. There were too many second chances. Everyone here is equal, which means everyone gets treated equally, for better or for worse. Sometimes people are jailed, sometimes people leave. If the crime was bad enough, there's always the death penalty. We've never had to use that though because people know there will be no exceptions. Occasionally we'll have to deal with wandering Nomads who are up to no good, and we do just that. We deal with them when the situation arises."

"Sounds like it could be a bit harsh. You don't ever have a dumb teenager make a mistake?" I questioned him.

"Not one that serious. What does the Compound do with people who disobey?" he countered.

Beckett was deflecting. He fully embraced the Open as the best option. That much was clear. And he would defend it fiercely at every turn, trying to convince me that the Compound was still an enemy. The truth was that I wasn't really sure what the consequences were. As far as I knew, there was no crime in the Compound. There was no need for it.

"I don't know," I answered truthfully. "I know that sometimes people have been banished to the outside, but I don't know what those people do or where they go. There hasn't been any crime to my knowledge where a punishment would be necessary. Why would anyone need to fight? We have everything we need in the Compound."

"Yeah," Beckett answered spitefully. "The Compound sure has everything it needs."

"Why do you hate the Compound so much?" I asked. "You don't even know what it's like."

"Eloise, you really do underestimate me," he replied. "I know a lot more than you think I do. Haven't you learned that by now?"

"If you knew what life was like in the Compound, you wouldn't be so proud of this dump."

I knew how to push his buttons and I was doing it intentionally. If he wanted to mess with my home, I would mess with his. Either due to the fact that he was more mature than I was, or maybe because Beckett really felt a little bit of defeat, he remained quiet.

While Beckett had educated me on a little bit of history, he still hadn't told me anything that explained what had happened earlier that day. I still had no reason for why my mind had been warped.

"What's any of this got to do with me?" I changed the subject.

Beckett's face brightened a bit, but it soon faded under a mask of what looked like internal conflict.

He looked up at me and gave me a serious, stern look. It was his no-nonsense look again.

"Eloise, this is where things are going to get a little bit confusing, a little bit harder to understand. You have to promise me that no matter what I tell you, you're going to believe me. No matter how ridiculous it may seem at first, no matter how improbable you think the truth may be, you have to know that it is the truth. You need to trust me and believe in me if you really want to understand what is going on. Can you do that?"

I didn't answer him right away. I didn't like to make promises if I wasn't sure that I could keep them. What is a person without her word? And this was a little more serious than promising my best friend she could borrow my favorite outfit, or promising that I would go to see a movie even though I had to study. Those were the types of promises that I was used to making. This was a promise that could quite literally be a life or death situation. Even with how bizarre the events had been recently, I was still so unsure of who was on my side. I felt as though I had to defend the Compound if anyone said anything bad about it, but at the same time I felt equally as loyal to Beckett.

There were pieces of the puzzle that I was missing, and I knew that. No matter if they were pieces of the Compound or pieces of the Open. Someone was hiding the truth, and someone was going to reveal the truth, and I didn't know which side was which.

So I told Beckett my own truth.

"I can't promise you anything," I said. "I don't really know what is going on or why I'm here. Or why I was even in the Compound for that matter, when there are other communities that I didn't even know about. My only truth right now is that I need to know both sides of the story. So I will listen to you, Beckett, and I will try not to make hasty judgments. That's all I give you right now."

I expected him to lecture me about all the things that had been hidden from me and how that was an indication that the Compound was not telling me things but that he was. But he didn't. Instead he nodded, which showed me that he respected my position. Whether intentionally or not, this made me want to listen more to what he had to say because he wasn't pushing me one way or another. If there was anything I knew about the truth, no matter what that truth was, it was that the truth was its own champion.

Beckett seemed to have found a new source of energy because he charged forward in his explanation.

"What I'm about to tell you is knowledge that is limited to a certain group of people. It's not something that you can discuss with just anyone, and one thing that you *will* have to promise is to not discuss this with anyone other than who I indicate as being in the inner circle. If you shared this information with others, we could create a pandemonium just like before. Can you promise me that much?" he asked

"I can promise you that I will never say anything that would cause anyone harm," I replied. It was a vague answer and I knew it, but I hoped it was good enough for Beckett to continue. I had to promise only what I could deliver, and if I was told information that was privileged but shouldn't be, I wouldn't keep it to myself. Just because Beckett deemed it confidential, that didn't mean that it was the right thing to do.

Beckett was satisfied enough with my answer and continued.

"Throughout history, there has long been a debate about something existing. Some have staunchly believed it exists, while others snub the idea and chalk it up to nonsense. It has been unable to be proven by the average physicist and therefore there has never been a confirmation of its possibility. It has, however, existed in confidential branches of the government, including that of the United States. It has been an ability limited to a select group of people and kept secret from the masses. It has changed the course of history, for better or for worse. You'll have to make that decision on your own. And you're a part of it all, Eloise. This is the reason you're in danger, and it's the reason why you're so important to either cause."

I looked at him skeptically. I was a teenage girl who had led a sheltered life. Maybe he was referring to the fact that my parents were physicists and maybe people thought I had some sort of information that I surely did not.

"Beckett, what on earth are you talking about?"

His eyes pierced mine. He held my gaze for a full moment, as if he were checking that he had my full attention, or maybe he was just doing it for dramatic effect. I almost opened my mouth and asked him what the hell he was waiting for, I was so out of patience.

And then he said to me as serious as the ground he stood on and the air he breathed, "Time travel, Eloise. You can travel through time."

I didn't even have a chance to register what he had just said. As he finished his sentence, the apartment door burst open. Instinctually, I threw myself to the floor and rolled over behind the end of the couch, crouching. Beckett had tensed and stood in front of me, in the ever protective manner that he had.

But it was only Mad-Eye. The first time I had met him he looked terrifying, but now I actually relaxed a little seeing that it was him. Only for a second. Then I realized that he was heaving from being out of breath and no longer looked terri*fying* but terri*fied*.

"They're coming for her!" he said frantically when he finally managed to get the words out. "They're coming for her!"

Beckett wasted no time. He turned, grabbed my arm, and tugged me to my feet. He sprinted the ten feet to the front door and didn't bother to close it. We ran down the hallway behind Mad-Eye, and half ran-half jumped down the flights of stairs. We were through the lobby and out to the car in a matter of twenty seconds, maybe less.

Mad-Eye opened up the trunk.

"Get in," he pointed and said to me.

"What? No. I am not getting in there by myself. Is this some kind of trick? I am not, no." I sputtered.

"Eloise, damnit, GET IN!" Beckett yelled at me, clearly impatient with my lack of cooperation.

"I'm scared of small spaces. I'll suffocate in there!" I whined.

"You're going to be a lot worse off if you don't get in the damn trunk!" scolded Mad-Eye. "Matter of fact, both of you get in there so we won't be noticed.... and stop wasting time!"

"Go on, El. I'll climb in too. The backseat pops open, don't worry. We won't be in there long anyway. Go! Before it's too late."

I wanted to fight this one tooth and nail. I wanted so badly not to get in that confined space and take my chances, but I also knew that Beckett's sense of urgency was no joke, and I had never heard Mad-Eye utter so many words before.

I hopped into the trunk and rolled over to make room. Beckett followed and Mad-Eye slammed the trunk shut. He was in the driver's seat and we sped off to who knows where.

It was dark and uncomfortable, and the only sound I could hear other than the hum of the engine was Beckett's breathing. I could feel it too, as we were facing each other so closely. I closed my eyes and tried to imagine that I was in a bed in a larger space at night, but my brain was not so good at convincing me.

Beckett sensed my panic. "It's okay, El. This is just until we get out of town and we're on a more open road. Then we'll be able to see anyone coming if they're coming, and we'll have time to hide again. Just concentrate on the sound of my voice. I'll keep talking if you want me to."

"Won't we use up the oxygen faster if we're talking?" I said, my voice shaking.

Beckett laughed softly. "Good point, Eloise. In fact, I think that the amount of talking we've done already may have done us in. We'll probably only last another minute or so. It's been swell knowing you."

I couldn't see him and we were in too small of a space for me to hit or kick him for thinking the situation was funny.

"I'm not laughing," I said.

"Oh, me either, sunshine. But if we're not going to make it, will you at least fulfill my last wish?" he asked playfully.

"What?" I was annoyed, but the distraction was helping me relax a little.

"This," he said, and then he kissed me.

I didn't know how he found my lips so quickly. He must have had his eyes open and adjusted to the dark. I also don't know why that's what my mind was concentrating on instead of the kiss I was receiving, but by the time it finally registered he had pulled away and it was over.

"Now I can die happy, Eloise," Beckett teased again.

I didn't know how to respond. I was a mixture of annoyed with him because he didn't know if I wanted him to kiss me and we were in such a small space that he left me with little choice, and thrilled because I had actually enjoyed it.

There was a thump on the backseat.

"Come on out, kids," Mad-Eye hollered.

"Watch out," Beckett said in a not-so-charming manner. Then he leaned over, half suffocating me, and pushed in the back seat. Light flooded the trunk and I had to blink to adjust to it again.

I couldn't crawl out to freedom quickly enough.

It was still cramped in the backseat because there wasn't enough room to push the seat back into place with our bodies in the way. That meant there was about enough room for our torsos and heads to be in the backset while our legs were still in the trunk. I still felt trapped not being able to move freely.

"Can we pull over, please, and fix this so we can sit right?" I begged.

"Sorry sweetheart, no can do," Mad-Eye replied. "Had to get out of the city without anyone seeing either one of you. We should be safe now, but I would rather put some more distance between us. If anyone is out here, it'll be easier for you two to go back into hiding the way you are now."

I swallowed hard and tried to think of wide open spaces. If I didn't calm down, I'd be having a full blown panic attack before long and that surely wouldn't be helpful.

I closed my eyes, rested my head on my arms, and took slow, even breaths. Pretending I wasn't there was easier than it had been in the trunk. Seeking comfort, I surprisingly pictured the familiar grounds of the Compound. From the athletic fields to the farmland, from the coziness of my bedroom to the clean lines of my classrooms. It was actually funny that I was comforted by the memories of a place that, unbeknownst to me, had been stifling my movement my entire life. If anything should have made me claustrophobic, it should have been thinking of the confines of the Compound.

Beckett remained quiet the entire ride. I didn't know exactly what he was doing because I kept my eyes closed the entire time, but I assumed his silence was provoked by the fact that he was on alert. Any distraction that caused him to miss something moving through the green blurs on the side of the road could cost us all our freedom. Finally I felt the car slow, almost to a stop, and then make a turn.

"You can open your eyes now, El," Beckett said.

I heard the click of the car door opening and then felt his body move away from my own. When I opened my eyes, there was a familiar sight before me. I was staring at Headquarters and it was no less imposing than the first time I had been there. Except this time, there were no cars lining the long drive, and the windows weren't all lit up from a party. No jubilant voices could be heard through the walls. It seemed like much more of a sad place being so vacant, like another abandoned piece of history left alone with its memories.

I climbed out of the car and looked around. I wondered why everyone felt like this was a secure place for Headquarters of whatever it was they were members of, because it was surrounded by woods and I felt like anyone could jump out at any moment. You'd never be able to see anyone coming with all the lush greenery, and there was only one way in and out, making it difficult to quickly escape. I hoped it wasn't something I'd have to experience firsthand.

Beckett and I began walking towards the house, but Mad-Eye didn't follow.

"Aren't you coming?" I asked him. I felt a strange softness for this strange man. He wasn't intimidating at all now that I knew him slightly better than when I had first laid eyes on him.

"Don't worry. I'll be around," he said vaguely as he leaned against the car.

I wanted to question him as to what he meant, but Beckett began walking towards the house again. When I caught up, I asked him instead.

"Why's he staying out here?"

"He...has some work to do," was all Beckett said. I really wished that everyone would stop giving me indistinct answers.

I turned back around to get one last look at Mad-Eye before we went inside. He was facing away from the house now towards the street at the end of the long driveway. At that moment, he adjusted his pants and I could see a gun tucked into the back of his waistband.

I had seen guns before. I'd even fired them at target practice in the Compound. But that was the only use that we had had for them. Out here in the Open, carrying a gun meant that the person probably intended to use it on a human being. I knew that it was for protection, for my protection probably, but it still made me uneasy to think that a human life could be taken so quickly. It also made me realize just how serious things were getting in my life, and that Beckett and his allies expected some sort of war to come before long. And it was all for me. I didn't know if I was ready for that, physically, mentally, or emotionally. I also didn't know why I was worth the effort.

"You coming? We need to get inside," Beckett said.

I hadn't realized I had stopped, still staring behind me at Mad-Eye vigilantly standing guard. Without a word, I turned back around and followed Beckett into the house.

* * *

The foyer was as grand as it had been on my last visit, but like it had seemed from the outside, it was lifeless. The party atmosphere that had existed seemed impossible now. The elegance of the mansion now seemed historically forlorn, a shell of grandeur instead of an eminence.

Beckett climbed the striking staircase and led me to the second floor, which I had not seen last time. The hallway was decorated with old floral wallpaper that looked like it was original. This was in contrast with the pristine, white wainscoting that crept halfway up the wall. Candle-less sconces adorned the walls next to paintings of people long dead. I found myself wondering who they were and what stories they would share if they were able to. I wondered what atrocities they had witnessed, and if they had even been able to imagine what would become of the world they once lived in.

We passed several open doors to rooms that, to my surprise, were not empty. There were a couple of people in each bedroom, and each bedroom seemed to be both sleeping quarters and workspace. Some people were hunched over computers, silently squinting and analyzing whatever was on the screen. Others were lifting weights or doing jumping jacks. Some appeared to be cleaning weapons. I made eye contact with a man cleaning a gun. He looked at me in an unsmiling way that sent chills down my spine, and for the first time I wondered if maybe I wasn't the only one questioning why I was worth a battle.

Finally, we reached the end of the hallway and stood in front of a bookcase. Beckett hadn't said a word as he led me down the hallway, and now he still stood without speaking. When I couldn't take the silence anymore (and couldn't figure out why he was staring at the books), I broke the stagnant air with the sound of my voice.

"Though it would be nice, I'm thinking right now probably isn't the best time to read," I said.

"Agreed," Beckett responded seriously.

He looked at me, with his full attention, for the first time since we had been in the trunk. The heat of the moment and the emotion behind the kiss had expired. This was business Beckett. Not emotional Beckett, not playful Beckett. I considered the possibility that the kiss may have been a ruse to distract me when I was upset. I was glad I hadn't outwardly reacted to it.

"Notice anything unusual about this bookcase?" he asked.

I examined it. There was something amiss or he wouldn't have asked me that question. I didn't like not knowing an answer, and I was usually pretty observant. But nothing stuck out to me. The bookcase was ornately carved on top and bottom and looked old like the rest of the house. Even the books on the shelves looked worn; not in a way that suggested misuse, but in a way that suggested that many years had passed since they had been written.

Grudgingly, I admitted defeat. "No."

"Good," Beckett said. "That's the whole point."

I raised an eyebrow at him and waited for him to explain.

He said no more, but reached forward and grasped the right hand side of the bookcase. With a gentle kind of force, he swung it toward us into the hallway. Behind it was a door with a short hallway that seemed to lead to another room. A hidden room.

"Well I didn't expect that," I said astonished. He gestured for me to walk in.

The short hallway was dark and the room beyond was even darker still as there were no windows. Unlike the rest of the house, the room was plain yet more modern. The walls were painted instead of wallpapered and the furniture lacked artfulness and charm. Its purpose seemed to be functionality instead of beauty. There was a bed, but no canopy with frilly coverings hung above it like I had seen in the other rooms we walked by. There was a desk with a computer, a storage unit, a small kitchenette. Something that looked like a telescope jutted out from one of the walls. There was one other door on the far side of the room. I was about to ask where it lead when Beckett began to speak.

"This room was an original part of the house. I would imagine that at one time it was used as a typical bedroom, but eventually it was sealed off with that bookcase there. We don't really know why the owner felt the need of this secret room. Some have spun a story that this is where the master of the house would meet his mistress so that his wife wouldn't know what he was up to. Others have suggested that some sort of fugitive of the law was housed here," he shrugged. "Doesn't really matter anymore because it serves a purpose for us. This house has been our headquarters for a long time, Eloise, and we anticipated that someday this room would be of some help. Now we know exactly what we can use it for."

He stopped, either to allow me to let it all sink in or for dramatic effect. I didn't say anything.

"That was a really close call this morning, El," he said, a look of concern briefly crossing his face. "We can't let it get that close again. There's still so much more I need to fill you in on, but with things being so unpredictable right now, this is the first order of business. This is your safe room. If someone gives the alert from outside, you come straight to this room. You don't look for me, you don't try to be a hero. You run straight in here and you shut that bookcase, and you lock both doors behind it. Then you don't let anyone in, even if it's me. No one, El, for no reason. Do you hear me?"

I nodded. I heard him. I just couldn't guarantee that I would listen if the time came. If everyone else was in trouble, how could I just go run and hide? If it came down to it....if they captured Beckett, I would trade myself. I would never let other people suffer in my place. So all I did was nod, because then I wasn't really promising much else besides the fact that I had heard him.

He nodded back and then continued. "All your basic needs are in this room. Technically, if the Compound showed up and took over Headquarters, you could exist in here for quite some time without anyone else knowing. The walls in here are soundproofed. You could probably scream and no one would hear you. There's food and water in the cabinet. The computer lets you connect to others in the Open in the event that you were stuck in here alone. Obviously the bed is for you to rest. There are books, a first-aid kit. A gun, even. Not that I expect that you would know how to use it, but it's there."

"I know how to use it," I said flatly.

"Really?" he asked, surprised. "Why?"

I shrugged. "The Compound taught us a little bit of everything. We took target practice."

Beckett snorted and shook his head as if he was disgusted. "Of course they'd teach you and pretend it was no big deal. Anyway, follow me over here and—"

"Wait, what do you mean, 'pretend it was no big deal'?" I asked.

"Eloise, does it even make sense for the Compound to have guns if you spent your whole life thinking that no one else existed? What would you need guns for if everyone was inside the Compound? They've anticipated they would need some sort of army at some point, so they've trained you how to use a weapon just in case. People in the Compound don't know any better, so they would blindly fight to the death for the place that keeps them ignorant. Those very people you trained with could be deployed all over the Open right now, ready to kill us, the 'threat'. Are you ready to face that? Could you kill your neighbor if your neighbor was trying to kill you?"

The conversation had turned serious very quickly and in a direction that I had not seen coming.

"Weapons were extracurricular to us," I tried to explain. "The first thing that we were taught were the dangers of them, how to stay safe when using them. But it was all done for sport. We never thought of guns' primary use being to harm other humans. We didn't question the walls that kept us in, or the sentinels keeping watch on the walls. Because we never had a reason to question it. It was what it was, and we were always happy and safe, so what did it matter to us? I understand your perspective now, Beckett, but don't treat me like an ignorant fool.

There's as much that you don't understand about the Compound as I don't understand about the Open. And my people wouldn't leave the Compound to kill others. They wouldn't have a reason to."

I was trying so hard to be reasonable, to see things from his point of view and not get angry, but he did not afford me the same courtesy.

"Are you joking, Eloise? After what I spent an hour explaining to you this morning, about human nature being inherently violent? Do you really think that your people don't have it in them? Look, I'm not saying that people from the Compound are suddenly going to be allowed beyond the walls and go on a killing spree for the sheer fun of it. If they've been directed outside the Compound, they've been given a specific purpose: finding you. They think you're in danger, Eloise. We're the enemy out here in the Open. They think that we are keeping you hostage, that you could be hurt or worse. They're going to feel like maiming other people is justified in order to save you."

I hadn't thought of it that way. There were many personalities in the Compound, some definitely more hostile than others, but no one was outwardly violent. It wasn't allowed. If you stepped out of line, you would have been thrown out. Or whatever it was that they did with people who we never saw again. But I supposed that being a rule-follower didn't mean that you didn't harbor feelings of anger deep inside you, that you wouldn't unleash those feelings once given the chance. Especially if you thought you were justified in doing so by having the right cause. Maybe it was true what Beckett said: people had a natural instinct for violence, whether it was done within what we considered to be reason or not. People were all too willing to hurt someone else having been given permission.

I couldn't really find any other words to say, being so struck by the way that Beckett had forced me to look at the situation. So I simply nodded again and that was good enough for him. He understood the weight of his words as well as I did.

"Now this is the one part that gets tricky," he said as he pointed at the other door. "Going to the bathroom and showering are a dangerous process around here. Water makes noises as it moves through pipes. There's really nothing that can be done to stop that. Chances are that possible captors wouldn't be able to pinpoint the exact source, but you never know. Even with the soundproofing, the pipes travel throughout the whole house, so you have to choose to flush or shower sparingly."

I made a face.

"Yeah, it's gross," Beckett admitted. "But if it's a matter a life or death, or in your case a matter of Open or Compound, it's a small price to pay."

He opened the door and revealed a tiny bathroom, hardly big enough to fit the toilet, shower, and sink and then have a person walk in and shut the door.

"There's not much I can tell you about this. You know how a bathroom works. If you get into a situation where you're locked in the safe room, try to only flush if you really have to. Shower for necessity rather than a matter of personal hygiene. Survival isn't about how pretty you look or smell," he gave me a pointed look and I rolled my eyes. "And this is the most important feature of all."

He pointed to a square on the wall that had a handle sticking out of it.

"What is it?" I asked.

Beckett pulled down the handle, revealing a hole just large enough for a human body to fit through comfortably. I immediately felt sick.

"Oh no," I shook my head vehemently. "NOT going to happen!"

"Eloise, don't be a child," he scolded me. "This is your escape route if you needed to get out of the house. And we need to practice so that you know where it leads."

I felt like I could burst into tears, and then I did. They flowed freely from my eyes without me really having any control over it. One claustrophobic space that day was enough. Never mind the coffin sized opening in the wall.

Beckett softened a bit. "I'm sorry. I know this is not ideal, but you never know when you're going to need this. And I would assume you might need it sooner rather than later. We need to be prepared. I'm going with you, but we obviously can't fit through this hole together. You need to be brave, and then I promise you won't have to do anything else today. We'll just relax."

There was no possible way that I was climbing into that hole. I would rather be taken back to the Compound kicking and screaming all the way than to stuff myself into that small space. But then I thought about all of the people I had passed in the hallway, all doing some sort of work that revolved around keeping me and Headquarters safe. I thought about Mad-Eye outside in the driveway, standing guard by himself in the face of possible danger. And all Beckett was asking me to do was climb into something.

I swallowed my fear and whispered a feeble, "Okay."

Beckett smiled at me and brushed a piece of hair out of my face.

"It'll be okay, El," he said gently. "Now this is just like a laundry chute or a slide.... I don't know if you know what either of those things are, but you're going to put your feet in first and push off. Gravity and the chute will do the rest for you. When you get to the bottom, there's a soft landing waiting for you. If you just close your eyes the whole time it'll be over before you know it. Do you want to go first or me?"

I ran my hands over my face and pouted.

"I'll go first," I said, cringing. "If you go first, I can't promise that I'll actually go through with it."

"Fair enough," Beckett answered. "So let's get this over with then. You're going to put your feet in first and get into a sitting position. Then, gently lower yourself into the chute. When you let go of the frame, give yourself a little push and you'll be off. I'll wait a few seconds before I follow you to give you time to get out of the way. Wouldn't be good if I fell on top of you."

"What if I get stuck?" I asked nervously. I began to panic as I pictured myself in the middle of the chute with no room to crawl forwards or backwards. It would be a living nightmare.

"It's not that small of a space, Eloise. I promise you that you won't get stuck."

With a sudden surge of adrenaline, I climbed into the chute, laid down, and pushed off. I went sliding down the chute at a reasonable speed, not too quickly but not too slowly. I kept my eyes closed the entire time not wanting to see the metal whiz by a few inches above my face. The cool metal under my body should have made me shiver, but I was sweating from anxiousness so it actually felt good on my skin. A few seconds later, I fell out of the chute onto a puffy landing pad and it was over.

I moved out of the way and waited for Beckett to follow. He landed with a *thwack* on the pad and looked bewildered.

"Jeez, El. A little warning would have been nice," he said.

"I felt a moment of courage, so I figured I'd better take it before it faded," I replied.

Beckett shook his head at me in disbelief. I shrugged at him and took in my surroundings. Where we had landed looked like a mixture between a basement and a bank vault that I had seen in old movies. The air was damp and cold, and the only light came from dull emergency lights on the walls. It was a big, empty room of stone and I had the eerie feeling that either a ghost or a rat would pop out at any second. Having just come through that chute, though, I wasn't uncomfortable in the least. This space was a lot larger than my body and I could stretch out in all directions without touching anything. That was enough at that moment.

"Anyway," Beckett said, recovering from my sudden leap. "This is underneath the house, but it's a part of the basement that is disconnected from the rest. So again, it's a secret unknown to most. There's a tunnel right over here that leads to the outside."

I gulped. "By tunnel you mean...?

"Don't worry," he smirked. "It's tall and wide."

I nodded and followed him. We passed through a large wooden door that was reminiscent of a castle.

"This is another security measure," Beckett explained. "Let's say by some chance you were followed down the chute. You run in here and close this, then swing the metal bar down. It'll buy you at least a little time before anyone breaks it open."

The metal bar screeched from misuse when I pulled it down. It was heavy, but I could manage to lift it back into place again.

"It's a little rusty, but it'll do its job," he admitted. "Now this over here is your go-bag. It has everything you need to survive for a couple of days on the run. We had to keep it light, so it only has the very bare essentials. There's a lightweight tent that you can pitch simply to create a barrier between you and the outside world. It won't be comfortable, it won't stop animals, and it isn't going to keep you very warm. There's some dried fruit and a bottle of water...maybe a couple of band-aids and a flashlight. If you ever need to, Eloise, you don't think twice about it. You grab this bag and you go. You run down that tunnel as fast as you can and you don't look back. Understand?"

"Yeah, I get it, Beckett. But there's one problem."

"What?"

"I don't know how to pitch a tent."

He laughed. "That's the least of your worries if you end up needing this bag, but I'll put it on my to do list: teach Eloise how to pitch a tent."

Beckett's easy laughter lasted only that second, and then he was back to all business.

"Ok, so I want you to try it on and make sure it's adjusted to fit you," he said. Then he watched as I put it on my shoulders and maneuvered the straps so that the bag would rest comfortably. It didn't feel all that heavy.

He always underestimates me, I thought to myself.

"Good? Good. Now see that little button down by the base of the strap?" he pointed to a spot on the bag that was below the natural resting place of your fingertips when you had on a backpack.

I reached for it.

"No! Don't press it now!" Beckett sputtered and then relaxed as I moved my hand away. "This bag is fitted with a GPS tracking system. When you press that button, it sends an alert to me and several other people who can then see your exact location. That way we can find you as quickly as possible should you need us to. Just make sure that you press the button as soon as you put the go-bag on. The sooner we know, the better."

"Who exactly will get the alert? And how do they get it?" I asked.

"Well, yours truly, of course," he said smugly. "Then there's Rose, Mad-Eye, a couple of guys on the security team who you haven't really met yet....Alistair." The last name was flung from his lips like a cuss. "They all have devices that will sound an alarm if you push that button."

"What if they don't see the alert? What if it doesn't work?" I questioned again.

"It'll work. And you can always count on me seeing and hearing it," he said as he pointed to the watch on his left wrist. "This isn't just a watch. That's why I never take it off. I'll always be paying attention, Eloise. You're always safe with me."

And there was the gentle side of him that made things slightly awkward. He looked at me intensely, and I believed that as long as he was in charge of my safety, I had nothing to worry about.

Neither of us said anything for a moment. It felt like there was a magnetic field between us, like we both wanted to close the space between us, but at the same time each of us held back. Finally Beckett gestured for me to hang the bag back up.

"We're almost done," he said, the authoritative tone now gone from his voice. "This tunnel stretches on for about a mile. We'll just walk through it once now so that you know where it goes."

"Seems a bit lengthy for an escape route," I said as we began walking. "It'll take me so long to get out that someone is sure to catch up with me. Running is not my strong suit, especially not if I'm carrying something."

"Well, first of all let's hope that none of this is ever necessary. It's really just a precaution. But the reason the tunnel is so long is that you need to surface somewhere the enemy isn't. If the tunnel was shorter, you'd end up in the gardens where they might be stationed. You need to get far beyond the house so that when you hit ground level, there's a less likely chance that you'll be captured."

I nodded. It did make sense. I just hoped that it would never actually happen. For all I had thought about escaping from Beckett and his crew and finding my way back to the Compound, I had never in my life been on my own in any part of the world. I didn't trust myself to make good decisions if I only had myself to rely upon while running around in the Open.

Beckett must have sensed my apprehension.

"It's alright, Eloise," he said. And then he reached for my hand. I didn't pull away.

We walked the length of the tunnel in silence, which was still only dimly lit by those amber emergency lights. I prayed that they would never go out and leave me stumbling in the darkness. Lost in my thoughts, I was surprised at how quickly we had reached the end. If I was in a hurry, it would take an even shorter amount of time. This gave me a little hope for my own escape....if it had to come to that.

In front of us there was a simple set of stone stairs that led to the ceiling of the tunnel. At first glance it just looked like a dead end with no exit. But as my eyes analyzed closely, you could see the outline of a rectangle with two handles and a seam down the middle.

"I half expected there to be a small space to crawl through to get out," I joked, feeling lighter now that we were about to resurface. "This just seems too easy."

Beckett smiled back at me. "I'm happy to report that it is this easy. You just have to climb the stairs, open the bolt, and push open the doors."

He led by example. Beckett slid across a smaller metal bolt and thrust the doors open. They were a little resistant at first, and I was glad that we had done this practice run. If the doors had gotten stuck when I was trying to open them alone, I would probably panic and curl up in the corner to cry.

As if reading my thoughts Beckett said, "Don't worry. They hadn't been opened in a long time."

He held out a hand for me to grab again and we climbed the rest of the stairs to the surface. When Beckett closed the doors again from the outside, I saw that they were covered in grass to camouflage them. They did blend right in once they were closed. If you didn't know they were there, you'd never even notice them.

"Sooo....how did someone bolt those doors shut?" I asked.

Beckett reached into his pocket and pulled out a metal object with a flat end. He reached down and felt around in the grass for something. When he located what he was looking for, he dug into the ground with the metal tool and moved it slightly to the right. I heard something click.

"It's a key of sorts," he explained. "This makes sure that no one could get in if they tried to. Let's say by some chance of bad luck the Compound knew about this door and you could hear them waiting on the other side. If they weren't coming from the direction of the chute, you could wait safely in the tunnel until we could come rescue you. No one else would be able to open that door unless they had this key."

Again, I found myself desperately hoping that I wouldn't be forced to stay in that tunnel for any longer than the time it took to walk or run that mile to the exit. It had felt wide enough today, but Beckett had been with me and I had just experienced a much smaller space, which made it seem not as bad. But I wasn't particularly fond of the idea of being underground.

"That's all there is to it," Beckett smiled. "Now I'm going to show you the way back to the house, obviously, because that's where we need to go right now. But for no circumstance would you *ever* turn back towards Headquarters if you had escaped. Tomorrow I'll show you how to get to the main road or to good hiding spots where we will know to look for you."

Night was falling as we walked the mile back to the mansion. Beckett made small talk and I tried my best to listen. He was explaining the dangers of the woods, plants that were safe to eat, plants to avoid, how to tell if certain animals had walked through and how to safely back away from them. I only caught half of it, but I nodded and commented back here and there to make it sound like I was doing a good job of listening. I felt guilty for not being attentive. Beckett could be sharing very valuable information that I needed to hear, and missing it could cost me greatly. But I just couldn't help it. There was so much to think about, to worry about. So many precautions had been put into place. Had they all been put into place for me? Or had they existed in general? It embarrassed me to think that I might have caused so much work to be done, and I still couldn't figure out what was so special about me. I was just another sixteen-year-old girl. There was no reason for anyone to-

I gasped and tackled Beckett to the ground.

"What the - ?" he said in an angry muffle, as I was holding his head down on the ground. "Eloise, I thought we were over the whole you beating me up thing."

"Shhh!" I reproached him.

All I could hear was the sound of my heart beat and Beckett's breathing as we lie flat on the ground. I watched the man that had appeared suddenly walk by us with a shotgun slung over his shoulder. He crept about as his eyes scanned the woods, and he passed within inches of my feet without noticing our bodies. Quietly, I sat up and watched him walk the way we had come. Suddenly he pulled his shotgun in front of him and fired at the air. I flinched and yelped.

"What the hell is the matter?" Beckett asked, clearly frustrated.

"The man, the man with the gun! Didn't you see him?" I whispered.

A look of understanding crossed Beckett's face, but he said, "No, El, I didn't see him."

"I thought he was someone from the Compound. He dressed a little funny, but he had a gun and he was coming right for us! It's the strangest thing. The man walked right by us, pretending that we weren't even here. It was if he couldn't even see us."

I was confused. I was seeing things again. Rubbing at my eyes, I tried to erase the vision of the man. He appeared out of nowhere just like the people in the factory had earlier that day. Wait...had that just been that morning? The day had been the longest in the history of days. Maybe it was just exhaustion. My eyes were playing tricks on me, that was it. But as I recalled the events of the day, I remembered what Beckett had said to me just before Mad-Eye had burst into the apartment.

"Beckett, you know why I saw that man, don't you?"

He sighed. "Look, let's get back. It's getting late. It's getting dark. We shouldn't be out here like sitting ducks."

"I am *so* tired of you dismissing me! You need to start answering questions. You need to start *telling* me what's going on!" I said through gritted teeth, annoyed, as I crossed my arms across my chest. "Or I'm not going anywhere."

Beckett looked like he wanted to argue with me, like he wanted to tell me what a child I was being. But he was clearly tired of that strategy.

"Suit yourself," he said as he stood up. "Stay out here if you want. I'm going back inside."

Damnit, I thought. He knew that I wouldn't stay out there, in the woods, in the dark, by myself. Beckett was winning this battle without even putting up a fight. Angrily, sulkily, maybe a little immaturely, I slapped the ground with both hands. Then, with little real choice, I stood up and followed him inside.

I could almost feel Beckett smiling to himself.

We entered the house through the gardens. I had run to catch up with Beckett after failing to get my way and passed him on purpose so that I could enter the French doors ahead of him, so as to close them promptly behind me. Though impolite, it was a small victory that let him know I was miffed and made me feel better.

As he reopened the doors behind me, I heard him mutter, "Charming as ever."

I didn't really know my way around the place, but I wasn't about to ask Beckett for directions, so I navigated using my sense of smell. Luckily, being the food-monger that I was, my nose didn't fail me. Rose and Alistair stood in the kitchen, and both were a welcome sight since I could hear footsteps following behind me.

"Hi, Eloise!" Rose said perkily.

"Hey Rose," I greeted her back with true warmth now that I knew she was Beckett's sister and not his girlfriend. Though at the moment, I was more inclined to flirt with Alistair than worry about Beckett's hurt feelings.

Alistair was leaning on the counter with both elbows and had clearly been attempting to sweet-talk Rose before we had walked in. Now, however, he turned his attention to me. I supposed that everyone in the Open probably knew Alistair's motives and girls like Rose would already be aware of his fox-like charms. Being the new girl, he probably considered me open season. And even though I *did* know better now after our last experience, I was angry enough to pretend that I didn't.

"Ah, Eloise," Alistair purred as he walked towards me. "It's been too long." He reached for my hand and planted a prolonged kiss on the back of my hand.

"Likewise," I returned and batted my eyelashes for all that they were worth.

"Oh, and you brought your puppy too," Alistair instigated. "Hello, Beckett. Lovely to see you." His voice was saturated with sarcasm.

"Alistair," Beckett grudgingly said back, surprisingly without a snarky comment. I could see the muscles in his forearms tense. As much as I was already irritated with Beckett, I didn't think a fistfight would enhance my evening, so I changed the subject.

"Rose, something smells delicious in here. What's for dinner?" I asked.

"Oh, thank you!" she said brightly. "I had to cook for the masses so we were a little limited as far as fanciness goes. I went for comfort food, you know, something I could cook in bulk. I figured everyone could use a little something homey to put them at ease now that we are all centrally located here until further notice."

Rose emphasized the last bit as she looked at her brother, clearly trying to send him a message to behave. I was sure she was all too familiar with his possessive mood swings and wanted to avoid any conflict as much as I did.

Beckett obeyed his sister and, ignoring Alistair, walked over to where she was standing in the gourmet kitchen. It really put the one in my apartment in the Compound to shame, even if it was operated by control panel and you didn't have to do anything for yourself. It was a work of art, and I noticed details that I hadn't the last time. The tile stone floor of neutrals contrasted perfectly with the ornately carved red sandalwood cabinets. One wall was completely stone with a welcoming fireplace, which matched the granite countertops that sparkled in the reflection of the light fixtures from above. Pots and pans hung over the large, centered island that had a six-burner range. The refrigerator was the largest that I had ever seen (not that I had seen many), and there were *three* fancy looking ovens. It made me want to learn how to cook, it was so beautiful.

"So where's the grub?" Beckett asked patting his stomach.

"It's cooking as we speak. I was just about to wash these pans," Rose answered. As she turned to move them to the sink, Beckett swiped a finger across one of them and then stuck it promptly in his mouth.

"Ugh, you know I hate when you do that," Rose scolded.

Beckett smiled and said exaggeratedly, "Mmmm, but it tastes sooooo gooooooood. Macaroni and cheese."

She rolled her eyes at him and he nudged her affectionately. It was so strange to see him in this family element, completely relaxed and normal, instead of on guard and bossy like he was when he was with me. It really showed how much he cared about his sister. And it was endearing. I tried not to let it affect me too much, as I was supposed to be irritated with him.

"Rough day today?" Rose asked gently as her arms were elbow deep in suds.

"Uh, yeah," I replied. "You could say that."

"Do you want to talk about it, girl to girl? We can kick them out."

"Oh, no, that's okay, really," I stammered. I didn't really want to explain that it had all started because I talk to strangers and see things that aren't there. "Here, let me help. I shouldn't just be standing here watching."

"You don't have to, Eloise," said Rose kindly. "It's been a long day."

"Really, I insist. It would be nice to feel helpful for once."

"Alright, if you really want to. Reach down into that drawer on the right. There should be some hand towels in there. I'll wash, you dry."

I smiled in thanks. It really *would* be nice to have a purpose.

As I bent down to open the drawer, I noticed a holster tucked into her boot which was semi-concealing a small pistol and I paused. *Even sweet Rose is ready for battle.* I tried to convince myself that they just happened to walk around like this all the time, and that it wasn't on my account that everyone was armed. At least I wouldn't have to worry about her taking care of herself if it came down to it.

"Did you find it?" Rose asked looking down at me.

She startled me out of my thoughts. "Oh, uh, yeah. Sorry, I was just, uh, tying my shoe." I reached into the drawer and pulled out a flowered hand towel.

Dinner went off without a hitch. We all gathered at the long dining table in the formal dining room to eat. Beckett made sure I sat at the end of the table with him to my left and Rose across from me. He acted like it was a coincidence, but I knew he was just trying to avoid Alistair being seated in my immediate vicinity. I rolled my eyes.

"Why are you rolling your eyes?" Beckett asked.

"Because for some reason you're the only male I'm allowed to talk to. I don't take kindly to being told what to do, you know," I replied.

He convincingly (if I didn't know better) furrowed his brow and tried to look innocent. "What are you talking about?"

I rolled my eyes again and took a sip from my water. Neither one of us said anything more.

Rose chattered on while we ate, keeping me entertained since we were removed from most of the rest of the table. She was a phenomenal cook too, and I ate so much that I felt like I would quite literally explode.

At one point in the conversation she lost me as I looked around the room. I envied how casual they all were with each other, a bunch of old friends gathered for a simple meal. It was almost as if there was no other reason for it besides to have a good time. You could *almost* forget that something horrible could happen at any moment. Except that as I observed more closely, you could see each person, though trying hard to feign ease, was on edge. One man with shockingly white-blond hair that I remembered seeing at the party kept reaching down to his side, unconsciously feeling for his weapon, as if to make sure it was still there. Another would inadvertently glance at the door mid-conversation, perhaps expecting someone to come barging in at any moment. There was a girl whose knuckles were white as she gripped her utensils, one in each hand. They were laughing and talking as if it *was* just a dinner party, but their body language suggested that everyone was equally ill at ease.

One person I didn't see was Mad-Eye, which prompted me to ask where he was.

"Oh, he's still outside with everyone else. They'll come in to eat for second shift when these guys are done," Beckett answered.

While I was glad he wasn't out there by himself for the night, it shocked me a little bit that a second shift was required for dinner when the table seated so many.

"What do you mean, *they'll* come in? I didn't see anyone else when we pulled up," I said."

"Eloise, do you really think Mad-Eye is going to stand guard of this entire property by himself? He is pretty formidable, but he's not supernatural," Beckett lectured me as if I had no common sense.

"I was just asking a question," I snapped.

Beckett nudged me with his elbow. "I wasn't trying to be rude. Lighten up, would you?"

I sighed. "It's not my fault that I don't know how all this works, and I'm tired of you talking down to me like I'm some ignorant child. If you want me to understand, then explain. Don't make cheeky comments."

"Sorry, sorry," Beckett put his hands up in surrender. "The house itself has more security measures than the actual premises. But the truth is, the Compound could attack from any direction, including from above. The helicopter you saw is the only one we currently have operating and it's not built for defense anyway. We're pretty limited with technology as far as defense goes. It's not like we can launch missiles or have access to satellite, not yet anyway. Maybe someday we'll build back up to that. So manpower is really our best option. Our people are strategically placed, camouflaged in trees and throughout the grounds, and they can walkie to one another if they see anything. Then we can at least get you out in time, even if everything else goes to hell."

"If everything else goes to hell," I repeated. "That sounds promising."

"You wanted to know the truth, El. The truth is, the Compound isn't going to come here and ask for you nicely. They already tried to surprise you, to get you to go of your own free will. But you ran, so they know they're going to have to take you by force. Things could get ugly very quickly, but that's what we signed up for. First, to protect our freedom and our rights as human beings, and now, to protect you."

"I don't like it," I shook my head. "Why would anyone risk their lives for me? You still haven't told me that part yet, Beckett. And it had better be a damn good reason."

He paused, looking at me, as if he were trying to decide how to proceed.

"You're right, I haven't. We were kind of getting to that part earlier before Mad-Eye came in. But I don't think this is really the best time for *that* conversation," he said, almost wincing, bracing himself for my response.

I nodded, surely surprising him with my civility. As much as I wanted to understand everything at once, even I knew that I had had enough for one day. There would be plenty of time all day tomorrow to talk about why I was turning into such a freak.

"Tomorrow," I said. "And no later. Because if the Compound could get here at any moment, I should at least know why before they arrive."

"I agree," Beckett said. "Tomorrow."

Part of me felt like that was what he kept saying every day. Tomorrow, tomorrow. Everything was always prolonged another day. Part of me was glad since every day my education of the Open was mostly full of new and unpleasant knowledge. I was frightened to think that I had lived my entire life ignorant of why I was special. How could I not know why these two entities, the Open and the Compound, were willing to risk so much to have me on their side? Whatever the reason, I had a feeling it wouldn't be uplifting.

I became suddenly aware that we had been having the conversation surrounded by friendly strangers, but they might wrinkle their noses in disgust at protecting someone who didn't even know why she was being protected. But it seemed like everyone had continued on their own conversations, oblivious to what we had been talking about. Rose was engaged with another girl in a chat about some sort of boots that they were both raving about. I could hear other seemingly normal conversations being had until a sudden bell dinged, signaling the end of dinner. Chairs immediately began noisily being moved and people stretched and exited the dining room, presumably to take on their positions, relieving the others to eat.

Beckett and Rose stood up too, so I followed their lead. They both moved to collect the dirty paper plates, plastics cups and forks, and used napkins off of the table, and I mimicked their actions. By the time we had the table cleaned and reset, the second shift began to stroll in from outside. Rose placed new, steaming hot pans of macaroni and cheese on the table, and I could now see what she meant about needing to cook in bulk. Considering the amount I myself ate, I could imagine that she must have been cooking for hours to feed all of us. I should have been more cognizant of the amount I put on my plate. The next time, I'd remember.

I continued to watch the others trickle in, purposely lingering in the corner of the room until I saw Mad-Eye. I didn't know why I was so particularly concerned with him getting a hot meal, but I couldn't rest until I knew that he was fed and able to rest for a while. Maybe it was because he was one of the first people besides Beckett that I had met in the Open. Maybe it was because he had whisked us away to safety that day. I couldn't exactly put my finger on it, but I had a soft spot for the gruff man who was a part of this strange journey.

"Everything look okay out there?" I asked him, trying to make conversation when he finally walked in.

"Mmph," Mad-Eye grunted and shrugged his shoulders. "S'okay for now."

He certainly wasn't a man of many words.

"The food is really good!" I tried again. "Rose is such a good cook."

I felt like an idiot, telling him something that he most certainly already knew. I was probably the only one who was newly acquainted with Rose's talent in the kitchen, but I was just trying to somehow let Mad-Eye know that I appreciated what he was doing for me.

"Yeah," he responded, stuffing his hands in his pockets and looking like he wanted to end the conversation.

"Alright then, I'll let you get to it," I said, feeling like a silly little girl who was seeking approval in a place she wasn't going to get it.

As I turned to walk way, I felt a hand on my shoulder. I turned my face back towards Mad-Eye. He nodded and smiled a small smile as he patted my shoulder, and then he sat down to eat. Taking that as a gesture of affection, I walked happily back to the doorway where Beckett stood waiting for me.

He was leaning against the doorway with his arms folded over his chest and a smug grin on his face.

"What?" I said quizzically, wondering what he could possibly be so amused by this time.

"Mad-Eye isn't a big talker," he said as we walked back out towards the foyer and the staircase. "You can't take it so personally."

"I don't know what you're talking about," I responded, blushing.

This time Beckett was the one rolling his eyes. "Okay, Eloise. Just know that Mad-Eye is the most loyal friend you have. He might have a difficult time showing it, but he is more vigilant than anyone else here, except maybe me. But, yeah. Just know that he does care for you, even if he's not a soft-and-fuzzy type of guy."

We walked silently upstairs and stopped in front of the door to the hidden room. I looked at Beckett, puzzled.

"What're we going in there for?"

"This is your room for the duration of your stay here," he said.

I felt the color drain out of my face. It was one thing to have to be in there for safety, otherwise it would feel like a sealed coffin.

"But I thought this was just for an emergency," I said unsteadily.

"Well, yeah, but we don't know when that emergency might happen," said Beckett. "It's the safest place for you to be. Say something happened in the middle of the night. All you would have to do is get in the chute."

"But it's not the middle of the night now," I whined. I was feeling claustrophobic just thinking about being shut up in that room by myself all the time. I'd rather risk being taken captive by the Compound than to have the walls closing in on me.

"It's not," he agreed. "But it's been such a long day you'll probably want to get to bed early. You don't have to shut the door yet. I can do that when you fall asleep."

Insensibly, I felt tears begin to well up in my eyes again. I had never been as emotional in my entire life as I had been since arriving in the Open. There was no real reason for me to put up such a fight about which room I slept in. I was safer there than anywhere else. But I think that all that had happened was finally catching up to me. I felt so overwhelmed and alone, and still so confused about all of the missing pieces to the puzzle that was now my life. My throat burned from trying to hold back the tears, desperately trying to be stronger and braver than I felt.

Beckett stared at me without saying a word as if I was something dangerous and combustible, like if he made any sudden movements or said the wrong thing he feared for his own safety.

"Will you stay with me?" I whispered, as that was the only level of speaking I could manage without bursting like a broken pipe. "I don't want to be alone."

Beckett seemed to instantly relax, his eyes smoldering with compassion. He threw his arms around me fiercely.

"Of course I will stay with you," he said as he buried his face in my hair. "All you have to do is want me there, and I'll be there."

We sat quietly reading our own separate books in my annex for a while until the words on the page began to swim and my eyes began to cross. When Beckett saw me put my book down and prepare for bed, he got up and locked the doors, and then he checked back at my facial expression before turning out the light, presumably to make sure I wasn't freaking out or having a panic attack.

Beckett crawled in beside me and planted a light kiss on my forehead. I reached for his arm and drew it across my waist. Being able to feel the weight of it throughout the night would keep me sane in case I woke up in a panic about where I was.

"Goodnight, El," he said, and I drifted off to sleep.

*   *   *

My room had no windows, so when I woke up I was disoriented without the sun to initially alert me to the time of day. Beckett was still next to me, his arm now like a leaden weight on my side. I sat there for a while, not wanting my movement to wake him. At first I thought it odd that I couldn't hear anyone moving throughout the giant house – maybe it was the middle of the night, I thought – but then I remembered the sound-proofing. There could be chaos going on around us and we would have absolutely no way of knowing.

I sat up suddenly in bed, carelessly jolting Beckett awake.

"What? What's wrong?" he bolted upright, questioning.

"Nothing! I don't think...I mean... I don't know if anything's wrong. It's just, I don't know what time it is right now and... how would we even know if anything was happening out there. I can't hear anything!" I sputtered.

Beckett's shoulders slightly relaxed and he ran a hand through his hair.

"Jesus, El, you scared me."

"Sorry. I just woke up and started thinking..."

He rubbed around his eyes and yawned. "It's okay, I get it. I have a walkie to contact everyone if necessary, and this watch would light up red and beep if something was wrong. I guess I probably should've told you that before."

"No, it's alright. You probably didn't expect to be trapped with someone who is going insane, so I don't blame you for not thinking of it beforehand," I replied bitterly recalling the events of yesterday.

"First of all, you are not going insane. Second of all, speaking of, we have a lot of work to do today so that you can start to finally understand everything." He looked over at the desk and the old-fashioned clock that we propped on top of it. "And it looks like it's about eight in the morning. Thank God, I'm starving."

His stomach growled then, as if on cue. He reached down on the side of the bed to feel around for something on the floor and came up with the walkie.

After Beckett turned a knob, it came to life with the sound of static.

"I turned it off during the night so that it wouldn't wake us. I figured if there was any real emergency, I'd hear the beep," he told me, and then continued to talk into the hand-held device. "Sorry if I'm waking anyone, but me and the little lady here are getting hungry. All clear through the night? Over," he said removing his finger from a button on the side.

The ten seconds of silence that followed made my stomach curdle. *Why weren't they answering right away?*

Of course I assumed that something had gone horribly wrong during the night and that we were somehow alerting the

Compound invaders to our location. Another second longer and I would have been on my feet with one leg in the chute. The sporadic waves of fear that came over me were so insensible. If worse came to worse, I would be going back to the place that I had lived my entire life. The rational side of me was sure that I was never in any *real* danger no matter where I was, but instinct and impulse told me otherwise. It was maddening to be in constant disagreement with myself. My mind was like a game of tug of war. But then a grainy, yet cheery voice answered back.

"No worries, brother," sounded Rose. "I'm in the kitchen cooking up some pancakes. Due to an uneventful night, there's plenty of time to sit down and have a balanced breakfast. I'll be waiting for you to come help cut up the fruit. Over."

Beckett smirked and shook his head. "Looks like we pulled fruit duty. Let's go."

He hopped off the bed and immediately headed to the inner door to begin to unlock it. I started to follow and then became conscious that I had just rolled out of bed. Suddenly aware of the foul taste of morning breath in my mouth, I breathed into my hand and tried to gauge the level of stench.

"Umm, can I just...?" I pointed towards the bathroom.

"Two minutes," Beckett warned.

I ran a quick toothbrush over my teeth, a comb through my hair to try and manage some semblance of tameness, and wiped off yesterday's barely-there, smudged eyeliner. After reapplying a quick new line to each eye, I glanced in the mirror. It wasn't my best look, but it was passable for breakfast. I had the feeling that I would be the only one who was too keen on her appearance anyway. In the Compound, how you presented yourself – how well you matched, the neatness of hair, the evenly applied makeup – was important. In the Open, being presentable meant that you were well-suited to taking action, being in survival mode.

"Okay, let's go," I said as I walked out and towards the door.

"I'm impressed Carlisle, very impressed," Beckett complimented me, teasingly.

It took me aback for a moment, the fact that he was calling me by my last name.

"Why'd you call me that?" I asked, scrunching up my nose as we emerged into the hallway.

Beckett shrugged.

"You've never done that before," I said quietly. For some reason it seemed so formal to me, like he was trying to keep me at a distance.

"Hey, hey. It's not a bad thing. It's like a nickname. Sometimes it means that you are being spoken to by someone of authority, but sometimes it's used when you're joking around with someone you're used to. In this case, I guess it's both," he grinned and nudged me with his elbow.

"Oh," I said.

It was so irritating to be unaware of all the nuances of the Open. I was used to being called by my first name by everyone. Even when he called me "El" it was unfamiliar, but the connotation was affectionate so it had been an easier transition. Calling me by my last name made me feel like I had done something wrong and was being disciplined. There was so much to get used to, every day. I wondered how long it would be before I was no longer full of unnerving malaise.

When we went down to breakfast Rose was alone in the kitchen with a spatula in each hand, pancakes browning and sizzling on a griddle.

"Good morning, kids!" she greeted us.

"Morning," I responded and observed the lack of bodies in the room. "Bunch of late sleepers around here."

Rose giggled. "Actually, you're the late sleepers. Most others have already eaten and left for work for the day. It's just you guys and some of the overnight crew that need to eat now."

"Sorry," I blushed. Being on time was a virtue that I usually upheld, even if I did cut it close.

"Oh, don't you apologize! You had an exhausting day yesterday. It was a well-deserved night of rest. I'll finish up with these pancakes, but if you guys could cut up the cantaloupe and wash the strawberries that would be a big help."

Beckett walked over to the monstrous refrigerator and took out the fruit. "I think it's best if I cut the cantaloupe and you wash these."

He handed me the strawberries. Because I could be incredibly stubborn, I wanted to argue that I could handle cutting up the cantaloupe, but truth be told, I had never had to prepare food for myself in my entire life. So it was probably best that I stayed away from sharp objects for the time being.

We completed our chore in just about the same amount of time that it took Rose to finish with the pancakes.

"Well now, that's done," she said as she put the plate on the island. "There's some maple syrup right there and butter in the microwave if you need it. I'd better get outside to meet with the daytime security team. You two enjoy!"

Rose flounced off to her meeting and left Beckett and I alone in the kitchen.

"Is she always that cheerful?" I asked, with envy in my voice.

"For the most part," Beckett admitted.

"She seems like she has a never-ending supply of energy," I said.

Beckett smiled and nodded his head as if he were thinking of the countless memories that served as evidence. "Rose is kind of like....the Alliance's mother. She's in charge of most meals when we're all together, and she's organized beyond belief. Rose can tell you where you left your shoes and the strategic location that you need to be in order to prevent the enemy from spotting you from afar. She can bandage you up and sing you a lullaby to calm your nerves. It's always been that way. That's just... Rose."

I smiled back at him, warm thoughts in my head. Rose could be a sister, a friend, and the mother I needed out here. She was slightly older than me, but she had more experience and naturally knew much more about the Open than I did. While I had been skeptical of her prettiness and jealous of her relationship to begin with, now I felt like I could trust her with just about anything. She exuded genuine friendliness and honesty with all the softness of a girl, but I bet that she was one hell of a warrior too. Otherwise the Alliance wouldn't value her quite as much. She did a lot, that was true, but I was intuitive enough to know that you had to be able to hold your own in a battle if need be in order to make it in this group too. And even though the Open supposedly embraced all, the Alliance was more of an exclusive group.

We ate in silence, Beckett and I, and then we cleaned up our plates. As we were walking outside, Mad-Eye was walking in.

"Morning, Eloise. Beckett," he nodded.

"Good morning!" I said, sounding more chipper than I had intended. *Why was I so eager for this man to like me?* "Going to have something to eat? You must be exhausted."

I knew that he must have been outside all night, standing guard against danger.

"Yea-p," he answered. "I'll have a bite before I get back out there."

"No sleeping?" I asked.

I wasn't trying to be pushy. I just wanted to engage in a conversation, but Mad-Eye remained silent for a minute, as if he were deciding if my question was worthy of being answered. I felt as if maybe I was prying into things that were none of my business. It was clear that he was a very private man.

"Sleep isn't really high on my list of priorities," he finally answered. "The enemy never sleeps, Eloise. You remember that."

"I will," I said curiously, and Mad-Eye walked away, ending the conversation.

When we were out of his range of hearing, I asked Beckett, "Does he sleep?"

Beckett laughed. "Well, like he said, it's not something he looks forward to like the rest of us. He doesn't sleep so much as he naps. Mad-Eye is extremely dedicated to his work. He doesn't want to ever miss any action and be responsible for something going wrong by not being there."

"Well that's admirable, but that can't be very healthy."

"No," he shook his head, "probably not. But I wouldn't try telling *him* that."

"Noted," I answered and sighed.

I couldn't put my finger on why it bothered me so much that Mad-Eye invested himself so deeply in this mission to protect me. Something had drawn me to him in the very beginning; not in the way that I was attracted to him -- he was old enough to be my father – but in a way that suggested familiarity. There was something about the brooding, silent man that piqued my curiosity.

I played out scenarios in my mind of why I felt such a connection. Could he have lived in the Compound at one point, been banished, and knew something that I didn't? It would explain why he approached his duty with such ferocity. Maybe he had known my parents and felt a loyalty towards me because of them. Had there been something that happened when I was very small that I could have forgotten about, or could there have been some trauma that caused my mind to repress the memory? It was unsettling that I couldn't figure out the association.

When I came out of my reverie, I grunted aloud in frustration and then noticed Beckett patiently looking at me.

"You good?" he asked me politely.

"Yeah. Yeah, I'm fine. It's just..." I started, and then abruptly stopped, not wanting to admit to any more inexplicable feelings. "Nothing. Never mind. Let's just get on with our day. Speaking of, what are we doing?"

"Well, I was thinking that as long as the grounds are secure, I could show you the safe points in the surrounding woods that you would go to in the event of an emergency," he responded in that business-like way that made him sound more like a walking instruction manual than a human.

I raised my eyebrows. "Beckett, no offense, but how about telling me what the hell is going on instead of taking me on another field trip?"

"Look, there's plenty of time—"

"NO, Beckett. Stop telling me it can wait. Later, later, later. You keep saying it and doing nothing about it."

"Eloise, I'm concerned for your safety first and foremost. So excuse me if I am trying to prioritize here when the Compound could flock down on us at any minute," he said, heatedly.

"Right. And if that did happen, I wouldn't even know *why* I am supposed to be running away from them. Maybe I should just go run out into the Open near the apartment and wait for them to find me!"

"So damn stubborn," he muttered. "I'm trying to keep you *safe*, to *prepare* you and you're yelling at me because it isn't story-time!"

"There you go again," I growled at him, "treating me like a child. I want to know *why* you turned my life upside down, *why* my home is my enemy, *why* I should even listen to *anything* you say! And if you don't have an explanation for me then maybe the Compound will."

Beckett turned his back on me, covering his face with his hands in frustration, clearly trying desperately to not start screaming and swearing at me I was sure. I was, after all, a very stubborn girl then. And dramatic to boot. When he didn't respond to me or turn back around quickly enough, I started to storm off in the direction of the front of the house and the car. Like the child that I didn't want to be, I was pretending to run away to expose myself to the Compound.

He grabbed my arm and spun me around.

"For God sakes, Eloise! What are you doing?!" he exclaimed. The fire in his eyes could have lit a match.

I knew he was doing what he thought was best, and I knew that I was being stubborn and difficult, but I was *too* stubborn and difficult to ever admit it to him. So instead of saying anything, I stayed in place, in Beckett's grasp, and didn't struggle to get away. When I didn't argue, Beckett's features softened and his tone changed.

"Can we at least compromise?" he finally asked, releasing his grip.

"That depends," I answered, still obstinate. I cursed myself in my head, knowing full well that the words fell out of my mouth, but that the answer was yes, yes we could compromise.

Beckett gave me a look but didn't scold me. "How about we walk out into the woods first, and then—"

I cut him off before he could even finish with a sharp, "No."

"Okay," he said through gritted teeth, yet still calmly. "Can we talk while we walk? I'd rather we sat down and focused on the information as I have a lot to tell you, but if you refuse to cooperate..."

"I'm not refusing to cooperate, I'm just sticking up for myself," I retorted.

"Do you have to turn *everything* into an argument?"

"I'm not turning everything into an argument," I began and then I caught myself...arguing about arguing. "Sorry. I'll try to work on that."

I looked away from him. Sincere apologies and admitting my faults were not my strong suit. Like the gentleman he was, Beckett didn't provoke me by pointing out that I didn't sound very convincing.

"Okay, then. Let's get a move on," he said and turned back towards the way we had come.

"Wait, where are you going?" I asked.

"Well, if you need to get to your escape route, you won't exactly be using the front door. Practice makes perfect," he said, and I could see him bracing himself for the tornado of a response that he expected from me.

I laughed and Beckett looked positively puzzled. Then I remembered the small space that I was about to crawl into again, and my face contorted into a grimace. He really must have thought I was losing my mind, my emotions changed so rapidly.

"Okay," I breathed. "Let's go."

Beckett shook his head in consternation and led the way upstairs.

Careening down the chute was no less pleasant than the first time, but at least at that point I knew what to expect when I landed. Beckett followed close behind and I began to walk through the door and down the tunnel.

"Forgetting something?" Beckett called behind me. I hadn't realized that he had stopped, and so I was surprised a little at hearing his voice at an unexpected distance. I turned around and he was pointing at the go-bag.

"What do we need to take that for?" I asked.

"Seriously?" Beckett asked. "I thought you Compound folk were supposed to be smart." Seeing my immediate defensive reaction, he threw his hands up in front of him in surrender. "I'm only teasing, El. Don't flip out on me again."

I crossed my arms and waited for him to answer my question.

"First of all, you need to practice carrying this thing the distance that you will need to travel so that you are aware of its weight as you travel over land. Secondly, you never know when something is going to happen. We might need this while we're out there today."

"Well...can't you just carry it?" I asked sweetly, batting lashes and trying to look as innocent as I could.

"If we were escaping together, I would carry it for you. You can be certain of that. But what we can't be certain of is that

I'll actually be there. So you need to practice moving under the weight."

"Fine," I conceded reluctantly, putting the backpack on my shoulders. "If I fall over like a turtle and can't get up, you'd better help me."

"What good would that do? What if that happened when you were alone? You'd need to know how to help yourself. So if it happens, I'll watch while you squirm until you figure it out."

My eyes bugged out of my head, but Beckett didn't wait to give me a chance to go on a tirade.

"I'm kidding, Eloise. You've really got to lighten up a little."

"*I* need to lighten up? You're the one who sounds like you're reading off of a teleprompter half the time…," I trailed off as we started walking. I must have been hyped up on adrenaline the previous day because the backpack was heavy already, and I could only imagine what it would feel like after a couple of miles. But I wasn't going to give Beckett the satisfaction of hearing me complain about anything else, so I kept my lips closed.

As we walked down the damp, dark tunnel, I waited patiently for Beckett to start talking. When he still didn't say anything after five minutes, I ran out of patience.

"Beckett," I said, trying not to say anything that could be construed as rude.

"What?" he asked.

It didn't take me long to get exasperated.

"What do you mean 'what'? You're supposed to be talking and you haven't said anything. You're so hesitant it makes me think that you don't even have a real reason for my leaving the Compound. Is this all some kind of charade? What are you so scared of telling me?"

He pursed his lips and then he said, "I can promise you it's no charade, Eloise, though sometimes I wish it was. It's not that I'm *scared* of telling you anything. It's just... complicated."

"Well you need to start uncomplicating things. Please, just start explaining," I pleaded. I figured that yelling didn't work, so maybe begging would. Either that was the ticket to success, or the timing was just finally right.

Beckett rubbed his hands on the side of his face. "Okay, you're right. Where do I begin?"

As he thought out loud, we reached the end of the tunnel and climbed to the surface. I thought about how much it would really suck if we emerged into the middle of a Compound encampment or something. Luckily, that wasn't the case.

"I promise I'm about to start, but it's important for you to listen to my directions first. When you get up to ground level, you can go in three different directions. The best option is straight ahead because it gets you the furthest distance from the house, and it's the easiest to find. The other two routes are diagonally right and diagonally left, but they aren't the best because one leads you closer to the road where you could potentially run into Compound soldiers, and the other leads you directly out from the garden, which would be an easy path for the Compound to sniff out."

He paused, checking for my attention.

"Okay, Beckett. I've got you, I'm listening," I said a little impatiently.

He nodded. "Right, so straight ahead in between those two tall pines. We couldn't take the risk of marking trees for you to follow because that would make it just as easy for the Compound to find you. I hope you have a good memory still."

"Still? What do you mean still?" I asked.

"Uh, nothing. Just follow me," he stammered unconvincingly. "Now if you pay close attention to your surroundings, you'll find this again easily if you need to. So you've got a pretty heavy task at hand right now. You need to pay attention to the landmarks that we'll be walking by while still following the information that I'm giving you about why you're in the Open in the first place."

"Yeah, Beckett. I know," I answered haughtily. Why did he always need to sound as if he was somehow insulting my intelligence?

"Okay so first a little history lesson," he began and I had a feeling that his way of sounding like a news reporter would quickly turn into sounding like a walking textbook instead. "I need to know, though: what exactly do you know about the Compound?"

I pushed air out of my lungs.

"Seriously, Beckett? Again? We've already been through this."

I was beginning to huff and puff a little as I talked and hefted the bag around at the same time.

"I know," he responded. "Just humor me. There's a method to my madness."

"Well, obviously the United States collapsed due to unfortunate, unavoidable circumstances. The Compound had been in construction before the subsidence of the nation, and the surviving population was escorted behind the walls for safety. The Compound has successfully existed in isolation ever since."

"*That's* what they told you?" Beckett guffawed incredulously. He shook his head with his mouth gaping open. "I mean, that's all? There's nothing else?"

"That's it," I shrugged.

"So, explain to me what life is like in there. How is it organized? Who do you see? What do you do?"

"It's just... life," I said, a bit exasperated. "You grow, you eat, you sleep. You go to school, you graduate, you get a job. You get married, you have a family. You get old, you die. It's the same everywhere, isn't it?"

"Well, the general cycle of life, Eloise, yes, it's the same. But how does your society function? How does the community work?"

"As you know, the Compound is enormous and self-sufficient. It provides everything that we need in order to survive: food, water, supplies, exercise, education, health care. It's... I don't even *know* how long except for estimating, which I would say is about a half mile on each side, and stories high obviously. There are certain wings and floors dedicated to living quarters, to recreational areas, the schools, the various areas of professions. You live with your family, you hang out with your friends. You eat meals, you watch movies, you do homework. I'm not really sure what else to say."

"Who is in charge? Who keeps order and makes the rules?" Beckett asked.

"The Council. I'd never really interacted with a member until the other day by the apartment. Rules aren't really an issue in the Compound. Everyone follows them for the most part, and if you don't..."

"If you don't, then what?" Beckett pressed on.

"Truthfully, I don't really know. It happened so infrequently that it has barely crossed my mind. I can only assume that those people are out here, wandering around in the Open. It's an unspoken assumption that people have been banished from the Compound before. At least, it's better than the alternative thought," I said. I couldn't quite admit to him that the Compound may have been responsible for the... disposal... of those who couldn't toe the line.

Beckett nodded. "It's all as we've expected. No question of authority because the Compound set itself up that way."

"How do you mean?" I asked him.

"The Compound doesn't contain the posterity of the survivors, Eloise. It is a population that was carefully selected to be saved, to be 'protected' from the rest of the world."

I stopped walking, pulling my head back and looking at him sideways. "I still don't understand what you mean."

"Keep walking," he commanded, and then continued. "This is where our new history lesson begins. We have to take a step back into the past for a moment."

I nodded and Beckett plunged into his lecture on the history of the United States.

"I don't know how much you know about the history of what was once our fine country, so I'm just going to start from the beginning, elaborating more than I did before. There was a point in time when this giant slab of land was mostly undisturbed. Nature was left untouched, and it was inhabited by the animals and scattered Native Americans. The short of it is that there was a group over in England unhappy with their lives, as I've told you before. So they took some boats to the 'new land' and created a new life for themselves. America became the land of opportunity and fresh beginnings.

Problem is, the newcomers eradicated the Natives in order to do so. The Pilgrims, as they were called, didn't trust the 'savages' that had already inhabited the land. So over time, they slaughtered them or chased them out into the west. They pretended to offer aid and instead handed the Natives blankets infested with the disease, smallpox. The Pilgrims nearly wiped out the entire population for the sake of 'freedom'.

That was the end of the beginning, El. We were screwed from the get-go. You can't found a country on bloodshed and expect things to turn out well. The hypocrites left England to escape persecution, and then they turned around and dished it out to someone else. Land of the free, home of the brave, my ass," he concluded. "Whoops, sorry for the language."

I smiled to myself in spite of the serious conversation we were having. Beckett spoke so passionately about the subject of the Native Americans' obliteration. It was a different side of him than I had seen so far, and I admired it. Beckett was dynamic, constantly revealing different shades of himself, peeling the layers of his personality like an onion. You could never call him shallow. I had a feeling there were depths of Beckett that I would never reach.

"Okay, so the United States was founded on the blood of the innocent," I recapped. I hoped my comprehension check was a subtle enough urge for him to continue.

"Yeah, that's the beginning of it. We're here," Beckett pointed in front of us to a cluster of entwined, snarled branches of unruly plants up against a large boulder.

"And why, exactly, is standing in front of this angry bush safe?" I questioned wryly.

"Well, that's the point," Beckett said. "It's not the front of the mess that we are concerned about. Gently now."

He placed one hand around the biggest branch of the bush on the right and another on the left, and then he carefully pulled them apart revealing the entrance to a small cave.

"Oh, *God!*" I recoiled. "Why do you keep insisting on putting me in small spaces? And what if there was an animal in there?!"

"Stop acting like such a princess. That's a risk you're going to have to take if you want to stay out of the clutches of the Council. I doubt that the cleanliness and creatures of this cave are going to be the first thing on your mind in a desperate situation," he said and held the branches apart for me to pass. I was about to retort that I still didn't even know if I wanted to avoid capture, but I actually refrained for once in my life.

"The trick is to make the branches once again look as if they had not been disturbed. Any good tracker will know right away that you have moved through those bushes, and I'm sure the

Compound has one," he said as he modeled manually tangling the branches. When he was done, I couldn't see past them into the woods where we had come from.

"Got it?" he asked.

I nodded and looked at my new surroundings. The small cave was not tall enough for us to stand, so we both had to crouch down to take a few steps into it. Instinctively, I turned on the flashlight that was hooked on the outside of the go-bag and turned it on to check for signs of living things. There were a few scattered, dried leaves that the wind had blown in and the floor was obviously dirt covered, but it was dry and obscured and looked devoid of any other life forms.

"Lesson number one," Beckett interrupted my observation. "Do not turn on that flashlight unless you absolutely need to, especially at night. During the day it won't cause too much of a distraction, but at night you will surely alert yourself to anyone looking for you. And that's a bad thing unless it's one of us."

Again with the dumbing things down, I thought to myself, but I didn't acknowledge it with actual speech.

"So this is basically it," he said. "You walk – or run if need be – to this location. Gently separate the entanglement by grabbing hold of the larger branches and pull apart. Get yourself safely through and then rearrange the limbs before positioning yourself in here. Then it's just a waiting game."

I nodded that I understood and Beckett started to untangle the branches again so that we could get out. I was grateful as I was predictably starting to feel claustrophobic with us both stuffed into the cave.

"Let's head back the way we came. It'll get you used to the sights," Beckett said and lead the way. "Oh, one more thing. Never, ever use those flares in your bag to try to attract our attention."

"Then what's the point of them being in there?" I asked, slightly bewildered.

"They're in there because we can't predict the type of emergency that you might face. If you fall and break your leg or almost get attacked by a bear, then it wouldn't matter who found you as long as you got to safety."

"There are bears out here?!"

"*Focus*, Eloise. No flares."

"No flares," I muttered. "Now back to that history lesson."

"Right. So after the colonists got the Native Americans out of the way, they realized that England was still sort of bossing them around from overseas. So they of course decided that that was unacceptable, and there was something called the Revolutionary War. The Americans fought against the British who didn't want to let the colonists become independent. La-di-da-di-da, the Americans win and their new home becomes an official country, the United States. Many men died fighting either for or against independence, so once again, bloodshed.

About another hundred years pass, and those years are really mostly uneventful for the *white* colonists. Because, you see, these men that were all about 'freedom' came up with the bright idea that they should have slaves do all their work for them. Again, hypocrites. Until finally the northern part of the country said, 'Hey, wait a minute. This isn't right'. The southern part of the country didn't like that because they depended on the slaves to work on their plantations. And so then the Americans were like, 'Gee we haven't had a war in a while. Let's do that again! It worked out well last time.' And there was something called the Civil War. It ended up being a big mess, pitting brother against brother as the north fought the south, and again countless lives were lost in the process. In the end, slavery was abolished and everyone was 'free'. Well, except for women who didn't even gain rights until decades later, but that's really insignificant compared to everything else."

I raised an eyebrow and curled my lip. "These Americans sound like real chumps."

Beckett nodded and shrugged. "Yeah, well, pretty much. But it doesn't stop there."

"Of course it doesn't," I said. "Let me guess, more blood and dying?"

"Ding, ding, ding!" Beckett pointed at me with both pointer fingers. "The country begins to somewhat get back together and we hit the turn of the century: 1900. Things look a little better for a little more than a decade, and then the whole world seems to go crazy, and there we have World War I. It seems as though it wasn't just the Americans that were bloodthirsty. All of the human race across the globe has a violent tendency. And now that the world became so much more connected, it was easier to get involved in everyone else's business. Inevitably, the United States joins the war – overseas this time – and over a hundred-thousand Americans perish.

You would think at this point everyone would realize that nothing really ever got solved by violence, and that people just kept on getting severely wounded or dying. But common sense and peace did not prevail. In fact, human beings liked death so much that they engaged in a *second* World War. And that time, weapon technology had advanced to the point where war was more deadly than it had ever been before. Planes could drop bombs on cities and towns from above, military and civilians alike in their paths, without ever having to touch the ground. Guns could shoot from a distance, virtually eliminating the need for hand to hand combat. Over 600,000 American deaths. Over one million soldiers total either dead or wounded. Families destroyed. Young guys, boys really, never getting to live their lives. It was unconscionable," Beckett said with a truly pained expression on his face.

"Sounds horrible," was all that I could muster. It was as if Beckett was having a personal and emotional moment, and I didn't want to be the one to disrupt his soliloquy, his tribute to the fallen. He was silent for a moment, but then he charged forward like a soldier into battle himself.

"It was horrible," he confirmed. "But that wasn't it, Eloise. The United States continued to insert itself into wars. There were the Vietnam and Korean Wars, the Gulf War, the war in Afghanistan, the war in Iraq, the War on Terror. There was a *third* World War and a *fourth* World War, Eloise. War, after war, after war. They never learned. They never learned."

I thought I saw tears welled up in his eyes, but then I blinked and he cleared his throat, and the evidence was no longer there. He seemed awfully affected, impassioned even, by the history of the United States, almost to the point where it was a little unreasonable. But at the same time it was endearing that he cared so much for humankind past.

I couldn't find the right words to say. Speaking, breaking the silence, seemed almost violent in itself at that moment. We kept walking back towards the hatch of the tunnel, I presumed, until I finally felt as though I had to say *something*. I had to try and show Beckett that I understood what he was telling me and what he was feeling. I, too, hurt for all of the death of the past.

"So, that's why there was so many of them," I wondered aloud, trying to demonstrate my comprehension.

"So many of what?" he asked.

"The graves. When we went to that cemetery," I said politely, but matter-of-factly.

Beckett stopped walking and looked at me with the saddest look of torture on his face. I wanted to wrap my arms around him, cradle him like a child and tell him it was going to be okay.

"No, Eloise," he said quietly.

I grimaced.

"None of those graves were the result of war. That's why it's so important that you never go back to the Compound," Beckett beseeched and then gestured in front of us. "We're back."

The revelation hit me like a blast of dynamite. There had been so many stone markers, how could they not be from a war? What could have happened to cause so many deaths?

"We have to go on to the next location," Beckett said. "Here, give me your pack."

Wordlessly, I shrugged the go-bag off of my shoulders and handed it to him. I knew that him carrying it for me was like a gesture of apology. Like he was unburdening me of the information he just relayed by lifting the literal weight off my back. But my shoulders still hung heavily, my chest felt laden with rocks. And it wasn't because of the trek with the backpack. It was the realization of my ignorance crushing me.

Beckett gave me a minute to recollect myself. I ran a hand through my hair, trying to imagine that some catastrophic natural event had claimed all of those lives. I knew, of course, that they hadn't perished in such a way. Otherwise Beckett wouldn't be so torn up about it. Obviously the Compound was somehow responsible for the carnage, and in turn I felt a sense of responsibility. I knew it had nothing to do with me personally, but somehow it felt like it did.

"El, we've got to get a move on," Beckett interrupted my thoughts. "Follow me."

He turned on his heel and began walking away, the emblazoned grief no longer etched on his face. I jogged a few steps to catch up with him, so that we were side by side. Being taller than I was, Beckett made it difficult to keep up with his long stride. I assumed that his pace had quickened due to the subject matter, but he betrayed no look of emotion on his face. In fact, he appeared to have never participated in the conversation at all.

"How do you do it?" I asked

"How do I do what," Beckett responded flatly, his eyes glued to the sea of trees ahead of us.

"Your emotions. They're constantly changing at the drop of a hat. One minute you're soft and fuzzy, the next you're all business and bossy, and then you're enraged. And then all of a sudden you're a tour guide again. I can't keep up with it all. How could you be so gloomy a minute ago, and now you're, I don't know, over it?"

It was exasperating. I wasn't the type of person who could let bygones be bygones. I felt everything deeply. When I was angry, I could give you the silent treatment for a week before I got bored. When I was sad, I could cry enough tears to fill a bathtub. Beckett's emotions were like a light switch that he could flick on or off at any given moment. It made him seem illegitimate, though my instincts told me otherwise.

"I've had a lot of time to think about all of this, Eloise," he replied.

I snorted. "All nineteen years."

Beckett opened his mouth as if to say something, but then he thought otherwise and closed it without a word.

"I mean, honestly, you act like my dad half of the time and we're practically the same age," I rambled on unknowingly, callously. "I'm the one who's a teenage girl here. You'd think it'd be my emotions that—"

Beckett gave me a tight-lipped, impatient look that stopped me short. Abashed, I lowered my head and concentrated on the ground. There I was accusing Beckett of being flippant with his emotions and I was a hypocrite. I sensed that Beckett wasn't feeling so motivated to continue with his story, but I had waited long enough. And now that I had part of the story, there was a need deep within my core to know the whole truth.

What did this all have to do with me?

I cleared my throat and pressed on. "So...I know that this hasn't been the most pleasant trip down memory lane, but I also know that's not the end of the story. What happened next?"

Beckett scratched his head, and then spoke, some lightness returning to his voice. It was clear that no matter how disturbing the content, when retelling history he was in his element.

"Right, so, there were a lot of wars throughout American history and people always could find a reason to support them. Don't get me wrong, not everyone did. But generally speaking we aren't talking about pacifists here. It was as if people were restless without any blood to spill. My point is – I feel like I am repeating myself – that wars can only happen when people have a tendency towards violence. Otherwise no one would sign up to fight them. So you have this...innate...aggression that all human beings have, some more than others. And you have the world evolving, but human beings don't really evolve.

I mean, think about it. Cavemen used to beat each other over the head with clubs over a piece of meat or the best cave dwelling. Sword-fighting virtually sustained the feudal system for hundreds of years so that a handful of people could be rich and powerful. Guns: pistols, shotguns, rifles, semi-automatics, automatics. Grenades, bombs, biological and chemical warfare. As time passed, what commonality do you see? It wasn't the human beings that were progressing, it was the technology. In particular, the weapons, which allowed us to continually express our hostility in more and more destructive ways. You follow?"

Beckett had become the professor again, wrapped up in his storytelling instead of the actual ending.

"Yeah, I guess," I answered. "I'm not going to say that I'm well-versed in weaponry, but I assume that they gradually got more deadly."

He nodded. "The problem was that it wasn't just the trained soldiers who had their hands on the guns. The wars weren't always being fought overseas. They were being fought on the streets of any given city in the United States by angry youths who didn't have an education. Some found themselves in an endless cycle of desperation. People were unable to dig themselves out of the holes that their predecessors had led them into, and so they resorted to violence as a means of survival. Some chose that kind of life for themselves, but most were born into it and it was difficult to leave behind. Gangs of young people senselessly killed each other all of the time over *nothing*. You looked at his girlfriend, disrespected him, walk in his neighborhood, stepped on his shoes. Didn't matter. That was how problems were solved.

Of course, they weren't really solved. As time went by, more and more people fell into this lifestyle of violence. People our age or younger, armed and dangerous, not knowing the consequences of their actions. Because, Eloise, there were no old gangsters. Do you know why?"

I assumed that the question was rhetorical, so I remained quiet, waiting for Beckett to answer his own question, the only sound the crunching of leaves and twigs underfoot. Meanwhile, I was trying to remember the way that we had traveled, considering that was the whole purpose of our journey. But I feared I was too enraptured by his tale to really concentrate. The good thing was, Beckett was so distracted I think he too forgot that I was supposed to be paying attention to our path, so at least I wouldn't be reprimanded for it.

"There were no old gangsters because they didn't *live* that long. It got to the point where if you lived past your twenty-fifth birthday in some communities, it was a miracle. Or it meant that you were in jail. And being dead or in jail didn't do anything to better society. It was on a rapid decline. The population of youths eighteen through twenty-five dropped dramatically, and as a result, so did the birth rate. Jails became so overpopulated that they had to convert old schools that had been closed into holding cells so that communities had convenient locations to divert the criminals. But the crime rate rose so high that there were not enough law enforcement agents to patrol, not enough jails to lock people up. So instead of making punishments harsher to try to dissuade people from committing crimes, the United States began to decriminalize. If you were mugged on the street or a store was robbed, they didn't try too hard to find the person so long as no one got seriously hurt. Fist fights and shootings were so commonplace that the general feeling became, 'if they want to kill each other, let them'. It got to the point where people thought you were nuts if you left your house after dark. Locking the doors didn't ensure your safety. You were grateful each day you woke up that you had made it through another night unmolested. And that isn't even including the drug problem."

Beckett shook his head in disgust.

"Drug problem?" I questioned. What did medicine have to do with anything? The population had declined and people were killing each other off, so medications saving lives couldn't have been a *problem*.

"I'm not talking curing sicknesses, El. I'm talking recreational drugs. Cocaine, heroin, LSD. Addictions to prescription medications. Not to mention the combinations that were born from the originals I just mentioned. Mutations of brain-addling drugs that ruined lives. People injected themselves, inhaled things, ate things that affected all of the body systems. And they were made of ingredients that kept people coming back for more, creating an addiction that took precedent over every other part of their lives. It contributed to the violence and the instability. People couldn't hold jobs or a roof over their heads. They would take the drugs while they were pregnant, creating generations of children who were afflicted. It was a downward spiral into the abyss. A rock on the gas pedal and no one at the wheel."

"Sounds ridiculous," I said, pigheaded in my youth. "It couldn't have been *everyone* who fell for the violence and the drugs. There had to be some good people still. The generations that followed couldn't have been totally hopeless. There still had to be people educating in the schools that could—"

"HA!" Beckett chortled, startling me. "Eloise, tell me what school looks like to you."

I didn't even want to answer his question. I knew that he was once again poking fun at my ignorance, and I didn't need to be reminded of it. But if I wanted him to eventually continue, I had no choice.

"Well, *Beckett*," I said through gritted teeth, trying desperately to keep the animosity out of my voice. "School is a place where students go to a classroom to learn from a teacher. They sit in desks, read books, calculate, research. Shall I go on?"

"No need. You could've stopped when you said students sit in desks," he replied.

I looked at him, puzzled.

"There was a time when students went to school to learn. To sit in desks, gain knowledge, and follow the rules," he admitted. "But that faded so quickly it's barely even a blemish in history. You see, with the decline of society, values also went by the wayside. It started off with a small percentage not caring about education, not being involved in school or teaching their children to behave. But eventually, there were so few parents who had high enough expectations of their children that the schools all had to close because they could no longer function as schools. At first, the children who had tough lives were coddled and catered to. Discipline eventually became nonexistent and it was the students ruling the classroom instead of the teacher or administration. People thought it was bad when elementary school students were fist-fighting and refusing to do work, or when high school students called in bomb threats every other day. That was only the beginning. Students of all ages were attacking teachers or the small group of students who still behaved. You couldn't teach lessons because students wouldn't stay in the school buildings, let alone their seats. It was anarchy. Anarchy in the schools just like the anarchy on the streets. They were forced to close."

"How can you close *schools*?" I wondered aloud, baffled. "Surely the troublemakers had to be the minority instead of the majority."

"Oh, I would be careful about how you're throwing those words around, Eloise," Beckett smirked and then looked quickly over his shoulder, as if someone was following us. I turned to look too. Playfulness returned, he smirked and said, "There's no one there. At least I don't think there is. I said that because racism became another unsolvable problem, or the accusation of racism, anyway. It existed. Prejudices always will. But the lack of education, the drug problems, the rising poverty level and violence... it all snowballed and people needed a reason for it. So everyone started calling each other 'racist'. You punished my child because you're racist. You arrested me because you're racist. You didn't vote for that candidate because you're racist. People didn't want to admit the fact that the child misbehaved, the adult committed a crime, or the politician didn't hold a strong platform. It was much easier to cry racism as the cause for it all. No one wanted to be held accountable for the reality of situations, and this sparked even more violence and unrest. Riots in the streets, looting and setting fire to businesses. More shootings and stabbings. Race was pitted against race and no one trusted each other anymore, not even a little bit.

The United States was thrown into utter chaos. It became impossible to hold on to some semblance of unity, some variation of an organized community that had once existed. Americans resorted to primitive, animalistic instinct that ultimately destroyed their home. And so it doesn't exist anymore, not in the sense that it once did."

I tried to think about my response before I said anything to Beckett. I still couldn't figure out how it was the Compound's fault that people went nuts killing each other. The graves made sense now, but you can't control the choices of other people. When you make poor life decisions, there are consequences that unfortunately affect many people. That seemed pretty straightforward to me.

"Well, that's awful," I said. "But you're making it sound like if the Americans chose to do the things that they did, they kind of had it coming to them."

I sort of winced at that point, expecting backlash from Beckett. I thought for sure he would think me insensitive.

"In a way you're right, El," he agreed, "but as human beings I feel that we have a responsibility to each other. It all could have been prevented if someone had stepped in and taken charge. If the government had stopped allowing for the violence to happen, stopped making excuses for people who had 'difficult circumstances', then it never would have happened the way that it did. Maybe the road to set things right may have been bumpy for a while, but the United States didn't have to completely collapse."

"I guess that's reasonable," I sighed. "So what does the Compound have to do with any of this?"

"The Compound was a secret project. The high-clearance security-level, kind of secret. Very few people knew about it. The military was involved and the government, of course. Various engineers and architectural firms. They risked termination if they spoke to anyone else about it, even their families. And when I say termination, I don't mean being fired. You see, the United States government watched their nation unravel in front of their eyes, and instead of fixing the problem, it decided that the elite needed somewhere to go when all hell broke loose. That's when the idea of the Compound was born."

"But no one even mentions the United States except for in history lessons at school," I said.

"Well of course they don't. They don't want the newer generations to know the cowardice their home was spawn from. They don't want to admit failure or to risk another all-out revolution if people realize that they can thwart the control. It's still a web of lies and secrets, Eloise. Haven't you ever noticed how you can't see anything for miles around from the Compound windows? Did you ever wonder what was beyond the walls that required stationed sentinels and security measures?"

"Well, I know it looks like a barren wasteland surrounding the Compound, but no. I never really wondered about the guns or the soldiers because I was safe and happy, as I've told you countless times before. I didn't have a *reason* to question any of it, Beckett. I had everything I needed. Why would I be looking for more?"

"That's because they didn't want you to think about it. How can people be so blind...," he began muttering to himself.

"Um, I'm right here you know," I reminded him.

"Yeah, sorry," Beckett said. "Anyway, the government built the Compound in secret when things really began deteriorating because they knew that they would need somewhere to go when it really wasn't possible to survive in the general public anymore. I don't really know if it remained a complete secret. It's kind of hard to believe that, with the number of people they had working on the place, someone wouldn't have slipped. My guess is that anyone who stumbled across the construction site on accident was probably shot immediately."

"Jesus," I mumbled, the hair of my arms standing on end.

"That's not the worst part of it," Beckett said gravely.

"Great. What is?"

"When the Compound was finally completed, there was no such thing as a functional society any longer. Businesses couldn't operate anymore, the schools had already closed down, and any part of law enforcement had long since given up on trying to keep order. So the government made a list, Eloise. A list of people who they considered worth saving. They took the best and the brightest and the most civil from all of the different professions that they would need in order to create a utopian society, protected behind the walls of the Compound. And that's just what they did. They barged into the people's homes who were on the list, and they weren't given a choice whether or not they wanted to participate. Because if they were invited and then denied the invitation, the word could get out about the Compound to others who were unwelcome, and they risked destroying their sacred new construction. So soldiers arrived at your door, gave you a half an hour to pack your valuables, and then you were escorted directly to the Compound, never to look back."

"I don't see anything wrong with wanting to protect the people who were still law-abiding citizens," I said. "They deserved to be separated from those other... those other animals."

"That's the argument that the Compound was founded upon," Beckett said impatiently. "But that's not the point. Yeah, sure, innocent people always deserve to be saved. The problem is, the government didn't save all of the innocent people. You had to be smart enough, useful enough, for them to even consider you. If you weren't selected based on their criteria, you were left to fend for yourself. The United States' government abandoned the people that they had sworn to protect and serve, Eloise. They left people behind just because they didn't think they were *smart* enough."

Before I could stop myself the words tumbled out of my mouth. "It's better for some to survive than none. It sounds like it was done for the greater good, so that *some* of us could have a future."

Beckett's eyes flashed. "Do you remember the Holocaust, Eloise? Hitler thought he was creating a superior race too. How did that turn out? Do you really feel that superior, that you would be willing to sacrifice others just to preserve yourself?"

"Do *not* compare me to damn Hitler!" I spat. "I wasn't *there*, Beckett, and neither were you for that matter. I just think that the United States' government must have made decisions based on what they felt was best at that time. Excuse me if you would have made better decisions in such a desperate situation. Plus, it would have taken ages to build more Compounds and they probably would have been discovered. How would the human race be doing now if no one had survived?"

He shook his head and flared his nose, disgusted with me and infuriated. I suddenly realized that we were standing still in front of a cluster of branches similar to the last hiding spot. *When had we stopped walking?* I wondered.

Anger emanated from us both, and we would have both been breathing fire if it were possible. Beckett started pacing in front of the bushes.

"What do you want me to say, Beckett?" I asked, throwing my hands in the air. "I feel awful that so many people died, but I'm not going to say that *I* regret being alive. I can't help where I was born or the kind of life that I have lived. Did we have it good in the Compound? Yeah, we had it damn good. And there are no uprisings and there's no violence. We coexist peacefully. We work together and we learn together and we live our lives without fearing being shot. Is that so bad?"

"No, Eloise," he waved his hand at me. "No, your life has not been bad. You've lived trouble free without a *clue* about what the people in the Open had to go through in order to just *make* it. These are survivors that you have met, survivors who are trying to return this place to something like what the United States was intended to *be*. But we can't do that, Eloise. And do you know why? Because the Compound doesn't *want* it to happen. They feel threatened by the mere existence of any other human life, never mind what they think will happen if we tried to resume some sort of structured community out here in the Open. Tell me, Eloise, is there really never any unrest there? Because the people who were originally selected to inhabit the Garden of Eden have long since died. You were living amongst the descendants of those who were plucked out of their homes, lucky enough to be worthy of the Compound. You can't tell me that everyone follows the rules, El. It's not in our nature to all be the same."

I avoided making eye contact with him, stubbornly reluctant to answer his question. I knew what he was getting at.

"Eloise?" he prompted.

"No, Beckett, not everyone follows the rules all of the time," I admitted grudgingly.

"What happens to them?"

"I don't know," I said, crossing my arms in front of me, trying to use my body to guard myself from his question.

"Eloise, what happens to them?" he growled.

"I. Don't. Know," I growled back.

"Yeah you do, El," he sniggered with a look on his face like he had a sour taste in his mouth. "You know exactly what happens to them. They're either sent into the Open with nothing but the clothes on their back. Or they just...disappear. Don't they, El? And the Compound likes to pretend that it lives in a world without violence, that they're superior to the rest of us. But it's all the same, the cycle. Admit it."

"I can't admit anything that I don't know," I retorted, fuming. "I'm just a sixteen-year-old girl from the Compound, and quite frankly, no one has ever considered me important enough to let in on all the secrets, including *you*. Arrogant bastard."

"Aw, God, come on," Beckett laughed sarcastically. "I keep putting myself through this, and for what? Will you ever change, Eloise? Damnit!"

He kicked at the brush around his feet and stomped around in frustration. I remember thinking about how ironic it was that he had been preaching about violence, and then demonstrating his own aggressive side so shortly afterwards.

"I don't know, Beckett, if I'll ever change. I don't really know how you can expect much from me in the three seconds that you've known me. Why are you putting all of this on me? How is *any* of this my fault? You parade around here, acting all high-and-mighty, blaming me for the downfall of the human race? Who's the delusional one? Not me!" I yelled back at him.

"Arghhh," Beckett grunted and shook his head.

"Tell me, Mr. I-Know-Everything. Tell me why you're constantly putting me d—"

"BECAUSE YOU CREATED THE GOD DAMNED COMPOUND, ELOISE!" Beckett bellowed at me.

For a moment, I forgot to breathe. And as soon as the words came out of his mouth, a look of regret immediately crossed Beckett's face. Before he could say anything more, I began to back away from him, shaking my head in confusion and disbelief. I stumbled after I had taken a couple of steps backwards, and then I couldn't look at him anymore.

I turned around, and I ran.

I didn't even know where I was running to, or what I was running from for that matter. Either Beckett was crazy or I was crazy, or maybe we were both crazy. As I ran through the woods to nowhere, twigs and branches flicked against my skin surely leaving marks, but at the time I was numb to everything around me. Lost in my own thoughts, I tried to understand Beckett's meaning when he said what he said. I was sixteen. There was no possible way that I had anything to do with the Compound. He must have meant that it was my people, or people like me. But what was that supposed to mean, people like me? Smart? Ignorant? Self-indulgent?

It didn't take long after my barrage through the trees to begin to feel my lungs burn under the strain. I would never been a good runner, no matter how good it could feel to have the wind crash into your face or your muscles contract with each step. I would always be easily out of breath, a fiery inferno ablaze in my chest. At that moment, my lungs were betraying me once again and I knew that I wouldn't be able to continue much further before I was really struggling for breath.

As if I had gone temporarily deaf for a couple of minutes, my hearing suddenly returned to me and I could hear Beckett calling my name behind me. He had to have been in better shape than me, and I could only figure he was behind me at all because he must have given me a moment before realizing I wasn't coming back. Soon, he would catch up to me, surpass me even probably. And then what?

Out of the corner of my eye I thought I saw a man with reddish-brown skin wearing animal furs skinning an animal. *Not again*, I thought to myself. *Not now*. I blinked and shook my head, and the vision was gone.

Ahead of me I could see a break in the tree line. Had I actually ran in the right direction? Was I approaching the clearing where the hatch to the tunnel was? If so, at least I now had a point of reference, not that it would do me any good. I couldn't trust anyone to tell me the truth at Headquarters any more than I could believe Beckett. I wondered if I was better off trying to find someone from the Compound to just take me home and have it all be over with. Maybe I had been horribly naïve to think that the Open's true initiative was to protect me. Maybe the whole thing had been a farce and I was really putting myself in danger by running away.

All of these thoughts swimming through my mind, I didn't see the knotted tree root sticking out of the ground. My steps had slowed slightly, making my gait a little less elongated, and I caught my left foot just right. I tripped on it and heard a *snap*, then hurtled forward into the clearing. Pain exploded in my ankle as I plummeted face first towards the ground. I caught myself with my hands mostly, but my head did thump a little on the ground as I landed.

Part of me screamed to get up and keep going, to drag myself if need be, to a place that was hidden from searching eyes. Was there anywhere that I could hide where Beckett wouldn't think to look? What about going back into the tunnel? Sometimes hiding in plain sight was the best way to prevent yourself from being caught.

But that part that was still plotting escape was very small, miniscule. Mostly, I just wanted to rest; to give my tired lungs a chance to regain normalcy, to close my eyes and wake up having had all of this been a dream. I curled up into the fetal position, wincing as my ankle made contact with my other leg or the ground, and waited. Beckett would catch up any second and there would be no point in trying to do anything. Somehow I had found myself in this strange new world, knowing supposed new and factual information about my home, and I didn't know if either side was completely telling the truth. I just wanted to lie in that field forever, to forget the tug-of-war game that the Compound and the Alliance were playing with me.

The dewy grass tickled my face, and I concentrated on watching an ant climb along a blade of grass as my breaths began to steady. How insignificant a life, I thought, an ant had. So fleeting, so monotonous, but yet so simple, so unaffected by trivial human problems such as who saved who, when, for what reason. No decisions to make, no one to disappoint. I envied that ant, so single-minded and trouble-free.

I began to cry, my first real tears that were not provoked by a weird vision since having been kidnapped from my home. How odd, I thought, to be upset now and not before. Before this had all felt like an adventure. Perhaps it had been just the fact that I had always longed for more after spending my entire life inside the walls of the Compound. And now that I had my freedom, I questioned why I had ever wanted it. No one in life is every *really* free. You are always tied to someone or something. Responsibilities will always keep you shackled. Before I had little choice about what I wanted to be or where I wanted to live. I had to go to classes, perform well, obey my parents. Now I was free to make decisions, but I was supposedly responsible for the heinous abandonment of an entire nation of people. If it were true, somehow, how could I justify ever going back to the cushy life that I had led? How could I live with the fact that I was at least partially responsible for more deaths than I could probably count? How do you move forward from such tragedy when you are the one responsible?

As I lie in self-loathing on the ground, I heard footsteps padding over to me.

"Eloise! Eloise, are you alright?" Beckett asked as he approached, not seeming the slightest bit out of breath, even with the go-bag on his back.

"Get away from me," I warned, as if he actually had any actual reason to be wary of me, being in my least formidable state.

"Aw, El, come on," he said gently. "I didn't mean to lose it back there. I can explain what I meant. Just come with—"

"I *said* get away from me!" I snarled.

Beckett moved, presumably to get closer to me rather than to follow my directions and leave me alone, and he tapped my foot as he went by.

"Ahhh!" I cried as a fresh wave of pain seared from the focal point. Instinctively, I reached for the tender spot. It felt warm and pulsated, and for the first time it occurred to me that I might have broken it.

"What? What's the matter?!" Beckett sputtered.

I glared at him and refused to answer. All I wanted was for him to disappear. I didn't even care if he never came back or if I ever saw him again. At that moment, I could have stayed in that field forever, fading away into the grass with the change of the seasons. It would be more pleasant to never have to deal with any of the visions or the accusations or the deciding between two worlds than to be stuck in the middle of the mess I was in.

Realizing I was holding my ankle, Beckett finally inferred that I wasn't lying down in surrender.

"You're hurt," he stated more than questioned. "Let me take a look."

As he crouched down and leaned in towards me, I attempted to roll or crawl away from him, but the slightest touch of any pressure on my ankle created by the movement made it worse. I whimpered aloud.

"Eloise, for once in your life stop being so difficult. There's plenty of time to be mad at me later," he responded to my obstinacy. He reached again towards the end of my pant leg and I didn't move. Beckett slid it up as gently as he could, but I still grimaced.

"It looks swollen. I'm not sure if it's a sprain or a break, but we have to get you back to the house so that someone can check it out," he said.

"Oh, sure, let's just walk on back," I said sarcastically, like the sullen child that I was.

"Well, no, Eloise, obviously you're not going to be able to walk there," Beckett returned impatiently. "We have to get out to the road so that someone can pick us up in a car. It'll be the easiest way, though we risk being spotted."

"I don't want to go. Just leave me alone."

"I am not going to leave you alone."

"I don't want any part of this anymore. Just leave me here and I'll find my own way," I said. I wasn't crying anymore. I felt stony, barren of any feeling at all.

"You'll find your own way, where? With a broken ankle? No money, no car, no roof over your head. You've never done anything alone before, Eloise. How would you survive?"

His questions taunted me. "I didn't ask you to protect me, to feed me, to clothe me. In fact, I didn't ask you to kidnap me. No one ever gives me the *chance* to do anything for myself. Get lost. I'll figure it out."

"You'll figure it out," he scoffed. "How?"

"I don't know, Beckett, maybe Squanto back there will give me a hand."

He scrunched up his eyebrows in confusion. "Squanto? What are you talking about? Did you hit your head when you fell?"

"Nope. I think the hallucinations started long before then."

"Oh," he said as if he understood what I was talking about. "Come on, get up. I'll help you to the road and we'll walkie for a ride."

Beckett slid a hand around my arm in attempt to get me up and I shoved his hand away.

"I'm. Not. Going."

"Don't you want to know the rest of the story?" he asked.

I gave him a look and then concentrated back on the grass.

"I've only told you the history, generally speaking. Don't you want to know *why* everything is that way it is? Don't you want to learn more about yourself? Why you see things?"

"You're not playing fair," I said flatly. There really was no way that I could resist knowing the truth. Or at least what he claimed to be the truth. I needed to fill in some of the pieces of the puzzle, to try to understand why people were so separated from one another by walls and fences and land. And guns. And sentinels.

"You at least need to come back with me until that ankle is healed. Hear me out. And if you don't believe me or don't like what you hear, then you can leave," he said.

I sighed. I knew that I couldn't just lie there, waiting to be eaten by God knows what animals lived in the woods. We hadn't seen any so far, but surely they were there, lying in wait for something delicious to eat. And I was kidding myself if I thought that a girl from the Compound, whose meals were cooked to order from a control panel, could rough it in the wilderness for even a single night and survive.

Beckett silently offered me his hand, and when I took it he offered me the other. He pulled me to my feet, or one foot I should say, and I was a little off-balance when I first stood up. I fell into him and he caught and steadied me, my face stopping just short of his. I could tell that there was a sense of longing. I had gotten used to that look on his face.

I looked into his eyes. "Who are you?"

He laughed, shrugging off my question and breaking the spell of the silent moment. "Are you sure you didn't hit your head?"

Beckett slung an arm around my waist and one of mine across his shoulders. I attempted to hop on one foot while he supported me. We didn't get too far before he stopped.

"This isn't going to work," he said. "At this rate, we'll be lucky if we even make it to the road by nightfall."

"Well what are we supposed to do?" I asked, slightly out of breath again from exerting myself so soon after the run. "It'll take ten times longer to try and get to Headquarters through the woods than it would to get to the road. I assume."

"I can run back and see if I can find a wheelbarrow or something to cart you back in," he suggested.

"And leave me here by myself?"

"Boy, you change your mind quickly. About two seconds ago you were begging me to leave you out here for good. Now you don't want to spend twenty minutes alone."

"Yeah, well, obviously we both know that wasn't really going to happen," I said. Why did he always have to point out my shortcomings?

"Yeah, I know," he said smugly, grinning. "I'll just have to carry you."

"It's too far. You've got that bag on your back... There's no way we'll make it. You'll end up with a hurt back and then we'll really be stuck out here."

"You underestimate me, Eloise Carlisle," he replied, and then he scooped me up before I could protest again and began walking.

Luckily at that age, at that point in time, I was quite petite, and we made it to the road much more quickly than we would have had I been hobbling along on one foot. By the time we got there, Beckett was broken out in a sweat. I almost commented on it, but I was too grateful to see Mad-Eye's car turning a bend and to be heading back to creature comforts, so I refrained.

When back at Headquarters, an older guy that I hadn't met before inspected my ankle. His name was Nigel, and he was apparently the resident doctor at Headquarters. He determined that it was just a sprain. The snap that I had heard had probably been a ligament and not a bone, and I would heal quickly enough if I followed instructions.

"Do you know who you are talking to?" Beckett teased. "She doesn't listen to anyone."

I rolled my eyes at him and Nigel smiled politely.

"I'm sure that's not true," he said in his British accent. "Keep this elevated when you can, ice on and off, and avoid putting pressure on that ankle. I'll wrap it with an ace bandage to keep it steady and that's really all that we can do."

I wondered suddenly if the same unrest had happened in Europe and the rest of the world that had happened in the United States. If so, how had the situation been handled there? If not, why hadn't anyone come to the aid of the crumbled nation? And better yet, how did Nigel even have an accent? He would have had to have been born in America since the nation collapsed so long ago. It didn't add up.

I was about to start asking Nigel questions, but then he stood up and said he needed to get back to his work. I thanked him, Beckett thanked him, and then he left the room.

"I'm hungry. How about you?" Beckett asked.

I hadn't been thinking about it, with the day having been so eventful, but at that moment my stomach rumbled as if on cue.

"Yeah, I could eat."

He helped me to the kitchen, adjusted my leg on the chair beside me, and reapplied the ice to my ankle. Then I watched him as he busied himself in the cabinets to prepare our late lunch.

We ate in silence, neither of us probably knowing how to carry on the conversation we had ended with before. Neither of us was probably sure if we really and truly wanted to. I was scared that I might learn something disturbing about myself, but I also knew the not-knowing would eat away at me if I tried to ignore it. On some level, I knew Beckett wanted me to understand, but he was also afraid of what my reaction might be when I finally did. We were at a stalemate.

After eating I was suddenly tired; from the hiking with the go-bag, from the exhausting running, from the injury, the information. I needed to take a nap to clear my head and recharge before I could even think about anything else.

"I need a nap," I declared through a yawn.

"Okay," Beckett nodded. "That's probably a good idea."

I had the feeling that he kind of wanted to escape from me for a while, to have a few minutes to himself where he didn't have to cater to me or worry about me...or get yelled at by me. And I couldn't really blame him. Having me in his life must have been nothing but a burden since that night in the helicopter. Probably even before that.

Slowly, we made our way to the main staircase, and I insisted on not needing any help. I hopped up the first two steps on one foot tentatively.

"Really, El?" Beckett said.

"What?"

"By the time you make it up these stairs, *I'm* going to be asleep," he said. Then, once again, he scooped me up into his arms, carried me the rest of the way to my annex, and plopped me onto the bed.

"Your arms are going to be killing you tomorrow," I said matter-of-factly as I snuggled onto the pillow.

"Probably. You're really going to owe me."

I smiled at him, feeling so opposite than I had a short while before. Beckett was able to bring out the worst of me so easily, but he also forgave me for it just as quickly. And he *seemed* to always have my best interests at heart.

"Have a good nap," Beckett said and took a few steps towards the door.

I sat up so fast I almost gave myself whiplash.

"You're leaving?" I felt pathetic saying it, but it frightened me to be alone in this strange world.

"Yeah, El. It is still daytime. I have things I need to do, people I need to check on. Don't worry, I'll leave the door open."

I nodded and lay back down. *Get it together, Carlisle.* Then I closed my eyes once again and slept.

A few nights later, I dreamed of the evening I left the Compound.

It started out much like it had taken place in real life. I was walking through the physicists' hallway, observing what I had observed before. I entered my parents lab, but unlike last time, it wasn't empty. They were both there, sitting in their swivel chairs by a Bunsen burner as if they were waiting for me to walk into the room. Their normally warm, friendly faces were stern and unmoving.

"Mom?" I asked. "Dad?"

They continued to sit there and stare at me without speaking, without even blinking. I took a few tentative steps closer, my hands gripping the straps of my backpack a little tighter. Still no response. I inched closer again and my mother's eyes narrowed. Neither of them had ever looked at me so coldly before.

"What's wrong? Why aren't you talking to me?" my lips quavered. "Did I do something wrong?"

My father spoke, one word only. "You."

I was so confused by the malice uttered in that one syllable, so hurt by the look of disgust on his face.

"I don't understand," I said, my eyes blurring with tears.

"It's all your fault," my mom accused.

"What's all my fault?"

In sync, they both stood and began walking toward me. I had never been afraid of them in my life, but at that moment I was terrified and matched each of their steps toward me with one step of mine backwards.

"You broke the world," they said in unison.

"What are you talking about?" I cried.

"You broke the world and you must pay." Their voices were robotic, and on some level I knew it was just a dream and that these people weren't my actual parents speaking to me, but it felt so, so real at the same time that I couldn't reason in my sleep state.

"Mom, Dad, please," I begged as they finally backed me towards the window I had fled out of in real life.

Just then there was the sound of the helicopter outside the window, and I was thankful that Beckett was coming to save me. The window shattered and I climbed up on the ledge to put some distance in between myself and my parents. The helicopter, which was much larger than I remembered, hovered outside, and when I turned to look Beckett was there. But he wasn't alone. Eleanora Blake stood beside him, and they both had their arms crossed in front of them as they looked at me with that same cold, empty look my parents had.

"What's it going to be, Eloise?" Beckett asked.

"Are you going to break the world again?" Eleanora chided.

In my dream, I screamed in frustration. What were they talking about? Why was Beckett willingly standing beside a Council member from the Compound?

"Eloise isn't worth saving," I heard my parents say behind me.

I turned to look at them just in time to see them push me out of the window. As I began falling towards my death, I woke up with a choked scream aloud. Tears were streaming down my face, a real feeling of betrayal and confusion turning my stomach. What had it all meant? Had I done something truly awful that was unforgivable? It was unconceivable from what I knew, but could I have really had something to do with the demise of an entire nation?

I lay there and let myself cry. When there was nothing left, I realized how silent the house was. Headquarters was always buzzing with quiet activity, but after that dream it seemed eerily more silent than usual. I was plagued with the sudden fear that my dream had somehow been connected to real life, that I had somehow slept through a Compound attack. Beckett would have wanted me to shut and lock the doors if he knew this was my instinct, but I didn't have it in me to run away when people who were fighting for me, people I cared about, could be in trouble. If I was responsible for something terrible before like abandoning my people, I wasn't going to repeat the same mistake.

Hurriedly, I stuffed my feet into a pair of boots – sorely remembering my sprained ankle - while rubbing the sleep out of my eyes and tiptoed out of my hiding place. I peered down the hallway before exiting my room, and seeing no one, I was no more at ease. Slowly and silently, I crept past room after room, all which were abandoned. My ankle loosened and felt better with each step. I had never really had an injury before, so I concluded that I had made it seem worse than it actually was. When I got to the top of the staircase, I pressed my back against the wall and looked over the side. No signs of life in either direction.

But then I heard laughter coming from somewhere else in the house and the tension in my shoulders relaxed a little. This was followed by more chatter, so judging from the twilight outside, everyone must have gathered in the dining room for dinner. I let out a breath and limped down the stairs much less cautiously about the sound I was making. When I walked into the room, my thoughts were confirmed by seeing Beckett, Mad-Eye, and Rose's familiar faces, among others who I still didn't know names for.

"There she is!" Beckett called and gestured to the empty seat next to him. Then he got up hastily to assist me. "You're not supposed to be putting pressure on it."

Over the last few days, he had been catering to me so much so that it had become annoying. He hadn't allowed me to do very much, so I had spent a lot of time reading. Since everyone was busy with their jobs, I didn't even get to know anyone.

"Honestly, it's feeling much better," I said, trying not to sound unappreciative. "I think I probably exaggerated about it in the first place."

A few people called a friendly hello. Alistair smiled dubiously from his place at the table and it made me feel uncomfortable for a reason I couldn't really define. I sat and began to serve myself.

"Sorry I didn't wake you," said Beckett. "I figured you could use some rest so I didn't want to disturb you."

"It's okay," I answered, secretly wishing he had woken me earlier so that I could have avoided that horrible dream.

"You alright?" he asked, assumingly noticing that something was bothering me. Care and concern were plastered on his face.

"Oh, yeah, fine. Just a bad dream."

Beckett smiled one of his winning smiles. "Oh, good! A little food and company will make you forget. I was just telling

Jessica over there – she's one of our marksmen – that maybe we should take you out one day..."

I tried hard to concentrate on what Beckett was saying. I nodded and smiled and hopefully made the appropriate comments that made it look like I was paying attention, but all I could think about was my parents' cruel treatment of me.

It's all your fault... You broke the world... She's not worth saving.

All through dinner I chewed and smiled and tried to engage in conversation. I learned a few names of a few new people, but forgot them just as quickly, too distracted to commit them to memory. Dinner should have been a pleasant break from reality – not that I was really sure what my reality was anymore – but I couldn't break myself away from the thoughts that were spinning around in my mind. I felt emotionally drained yet motivated at the same time. I had waited my entire time in - captivity? I wasn't sure if I could even call it that- to figure out why the series of events had occurred in the first place, and I couldn't just throw in the towel now that I was finally getting some answers. I needed to hear the whole story, all of it, no matter how much it may upset or surprise me, and I needed to hear it sooner rather than later.

In fact, I didn't want to wait a single second longer. I had the urge to drag Beckett out of the room then and there and demand that he continue his story. And not the history part of it either. The part that involved me. Having been brought up with better manners than that, I gripped the sides of the chair with white-knuckled hands, literally anchoring myself so that I didn't pop up out of my chair. I was teeming with impatience, an energy coursing through my body like volts of electricity through a live wire. *The one night everyone has the time to sit around and chat!* I thought to myself.

While everyone else was engaged in conversation, I was trying to devise a way to get Beckett to leave the room. If I said I didn't feel well, he might just tell me to go rest in my hidden room by myself, and that wouldn't get me anywhere. If I didn't give him a reason, he'd probably say that whatever it was could wait, that I should get to know some of the people who were willing to risk their lives for me. I blew a piece of hair out of my eye in frustration and then quickly looked around to make sure I wasn't being too obviously bored. No one seemed to notice. All were thoroughly enjoying their time to rest before what I was sure would be a long night of vigilance.

At one point, Alistair got out of his chair and tried to talk to me.

"Hello, Eloise," he said greasily.

I didn't know if it was Beckett's influence since he disliked the guy so much, but Al was starting to give me the creeps. Maybe he just didn't have any experience with talking to girls, or maybe his personality was just naturally awkward. Or maybe he was just a total creep. I couldn't tell, but I didn't find him as charming and alluring as I had on that first night that we met. I felt like his eyes were always on me and Beckett when we were in the same room. When Beckett and I were alone in a room having a conversation, we had often run into Alistair as we exited. It was as if he was listening for something, spying on us. Beckett didn't say anything, but I know that he noticed. I wondered what he thought of the situation. Maybe I was being overly cautious and paranoid.

"How are you settling in?" Alistair continued, even after all I did was smile in response to his first address.

"I'm fine," I replied curtly.

"I hope that Beckett is showing you the ropes properly, you know, teaching you everything you need to learn," he said as he scratched his chin.

"Beckett's a great teacher," I said, trying to get Alistair to take a hint. *What was he getting at?* I looked at Beckett, sure that if he was listening to the conversation he would be ready to step in and save me. But for once he wasn't listening. He was in a deep conversation about perimeters and formations with Mad-Eye. I could only assume they were discussing security protocol. I reluctantly turned back towards Al.

"I don't know," he said. "Old Beckett can be a real uptight guy sometimes. I was thinking that if you wanted take a walk sometime or something, I could tell you lots of information about the Open, stuff that grumpy over there wouldn't."

Part of me lurched inside at the chance to know something that Beckett wouldn't willingly share, but I also had the instinct that something with Alistair just wasn't right. There was also my tentative loyalty to Beckett to consider. They obviously had some sort of history together, and I wasn't about to get in the middle of it. Plus, Al had become shifty. He was no longer the statuesque picture of romanticized manliness.

"No, Alistair, but thank you for offering," I said, ending the conversation.

"Okay, Eloise, but I really think you're going to regret your decision," Alistair replied mysteriously, and then he walked away. His last remark left me uneasy. *What was that supposed to mean?*

Rose had made brownies for dessert, apparently a rare delicacy at Headquarters, and I would have been annoyed with her for prolonging the meal if they weren't so good. Not much topped my gourmet, control panel service at home, but this time I was pleasantly surprised. In awe, really. The brownies were so fudgy that they tasted like brownie batter instead of ones that were cooked.

There was an option in our kitchen to select such a treat at home, and I indulged myself as often as it would let me, which was not very often. The Compound was strict about keeping its inhabitants healthy by limiting selections on the menu. For example, if you ate too much red meat, that option would disappear for a while until you began to widen your intake. The way it kept track of portions, calories, and nutrients was all quite fascinating, but it was also extremely annoying when you were in the mood for something it wouldn't let you have. It was another way the Compound had controlled us that hadn't seemed like a big deal at the time, but I was starting to see just how little choice I had about anything I did in my life.

I could've eaten the entire plate, and the only thing that stopped me was the fact that they were in demand. The brownies weren't there in surplus, so by the time everyone grabbed one there weren't any left. Feeling selfish wasn't something I was completely used to, but I was sorely disappointed that there weren't second helpings. And then I felt ashamed for wishing that I had more than everyone else. They probably already thought of me as a princess. I didn't need to contribute and make that image come to life.

After dessert, the conversation began to wind down and the others slowly started filtering out of the room. Beckett was still talking to Mad-Eye as Rose began to clear the table, so I figured I might as well help her. Trying not to appear too anxious – I didn't want Beckett to know my plan of action before I could even carry it out – I took my time stacking paper plates and collecting plastic silverware, commenting to Rose about how delicious her brownies were. By the time I had assumed my role of drying the dishes while she washed, Beckett was finished talking. I couldn't exactly ditch Rose in the middle of dishes (as much as I really did want to), so I finished what I had started, all the while tapping metaphorical fingers in my head.

"Boy am I tired today," Rose said through a yawn as she handed me the last plate, turned the water off, and leaned against the counter. "I think I'll go read a book until my eyes cross. Later."

As she walked away, I silently thanked whoever was listening for the rare gift of things going my way. One struggle down, one struggle to go: how to approach Beckett.

I took a deep breath as he bent down to tie his shoe.

Before he could stand up and make eye contact with me, I let out my plea in one astonishingly fast, rambled breath.

"Beckett, we really need to talk. I know you probably don't really want to talk about anything else today, but I can't get all of this off of my mind and I really just want to know and understand everything. If you'll just sit down and finish telling me everything there is that I need to know, I promise that I won't freak out on you or anything. Please?" I finished and caught my breath.

Beckett raised an eyebrow. "Okay."

Ready to fully protest his denial, I was taken aback by his simple response in my favor.

"Okay?" I asked.

"Yeah, okay. I know I haven't been as forthcoming about ...stuff as I could have been. And you really do need to know the whole of it in case... in case anything did happen. I want you to be able to hear me out before anyone else tries to sway you otherwise."

It was a bit vague, but he agreed to grant my wish so I decided against questioning him any further.

"Let's make some coffee," Beckett said. "This might take a while."

"I don't really drink coffee."

"No?" he asked, seeming surprised. "Hot chocolate then?"

"No, thank you. I'm all set for now. Maybe I'll just have water." I doubted that I'd remember to drink anything while it was still warm once he started talking. Might as well just start off with a cold drink.

I waited for Beckett to make himself a cup of hazelnut coffee (even though I didn't drink it, I would know that smell anywhere- it was my mom's favorite) and add milk and a little sugar. Then he led me off to the other side of the main floor, to which I hadn't previously had a reason to venture.

Two, large wooden double doors with the same intricate symbols carved on each stood in front of us. The fleur-di-lis I recognized right away. I knew from my lessons that it had traditionally been used in French royalty, and had become a symbol of status in general over time. I had to pause and think about the other two symbols, to search my brain for where I had seen them before, until I could place them. The second symbol was a lotus flower, a Buddhist symbol that championed rising above the mud and murk of life to reach enlightenment. And the third I happened to know just by chance. For a history class, I had chosen to do a project on the Druids. History – not "modern" history, like Beckett had carried on about but *ancient* history- had always fascinated me. The way that people were able to survive with such little knowledge of the world they lived in- it was awe-inspiring.

During my research, I had come across a Druid symbol called "Awen". It was a very simple symbol: a circle with three smaller circles inside at the top, and three lines originating from the smaller circles spreading out and thickening as they moved downward in the circle. That was it. But the symbol carried a very powerful meaning: the unity of the forces that be. Some interpreted it as the earth, the sea, and the air. Others believed it represented body, mind, and spirit. And still others understood the symbol to stand for love, wisdom, and truth. The general idea, no matter which theory you follow, is that one force cannot exist without the other two. In order to prosper, all three had to be present. And there it stood before me, a symbol I had learned and forgotten, returning to my life at such a crucial time.

The final detail that completed the prominent set of doors was the handles. The two met in the middle so that you almost couldn't even see the seam, and together they created the symbol for infinity. It was as if the door was a prophet delivering a message, that the symbols themselves would forever be applicable to life, that they would endure across time and space to guide humans through dark times.

This is one seriously deep door, I thought to myself. I began to wonder, again, who had owned the house. What intellectual mind had taken so much time to make a door be such a statement piece? I admired the choice and I relished meeting the divine being who made it. And then I began to wonder, what sort of room would call for such an entrance? Beckett grasped one half of the infinity symbol and pulled the door towards himself, allowing me to be the first one in the room of mystery.

My jaw dropped in appreciation as I laid my eyes upon the grandest library I could have ever imagined. The smaller library I had seen in Headquarters paled in comparison, though it had been admirable at first. The Compound had an extensive library, but it was cold and unwelcoming. *That* library made knowledge seem like nothing more than alphabetical organization of words on pages. At Headquarters, I felt like I could live in that one room for the rest of my life and never feel a need to leave. Books lined the walls, shelves stretching all the way up to the cathedral ceiling, covering every inch that weren't broken up by floor-to-ceiling windows. Crimson velvet curtains were tied back by golden tassels alongside each window. A couple of ladders led up to a catwalk that lined the perimeter of the room, making it easier to reach books that were higher up. On the catwalk there were still a couple more ladders secured to the shelves on tracks to move with ease to the second tier of books even further out of reach. Expensive, antique-looking armchairs and sofas were centralized by the fireplace or spread throughout gymnasium-sized room.

"Beckett!" I exclaimed. "*Why* haven't I been in this room before now?!"

He smirked at me and slipped his hands into his front pockets. "I knew I'd never get you to leave."

"You might be quite right about that," I murmured as I walked around, exploring further.

There were texts of all ages on the shelves. I could tell by the layers of dust or the lack thereof, the bindings that were more tattered than others. I wanted to run through the room, letting my hand glide over each spine and literally touch history. I could only assume from the look of some of the embossed scripts that there must be original copies of some books in the library. I found myself wishing I could be locked there at night instead. Of course, then I would never sleep again.

Beckett indulged my admiration while he got the fireplace started. It was a bit drafty as it was such a large room. *How had I not noticed it from the outside before?*

When he was done, though, he brought me back down to earth.

"El, did you forget the whole reason we came in here?" he asked.

"Yeah, kind of," I responded, still only partially interested in the fact that he was speaking at all.

"Well, if you aren't interested we can always do this another day," he said.

"No!" I said, suddenly snapping myself back to reality. If things worked out and the Compound didn't whisk me away again, I could spend as much time as I wanted in the library later. "I want to know. Now."

Beckett held out his hand, gesturing for me to sit down in one of the armchairs nearest the fireplace. He took the other, opposite me. Feeling chilly, I wrapped myself in the blanket slung across the back of my chair, though I was sure it was actually meant for decoration.

I pulled my knees up to my chest and said, "So, where do we begin?"

"That is a good question. Actually, before I tell you anything else, raise your right arm please," Beckett directed. I furrowed my brows and he nodded at me. "Just go on."

I raised my hand above my head, as if I were answering a question in school. Beckett laughed. "Not like that." He modeled what he wanted from me: an arm half-raised, held out on the side of my body like a pledge.

"You've got to be kidding me," I said.

"Oh, Eloise, I am not in the least bit joking. If I am going to fill you in, there have to be some rules. Well, not rules. Guidelines. You aren't the easiest person to explain things to."

I rolled my eyes, but I followed his directions and repeated every word he said.

"I solemnly swear that I will not freak out, run out of the room, swear at my friend, get angry, yell, or scream, no matter what I learn here today. Is that all....*sir*?" I asked sarcastically.

"Oh, and don't interrupt me while I'm trying to explain. I know you'll have questions, and I'll stop and let you ask them, but don't start jumping down my throat mid-sentence. Give me a chance, okay?"

"*Now* is that all?"

Beckett looked out of the window, as if he were counting to ten or something before answering me. Then he looked back at me and said, "Yeah, El. That's all," as if he were trying extremely hard to be patient. I made a mental note to try to not be my usual, pushy self.

"I'm listening, I promise," I said, trying to let Beckett know that I was on my best behavior.

He nodded and began.

"I sort of jumped the gun a while back, you know, when I mentioned something about time travel. And I apologize for that," he said.

I snorted. "It's okay. I knew you couldn't be for real."

Beckett sort of winced then. "I didn't say I was making things up. I just shouldn't have said it the way I said it."

I tried to make my face emotionless, but all the while I was thinking to myself that I wasn't the only person who was crazy.

"Okay," I managed with a straight face.

"So, you'll obviously remember everything that I told you about the history of the United States," Beckett said, and I nodded. "Well, as things consistently worsened and life became more and more bloody, a faction of the national government decided that something had to be done about it. That faction was broken up into different sub-groups who were searching for answers, and one of the sub-groups was a team of physicists. Those physicists were researching time travel as a means of fixing the mistakes that were repeatedly made throughout history. They thought that if they could figure out a way to go back, they would be able to sort of undo all of the death and destruction that humankind had caused. You know the saying, 'Hindsight is twenty-twenty'? The physicists thought that if they were able to analyze what had gone wrong, lives would be saved and the earth as a whole would be better off. Are you with me so far?"

"The government wanted to figure out ways to improve life, or I should say, to fix the many problems in the nation. So they developed teams to come up with different solutions, one of which was a team of physicists who were studying time travel," I recapped.

"Right. I'm going to give you the short version of it, since I still don't really understand how it all works. So if there are gaps in what I'm saying or something doesn't really make sense, by all means ask me anything you want. The area of physics that studies time travel is called quantum physics, which you may have learned the very basics of in your study of science at the Compound. That part is knowledge available to everyone, but not everyone has access to what I'm going to share with you today. Have you ever heard of Albert Einstein?"

"Is there anyone who *doesn't* know who Albert Einstein is?" I asked, probably a little cheekier than necessary. I made a mental note – again – to watch the way I responded.

"Well, there was a time when his name was known in every household, but I wasn't sure that he was still popular in the Compound considering..." Beckett trailed off.

"Considering what?"

"Well, considering what we're about to get into. Einstein, as you know, is remembered as the Father of Modern Physics. Except what you've learned in school is just that he is credited with many theories; they don't teach you what he actually discovered. In his early days, he wrote that he was disturbed that the equations he had developed allowed for time travel. That is also common knowledge. But after he wrote that, he poured over those equations, El, and he made them a reality. He just didn't know it while he was alive, but his work was used to make it real. That's what they don't tell you in school."

I was silent for a moment, and then I said skeptically, "People can time travel."

Beckett threw his arms in the air and shrugged. "People can time travel, El."

"How is that even possible?" I asked.

Surprisingly, while I still thought there was a real possibility that Beckett was a part of a group of psychopaths who had kidnapped me to fulfill their delusion, I was more inclined to believe what he was saying. Sure, I had seen and read plenty of science fiction that imagined such a reality, but I had never given a whole lot of thought to it actually *being* a reality. Then again, I had never completely dismissed it either.

"This is where it gets difficult for me to explain because I'm truthfully not an expert on the subject," Beckett admitted.

In my head, I made some snarky, sarcastic comment about how uncanny it was, then, that he was entrusted to explain it to me considering he didn't know what he was talking about. But I practiced self control – it didn't come naturally to me – and patiently waited for him to continue.

"Initially, the group of physicists determined that in order to time travel, there would have to ultimately be some sort of time 'machine' that would transport you to another era. In order for this to happen, they would need what they referred to as 'fabulous amounts of energy' to run on, energy from a start, or a source of negative energy. Eventually they verified the latter and called it the Casimir effect: energy created by two parallel plates. What this means is that there would have to be two uncharged metallic plates in a vacuum. Not the kind you use to clean, but the kind that means there's a space that has no matter. And these two plates had to be placed two nanometers apart. If this happened, they would no longer have to obey the traditional boundary conditions of space and time. Does that make any sense?"

"I guess," I said, wishing my parents were around to explain instead. They would've known exactly what Beckett was talking about *and* been able to put it in simpler terms. "I mean, not really, but I'm not a physicist. I'm following you well enough, though."

"Sorry, I'm sort of just repeating what I learned myself. I never have really gotten a grasp on the scientific explanation of how it all works. Anyway, when the conditions were right for the time travel to occur, black holes or 'worm holes' would be created, and once they were stable, they would allow people the ability to travel at the speed of light either backwards or forwards in time. These holes were like shortcuts through space and time, allowing the traveler to stay youthful, virtually unchanged, throughout the experience," he paused. "What do you think?"

"I think I'd like to find a book in this library and study the topic myself so that I could better understand what you said, but generally speaking I don't think you sound like a lunatic," I said frankly.

"Good enough for me," Beckett smiled. "Moving on, that's the theory that the team of physicists brought to the table when all of the teams convened to present their solutions. They suggested, that instead of attempting to rectify the present, we should just go back and fix the problems before they could occur, which would also solve the present-day chaos. Some of the other teams laughed in their faces, others were interested in hearing more. There were those who argued that it wouldn't work, because if it had, we would have already had visitors from the future. The physicists countered with the fact that if they were about to go through with altering the course of history, when you arrived in the past you wouldn't really benefit from announcing yourself to be someone from the future. If it was to all go smoothly, it would have to be a top-secret initiative limited to the people that were currently in the room. Sharing the knowledge with the masses would undoubtedly create even more problems."

"That makes sense. I can imagine lots of angry folks wanting someone to go back in time to avenge misdoings or to abuse the privilege," I wagered. "So, I assume that the physicists won the bid to fix the world's problems since we're now having this conversation."

"You would assume correctly. However, it wasn't solely because the team of scientists had the very best solution. It was the cheapest answer. Since the physicists were already being paid well, it wouldn't cost the federal government any more money for them to go back in time. Manipulating energy might require some laboratory resources, but nothing more. And if the plan backfired, the worst that could happen was that they would try one of the other solutions. At the end of the conference, the physicists were motivated by their victory, and surged forward with preparations. What points in time would they want to return to? Could they pinpoint a precise time to travel to, or would they only have a vague number of years to aim for? And *who* would be doing the travelling? What were the possible repercussions of altering history?

These were all questions that they attempted to answer – usually unsuccessfully, I might add – but not enough so to cause the slowing-down of progress. Lost in excitement, the team of physicists didn't spend any real time trying to consider the ramifications. And the government, eager to tame the masses, didn't really question *anything* they were doing."

"I'm not a psychic, clearly, but I feel like this lack of preparation you're talking about is leading to a not-so-good outcome," I said.

"Well, you'll have to decide that for yourself when we're done, Eloise," Beckett said mystically. "Anyway, the team may have not developed any *real* answers to their questions, but there were *some* answers based on the knowledge that they had at the time. There is a success story as far as exacting the point in time that was to be traveled to: they were able to narrow their destination to an exact month and year after a series of trials and errors. However, when they began sending themselves back in trial travels, they discovered that some returned to the present intact, while others got their brains scrambled. Excuse my being cavalier, but it's true. There were people who were able to travel seemingly unaffected, and others were never the same upon their return.

So, our physicists decided that there had to be a reason for this. Time travel trial runs were halted briefly, and they invested in help from biologists who were beginning to study genes. It was thought that there had to be something genetically different about those who were able to successfully travel and those who weren't, and they were right. After examining the genetic material from the travelers and comparing it, the geneticists discovered that there was a gene on a certain chromosome that the survivors had that the frazzled didn't. When they discovered this, they began testing candidates' DNA before allowing them to travel. If you didn't have the right genetic material, you couldn't go. At least they had *some* morality in all of this," he speculated.

I was enthralled by what Beckett was saying. With how much I loved history, my body was almost humming with excitement, thinking that maybe *I* could travel.

"Does this mean that I can go back in time, Beckett? Can I visit the Egyptian pyramids as they're being built? Can I dine with kings and queens of the fifteenth century? Would I be able to see the United States as it was?" I was swooning at the thought.

"Whoa, hold your horses, sister," Beckett said, using his hands as stop signs. "I'm not finished yet. Like I said, the tests determined who was allowed to go and who wasn't. Those who tested positive for being candidates then went on trial runs to the past. This was also successful for a while, and the physicists felt that they could finally move forward with their solution, but-"

"But something went wrong!" I interrupted, on the edge of my seat. "Whoops, sorry."

"It's okay," Beckett said patiently. He must have been impressed that I was being as cooperative as I was. "As I was saying...but then something started to change. Little by little, travelers started to return not as whole as they used to. People started having difficulty breathing upon returning. They were experiencing heart palpitations and memory loss. The more that a single traveler continued to go back in time, the more fractured his or her psyche became, until finally his or her mind was as shattered as the original candidates who had failed. And it wasn't pretty, El. We're talking completely mentally unstable, dangerously so, or in some cases people became empty slates. Drooling and carrying on without any awareness or inkling of the life they had left behind. Scary stuff.

So once again, the team was back to the drawing board. What had gone wrong? Why were people suddenly frail after traveling? They began to chart data, and they kept statistics on what years people were traveling to, how many times they had traveled, what experiences the travelers had while in the past. The only commonality that they found was the frequency. It seemed that even if someone was initially genetically 'correct' for traveling, that gene did not sustain them if they continued to travel. Some people only lasted three travels, while others could make it to ten. There was no way of telling when it would happen, no exact number to indicate mental instability. It was a crap shoot."

"Strange. Did they end up figuring it out? Determining another gene or finding a smaller pool of people who were even more qualified?" I asked.

Beckett shook his head. "The government began to get impatient as the nation continued crumbling, so they went ahead with their time travel trials. They developed a vocabulary to discuss time travelers. Those who could travel time, the ones who were verified by their DNA, were called Stringers, after the initial name of time travel, 'String Theory'. Stringers would continue to go on these missions backwards in time, sometimes just traveling in general, other times slightly altering one person's life to study the effects in the future. That was how they determined it was safe to make changes, by the way. Just by returning someone's lost wallet or preventing a car accident from happening. Stringers studied a lineage beforehand, altered the life, and then studied the changes in the future of that family once returning to the present. It was quite the process, a lot of paperwork and documentation. I might mislead you to think that everything was done on a whim over a month's time, but that wasn't the case. There was a lot of time and effort put into this project.

But I digress. So there were Stringers, active travelers. And the poor souls who lost their minds or went insane from the traveling were known as 'Strung'. The Strung were out-casted. The government couldn't admit to having anything to do with a person suddenly going crazy, so they cast them out into the world and people assumed the Strung just had mid-life crises. These people had given up their entire lives- their families even- for their work, and then they were just tossed aside like old rags," Beckett said with a look of disgust.

"It sounds rough, but that was the choice those people made. Surely they would have known that getting involved with something like time travel was risky," I reasoned. Instantly I knew that was the wrong thing to say, as Beckett's eyes flared with anger.

"So soldiers chose to fight to protect the freedoms of countries. When they got wounded, should we have just left them to die?" he retorted.

"No, I understand where you're coming from," I said, just to keep the peace. "What happened next?"

Beckett accepted my white flag and his eyes cleared again.

"Geneticists continued to research the genes of the team, of all the Stringers and possible future Stringers, trying to divulge the secret to traveling without being affected. The head physicist, the one who lead the team and ultimately made all of the big decisions, hadn't traveled as of yet. She was busy organizing and planning and directing, so there had been no need to test her genes. Don't ask me why no one had though to do so before, but finally curiosity got the best of her. There was one geneticist who she had become close to, fond of even, and she secretly began working with him to study herself. When the geneticist examined her genes, he discovered that she was quite different than the others. She had a sort of super-gene that was superior. So the geneticist and the head physicist spent countless hours together, long after the regular work-day ended, to decipher what it all meant. Then, they finally sent her on secret time travels when no one else was around. Each time, they would take a new sample and analyze the gene to see if it had at all mutated from the traveling. It hadn't. They had found someone – the head physicist – who would be able to move through time without consequence."

"That seems an odd coincidence," I said skeptically.

"It sure was. Pure luck, but the physicist thought it was fate, that her destiny was to be a part of this great mission to change the course of history," Beckett replied.

"She sounds pretty uppity. A little self-righteous, if you ask me. Who was she?" I asked.

"Well, Eloise," Beckett hesitated and scratched his head. Then he looked me square in the eye and said, "It was you."

Keeping my promise, I didn't freak out. I think that part of me knew it was coming, that I would have something to do with the beginning of it all. Ever since Beckett had blown up at me in the woods... since I had the weird dream... I knew I had to play some significant role in *something*. I just didn't know what that something was. I was still a little fuzzy, at that point, about my actual role in the events that followed. So far, Beckett had said that I had kept it all a secret, so why would I go off and ruin it by sharing? It didn't make sense.

He had been patiently waiting, probably bracing himself for my reaction, but Beckett finally broke the silence. I wondered what my facial expression looked like. I felt actually rather emotionless for having had that bomb dropped on me, and usually my face betrayed every single emotion that I had. In that case, I must have looked comatose.

"El," Beckett said quietly and gently. "What are you thinking?"

I burst into a fit of uncontrollable laughter. It was the fact that the whole idea of time travel – and that I had been a part of it – was so ridiculous to even imagine, never mind live, combined with the priceless look on Beckett's face, like he was entering a lion's cage with a piece of meat. He smiled and giggled nervously with me, clearly unsure if I was just taking it well or if I had finally lost it.

"It's just... I mean this as all...so...so," I tried to express myself in between laughs. "So...you know?"

Still smiling cautiously, he said, "Believe me, I do."

He let me continue on with my ludicrous, manic laughter until I finally caught my breath and calmed down. As insane as I must have looked, sitting there in the middle of a classic, dignified library, laughing my head off inappropriately, it felt so *good*. It was euphoric to have that release after having been so angry, then so lost and confused. There was a small part of me that was trying to be practical, a voice in my head saying that this was all becoming believable just because it appealed to some weird desire to *be* somebody other than Eloise from the Compound. At the same time, it all kind of made sense. I had always had a family who loved me and I had been socially accepted by my peers, but I also always felt somehow out of place, like I didn't belong. This was why.

"I'm sure you must have some questions," Beckett said, business-face returned.

"That's an understatement," I giggled again, and covered my mouth the stop up any more fits of laughter.

"You're taking this a little differently than I had imagined, and it's actually making me *more* nervous than you yelling and storming off."

"I'm sorry, it's just a lot at once, you know?"

"Don't be sorry," Beckett said. "It's good to see you laugh again."

There was an awkward pause, and suddenly I didn't feel so giddy anymore. Beckett was looking at me in that weird way that somehow made me uncomfortable and curious at the same time. I diverted the conversation back to where we had left off.

"So what you were saying was that I was a power-hungry, bossy woman who put myself on a pedestal?"

"I didn't use those words."

"No, but I am. And I don't like myself very much right now."

My words caught my funny bone, and again I had to stifle a laugh. I clapped my hand over my mouth and held up a hand in apology.

"Don't be so hard on yourself," Beckett said. "You had every right to be proud and to be in the position you were in. El, you had a higher security clearance than almost anyone in the government. You were the mastermind behind the entire time travel project, *and* you actually got it to work. Then you figured out that you were the only one who could travel without consequence. That's a pretty lofty finding. And you actually exposed yourself as a good deed. You didn't want any more Stringers to be harmed, so you called off all further travel except for yourself."

"Alright, well that sounds slightly less obnoxious," I said with relief. I didn't want to be a total jerk in my past life. Then it dawned on me. "So, who are you really? How do you come into play in all this?"

Beckett smiled widely and his eyes twinkled. He was clearly proud of himself for something. "Who do you think your geneticist sidekick was?"

I considered this. If he had followed me through time and space to be together again, there had to be a reason besides the fact that we were coworkers. "Beckett, were we....?"

"Together?" he asked. And then he blushed before continuing, actually looking bashful. "We were, very much so. But you don't have to worry about that part right now."

He looked away from me, as if too embarrassed by the turn in conversation to meet my eye. I studied him for a moment.

"You're...different. Dynamic," I concluded after my observation.

"How do you mean?" he asked.

"There are so many sides to you that I don't even know who you really are. When we first met you were this dangerously cool stranger busting through my window, hanging from a helicopter multiple stories off of the ground. Then you were trying to be my friend. As if a switch flipped, you could treat me like a prisoner or like I was just your job, you know- like it was strictly business. Then sometimes you look at me strangely or kiss me. And I couldn't see it before, but now you seem much more the scientist than dangerously cool. What gives?"

"We've been through a lot, El. And I have a lot of memories that you don't have anymore, which is sad really. But we've lived apart for the past sixteen years and my life in the Open was a lot different than yours in the Compound. I've learned to be adaptable, depending on the situation I'm facing. Sometimes I feel the age my body is, but sometimes I feel like a geneticist with more life experience. My brain can revert to that teenage state and back again. Time travel is strange like that. We're just not the same people we used to be."

"No, I guess we're not," I agreed. "But something tells me that in some ways maybe we still are."

There was another awkward pause. I felt a little guilty, sitting there with someone who I still considered a stranger, but who I had actually been in love with at some point in time and couldn't remember. Beckett had to have been overflowing with emotions during the past couple of weeks we had spent together, and he couldn't even say anything to me about them. I realized then that I had behaved so impolitely, so aggressively at times, that it was a wonder he hadn't given up and shipped me back to the Compound, a lost cause.

"Do your genes test the way that mine did? Is that why you're able to travel through time?" I asked before things got any more awkward.

Beckett looked like he was glad to be changing the conversation, but his face changed quickly and I couldn't quite read why.

"Ah, no, I didn't have genes like yours," he said. I was inclined to interrupt and ask why, but I resisted the urge and patiently waited for him to explain. "I'm not innocent in all of this, Eloise. So don't think that you were alone in the decisions that you made. Once we discovered your own ability, and things got... serious between us, I began to do more research...research about how I could replicate your DNA."

I looked at him quizzically.

"You were the brainiac physicist, but I was your equivalent in the field of genetics. I used what I learned from your body to give myself gene therapy so that I, too, would be able to travel through time unmarred. We never told anyone, which was selfish and irresponsible, Eloise, and I want you to know that I have always regretted it. Driven by our genius and our desire to travel together, we didn't allow anyone else to gain our ability. They all just assumed that I had been naturally inclined like you, and we rode the wave of power together."

"It's funny," I said, thinking aloud.

"What's funny?" Beckett asked.

"If I had stayed in the Compound, with my physicist parents, I was slated to follow the same career path. And I had absolutely no desire to do so. Weird, isn't it? That I wouldn't have the natural desire to be who I was before?"

"It's not all that strange to me, but I already know the rest of the story," he responded.

I should have asked for the ending, right then and there, but my mind had already jumped backwards. "You know, speaking of physicists. My 'parents'...who are they?"

Beckett laughed. "I'm sure you've guessed as much, but they're not actually your birth parents. They passed before you had found a way to time travel. Barnum and Mildred Carlisle were friends of ours, good people."

I nodded, then blinked and shook my head. This was all too strange, my parents not being my parents. The two people who I had lived with for the past sixteen years had no relation to me. What a revelation.

"So, how did I end up...here, in the future-present? As a teenager again? And how does that work? Does it mean that we live forever?" I tried to picture a life where I would constantly be able to revert myself to any age I wanted. I could live to old age and start over from scratch any time. But, would I want to? Did I have a choice?

"We have to take a step backwards in time again – not literally – to answer that series of questions," Beckett responded and leaned forward, his elbows resting on his knees. "Once we had both been secured to travel, we began to conduct trials with ourselves again. We studied the patterns of these seemingly small, insignificant changes and determined that we were successful, that we had improved the future of the folks we messed with. And then we came up with a brilliant idea. What if we were able to change a major event in history? We decided to start with the Holocaust."

"Well, clearly we were unsuccessful with that, since it's still in my history book," I said.

Beckett shook his head sadly. "What you've read about is the result of our actions. We returned to the Holocaust twice, Eloise, and tried to fix our mistake. Originally, Hitler had managed to carry out his plan, but to a lesser effect. Before we changed anything, about one million people had died. You and I, we saw that as an opportunity to save a million lives. So we went back and we tried to assassinate Hitler. I know, it sounds crazy, but we were young and on a power-trip, and we believed, I mean really believed, that we were doing something for the good of all of mankind.

But when we returned from the past, we ended up in a present where we had successfully eliminated Hitler, but we didn't make things better. Instead, Hitler's successor had been far more deadly, and all of Europe was under Heinrich Himmler's thumb. Devastated by how much worse suffering Europeans had experienced, we went back yet again to try and correct our mistake. The result is what you will find in your textbook: the deaths of six million people. As you can see, our glorification of our roles in the universe caused five million more people to die than originally had died. It was our first dance with a major historical event, and we told ourselves that maybe it was meant to happen. That possibly we were solving the problem of over-population of the world that could happen someday. We did everything but admit that we had done no good by our work."

This new information was horrific. With my extensive knowledge of history, I knew the terror written about the concentration camps, and I felt nauseous at the thought that I was as bad as Hitler, equally as responsible. Part of my original self must have been subconsciously present, because I still didn't want to admit or to feel accountable for any of it.

"Maybe we did solve the problem of overpopulation," I offered weakly.

"I hope you don't really believe that, Eloise," Beckett replied solemnly.

"Well, you never know," I insisted, and I didn't know why I was pushing back so much. I didn't even believe the words that were coming out of my mouth.

Beckett did that thing again where he looked like he was counting to ten. I knew I had to get us back on track or we would be heading down a path that resulted in arguing.

"What happened after that...failure?" I asked, choosing my words carefully.

"Everything that happens in history, Eloise, has a direct effect on the future. We tried to tell ourselves that that wasn't true at first, but the Holocaust debacle proved otherwise. Our government – our bosses, really – were furious. Before we traveled, we had written everything down in a secret file. We knew that anything was possible, and that we could affect the government itself, which we had. There weren't the same members to deal with when we returned, but they had the file to fill them in and the select few that understood what we had done were demanding answers. The country was in worse turmoil as a result of our tampering, and they grew impatient.

We were temporarily barred from traveling anymore, and the government insisted that we send other Stringers to conduct specifically chosen missions – by the government – in our place. They didn't care what the risk was anymore because they were so desperate to inspire some sort of positive change. Since we had our tails between our legs, and it wasn't really up to us, we had no choice but to listen. We became overseers."

"And how did that go, sending regular Stringers into the past?" I asked.

"Not well," Beckett said bitterly. "The results ranged from pathetic to catastrophic. At first, only a handful of Stringers were sent back at a time. We tried to explain that there was no telling what these people would do if they made parallel changes, but no one wanted to listen to us anymore. Of course, nothing good came of the Stringers' journeys, but instead of learning from their mistakes, the government sent more and more willing Stringers back. And what had started as a secret mission was losing its prior invisibility. If you take a look at your history textbook, you'll find a series of Stringer errors. Sometimes it was the actual Stringer that went missing, but sometimes the altering caused civilians of the actual time period to just disappear. I'll give you just a few examples.

Amelia Earhart, first woman to fly solo across the Atlantic Ocean. She—"

I interrupted. "She was a Stringer?!"

"No," Beckett said pointedly, giving me a look. He could be so edgy sometimes. "She was not. Her plane didn't go down in the ocean though, either. Amelia just had some bad luck was all; flew in the wrong place at the wrong time. While she was en route, a Stringer had opened a black hole and she happened to disappear into it.

Sean Flynn, a photojournalist for TIME Magazine. He disappeared while on assignment in Cambodia, remains never found. The public assumed he was killed by a rogue criminal there and disposed of. Harold Holt, an Australian prime minister. He went swimming in the ocean and was never seen again. They assumed he drowned. Dorothy Arnold, a wealthy socialite, disappeared on a shopping trip and never made it home. They assumed she was kidnapped and murdered. Assumed, assumed, assumed. Civilians can find probable cause for just about anything, but the truth was that they too were casualties of our genius.

Those are just a few examples of individuals. We affected entire locations on the earth. Think Bermuda Triangle. Coincidence that there is so much history about strange disappearances? Not really. There are certain coordinates, certain points, where Stringers enter from a black hole before softly appearing on ground level. There's also the Bennington Triangle in Vermont where 'various unexplained disappearances' occurred over three decades. Stonehenge in England. And that's just to name a few. All chalked up to inexplicable, coincidental happenings...all *actually* because of us."

I didn't like the heaviness that I felt throughout my entire body. How could it be that just a couple of weeks ago all I had to worry about was getting to class on time? I kept on looking at Beckett, half hoping he would fill the void with his voice, half hoping that he wouldn't have anything else awful to say. But he just waited. Waited for me to process all of the information. Now that I look back, I think he was hoping that I would be horrified by myself, ashamed of our actions and their consequences.

Due to sheer stubbornness perhaps, to denial, or due to the fact that I ultimately felt so far removed from all of it, I couldn't tell him what he wanted to hear. I couldn't apologize for things that I didn't even remember doing.

"Then what happened?" was all I could manage.

"The time travel project was out of our control," Beckett continued, "and we knew that the United States was getting worse and worse with each travel by an inexperienced Stringer. Not to mention that the streets of the cities were now full of ex-Stringers, out of their wits and left to wander aimlessly. People just thought they were homeless, insane. The general public just considered the increase an effect of the decline of society as a whole. It only made matters worse.

Knowing that we couldn't just keep standing by watching the nation unravel from the fruit of our efforts, we organized a presentation to the government. After our fall from grace, our demotion, we had to regain their trust and try to right some of the wrongs we had caused. Our timing was impeccable, as the President and Congress no longer knew what to do with the unrest they were supposed to be managing, so they allowed us to travel again.

After conducting some research about the other Stringers' travels – the information that we actually had, anyway, since most were never sane enough to record their experiences- we went back, together, and much more cautiously than before tried to repair what we had broken. We actually had some small successes, but ultimately there was nothing that we could really do that would be enough to save our country. So when we realized this, you developed a different plan, a plan that assumed the ultimate demise.

After drawing up lengthy plans and creating a proposal, you approached the government with the blueprint for the Compound. You admitted defeat and suggested an alternative: a way to save the best of the best, to create a place where an orderly way of life could be resumed. It was adopted, funded, and as you know, built. What I told you before about the selection process was all true, all accurate. And by the time it was built and occupied, the general population was in a fierce civil war. That's what I meant when I said you abandoned them to die. I just failed to mention that I, too, had been a part of it."

I was a little annoyed that Beckett had tried to initially pit the whole thing on me when we had been partners, and on top of that, I was perplexed about how I was sitting there as a sixteen year old if I moved to the Compound in the past as an adult.

"I'm following you, but how am I sitting here now?" I asked.

Beckett sighed and looked wistful as he sifted through his memories.

"After all was said and done, when the Compound was built and it was time to move in, you were no longer proud of what you had accomplished. You were emotionally drained and full of guilt for what you had made possible. You were afraid that if you lived in the Compound as the adult physicist, the government might decide to again employ your talent for traveling, and that you might again cause turmoil in the world. So you decided that you wouldn't go to the Compound after all, at least not as an adult.

We hatched a plan together, and enlisted the help of a few of our dearest and most trustworthy friends. Neither of us wanted to be protected by the walls of the Compound after what we had done, but you didn't even want to be *you* anymore. So Mildred and Barnum agreed to help us. They would go on to the Compound as they were asked to do, but you and I would remain on the outside for the time being. The government would assume that we had either disappeared into the past or into the present. Fortunately, Mildred and Barnum were a couple of the lucky

Stringers who had virtually been unaffected by traveling, though they didn't go often. So when a certain amount of time had passed, they would travel to the past –they had barely aged in the time that had gone by, traveling can be weird like that- collect the baby version of yourself, and bring you forward to the present as an infant. Just in case things went wrong, I would remain in the United States with the old version of you. We promised that we would meet up again in the future if it all worked out."

"Wait, wait, wait," I shook my head. "This doesn't make sense. If the baby version of myself had been brought to the future, my original life and all of the things that I had done should have never happened, right?"

Beckett smiled at me sadly. "That's what you were counting on, but toying with time is unpredictable."

"But it didn't work that way," I murmured. He shook his head. "So, if I went back to the past again, would I meet myself?"

"Wouldn't that be a sight," Beckett smirked. "I don't know how well two versions of you would get along, but you don't ever have to worry about that. As soon as your baby self made it to the future, the you in the past disappeared. That's how I knew it had worked."

"And what about you? How are you here as a teenager again?" I asked.

Beckett blushed again. "I sort of had to play around with traveling a lot. Once I found grown-up you on the spectrum of time, I wanted to be relatively the same age again."

A sudden understanding dawned on me, and that bad temper that I possessed began to flare up inside me. "Are you telling me that you found me and plucked me from the Compound and told me all of this just so that we could be together again? To fulfill a selfish wish, when all I wanted to do was forget?"

"No, Eloise!" Beckett said, looking pained. "I loved you. I love you. I would never do that to you again."

I was taken aback by the l-word and tried to pretend that I hadn't heard it.

"So then why am I here?!" I exclaimed, exasperated.

"You have to understand that the government who we had worked for – the ones who had first moved into the Compound – they've already died. So we didn't have to worry about anyone recognizing you when you grew. But the Council that you know is made up of the same type of people that we worked for so many years ago. And having lived in a perfect little, enclosed world, they were itching to toy with time travel. Mildred and Barnum got wind of this and began to worry for you. If they did genetic testing again, they would find that you were the Harp and they would use you to travel. They didn't want you to have to go through that again, so they got word to me. Oh, I forgot to mention the fact that I made contact with them when I arrived in the Open, so they knew I was here."

"People really don't learn from their mistakes," I muttered to myself. "Wait a minute, what did you call me?" I said, now addressing Beckett.

He smiled at me in a way that made my stomach flutter strangely. "The Harp. It was the name I came up with for you after we discovered your ability. Stringers were your average time travelers. You were something much, much more than that. Your strings could be played, so to speak, to create beautiful music, rather than just to be plucked one at the time. It's just a stupid metaphor."

Beckett became self-conscious as he reminisced; I must not have looked very amused.

"It's not stupid. The Harp, I like it," I said, feeling the need to lift him back up. "It's actually quite beautiful. Just probably not a word with a connation that I deserve."

"Aw, you do though, El," Beckett said with love clearly in his eyes. "You never could have known what would happen. You wanted to use your ability to do the world some good."

I shifted uncomfortably in my seat, and not just because I had been sitting there a long time. I didn't want to hurt his feelings, but I didn't share his level of affection. I wasn't sure if I ever could, after all that had happened. I wasn't Old Eloise. Beckett didn't come into my life under the same circumstances as the first time, and I felt that too much had passed for things between us to ever be as they once were.

"Thanks," I said. "So you really did kidnap me for my own good?"

I wasn't trying to act like I had taken the whole conversation lightly, but I *did* feel the need to lighten the mood a bit.

Beckett nodded and smirked, though not whole-heartedly.

"Don't take this the wrong way, but you never answered my question about living forever," I risked pointing out.

"Right, sorry, I forgot," Beckett replied evenly. "Truthfully I don't really know the answer to that. As far as we know, you're genetically built to travel through time as much as you like, but we don't really know if that luck will ever run out."

I nodded. I didn't know if I'd want to keep reliving anyway. The more time I spent on the earth, the more heartache and pain it seemed I was likely to cause.

"Where did you get all of this help from? The Alliance, why are they so willing to risk their lives to protect me?" I asked.

"It was simple really. Once I established myself in this community and learned about it, I figured out who I could trust. I became a regular member and began to study people; their strengths, their weaknesses, their usefulness. When I figured out who would be the best fit for the cause, I exposed the Compound, which no one here in the present even knew existed before, by the way. And I explained everything to them: about you, about the history, the time traveling, the Council. As crazy as it sounds, they all bought into it. I don't know if that should've made me trust them less, but we've established a family now that I trust my life with. Oh, I almost forgot. There was one person I didn't have to explain it to, because that person traveled with me. Venture a guess?"

Beckett was smiling at me like a mischievous child, baiting me with the secret. He didn't tell me who it was; instead, he waited for me to figure it out. Who could have known me in my past life?

I gasped when the light-bulb went off in my head. "Mad-Eye! That's why he seemed so familiar!"

Beckett laughed and nodded.

"But is he like us? He can travel through time unaffected? And wait, who is he actually?" I asked excitedly.

"No, Mad-Eye is just a regular old Stringer. That's how he became blind in one eye by the way, time travel accident. Arrived in the wrong place, at the wrong time in the past. But he was just a close friend, like an uncle to you. That's why he is so vigilant. He cares a lot about you. In fact, he'll be thrilled that you know who he is again, though he'll never show it, tough old bird."

"What about Rose?" I asked, curious now about her identity.

"Rose is *not* actually my sister," Beckett admitted. "I met her here, in the Open, and she became like my kid sister."

I nodded again in understanding. There were so many pieces to this confusing jigsaw puzzle.

"What was it like, getting to know a different me?" I asked Beckett quietly, curious too about how he could handle all this so well himself. I wondered who he liked better, the old me or the new me. I wasn't really sure I wanted to know the answer.

"Strange, man!" Beckett laughed and shook his head. "I mean, your face is the same. Younger, sure, but the same. But it was so weird that you didn't know what anything was, what anything was called. I was beginning to think that reacquainting myself with you was going to be much harder than I originally planned. But as much as you were oblivious to begin with, it was like some part of you had remained intact that allowed you to remember little things. Think about how quickly you didn't have to ask me a million questions. You went from not knowing what a toaster was, to navigating the Open without a problem."

It was true, when I thought about it. I had gotten familiar with all of the sights and "new" experiences with ease. I supposed that, though I had forgotten much of my former life, there must have somehow been some form of memory tucked away in my brain from my former self.

"Oh my God!" I shouted suddenly, my brain switching topics faster than I could flip a switch.

Beckett jumped and half-stood up, startled. "What?!"

"That delusion I had in that old factory, and all of the seeing things that aren't there...did that have anything to do with the time traveling? Or am I still just crazy?" I asked, looking at him sideways.

"Jesus, El, are you trying to give a guy a heart attack?" he said and sat back down. "But yeah, actually, it does. It's a side effect of time travel. If you aren't careful to shut it out, you can have visions of what once was wherever you are. It happens to me too, but the difference is that I know why it happens. I couldn't exactly tell you before explaining all of this."

"Ha! I'm not crazy," I said, feeling victorious.

"Well, that's debatable, but for other reasons," Beckett teased.

"How do I get control over it? Can I look into the past at will?" I asked, now curious and excited about my bizarre behavior of late.

"There's no hard and fast rule about when and where it happens. Just from my own experiences, it seems like it's more likely to happen when you are feeling vulnerable or frightened. I've also found that it happens more frequently if I have been to the place at some time in the past. But you can't exactly control or predict it as far as I know. At least now that you know it's coming it won't be so... debilitating."

I yawned. We had been talking for a long time, and the content itself had been exhausting on top of the fact that it was late in the day.

"I'm tired. I think it's time for bed," I said.

"Agreed. I'm glad you handled all of this so well," Beckett said, standing all the way up this time. "I thought this would go much differently, and not for the better."

"Ye of little faith," I replied, wagging my finger. "I guess I knew this was all coming, on some level. And I feel so distanced from the person that I used to be. She didn't exist for me, you know? So as awful as everything was that you told me, I guess it just doesn't affect me as much."

My cavalier attitude was a mistake, but I wasn't trying to say that I didn't care. I just honestly felt that disconnected from Old Eloise. Beckett stopped in his tracks on the way to my new favorite door, and looked at me.

"Eloise, you can't tell me that you don't think that it's a big deal that we ruined the world," he said.

"It's not that I don't think it's a big deal, but I guess I still believe in fate, in things turning out the way that they're supposed to be. It didn't end so badly for the two of us," I shrugged, digging myself into a deeper hole.

"It's not *about* the two of us. What about everyone else?" He was irritated. I knew enough to drop the subject before it became a battle.

"You're right," I surrendered.

Beckett's shoulders loosened and he turned and walked toward the door again. As it shut behind us, I glanced again at the meaningful symbols.

"Hey," I called to Beckett. "I've been meaning to ask you. Who used to live here?"

Beckett raised his eyebrows. "Once again, Eloise, it was you. Now you can see that you were a bit over-the-top. And a bit paranoid," he said as he pointed upstairs to the annex.

I smiled to myself. I wasn't going to risk setting Beckett off again since he seemed to remember my faults so well, but I was proud of my former self for several different reasons, all of which would have made Beckett fume. *Old personality traits die hard too*, I thought to myself.

Having slept peacefully after receiving answers, I awoke the next morning feeling particularly refreshed. It is a bit strange, looking back, that I wasn't more overwhelmed by all of the new information that had been thrown at me. I attribute it to the fact that, on some deeper level, a part of the old me existed in my psyche and allowed me to synthesize it all so quickly. I also think that I had such a need to feel a sense of belonging that I would have believed *anything* Beckett told me. Life in the Compound had been protected, safe, logical. But it had also been monotonously familiar, lacking in some way that I could never put my finger on. There was nothing that I could really complain about, but it had never been enough. I always found myself wanting something more. Not wanting to accept my chosen path in physics had made me feel different and scared. Now I understood that I probably had an innate aversion to the subject due to my former life. It was pretty serious that I had wanted to erase myself, the guilt taking me over so much that I didn't want to exist. As the recreated "me", I subconsciously didn't want any part of my past life. Now it all made sense. Now I understood it all.

The new knowledge was empowering. I had discovered things about myself that I had never known. I had seen places and people and things that I didn't know I had seen. I had been someone that I didn't even know existed. It made me wonder why I had never read about myself in any of the textbooks, but then I remembered that once I had been brought to the future, my former self never existed. That was the only part that I couldn't figure out. How had *I* disappeared, but not everything that I had done to the world? Why didn't the world revert to the way it would have been without my discovery, or my existence even? It seemed to defy the very purpose of time traveling.

I suppose that, while I was energized, my mind wasn't at rest that morning. These were the thoughts that were flitting around inside my head: questions as a result of the questions that had been answered. I had wanted to wake Beckett straight away and begin my onslaught of inquiries, but he wasn't in the annex. On previous days, his absence may have made me wary or uneasy, but I had learned that he was an early riser and I no longer felt alone and afraid. Whereas the Alliance had been a foreign entity before, I was now an informed part of it. No longer did anyone have the one-up on me about my own past.

I took my time getting ready, knowing that I didn't need to be in a rush to get breakfast. There would be a plate for me whether I was on time or not, and I was already late. Why hurry?

With a little extra effort, I looked a bit more like the pristine, Compound version of myself than the ragamuffin girl that had been wandering around the Open. I felt strong and confident armed with the truth of my past. The bits and pieces of my story flowed through me in pulsating waves like currents of electrical energy. Fueled by this new self-confidence, I felt ready to go downstairs and begin being an actual part of the movement.

When I entered the kitchen, I couldn't hear much noise coming from the dining room so I knew that I definitely must have been late. Rose had her back to me, busy cleaning up the remaining dishes in the sink. Beckett was sitting at the island reading something and looked up when he heard me walk in.

"I was wondering how late you were going to sleep in, but now I see that it wasn't sleeping that was holding you up," said Beckett.

Rose turned and looked over her shoulder. "Good morning!"

"Morning, Rose," I said cheerily and then turned towards Beckett and changed my tone. "I'm not really sure if that was supposed to be an insult or a compliment."

It was certainly not the reaction that I was expecting. Not that I was expecting a reaction.

"Whoa, now, don't get all Eloise-in-the-RV on me," he said with his hands up in surrender. "I just think that you might want to change before we go on our little field trip today."

"And, pray tell, where would that be to?" I asked, crossing my arms.

"Somewhere you might need to worry about moving quickly rather than looking pretty," he responded.

"I can move just fine in this," I retorted stubbornly.

"It's your call. I don't want to hear about how uncomfortable you are or how your nice light pink shirt is covered in dirt or blood," Beckett said ominously. "I myself wouldn't be very scared of you in that outfit."

"I don't really know why I would want anyone to be scared of me, but I'll go change just to make you shut up," I responded icily.

Beckett rolled his eyes and shook his head. I could hear him muttering something about how familiar the conversation sounded. Why couldn't he have just told me I looked nice and then suggested that maybe I should change? As my mother – or my fake mother – always said, it's not always *what* you say, but *how* you say it.

I stormed upstairs and tore off my clothes. If he wanted me to look scary, he was going to get scary. I dressed myself in black from head to toe, including the combat boots on my feet. My hair, which had been down, was gathered into a high ponytail on top of my head, and then I braided it so tightly I was afraid my scalp would come off. I didn't feel like it was necessary to remove my makeup, so instead I added a little something to it: I smeared black eyeliner across the tops of my cheeks the way I had seen men do in movies. When I reassessed myself in the mirror, I no longer looked the picture of prettiness. I looked fierce, and I felt fierce. Strong. Confident. Things I hadn't really felt before. It may have been a bit over the top, but according to Beckett that was characteristic of me anyway.

When I went back downstairs, Beckett didn't have any words at first. I couldn't tell if he was trying to manage his temper or if he was impressed.

"That'll do," was all he said. "Let's go."

"Where exactly are we going?" I asked.

"To lasso some more truth," he responded.

I rolled my eyes. Why did he need to be so vague about everything? Would it really be so difficult to just get straight to the point? Sometimes I swore it was all a game to him, that he enjoyed me being in the dark a little more than he should. I wondered if he would keep bits and pieces from me just so he would always have something to reveal.

That little annoyance triggered trust issues within me again. I never could quite level with Beckett. My first instinct in the Compound was to trust him; then I changed my mind when it was too late. In our short journey to the Open I had assaulted him, and then a few short hours later we were making lunch together. I had leaned on him in times of fear and uncertainty, and bucked our friendship the second I felt comfortable again. Was this what it had always been like, a constant tug-of-war?

Beckett had made it sound like we had been more than just friends or colleagues, but I couldn't imagine having been compatible at all. It seemed impossible for us to last a full day without getting angry at each other. I had my moments when I had softened, got caught up, but the intensity of those rare occasions seemed to be lessening in frequency. Was I a different person now, unable to feel what I had once felt? Or was I always cold and unmoving and Beckett had loved me anyway? I wasn't sure if I wanted to know the answer. It made me uncomfortable to think that I could feel a sense of belonging in the Open, but no particular, lasting allegiance to my savior and longtime companion.

I followed Beckett outside to the car. I admit that I was relieved to not be trekking across the forest again. While my ankle felt stronger, I wasn't ready to risk tripping and reinjuring it. Plus, I was truthfully *still* not used to as much exercise as I had been getting.

As if reading my mind and purposely wanting to push my buttons, Beckett said, "We'll be taking the car for a part of the day, but we'll have to get out and walk the rest."

I tried to keep my sulking to a minimum, not wanting to give him a reason to lecture me again. He needed to stop seeing me as a weak little girl who needed protecting. From what I had gathered, the former me didn't sound like a meek and mild person. That made me wonder if Beckett was asserting power now because he didn't have any say then. If he thought he was going to wear the pants, he had another thing coming.

I got into the passenger side and rested my head on the seat as Beckett pulled down the long, gravelly driveway and out onto the main road.

"It's going to be a bit of a drive," he cautioned me. "So if you want to take a nap or something, I'll wake you up when I need to."

"I think I'd like to stay awake, thank you very much," I said.

"El, why do you have to make everything a fight? I was just trying to be polite."

I bit back my stubbornness and a biting comment. "And I just would like to get used to these surroundings. I don't want to miss anything."

"Well, I guess it's a good thing that you want to pay attention today because you might need to," he replied with a serious look on his face.

"And why is that?"

"We're driving towards the Compound."

"Are you serious? Why on earth would we do that? I thought the whole point of living at Headquarters was to *avoid* the Compound," I said exasperatedly.

"I didn't mean that we were driving *to* the Compound," Beckett replied. "We're just driving in that general direction. We can assume that if they have a camp set up anywhere it's probably this way, so we just need to be on high alert today."

"I still don't get why you're putting us in that position. Wouldn't it make sense for us to drive *away* from the Compound for our little outing?"

"That would make sense," Beckett nodded, "but what we need to see isn't in any other direction. We don't have any other options. Not that I know of anyway, and our intelligence is pretty thorough."

I could clearly see that the whole cryptic speech thing wasn't going away, so instead of frustrating myself further or saying something that would ignite a feud, I closed my mouth and let him drive.

The road we traveled wasn't very exciting, and we – thankfully – didn't run into anyone as we drove. When Beckett began to slow down, I recognized the hidden driveway of the cemetery. He pulled in.

"Couldn't you have just told me that this was where we were going? It's not like I haven't been here before. And I wouldn't exactly put this in Compound territory," I said.

"This is just a pit stop before we get to where we need to go," he answered.

"Are we visiting relatives then? Because I've already seen the body count. I get that a lot of people died."

Beckett looked at me sidelong, and I could tell that he needed to collect himself before responding to me.

"No, Eloise, we are not here to visit anyone. Though there are countless people who haven't received visitors in years upon years. Because, you know, their relatives are all dead too," he said sarcastically. Then he cleared his throat and gathered his patience again. "I know that we've been here and I know that last time you seemed emotionally unhinged by it. But I'm afraid that the gravity of the situation has left you now that you know the truth. The girl that I brought here originally was appalled by what she saw. Now you're a bit more... callous."

"So you're trying to say that I'm acting like my old self instead of my new self and you don't like it. I'm sorry that I can't live up to your expectations, whatever they are, since they are constantly changing."

"Argh!" he grunted as he hit the steering wheel once, sounding a *beep* and alerting the dead of our presence. "I'm not trying to insult you, Eloise! Damn it! What is it about me lately that puts you on the defensive? It's like you're trying to distance yourself from me with this... this new act or something. I'm not the bad guy here. I'm your friend, I'm your... well, never mind that. I'm here for you. We're supposed to be allies. We're supposed to work together. One minute you're smiling at me and accepting my help and the next you're looking at me like I'm an insect you want to squash. You say that I'm constantly changing, but what about you? I mean, who are you?"

I flinched.

The car was stopped, the engine running the only sound to break the silence. Beckett sat in his own frustration after his speech, gripping the steering wheel with both hands and staring straight ahead. I looked straight at my lap at my fingers twiddling, dancing in embarrassment.

I didn't know how to answer that question. *Who was I?* Up until a few weeks ago, I thought I had somewhat known. Now I knew that I had existed as a different version of myself in the past, with only the memories of the version I was now. How do I reconcile with myself? How do I make both versions a part of me? Being scared and confused had made me feel insignificant and alone. With the knowledge I had gained the night before, I felt powerful, but it was going to cause me to be alone. I was battling myself and I didn't know how to stop. I didn't know how to be both versions without destroying one or the other.

Covering my face with my hands, I began to silently cry.

It didn't take long for Beckett to notice. Not that I was doing it simply for effect. I was genuinely lost and ashamed of myself.

"El, I'm sorry, I didn't mean to make you cry," Beckett said more softly, but his voice lacked the empathy that it was usually flooded with.

"It's not your fault," I sniffled. "I don't know who I am."

There was silence for a moment, either because Beckett was giving me a moment to recover or because he was thinking about my answer. But finally he said, "Is that what all is this about, this hot and cold? Because you don't feel like you know who you are?"

He still wasn't looking at me, but his voice had lost the sharpness.

"I...I don't know," I sobbed. "I don't know why I'm acting the way I've been acting. I can't figure out who to be, what to be. I've never been a mean person. I've always held my own, sure, but I've never been so...so p-petty. Oh, I don't even know if that's the right word."

I wiped at the tears on my face and hoped there was nothing falling from my nose. I was aware that I was sort of babbling rather than give any explanation for how I was feeling or what I was thinking. I tried to calm myself down.

"Was I like this before?" I asked, my voice coming out all nasally due to my head being full of fluid.

"Everyone's a little pushy sometimes, El. We all have our bad moments. But no, not like this. Never this ready to argue over every little thing. You've always had a strong personality, but now it's almost like your trying to take it to the limit."

I didn't know what to say. I wasn't trying to be a pain. I wasn't trying to lose the few friendships that I had. I didn't know what I was trying to be, or rather I didn't know who I was *supposed* to be. My second life had to have a purpose of some sort – I believed everything happened for a reason – but I didn't know what that purpose was exactly. Was I supposed to be a leader or a cog? A force to be reckoned with, or a reckoning of the force? The truth was, I felt like I didn't have a place anymore. I didn't belong in the past, but I didn't belong in the present either since I was only there due to my freak-of-nature genes that allowed me to be.

I sat deep in thought of all of this until I realized Beckett was probably waiting for me to respond or move or tell him to go on.

"I'm sorry," I said, and I felt very small.

"It's okay," Beckett said as he shifted the car back into drive. "I'm sorry for not being patient. I should've explained things to you sooner and maybe you wouldn't feel so lost with all of this."

"Don't do that," I said, immediately resuming bossiness.

"Don't do what?"

"Don't keep making excuses for me. Technically I got myself into this, so I can handle it. There are plenty of people who go through hard times without becoming a complete... a complete ass."

Becket laughed. "That's true."

"What's so funny?" This was exactly why I got so moody and irritated, I thought to myself. He's always treating me like an errant child, never taking me seriously.

"It's just that I don't think I've really heard you swear in the past couple weeks," he said.

I pondered his observation. It was true; I had never been one to use that kind of language.

"Did I used to swear?" I asked. I could only assume that all of these foreign pieces of me used to belong to the girl that was before.

"A lot," Beckett admitted. "For an educated person, you could rattle them off as well as anyone. Don't worry though, your ability to sometimes be down-to-earth is what made a lot of people like you."

"Have you always made excuses for me?" I asked. I knew it would create an awkward moment, but I was still trying to recreate a sense of our former relationship.

"I wouldn't call it that, but yeah, I suppose."

I nodded and looked out of the window at the rows of gravestones, lined up in perfect measure like soldiers at roll-call. Part of me wondered if Beckett had followed me out of love, or if he feared that I would make the same mistakes again and wanted to prevent it. Was I even capable of doing the right thing? Maybe I would make all of the wrong choices again, given the chance. Maybe Beckett was now more like a babysitter than a friend. It made me sad to think of how alone I could really be in the world- no real family, no real friends.

"Are we through with the Inquisition now?" Beckett said lightly, interrupting my morbid thoughts.

"Yeah, let's go."

We drove forward and up the hill that I had insisted on mounting the last time, but we hadn't gone any further than that. Beckett paused atop the hill again.

"The reason why I'm taking you here is just because I want you to be able to understand the true impact that our decisions had on the world. Sometimes that's hard to do unless you have a visual," he pointed out over the steering wheel to the horizon where the stones seemed to meet the sun. "I just want you to observe."

Beckett drove onward for a solid ten minutes. He wasn't going very fast, and he did weave in between rows where there was a clear path wide enough for a car, but the little stone markers never ended. Closer to the entrance of the cemetery there had been a variety of shapes and sizes, but from that point on there had only been rows of the same square slabs.

"Why do the stones at the beginning all look different?" I asked Beckett.

"Well, there was an era when people had time to mourn the death of a loved one, to prepare and plan. When things got bad, they couldn't create these fast enough. It was lucky that people were buried individually with identification in the end."

"Beckett, was it really that bad? I mean, you say that the population was incredibly high, but still. How is it possible that people were dying that quickly? No voice of reason put a stop to it? It seems a little far-fetched."

"I can see why you'd say that. But unfortunately it's not far-fetched. Violence became commonplace in cities and towns across America. These graves didn't get here in one day. If that was the case you could be sure that this orderly cemetery wouldn't exist. So yes, Eloise, it really was that bad... over time. That's why I want you to see this. I'm not saying that our choices were the sole cause of all of the chaos that led to these lives ending early. What makes us human is that we have free will. We have brains that allow us to make our own decisions. We can't make other people make good ones. But we did play a part. We made things worse for people by playing with time instead of making things better. These were people with families, with individual stories, with history. They loved and were loved. People missed them when they were gone. We can't let that happen again. We can't cause the destruction of lives. We can't repeat history. No matter what."

I didn't have a chance to answer him before he pulled over – as if there was a chance of anyone needing to pass us – and unbuckled his seatbelt. Then he opened the door and got out. I followed suit, assuming I was expected to do the same.

"What are we doing?" I asked, wrapping my arms around myself in the sudden chill. "And why is it so cold all of a sudden?"

I didn't remember it being frigid when we left Headquarters.

"Why do you think, Eloise?" said Beckett, as usual not answering my question.

"I don't know. Global warming?"

"I would agree, but that slowed down a bit with so many less people to pollute the earth."

I shrugged at him and waited for an answer. I was tired of playing the guessing game already.

"It's another side effect of your time traveling. You're in a place where the remains of thousands upon thousands of people were laid to rest. They may not exist in your world today, but these people existed in your world once. And that's a lot of death to be surrounded by, a lot of souls that lack the warmth of a body."

I wrinkled up my face. "I'm not trying to take away from the seriousness of the situation, but that's super creepy."

Beckett ignored my remark. "And the reason why we are here is because I want to show you something. Take a walk all the way down this aisle and then back up the next one and examine the stones. Take your time. I'll wait for you here."

"I'm not going to find a freshly dug hole that you're going to push me into, am I?" I joked.

He smiled at me close-mouthed and half-heartedly and gestured for me to go forward.

There were about thirty stones in each row, all identically jutting out from the ground like planned, gray weeds. They were symmetrical and exactly the same height, which suggested that while they may have been rushed into production, someone or something had measured them precisely, to the nearest sixteenth of an inch. The only difference was the name that was etched into each one. There were names of both genders, but none of the stones bore the same surname. There were all nationalities and I couldn't find a single commonality. Had Beckett stopped here for a particular reason, or was he just trying to point out how many different families had been affected by various tragedies?

When I finished my sad, little tour and stood before Beckett, he was waiting with his thumbs in his front pockets, leaning against the car.

"So?" he asked, expectantly.

"So what?" I didn't know there was going to be a test. Though, knowing Beckett, I probably should have.

"What did you notice?" he asked as if he were a teacher prompting me for a correct answer.

"Mr. Beckett, I noticed that there were a bunch of gray stones next to each other in a line. They were all the same size, had different names, genders, and nationalities," I replied mockingly.

"And the dates?"

I hadn't paid them any mind, truthfully. My eyes had been drawn to the names of the people, the identities of those who I had played a part in killing.

"I didn't notice them," I admitted. "But I assume they were all close together."

"Take a look again," Beckett instructed. Seeing my reluctant face, he added, "You don't even have to go all the way if you don't want, princess."

I gave him a look and then began to walk down the first row for the second time. I squinted at the dates, some stones not having been chiseled as clearly as others. I really did need to stop being so lazy, I was thinking to myself when I got to the third marker. The birth dates and death dates had been close together for the first three. I picked up my pace, examined the next few, and found the same result. I began to jog down the rest of the row, the numbers jumping out at me now like I had bionic vision. By the time I ran down the next row and got back to Beckett, I was out of breath from my sprint.

"They're...all...children," I panted, hands on my knees. "What...happened?"

He patted a spot on the hood of the car for me to lean on.

"It wasn't just a lack of respect or decline in general society that caused this cemetery to be so full," he began quietly. "The reason why I say we played an even larger role in all of this is because we are responsible for the Strung- the people that we sent back into the world, addled and alone. As no one knew about the traveling, the rest of the country thought that there was just a sudden increase in mental illness. But the truth was, at the apex of the traveling there were so many people being added to the Strung population that we couldn't have kept track of them even if we tried. You see, there was no harm for us in letting them go back to the public because they couldn't remember anything about time traveling. And even if they could, people would have chalked it up to the ramblings of lunatics.

But what we didn't realize was just the damage that the Strung could do. We thought that they would walk aimlessly about the earth mumbling to themselves and drooling and acting strangely, and no one would be the wiser. Eventually they would die and no one would be affected. But we gravely misjudged their capabilities. Some were able to lead semi-functioning lives, to blend into society a bit. They were able to become conspirators when they found one another and get their hands on weapons. And what you see here is the result of one such group of the Strung."

"The Strung killed these children?" I asked.

Beckett nodded. "There was no evidence left behind about why, but we can assume that the Strung who committed this act got it into their heads that children were the enemy. Or that they had some notion of what they thought the world would turn out to be and were trying to save them from growing up. We don't really know. But they walked into a densely populated school and opened fire in all of the classrooms. There were barely any survivors. You can walk these rows for a while and you will find the same short life spans etched into the stones. They were all buried here."

It was a sobering conversation, to think of all of the young lives lost. To think of all the potential that never got fulfilled. To think that these children didn't even get to live one lifetime, and I was already on my second. It gave me a slightly different perspective about time travel, knowing that an incident like this was actually directly related to the choices that we had made. But there was one thing that I didn't understand.

"Beckett, now don't take this the wrong way. I have a serious question. If we know better than to let the average Stringer continue to travel, and we know that if someone becomes Strung he or she cannot rejoin society unsupervised, couldn't we prevent this from happening? You know, even if we traveled again."

"Yeah, El, it's always a possibility that we would learn from the mistakes of the past. But it would be the first time. When someone comes into a position of power, it somehow usurps his entire being. You aren't the person that you would normally be. You don't make the decisions that you would normally make. I mean, just think about how you've been acting since you've learned about the Open and all of the history behind it. It's not a risk worth taking."

"I understand," I said. And on some level, I did. But I couldn't help wondering if Beckett was being overly cautious, if he had become so self-righteous out of necessity or overzealousness.

"Right, well, I said this was stop number one so we'd better get a move on," Beckett said as he stood up and opened the car door again.

I climbed back in the passenger's side. "Where are we going now?"

"We're going to go see first-hand what happens to people when they become Strung," Beckett said. "Buckle up."

It took a minute for me to register what Beckett had said. If we were going to visit the Strung that could only mean...

"Beckett, are you telling me that people are still traveling?" I asked incredulously.

"That's exactly what I'm saying," he said. "It's happening right inside the Compound to your own people- people who aren't fit to travel."

"That's impossible. I've lived there my entire life and never heard of such a thing. My parents surely would have known about it."

"They did know about it, El. That's why they wanted to get you out. They knew it was only a matter of time before the Council found out about you and used you. There was a very short window of time when traveling was frowned upon. The Compound picked up where we left off. They didn't learn from our mistakes."

I was shocked and disgusted, wondering how many times my present life had changed without me knowing. Surely if people were traveling, life at the Compound would be affected by the thing they went back to try and fix.

"How do you know for sure? How do you know that people are still traveling?"

"Mildred and Barnum confirmed it obviously, but when you see the Strung for yourself there's no doubting it. You might even recognize some of them."

There were so many people living in the Compound that it was possible there were plenty of people who I'd never even come into contact with.

"But how is it possible that people are traveling and nothing in the Compound has changed? Don't you think that *something* would be seriously affected by it?"

Beckett sighed. "No, El, you wouldn't notice. Because if people traveled and significantly affected your ancestors or your neighbor's ancestors, your memories would automatically alter to fit the new truth created by the traveling. Your life could have changed drastically and you wouldn't know because you wouldn't remember any differently. Considering nothing catastrophic has happened, chances are that people either don't travel all that frequently or they're only making minor changes, like the ones that we had started out with. The Compound lives very comfortably right now. There's really no reason for them to want to alter history in a big way. And there's always the chance that things could remain somewhat unaltered. You're a walking example of that. Your past life was not completely undone, as the results of your actions remained."

I felt powerless and betrayed. What if travelers had affected my life, for better or for worse? My memories could have been stolen from me without me even knowing it. My former self was still ruining my life – our life, I guess – and there was nothing that I could do about it. I had created such severe consequences by my actions that I felt there would be an endless cycle of travel propelled by a perpetual desire of people in power to have control. Was it even *possible* anymore to stop traveling from happening?

"This is serious," I said. It was one thing for other people's lives to be affected, but once I knew that I could also be a victim, I was much more invested.

Beckett looked at me wordlessly and then focused back on the road. I had a feeling that this was the exact result he had been hoping for. There was a small, stubborn part of me that wanted to be mad at him for manipulating my emotions that way, but I was starting to understand his viewpoint, his passion to stop this vicious cycle that could never end well. I was beginning to connect with his seemingly infinite obsession with stopping time travel.

"This is the part that's going to be a bit of a drive, about two hours," Beckett said.

I nodded. I knew he was telling me that I could sleep if I wanted to, probably even hoping that I would instead of staying up to ask questions, or even worse, to possibly argue. But I didn't have any fight in me at that moment. My mind was too full of what-ifs, a whirlpool of questions about my past and present. How many pasts had I even had at this point? How old was I? Sixteen? A hundred and sixteen? I didn't even know. Was my birthday even my birthday?

"Beckett, when's my birthday?" I asked.

He smiled that carefree smile that reminded me he was handsome and his eyes crinkled quizzically. "Random. June twenty-third."

"Okay," I said. At least some things remained the same.

And then we were quiet for the rest of the ride. I was lost in my thoughts, and I presumed that Beckett was lost in his. I wanted to crawl inside his mind and see if he was thinking about our past together and how things used to be, or if he was focused on the present, looking for an attack or preparing his next speech when we arrived at the Strung. I wondered how much he had lost in all of this, in family, friends, and himself. Considering he was sitting next to me, also younger than he was supposed to be, alive instead of dead, he must have had a long and difficult journey to get here. Alone through the years, except maybe for Mad-Eye, all in his desperation to stop time travel. And to find me. No matter how much I questioned his motives from time to time, it really did speak volumes about his feelings that he had defied what was once believed to be the laws of physics in order to be with me. I had to try to remember that next time I felt unreasonable anger bubbling up in me.

It made me wish that there was some sort of evidence of our relationship, some clues to fill in all of the blanks. It was odd to have loved someone you couldn't remember. Granted it had been years since we had had any sort of relationship, but I wondered how difficult it was for Beckett to play the role of a friend. I wondered if he still had the same feelings for me, or if time and differences in me had allowed them to ebb. I wondered if there were moments where he wanted to fold me into his arms, to return to a time that had now actually never technically existed since my first life had been erased. I thought I could answer the question myself, since Beckett and I had those few tender moments before I knew any of the truth. But something had changed. The distance that he had mentioned before was palpable, and I think that we were both to blame for it. And I wondered if it would be a good thing or a bad thing for our love to be lost. It had created so much tragedy the first time, maybe it was for the best that we didn't tornado our way through the Open. Or maybe everything that we had gone through would make us a force of good rather than evil.

I felt an inexplicable sadness, like I had lost something, but I never had the something in the first place.

My throat began to burn in that familiar way it does when you're trying not to cry. So before my tears became an unwelcome passenger in our car, I pushed the thoughts out of my mind and tried to focus on the part of the world we were driving through that I had never seen before. The Open had allowed my world to become so much bigger, I felt the need to observe as an offering of thanks for finally being a part of it. The thought of the walls of the Compound now seemed as claustrophobic as the annex and the chute had felt on that day at Headquarters. Who would want to live that way when there was this wide-open world to explore? I didn't think that I could ever go back now that I had this freedom.

Whereas the road closest to Headquarters had been thickly tree-lined from the surrounding forest, we seemed to be driving through a more rural area. There were flat fields as far as the eye could see of overgrown grass. *Must have been farm land once.* The thought popped into my mind and it was as if it wasn't my own. The only concept of farm land that I had was what we had in the grounds of the Compound, and that didn't look anything like the rolling land that was before me. I picked up on what Beckett was talking about now about how certain things had seemed to creep back from locked-away memories. It was possible that I had seen farmland in the movies that the Compound possessed from American theater, but the thought had come so naturally I believed it belonged to Old Eloise.

As we drove further, the rural area turned into what must have once been a town. Dilapidated houses got closer together and the open spaces became less frequent. Beckett turned off the main road and we drove through the town. You could tell that the homes were abandoned long ago, as they looked weathered and beaten. Windows were broken, and gutters and siding were peeling off and hung limply on the sides of the houses. Broken fence posts littered front yards and front doors were wide open. Cars whose owners had long passed sat eerily in driveways like strewn toys left behind by a child. Some doors hung on hinges and some were missing tires, but others sat untouched as if frozen in time, as if there was still a family inside that would pile into it and take off to a baseball game. But I knew that there were no block parties happening there anymore, unless there were ghosts in attendance.

As the thought of ghosts crossed my mind, I blinked and saw a little girl in a white cotton dress holding a blanket with a thumb in her mouth on the farmer's porch of a house. I almost yelled at Beckett to stop the car, that there was a lost little girl all alone out there, but she faded as quickly as she had appeared, and I realized that I had seen someone who once was, not someone who was anymore. It was strange to be able to see the past, but I was at least thankful for not feeling insane. The odd experience was much easier to handle knowing what I was seeing.

It gave me an idea.

"Beckett, can you just stop the car for a minute?" I asked calmly.

He came to a slow stop and said, "Is everything okay?"

"Yeah. Yeah, everything's fine," I replied. "I just want to...test something out."

Beckett looked at me strangely, trying to figure out what I was up to, but he didn't ask any questions. He pulled over to the side of the road.

"Do you really think that's necessary?" I asked wryly.

"You never know," he shrugged and then admitted, "Old habit."

I closed my eyes and tried to think about the past, which was difficult to do since I had no memory of it. But I knew that Beckett had said that if I learned how to concentrate, I would be able to control the visions, to avoid them. I wondered if it worked the same way with *wanting* to see. I crossed my fingers and hoped that when I opened my eyes I would find a vibrant neighborhood instead of one in ruin.

Slowly, I lifted my lids, and saw a man on a bicycle coming straight towards our car. I gasped as he was about to crash head on, but he suddenly disappeared. And when I looked behind us, there he was, continuing on as if he had gone right through. The picture got a little bleary for a moment, and I had to remind myself to focus on seeing what I wanted to see. The color on the houses came back vividly, and the yards were finely manicured instead of drab and dead. Flowers bloomed in gardens and in window boxes, and there were wreaths on doors or flags blowing in the breeze on poles. A mailman was delivering mail on a walking route, and I watched him curiously as he went up to a mailbox and slipped a few envelopes in, clear as day in front of me. Clear as if he was actually there.

I heard raucous laughter and I turned to my right, seeing children chasing each other across the neatly mowed front yard and into the back. They were wielding squirt guns in one hand and popsicles in the other. I smiled in spite of myself, knowing that it wasn't truly happening, but appreciating that the innocence once was real.

"Drive," I whispered to Beckett, afraid that if I made too much noise I would ruin the movie that I was taking part in. He obeyed and pulled away from the curb. As we gained speed, the picture began to jump in and out of focus to the point where I almost lost it completely. "No, no. Slowly."

The world became clear again and I could hear birds chirping, a radio playing in a man's garage as he washed his car in the driveway. I could see a woman jogging down the street with headphones in her ears pushing a baby stroller. I could smell something cooking on a grill. These once-common human experiences came back to me like a tsunami of memories. I didn't even have to question any of it because it was as if I had lived it all before. It was surreal. Surreal perfection, and everyone looked so happy it made me yearn to be a part of it. The quiet neighborhood was so at peace, yet so lively at the same time. I was so used to people behaving robotically within a community, and it didn't seem like that fluid coldness there. They did not operate as if by the control panels that chose their clothes or their food. These people were so free.

Beckett continued on driving without saying a word, letting me take in the surroundings in my own way. I was sure he probably thought I was in awe of how broken-down it all was, but I couldn't wait to share with him what I had seen. Then, we came to an enormous clearing where there was some sort of fair going on.

"Stop," I whispered to Beckett again, and I smiled in awe at the crowd.

There were so many people crowded into the area. Some were lined up at the ticket booth at the entrance, children practically bouncing on their feet as they waited to get in. I could smell popcorn and soft pretzels and cotton candy. There was a Ferris wheel that towered over a variety of other rides. I could have sworn a little boy waved to me from the top, but I knew that he was waving to someone else in the past, maybe his mom or his dad. There was carnival music playing and shrieking as kids wove in and out of the crowd chasing each other to the bounce houses. A couple asked strangers to take their picture, and then they put their faces and arms through a wooden cutout of a girl in a bikini and a surfer dude.

I watched them all going about their business, laughing and enjoying themselves, blissfully unaware of the girl from the future watching them. I watched their body language as they held hands, hugged, leaned on one another. There was love there, friendship. These were not violent people. I wondered what Beckett possibly could have been talking about.

And then the gunfire began.

At first, I thought that it was the noises of a ride or a game. Maybe someone was about to light up the sky with fireworks. But then I heard the terrified screams. I saw people begin to run towards the entrance frantically. Mothers were screaming for their children. Young children were wailing. And then I saw figures dressed all in black wearing clown masks and toting semi-automatic weapons, walking through the crowd and firing randomly.

I screamed. I scrambled to get out of the car, and on the edge of my hearing I vaguely heard Beckett ask me what I was doing.

"No! NO!" I yelled as I ran towards them. I wasn't thinking about what I could possibly do to stop the savages from doing what they were doing. I was just thinking that I had to save these people, these innocent families who were just enjoying a nice, summer day out.

The figures in black were getting closer, or I was closing in on them, but I wasn't struck by a single bullet as I ran full speed ahead. A blond toddler was thirty yards in front of me to the left, standing all alone as people ran in different directions trying to escape, to find safety from the barrage of bullets. I sprinted towards him, to get him out of harm's way. But I wasn't fast enough. Just before I reached him, my ankle gave a twinge. I slipped on something wet and he tumbled to the ground.

"NOOOO!" A strangled scream escaped my lips as I hurdled to the ground and tried to cradle him in my arms. But he was nothing but air, and when I blinked angry tears out of my eyes the whole horrific scene had disappeared. One second I was staring at my hands covered in red, and the next second my skin was clean.

I patted the ground where the boy had been seconds before, feeling around as if he had somehow slipped into the earth, but there was nothing there. I had forgotten myself. I had forgotten that I wasn't really there, that he wasn't really there. Not anymore. The massacre had happened long ago.

I put my face in my hands and sobbed, rocking back and forth on my knees and shaking. I heard footsteps padding behind me and instinctively covered my head, as if it were the shooters that had materialized and were coming after me.

"Eloise! It's me! It's me!" Beckett said as he dropped to his knees and grabbed me by the shoulders. "It's okay! What just happened? It's alright now, it's alright."

I curled my fingers around his shirt and buried my face in his neck and sobbed. I wailed aloud, and my body trembled uncontrollably as he held me and whispered that everything was okay. When I had finally somewhat calmed down, I pulled far enough away from Beckett to speak to him.

"I could see them in the p-past. I started to see w-what this town u-used to look like, and I w-wanted to see," I started to say, still unable to get the words out clearly through my crying. "Th-there was this fair, and people were s-so h-happy. There were rides, Beckett, and I could s-smell the popcorn so much I could al-almost taste it. They were all l-laughing and the k-kids were so excited, you know? And then all...all of a sudden out of n-nowhere there were p-people dressed in b-black and they had g-guns. And they just started sh-shooting everyone and th-there was this little b-boy and he...."

I brought my hand to my mouth and tears started streaming down my face again as I relived it in my mind. I closed my eyes and shook my head, trying to get the images out of my mind of the bodies strewn on the ground, of the golden straw underfoot that had become red.

"It was so awful," I cried. "It was so awfully real."

"Eloise, I'm so sorry. I'm so sorry. It's okay, El. Shhh, it's okay," Beckett kept repeating as he stroked my hair and tucked my head under his chin.

A sudden realization dawned on me.

"Wait a minute. D-Did you know? Did you kn-know I was going to see that?" I pushed him away and asked angrily. He had said we were going to see what it was really like to be Strung. Did he take me to this place on purpose, knowing that I was going to see the carnival disaster?

I could see a mix of fear and sadness in his eyes. "No, Eloise! No, absolutely not. I had no idea. We aren't even there yet. I would never do something like that, I promise."

Sensing that his reaction was sincere and his emotions were real, I believed him, and I rested my head on his chest again.

We sat there like that for a while until my chest stopped heaving and I had no tears left to cry. I had a feeling it would be a long time before I would try to see the past again on purpose.

I lifted my head and Beckett's t-shirt stuck to my face for a second. There was a big wet patch where I had cried on him.

"I'm sorry. I got your shirt all wet," I croaked.

"It's okay, El. You have nothing to be sorry about," he said softly. "We don't have to keep going, you know. We can just go back to Headquarters. I think you've seen enough to understand what time traveling can do to people. I mean, I don't know if the people you saw were Strung, but it gave you a pretty good enough idea."

"No," I shook my head, wiped my eyes, and sniffled. "I need to see them. I need to understand it all. Let's go."

I stood up and my legs were a little bit shaky, but I had a strong desire to gather more proof to completely be on Beckett's side about traveling. The truth came in all shapes and sizes, and it wasn't always pretty. But it was important to know the truth of the past in order to know how to move toward the future.

"Are you sure?" Beckett asked.

"I'm positive," I said resolutely.

Tentatively, Beckett laced his fingers through mine and I accepted. I felt the jolt of electricity that I had felt the few times before. It had been a while and it reminded me that I had started to have feelings for Beckett before I knew who he really was.

When we got back to the car, Beckett walked me around to the passenger's side and opened the door for me. I climbed in and he closed it, and then he walked to the driver's side and got in.

"We're not going too much further anyway," he said. "There is an old city about ten miles down the road from here. We think it's where the Compound must drop the Strung when they're through with them."

"Aren't you worried that they could be dropping someone there today? Or that they might be camping there, if it's a common stopping place?" I asked.

"We think that they may have put the whole time traveling thing on hold while they're out looking for you. And I highly doubt that anyone from the Compound would want to be camping out anywhere near the Strung."

"Because they're dangerous?"

"Some," Beckett admitted. "But let's just say that the living conditions are also not quite up to par for them."

It *was* actually quite hard to imagine anyone from the Compound slumming it in the Open. I was sure there were probably teams within the Compound's military that were a little less averse to roughing it without the luxuries, but I still didn't see them without control panels and pristine white walls all around. They held themselves in too high of esteem to fathom sleeping among the lesser class. They didn't know any differently.

Beckett pulled into the parking lot of what was once a supermarket and parked the car neatly between two white lines, as if anyone would be there to notice if he parked diagonally across four spots.

"We're walking from here," he said as he turned the key, shutting off the ignition. "We need to gear up, just in case."

I looked at him quizzically as he exited the driver's side and walked to the trunk. I followed and stood next to him as he popped it open. There was one small leather bag sitting in the center. Beckett pulled out a pistol in a holster, attached it to his belt, and pulled his sweatshirt down over it. Then he pulled out another and held it out to me.

"What do you think I'm going to do with that?" I asked bewildered. It was one thing if he wanted to carry one, but I had never even touched a gun before except for recreation. It was a different story to contemplate aiming it at a live being.

"You need to conceal it on your person for your protection," he said waving it in front of me.

"Beckett, I've taken target practice for sport, but it's been a while and I'm not an expert..."

"This is the safety," he said, clicking something off towards the back of the gun. "You flick it off, and you pull the trigger if need be. It's very simple. As to your aim, this is only a precaution. You shouldn't actually need this. But in the event that you do, I'm hoping that your memory will come back to you. But it doesn't really matter because firing it into the air will probably scare most Strung away enough anyway. Needing to aim is almost completely unlikely."

Reluctantly, I took the pistol from Beckett and hooked it onto my pants. I now understood why Beckett had suggested I wear my jacket even though it was pretty mild out. There would have been nothing to hide the weapon otherwise.

Beckett closed the trunk and locked the doors, which again made me smirk. I wondered how many car thefts happened in the Open, considering there was probably no one out there besides the Strung within a thirty mile radius at least.

We walked the city blocks side by side without talking. There wasn't much to say at that point, and I had a feeling that Beckett was on alert. He wasn't just my companion; he was on patrol, leading me to an investigation, both partner and bodyguard. As we walked further, taller buildings became more frequent and more densely packed. I began seeing graffiti spray-painted on everything and anything. There were just shapes and random lines at first, and then the marring took on word form. The words "THIS IS THE END" loomed an inevitable omen on one brick building as we turned a corner. It sent chills up my spine and the hair on my arms stood on end as I thought of how true it seemed, witnessing the barren streets. It was like walking through a ghost town, with windows smashed like they had been at some of the houses in town earlier. The only signs of life were birds or an occasional squirrel, an odd sight in the middle of a city. But it was a city no more.

When we reached the wrought iron gates of the city park, I could hear strange noises that could have been human or animal.

There was some sort of wailing, a clucking noise, and maniacal laughter. We had found the Strung.

Beckett paused in front of the gate. "Before we go in, you need to promise me that you'll follow my instructions. The whole time. The Strung are unpredictable and I need you to trust me. And *I* need to trust that *you* are going to listen to me for once."

I raised my hands in surrender. "Okay, okay."

Beckett raised his eyebrow, as if he wanted me to say something more.

"Seriously?" I asked. I raised my right hand in pledge. "I solemnly swear to be a good girl, behave, and do what you tell me. Good enough?"

Beckett nodded and I rolled my eyes.

"Come on," he said and gestured for me to follow him.

At first, all I could see was overgrown grass and trees. There were some scattered wildflowers here and there, but I could only imagine that the park was a shadow of what it once was. We followed a dirt path, which had clumps of grass growing in spots, a sure sign that it had been a long time since anyone had taken care of it. Part of me wanted to pause and try to witness what it had looked like in its glory days, but I knew that Beckett was on a mission. And I was sure neither one of us was ready for another emotional meltdown just yet.

As we continued down the path, the sounds got louder and more bountiful. There were more than the three or four voices that I had heard at the entrance. We passed a cluster of trees and the path opened into a clearing with a fountain that was no longer functioning in the center. My breath caught in my throat as I took in the scene before me, and for a moment I was certain we had stumbled into a horror movie. I froze behind a tree and observed, not ready to take any more steps forward. Beckett realized after a moment, turned around, and ducked behind the tree with me, allowing me the brief pause to take it all in.

There were about twenty to thirty Strung spread around the vicinity of the fountain, and they moved zombie-like, body movements unintentional and spastic, not their own. They were unkempt. Some wore more clothes than necessary while others hardly had any on at all. An assortment of bizarre behaviors kept them occupied, providing reason for not having noticed us approaching. The cacophony of noises sounded like an ethereal tribute to circus animals, both otherworldly and animalistic at the same time. I looked at Beckett and he jerked his head back towards the path, suggesting it was time to go on.

We stepped back onto the path and walked towards the Strung. I couldn't help feeling a bit frightened, my hand instinctively resting over the gun.

"Don't do that," Beckett said. "If they feel threatened right away, it'll only rile them up."

I removed my hand reluctantly and tried to convince myself that these people were just unstable, not ready to lunge at me.

When we got close enough to be in the thick of things, some Strung appeared to notice us while others made no acknowledgement of our arrival. There was a man sitting in the murky water of the fountain, naked from at least the waist up from what I could see. He kept scooping water up above his head with his hands and letting it trickle back down to the pool, intent on watching the dancing drops as if it were magical every time. I shuddered as he examined something that lingered in his hand once all of the water had fallen, held the algae up for further scrutiny, and then ate it.

The fountain Strung wasn't the only one with an outward expression of lunacy. A woman sat against the base of the fountain, rocking back and forth while chanting gutturally, shaking her head from side to side and alternately patting her hands on her cheeks. An older man, the voice of the loud wailing, stood with his arms wrapped around a tree, clinging to it like a life preserver. A girl who looked slightly older than me – but whom I did not recognize – sat on a patch of grass with a circle of earth dug out around her. She was smearing the mud she had dug on her face and doing the maniacal laughing. Another woman stood muttering rapid-fire numbers to herself, a code that only she could understand.

There were many others who were just walking around aimlessly, silently, without a purpose. They looked like lost souls in purgatory, unable to find their way to salvation or damnation. It was almost as if there was an invisible fence that corralled them all, because they did not venture any further than the area of the fountain.

I heard the clucking almost in my ear, and I looked around trying to figure out where it was coming from. There was a sudden thud on the ground beside me and I let out a slightly audible scream. I wasn't sure how the Strung would react to loud noises and I wasn't about to test it out, so I tried to minimize my volume. A bearded man in his twenties, tall and willowy, stood beside me in a flamboyant array of colors. He was the culprit of the clucking noises, and he had been perched in the tree above me.

"Becky, Becky, Becky, Becky," he repeated over and over as he stared at us.

"Does he know you?" I whispered, as if speaking normally would insight a riot.

"Hi, Phoenix," Beckett greeted the man and then turned to me. "Yes, I know him. He's the sanest one here, believe it or not. The only one that always recognizes me and remembers my name. We come here occasionally to make sure that they have food, that everyone is still alive. The one thing that the Compound does is drop off shipments of food. We just monitor to make sure that they continue."

"But if you know they're here and you don't like that the Compound just left them here, why don't you take them back with you?" I asked. Beckett was so self-righteous all of the time, it was a bit shocking that he hadn't created some sort of facility to keep them in.

He shifted uncomfortably from one foot to the other. "Well, there are a couple of different reasons. In the Open, not everyone agrees on my assessment of their level of dangerousness. Some think that they are a threat and fear for their children if the Strung were brought back. They have been known to set random fires, occasionally lash out at one another. I would give it a try, but everyone else isn't willing to take the risk. The other reason is, for some reason they won't leave this area. If you try to lead them past a certain point, they start freaking out. Screaming, clawing at the earth to go back. I don't know what it is, but it's like they're bound to this place."

I was so ready to be able to find a fault in Beckett in his unwillingness to care for these clinically insane people, but not even this was at all his doing. He truly wanted to be the white knight all of the time, and he was doing the best he could by making his appearances however often he came to visit the Strung.

There was a man about twenty yards away who caught my attention. His back was to me, but when I squinted there was something familiar about him. I half walked, half jogged towards him and Beckett was at my side.

"What's the matter? Do you know him?" he asked.

"I don't know. I don't think so. It's just that he looks—," I stopped short when the man turned around as we approached him. "Professor Hunter! Beckett I thought you..."

The night that Beckett had whisked me away from the Compound in the helicopter, Professor Hunter had tried to stop us. Beckett had shot him. A lot had happened in the last few weeks, but of that I was positive. And here he was in front of me.

"I did shoot him," Beckett admitted. "But not with real bullets. In the Open, we don't kill unless there is no other choice. Hunter wasn't a real threat. I just needed to stop him from trying to keep you in the Compound."

I felt a rush of gratitude towards Beckett and gave him a kiss on the cheek. He was taken aback, but before he had the time to really react, I turned back to Hunter.

"Professor Hunter, it's me, Eloise," I said to him gently.

Hunter turned his head so that he was completely facing me. For a half a second, I thought that there was a spark of recognition, but he just stared at me blankly. His mouth was gaping open and he began to drool. It hung from the corner of his mouth, slowly creeping towards the ground until it broke off.

Saliva soon pooled again and begun to hang where the other had fallen. Hunter was just a shell of the man that he was before. He looked at me for just a brief second longer, and then shuffled a few paces away and stood idly in the new spot, staring into oblivion.

It pained me to see that my favorite teacher had become Strung. I had had enough.

I turned to Beckett to tell him that we should go, but the woman who had been playing in the dirt came up to us, startling me. She now had mud caked in the corners of her mouth, matted in her hair, in between her teeth, and caked underneath her fingernails. I thought of myself as a caring person, but at that moment I wasn't beneath wanting to run away from her.

The woman's eyes took on a gleeful glean. "They're coming!" She cackled. "They're coming, they're coming, they're coming!" She began clapping her hands loudly, dancing around laughing hysterically. The other Strung were suddenly restless, upset by the woman's noises. Some covered their ears with their hands, others began wailing along with the man hugging the tree. Some Strung began screaming and screeching as if they were being tortured.

"Time to go, Eloise," Beckett said as he grabbed my arm and tugged it. Our pace was quicker than it had been on our way in, and I sensed that he wasn't very concerned about how the Strung would react anymore.

"Who's coming? Does she know what's going on?" I asked worriedly.

"I don't know," Beckett sounded concerned. "But I'm not about to stick around and find out. As a matter of fact..."

He didn't finish his sentence. Instead he began to run, still clinging to my arm, forcing me to run with him. We sprinted a few city blocks away and then ducked behind a building. We stopped for a breather. Once again, I was hunched forward, hands on my knees. Beckett peeked around the corner towards the park. He flung his head back behind the building.

"We have to go," he said authoritatively.

"Can I just catch my breath first? Running isn't really my thing."

"No, Eloise, now. The Compound is here."

"What? But you said—"

"There's no time right now!" he commanded. He grabbed my arm again and we began to run in a different direction than we had come. "We have to get further out of sight before we can dart across. I want to look like ants to them, or like nothing at all on the horizon."

He pulled me along and I did my best to keep up, panting and wheezing. I looked back over my shoulder as we ran, and I could see white suits scattered among the Strung. Had they known we were there, or was it a regularly scheduled visit? Even as far as we were away, I could have sworn that one of them was looking in our direction. I snapped my head back around, and we ran until my lungs were on fire and I felt like I would collapse.

"Beckett....I can't," I gasped.

"Just a little further, Eloise. We're almost to the parking lot. Then you can rest the whole way back to Headquarters."

He wasn't exaggerating for my benefit. We reached the run-down supermarket thirty seconds later. Beckett unlocked the car and I threw myself inside, slamming the door behind me. I slumped in my seat and struggled for air as Beckett turned the car on and sped out of the lot. We weren't on a scenic tour anymore. We were fleeing. The car was speeding through the streets so fast that everything out my window was a blur. Between being out of breath and the movement of the car, I was feeling terribly nauseous, and there was no way Beckett was going to stop the car so that I could be sick.

I closed my eyes, put my head between my legs, and tried to concentrate on my breaths. In, out. In, out. When I felt better I sat up. At some point my breathing must have regulated, and I fell asleep. When I woke up, we were pulling safely into the gravelly driveway of Headquarters, Mad-Eye standing sentinel in front of the house.

I could tell that Beckett was breathing easier, being back, being surrounded by our allies and protectors. I rubbed sleep from my eyes and yawned as we got out of the car.

"Eloise," Mad-Eye greeted me and then turned to Beckett. "How'd it go? Any incidents?"

Beckett let out a sarcastic laugh. "I guess that depends on your definition of 'incident', but we made it back in one piece."

Mad-Eye didn't find Beckett's humor in the situation. I could see his shoulders stiffen and he had a serious glint in his eye. The pride and seriousness he took in his job shone through his every muscular movement.

"Tell me what happened," he demanded.

"I think it's a good time to have a meeting," Beckett suggested. Mad-Eye nodded at him and pulled out a walkie, barking commands into it. "El, you're welcome to join, but you kind of already know what's going on, so if you want to just go inside and find Rose or something..."

"That sounds like a good idea," I took him up on the offer as he trailed off. I had had enough of the Strung and close encounters with the Compound for one day. No need to relive it.

I climbed the stairs to the house, walked through the foyer, and sure enough, found Rose in the kitchen in full dinner-making mode.

"Hey, need some help?" I said from behind her. She jumped, putting a hand to her chest. "I'm sorry. I didn't mean to scare you."

Rose turned around, smiling. "It's okay, Eloise! I just didn't hear you come in. But sure, I could always use some help feeding the masses. Catch."

She tossed me an apron. I put it on, though I felt a little ridiculous. I certainly didn't have the domestic tendencies that she did. I walked over and stood next to Rose, waiting for directions.

"Is everything okay?" Rose asked. I realized that I was playing nervously with the necklace that I was wearing, and I had been dazing off a bit distractedly.

"Oh, yeah," I sighed. "Long day. What can I do?"

"Well," Rose started as she assessed the area. "If you could finish peeling these potatoes, I would be eternally grateful."

"Sure thing," I responded, thankful that she had given me an easy task, and also thankful that she didn't press me to talk about the day. Rose had a sixth sense for reading me. She smiled and then left me to my thoughts aside from the song she hummed as she worked.

I glanced over occasionally as I peeled the potatoes. I thought about how jealous I had been of her striking beauty when we first met and smirked to myself. There had been so many changes in the short time that had passed, but Rose's kindness and maternal way had not ebbed. Beckett had said he met Rose in the open, but as I watched her flit about the kitchen adding ingredients and adjusting pans, I couldn't help but wonder. For a girl who was supposed to be about my age, she behaved like quite an older soul. I had a feeling that the secrets weren't all aired yet, but maybe it wasn't Beckett's story to tell. Maybe Rose had a secret history all her own.

The next morning I awoke to what I thought was the sun flickering across my face. But then I remembered that there were no windows in the annex. I blinked and yawned. Beckett was sitting on the edge of the bed fiddling with a mirror by the light of the lamp.

"Were you trying to get me to wake up through Morse code?" I asked groggily.

"Sorry, did I wake you?" he asked. He was already fully dressed and appeared to have been awake for some time as his eyes were bright and ready. Part of me wondered if he ever slept.

I sat up on my elbows. "I suppose I must have been close to waking up anyways. What's going on?"

Normally he would have left me to sleep and went about his business until I woke up, but it looked like he was specifically waiting for me.

"I thought we could have some fun today," Beckett said with a smile. "Yesterday was a little rough, so I though today we'd just enjoy ourselves."

"And your idea of enjoying ourselves is getting up at the crack of dawn?" I asked, eyebrows raised and yawning again.

"Didn't you have a strict schedule or something in the Compound? I'd think you'd be used to getting up. And it's not the crack of dawn anyways. It's nine o'clock."

"Already?" I asked. Since I had been in the Open, I had felt unwaveringly tired all of the time. I always had enjoyed my sleep, but I couldn't seem to get enough lately.

Beckett nodded. "So get dressed and meet me downstairs."

Though I normally would be annoyed by his bossiness, there was a note of excitement in his voice that was contagious. I couldn't help but be curious myself about what he had planned. Knowing Beckett, we would have a detailed itinerary, which made things a little less loose, but as long as it didn't involve witnessing horrific past events, encounters with the Strung, or running away from the Compound, it pretty much had to be a good time. Or at least it would be compared to what one of our "normal" days looked like lately.

I threw on a pair of faded jeans, a t-shirt with the logo of a bygone sports team on it, and pristine white sneakers. I gathered my hair into my new staple high ponytail and braided it tightly. You never knew if Beckett's idea of "fun" and "relaxing" would involve some sort of physical activity, which in hindsight made the white sneakers a moot point. I was tempted to bring other various layers of clothing, just in case, but I assumed that Beckett would have told me had they been necessary.

After brushing my teeth and quickly applying a little makeup, I met Beckett in the kitchen where he was already eating.

"Sorry. Cou'n help m'self," he said through a mouthful of waffles. He swallowed. "Never know how long a girl is going to take to get ready, and these are too good to keep waiting."

I shook my head and rolled my eyes. Then I sat down with my own plate and heaped the waffles with maple syrup.

"Pretty sure that negates any nutritional value that those waffles once held," Beckett said.

"That's okay. I'm not going for nutritional value. I'm going for taste bud value," I said.

"Amen," Rose said as she walked in the room and gave me a high-five. "Grandpa over here should worry about his own nutrition. Oh, you've got a little syrup."

Rose dabbed at my face with a napkin.

"And you're calling me grandpa?" Beckett teased and Rose stuck out her tongue.

I laughed at them both. Maybe today *would* be a good day.

I had barely put the last forkful of waffle in my mouth when Beckett was already hopping off of his stool. He clapped his hands together and looked at me mischievously. "Time for an adventure."

"Let the girl chew," Rose clucked.

"She can chew on the road. No time to waste, Eloise! Let's go have some fun! Now."

Rose gave me a look that told me she was also used to Beckett's constant need to be in charge. "Good luck."

"Thanks. I have a feeling I'll need it," I said as I dabbed at my mouth with the napkin one last time, and then jogged to catch up with Beckett.

He strode to the car and immediately got into the driver's seat and started the engine. I thought it was just as likely for him to wait for me as it was for him to leave me in the dust. Whatever he had planned had him acting with even more of a sense of urgency than usual.

"What's the rush?" I asked, clicking my seatbelt into place as Beckett began driving.

"We have a bit of a drive again and I want to be able to enjoy as much of the day as possible. That's all I can tell you for now." He was grinning like a child about the secret he knew that I didn't. He was just about bursting with wanting to tell me, too.

I smirked at him. The sparkle in his eye was endearing, and it made all of his irritating qualities a little less irritating. I reminded myself that this whole day was about making me feel better. It was so easy to remember all of the things Beckett did to make me angry, but I had an easy time forgetting how much he had risked and given up for me. We can always list someone's faults before we attempt to acknowledge the good.

I fell asleep for a while, lulled by the movements of the car like a baby, and was then thankful for my lethargic behavior because the drive passed quickly. When I opened my eyes, the scenery had changed. The thick forests no longer lined the road, and the dewy, soil smell had been replaced with a distantly familiar scent that I couldn't put my finger on.

We were in a residential area, but the homes didn't look like they had in the neighborhood the day before. The outside was layered in shingles instead of siding, and there wasn't much lawn to speak of to imagine it would have ever been manicured. They were also up on stilts instead of flush to the ground, which was odd to me as I didn't remember seeing homes like that before. Some were clearly abandoned, overgrown and falling apart, whereas others looked slightly lived in. A bicycle that didn't look rotted leaned against one house, a pot of fresh flowers growing by another. I wondered if it was coincidence, squatters, or if there was a community of people living there like there had been in the Open. I remembered that – what seemed like ages ago already – Beckett had mentioned there being clusters of people living throughout the land. I wanted to ask if these people were an established group or if they were just trying to silently exist in the background. Part of me also wondered if I was seeing real time or if the more vibrant-looking houses were glimpses into the past. I squeezed my eyes shut and shook my head, not wanting to have any more experiences with times gone by nor *any* conversations with Beckett that would ruin our day.

As we kept driving on the main road, the air became thick and damp against my skin with the windows rolled down. It immediately made me feel like I needed another shower, but in a good way. I closed my eyes again and leaned my head back on the headrest, feeling the warmth of the sun on my skin and the moist air caress my face.

"Don't fall asleep on me now. We're almost there," Beckett's voice broke the silence.

"I'm not sleeping," I muttered dreamily. "I'm just enjoying."

I could almost feel Beckett smile at me through his lack of response, already taking pride that his day was going according to plan.

I felt the car shift, indicating that we were taking a turn. Two minutes later, there was another and then the car stopped.

"Here we are," Beckett said and hopped out of the car.

I opened my eyes and all I could see were piles of sand strewn with tall grasses and an old worn-down wood picket fence. We were parked in an abandoned parking lot. There was a building nearby labeled "Restrooms" to the left, and behind us there were a few businesses that had once serviced visitors. Most of the signs were so faded you couldn't read what they said, but it was clear that at one point you could get a glass of fresh lemonade, slices of pizza, and ice cream in twenty flavors. The doors were wide open, and there was scattered merchandise coming out of one door: broken chairs and umbrellas, bottles of lotion, toys.

I spun around and faced Beckett, the pieces of the puzzle clicking together. Now I could legitimately share his excitement. Without uttering a word, I sprinted towards the hole in between the mounds of sand and ran along the sandy path.

Before me lay a stretch of beach and beyond it the vast ocean. I had never actually been to the beach before having never left the walls of the Compound – not in this lifetime anyway. But I had seen videos and read about them in books, and there had been that nagging feeling that the smell had brought on, like I recognized it and didn't know why. The salty sea air filled my nostrils and I breathed deeply, welcoming its presence. I plopped down in the sand and spread out, creating a letter X with my body. Just as soon, I sat back up again and couldn't get my shoes off fast enough. I removed my socks and shoved my toes into the sand, wriggling them and letting the grains fill the spaces in between. Closing my eyes, I smiled. This was happiness. This was peace.

I didn't notice Beckett approach, but he dropped a bunch of stuff on the ground and sat down next to me.

"So did I do good?" he asked.

"You did good," I admitted. "Very good."

We sat there for a while, Beckett letting me soak up my second "first" experience by the ocean. It was hard to imagine there having been any sort of chaos, any malevolent behavior in that moment on the beach. It was so peaceful, listening to the waves roll onto the shore and a few birds squawk as they flew overhead. I burrowed my feet in the sand up to my ankles and breathed deeply again with my face upturned towards the sun. It was truly a little slice of heaven on earth.

"Let's stay here forever," I mused as I lie back down.

Beckett laughed. "That would be nice."

A thought occurred to me in my youthful ignorance. "Why couldn't we? We'll just fix up one of those nice little houses we drove by. We can hide out, do what we want without worrying about the Compound or the Alliance or any of it! Just spend our days enjoying life and relaxing on the beach. Think about it! You and me and no worries..."

I could see a flicker of emotion on Beckett's face, as if that was exactly the kind of life that he had always imagined, not just for himself, but for the two of us. But it was gone as quickly as it had come.

"El, it sounds great. Perfect even. But we have responsibilities, even if we'd rather not admit it. We have to make up for what we did before. We have to make sure history doesn't repeat itself, again. It wouldn't be right to just walk away from it all, from the people we care about, no matter how good it sounds right now. And plus, where would we get our food? Running water? Electricity? I'm not sure there's any of that out here. If there's anyone living here, they don't want us to know it. They're just existing, El. There's no safety in any form, food or otherwise. It just isn't possible for us right now, but maybe someday," Beckett said gently.

I could tell that it pained him to say it as much as it pained me to realize he was right. Beckett was chivalrous and selfless, and he wasn't going to walk away. Even if I felt like I would be able to do it without regret – and I did – I would never get him to agree to it. And what was I going to do? Live out here on my own? Try and make new friends? It wasn't sensible. It wasn't plausible.

I felt the surge of excitement fizzle out of me, causing me to feel glum in general. The realization that there seemed to be a never-ending sense of duty to the community wasn't a pleasant prospect. I might have been someone who had a civic responsibility before, but I wasn't that person anymore. I just wanted to be myself, not a shadow of a person that used to be.

Sensing the deflation, Beckett stood up. "But while we're here, we have loads of fun things to do. Come on."

He offered me his hand, which I accepted, and he pulled me to my feet. Either one or both of us had a bit more energy than expected, and we ended up face to face in an awkward way...again. I knew that Beckett wanted to kiss me, but I turned away. His face fell, and I was sure he didn't intend for me to see.

Beckett recovered quickly and said, "Race you to the water!"

The tide was out, so the water was about fifty yards away and I had enough ground to sprint. Obviously I normally loathed running, but when the wind was in my hair, the sand under my toes, and with no one chasing me, I felt so free. I ran with my arms extended out at my sides, taking in the warm, salty air. There was no annex, no walls of the Compound to box me in. Just the beauty of the nature around me, welcoming me. Even as my toes met the icy ocean water, I didn't feel the need to cringe or back away. This was what life was supposed to be: open land, open sea, quiet, peaceful.

I looked at Beckett beside me, staring out into the horizon and lost in his thoughts about a better world. I knew his perspective was honorable, selfless, and benevolent, and that he was trying to make up for the people we had been. But I didn't feel the sort of connection that he did. I didn't feel the need to throw myself in the midst of the chaos, to devote my life to making other people happy. I wanted time travel to stop. I wanted there to be no more suffering or violence, but I also wanted to isolate myself from the world. Find a little house in the middle of nowhere and not worry about time travel or government scandal or revolution. I wanted to leave that life behind and just be *me*. This version of me was the only one that I knew. Punishing myself for Old Eloise's actions would be like taking the blame for a completely different person. Call it cowardice or bravery or both, I didn't feel that it was my battle. I couldn't fix what was broken. Besides, I had already messed things up once. Who was to say I wouldn't do it again?

"What're you thinking about?" Beckett interrupted my thoughts.

"Nothing," I lied and smiled. He was the closest thing I had to an ally at that point. And I didn't know how much that said about my relationships considering he had kidnapped me and then told me about a double life and experiences with time travel. But I could call him a friend. And even still, I couldn't even tell him the truth about how I felt. Beckett was on a self-righteous journey to right wrongs, and it wasn't in his nature to just move on. It was a lonely thought that not one other person on the planet was completely on my side.

I took a couple of steps back – just far enough so that the water was out of reach – and plopped down in the sand. Beckett followed suit and thankfully didn't say a word.

Thoughts about being alone had dampened my mood. I recalled my supposed actions in the past. I had wanted to erase everything that I had been for the good of all, so I couldn't have liked myself very much in the end. And so I had planned to send myself to the future, to grow up in the Compound as a cog in a machine. There must have been some thought that there was a possibility everything we had done in time travel wouldn't be erased, no matter how hopeful I was for it to be otherwise. Did I think, in the event that history remained unchanged, that I was creating a better life for myself? Did I anticipate essentially being locked away and limited to one tiny piece of the world for my entire life? Did I think that was safe? A punishment? What purpose did I intend myself to serve as this new version? Would Old Eloise have wanted me to run away from it all, join the

Compound, or become a revolutionary leader? So many questions raced through my mind I began having stress palpitations. *So much for this day being fun*, I thought to myself.

As if reading my mind, Beckett leaned over and nudged me with his shoulder. "You don't look like you're having much fun."

I tried to think of an answer that would explain my disposition without causing an argument.

"I know, sorry. It's beautiful here. Peaceful. Quiet. Makes for a good environment to think," I smiled, trying to keep it light.

"That's what worries me, the thinking," Beckett said. "What is going on in El's head? That's what I'm left to think about. And we both know that's as big a mystery as any."

I nudged him back and smiled again. "I'm just thinking about...how small we are. You know, philosophizing. I've spent my whole life – well, *this* whole life – having no idea how big the world is. Sure, I've seen maps and movies and pictures, but it's really another story to experience it. Never mind the land, just look at this ocean. I know it doesn't, but it appears to go on forever. Just miles and miles of nature left to its own devices, its own secrets and mysteries. It just gets to be, without any disruption. I envy that. When you think about how many creatures and people have lived on this earth, the choices they've made and how they've affected one another, it gets a little overwhelming."

"I get that. I can't imagine the adjustment that it must be to have gone through the past couple weeks. But that's why it's all worth it, El. There's so much to be in awe of. Don't you want to keep it that way? To make sure that we're not the last ones that get to enjoy it? Our actions set off a chain of events that almost wiped out the human population. That's a pretty big 'oops'."

The conversation was teetering on the dangerous and precarious edge of friendly chatter and incendiary. Unlike Beckett, who was so set on his planned agenda of saving the world, I took the time to choose my words. I wasn't looking for a quarrel, not anymore. It was clear to me that we were of two different mindsets, and that was okay as long as we didn't have to talk about it.

"I know. We made a lot of mistakes and there were consequences. But look around you at this testament of survival. Humans have done so many things to each other and to the planet, but still it goes on. The clouds are above us in the blue sky, the sand on this beach is still nature's pillow, the ocean still a force to be reckoned with, a power to respect and admire. Isn't that something to celebrate?"

I wasn't sure how he was going to answer. I didn't completely oppose his views, but I wouldn't altogether give in to them for the sake of making peace either. There had to be a middle ground and I had to find it.

"Speaking of celebrating, we're supposed to be having fun! Do you want to go on a hunt for the perfect seashell first or play a game of Frisbee?"

Thankful that Beckett changed the subject, I chose to look for seashells. It would allow me some more quiet time to reflect on everything, or to think about nothing if I wanted to. We took a long walk at the water's edge collecting smooth rocks and intact shells, leaving the broken ones discarded on the sand. I couldn't help but think as I tossed the chipped pieces of seashells that were once whole, that they were so like the Strung, broken and unwanted. I shook the thought from my mind, focusing instead on the ones that had survived the weathering of the ocean.

We spent the remainder of our time at the beach that day not worrying about the future or the past. After our walk we ended up playing Frisbee, or at least attempting to play. I wasn't very good at aiming, and Beckett tried valiantly to chase down my erratic tosses to no avail. But we *laughed*, the kind of laugh that makes your stomach hurt and tears spring in your eyes, and it felt good.

He had packed us a picnic lunch. We spread an old blanket on the sand and ate sandwiches and fresh fruit. I learned quickly that it was nearly impossible to avoid crunching on some sand or eating wisps of my own hair in the process, but I couldn't be annoyed. We were being human, doing normal human things. There was no one to save, and we didn't need to be saved. I could try to teach Beckett to do a cartwheel or splash in the water without looking over my shoulder.

When Beckett looked at his watch and announced that we had to start driving if we wanted to be back before dark, I wanted to sulk and stomp like a toddler, refuse to leave. Why couldn't we have more than one day like that? I supposed, though, if we went on any sort of extended trip I would never want to go back. After one afternoon I was ready to abandon everything and everyone I had ever known, in the Compound and in the Open. I wasn't sure where exactly I belonged, but deep down I knew that I had to make a choice between the two. Becoming a lone ranger wasn't an option.

I helped Beckett pack up our toys and supplies, and we put them back into the trunk of the car. Then we drove back to Headquarters in silence, both of us already reminiscent of our carefree day. I was nervous and skeptical and confused about the path that lay ahead of me, and I didn't know if Beckett and I would continue on it together or separately, but I was grateful at least for that one day where all I had to worry about was a little grit when I was trying to eat my sandwich.

Our ride back was uneventful. When we pulled into the driveway, Mad-Eye was standing guard as usual. As soon as we had parked he began walking towards us.

"Everything go okay? See anything out of the ordinary?" he asked urgently.

"Nope, not a thing. Just a little fun in the sun," Beckett winked at me conspiratorily.

"You're sure?" Mad-Eye asked. "Were you paying attention?"

Beckett and I exchanged a confused look.

"Yeah, I'm sure. Why?" he asked.

Mad-Eye shook his head and looked around. "Something's not right. Something in the air. Something's wrong."

Beckett clapped him on the shoulder. "Don't worry, old friend. Nothing gets past you."

We walked back towards the house. It was clear that Beckett didn't pay much mind to Mad-Eye's warning, but I felt ill at ease.

"What was up with that?" I asked.

"Don't worry about him," Beckett shrugged. "He's a little paranoid sometimes. That's what makes him such a great head of security. No one is more alert or prepared. If anything was to happen, Mad-Eye would know before anyone. But he also always thinks something is about to happen, so you have to take what he says with a grain of salt."

"How do you tell the difference? If it's a serious threat or not?"

Beckett scratched his head with one hand as he opened the door with the other. "To tell the truth, nothing major has happened yet. But this isn't the first time Mad-Eye has been on high alert. So far it's all worked out."

"That doesn't sound like a very solid piece of evidence," I said skeptically. No matter what I might have spent the day debating, I wasn't ready to make a decision. And I didn't want the decision to be made for me.

"Maybe not," Beckett admitted, "but we'll cross that bridge when we come to it. If we have to."

I nodded and my stomach rumbled simultaneously. It didn't seem like lunch had been all that long ago, but considering the drive had to have been two hours in itself, a good chunk of time had to have passed.

"Judging by your angry stomach, I guess our first stop should be the kitchen," Beckett said.

"That's probably a good idea."

In the kitchen, Rose was spreading sauce over pizza dough and looking haggard.

"Yikes. You alright?" Beckett said. With all of his experience on the earth, he clearly still lacked the ability to choose his words carefully with women. I whacked his arm with the back of my hand.

"It's been a long day," Rose said tiredly, but still with a smile. "Mad-Eye is all uptight about who-knows-what. He's had us all doing security and perimeter checks all day. I've been running around the woods with everyone else making sure his imaginary assailants aren't there. Then I had to come back here and make sure I had dinner ready. Don't worry, I'm fine."

"Why don't you go relax?" I suggested. "I can take it from here."

Secretly, I was glad we were absent for Mad-Eye's directives, but I also felt too guilty to have had the day to myself and then stand and watch Rose work.

"Thanks," Rose said gratefully. "Normally I wouldn't say this, but I sure wouldn't mind putting my feet up."

"No problem," I smiled warmly at her.

She walked into the formal living room which was nearby, and when Beckett went to check on her a few minutes later, she was sound asleep in an armchair.

"She's earned it," I said to Beckett. "I don't know how she's always full of so much energy. It's bound to catch up with her at some point."

Beckett helped me finish putting toppings on the eight pizzas and begin to put them in the oven. I was glad Rose had picked something simple to make that day so that I could handle it. While old skills might be slowly coming back to me, never having to cook for myself definitely affected my performance in the kitchen.

We were just sitting down at the island and Beckett was talking about teaching me how to cook a mean omelet when we heard loud footsteps come padding towards us.

Mad-Eye came storming into the room at full speed, strands of his black hair in his eyes which were wild.

"WHAT ARE YOU DOING HERE?" he bellowed.

Beckett looked like a frightened school boy. "What?"

"WHERE'S YOUR DAMNED WALKIE? THE COMPOUND HAS BREACHED! YOU NEED TO GET HER OUT OF HERE, NOW!"

I tried hard to swallow the lump in my throat. Was this for real?

"Mad-Eye, slow down," Beckett said calmly as he felt for the walkie that was missing from his back pocket. It must have been with the gear in the trunk of the car. "Are you sure?"

"We don't have time to slow down!" he growled. "I walkied you fifteen minutes ago! I don't know where they came from, but they've got the whole road blocked in both directions about a mile down the road. Spotters just reported to me, they're coming on foot. Probably trying to take us by surprise. Move!"

"Eloise, get to the annex and go," Beckett commanded.

"Knew something wasn't right," Mad-Eye mumbled.

"But aren't you coming with me?" I asked, panicked. Everything had happened so fast. We must have just missed the

Compound soldiers when we were on the road. Had they been watching us? Did they see us come back?

"I'll be right behind you, but you need to go now," Beckett said impatiently.

"But—"

"Eloise, NOW!" Mad-Eye and Beckett said together.

I clenched my teeth and my fists, stubbornly stared at them for a moment longer, and then turned around and began to run to the stairs.

"Go right, Eloise! Stay away from the road!" Mad-Eye called after me. "BE SAFE!"

What a bizarre day, I thought to myself as I took the main staircase two stairs at a time. Just a short time ago I was playing a game on the beach and collecting shells. I felt for the collection I still had in my pocket, a reminder of a short-lived happiness that was too good to be true.

This is it. It's actually happening.

I reached the annex bookcase, entered and locked the first door. Then I closed and locked the inner door as well, just like I had been instructed to do. I stood for a moment in the annex by myself and considered just staying there. I mean who really knew anything about it? I could just wait it out. The Compound most likely wouldn't gain any ground anyway, and I'd just be wandering around in the woods by myself for no reason. The way I saw it, I had a better chance of staying safe if I just waited it out. Eventually Beckett would have to come this way, and then we'd either leave together or there would be no need.

But then I heard the first gunshot and realized that maybe I wasn't taking the situation seriously enough. I panicked, wondering if they were real guns or not, wondering if anyone I cared about had been struck. I could have run back towards the fracas. My instincts told me not to abandon the Alliance; instead, I should be joining them. Just because I hadn't committed to a particular side yet didn't mean I thought what the Compound was doing was right. But then I thought of how everything that had been done, had been done, at some level, for me. I had no training. I hadn't sat in on any meetings and didn't know any of the plans if something like this were to happen. The truth was, I could put more people in danger by staying than if I followed orders like I was supposed to.

Torn in half, I retreated to the chute. Before I could think any further, I slipped my legs in first and then pushed off. I didn't have the wherewithal to be afraid of the small space. My fears had a new home. I landed with a dull *thud*. Instinctively I walked over to the wall where the go-bag should be, but it wasn't there. Had we forgotten to put it back after our last excursion? It didn't seem like Beckett to forget something like that, but no one is perfect. I quickly scanned the room, but as it was empty there weren't many places for the backpack to be hiding. Knowing there was nothing I could do about it, I decided to just keep on going. What was the chance of me getting stuck in the woods and needing supplies? A very slim one, I hoped.

I walked the tunnel at a brisk pace instead of a run. I could hear Beckett telling me to move it in my head, but nothing or no one was chasing me. I would conserve my energy until I needed it. It certainly was helpful to move without all of that extra weight on my back, and I was almost grateful that the go-bag was missing. I just hoped that I wouldn't pay for it later.

Time passed slowly and the tunnel seemed to have tripled in length since the last time I had walked it. I supposed that without a companion any journey seemed more tedious.

All was quiet behind me as well as ahead of me, and it was eating at my very core that I didn't know what was going on above ground. Where were Beckett, Mad-Eye and Rose? What about all of the other Alliance members that I could never remember the names of? Had they driven the Compound back or were they inside my house? (It was still technically my house, I thought, since it had been mine originally.) Was it all over? Had it just begun? Who was going to be waiting for me on the other side of the hatch? The Compound, the Alliance, or no one?

What would my reaction be to whoever *was* waiting for me, if anyone? Did I want the Compound to find me so that everyone from Headquarters could go back to their own lives instead of worrying about me? Did I just want to get back to *my* old life and forget all of this ever happened? Did I want the Alliance to be there, to have time for them to teach me the ropes- how to really be able to fight for the next time? I didn't have a sure answer to a single question.

Luckily, or maybe unluckily, I had reached the end of the tunnel and didn't have time to ask myself any more questions or attempt to answer the ones I had already asked. I paused and listened, hoping that my hearing would be keen enough to determine if someone was on the other side. Even if there was someone there, what would I do? There was only one way out. I had no food, no water, no anything. Waiting the siege out in the tunnel wasn't an option.

I crept as quietly as possible up the stairs. I sat and listened for any sign of life on the other side of the hatch for what seemed like a good ten minutes. For all I know it could have been three.

It is difficult to keep a sense of time in emergency situations. Settling on the fact that there was no one there, I gathered my courage and worked myself up to opening the hatch. *On the count of three,* I told myself. *One…two…three!* I thrust my body upwards, leading with my shoulder, and crashed into it. It didn't budge because I had forgotten to unlock it. If stealth mode had worked for me so far, the jig was up if anyone was nearby.

Knowing I had blown my cover, I unlocked the hatch and opened it without much ceremony. When I peered 360 degrees around the perimeter of the opening, I realized that there was no one around. Or if they were, they were completely covered by shrubbery and didn't want me to see them just yet. I climbed out into the open air and took a deep breath. Though I hadn't been focusing on the claustrophobia, I could feel my body slightly relax being above ground again.

You don't have time to relax! I reminded myself.

Mad-Eye had told us that the road had been commandeered by the Compound, and he had yelled after me to go to the right. I began walking diagonally to the right. The problem was that that was the one direction we hadn't practiced walking, and I hadn't paid very close attention to the directions Beckett had been given about the secret clues to follow to ensure I was going in exactly the right direction. For the first time in my life, I wished I had been a better pupil.

I tried to follow what looked like an unmarked path. One thing I did know was that you could tell when humans consistently traveled in the same direction; the grass or dirt would be packed down, there would be snapped twigs and branches to create spaces wide enough for a body to walk through. I really wished that I had the compass in the go-bag. At least then I would know if I was walking in a straight line. Instead I just had to hope that by some miracle I went in the right direction without being caught.

Never having spent much time in the real outdoors, I was suddenly aware of all of nature's noises as I walked. Flies buzzing by would cause me to slap at my own ear if they got too close. In the damper spots I had to swat away mosquitoes. I scared myself half to death every time I stepped on a twig and cracked it, jumping in fear that someone was behind me or about to jump out from behind a bush. There were other critter noises besides the birds singing songs, and I hoped that they were all smaller than I was. Had Beckett mentioned anything about bears?

Beckett. What was going on? Was everyone okay? Was it over? I hated the not knowing, so much so that I didn't even feel the scrapes that were collecting on my legs as I carelessly brushed past countless tree branches or picker bushes. It was dark around me for still being daytime, though I supposed that the light would fade soon. The woods were packed so tightly that only crevices allowed sunlight to reach the floor.

If it was over, wouldn't I have run into someone by now? Isn't there supposed to be a whole crew that would be on the lookout for me in this situation, if the Compound lost and retreated?

Lost in self-centered thoughts, I almost walked straight into what appeared to be a large bush or small tree. After instinctively wiping at my face for any stray insects or leaf parts, I realized that I was actually looking at something familiar. The way the branches had been placed *should* have looked natural to the average person, but the particular array in front of me looked awfully similar to the two that Beckett had shown me. Gently, I unwove the branches to see if there was anything hiding behind the curtain. There, in front of me, was a human sized space burrowed into the ground. It must have been deeper and wider than it looked, or at least I hoped for my own sake.

I had actually found the third hiding spot, all on my own! I wanted to whoop for joy aloud, but caught myself at the last second. I would have been pretty angry if I alerted anyone to where I was after all of that. I climbed over the branches to the other side and rearranged them like Beckett had shown me. Then I looked hesitantly at the space I was supposed to climb in to hide. I had made it this far without incident. Did I really have to climb in there? There wasn't even anyone around. Who would be the wiser if I didn't?

Though tempted – as usual – to disobey the command I had been given, I could see Beckett's irritation in my mind and decided that I might as well see the whole thing through the right way. *Please don't let there be a snake*, I cringed as I gingerly arranged my body in the small cave.

I sat in the cramped space and waited. I became finely attuned to the sounds of the forest again, no longer frightened by a stray leaf that might be blowing by. A squirrel scampered across the ground here and there, and birds continued to chirp cheerful melodies. Once I thought I heard something slithering, but I concluded that it was my imagination. I never did see a snake so I couldn't confirm otherwise. It became clear that there were a lot of normal rustling noises, as the day was a bit breezy, so I began to calm down more and more with each passing sound.

Suddenly, there was a louder crunch that sounded like a footstep. I froze and my ears perked up. A pause, then another crunch. The noise had definitely come from either a human or a large animal and I winced. I was pretty sure that if it was someone from Headquarters, they would have identified themselves by that point. Another crunch, closer than before.

My heart began pounding in my chest, and I tried to think about what I could possibly do if it was someone from the Compound lurking outside my little cave. With my eyes adjusted to the dim light, I looked around the small amount of space for something I could use as a weapon. All there was in sight was a small stick and a couple of pebbles. I felt like I was breathing so loudly that the whole forest could hear me.

The crunching continued right outside of the bushes that I had thought I made unnoticeable. I clapped my hand silently over my mouth, trying to prevent any accidental sound from coming out. The branches began to rustle, and I wondered if I should scream. Someone from Headquarters could be out there looking for me and would hear the alert. A face emerged through the branches.

"Alistair!" I said relieved as my heart returned to my chest. "I thought you were someone else."

"I was starting to think I had the wrong spot. I haven't been out here in a while," he replied with a devilish grin.

Offering me his hands, he helped pull me out of my burrow and the bushes.

"I'm so glad to see you. I wouldn't have lasted very long in there. Roughing it isn't really my thing."

Al looked at me with a strangely satisfied expression.

"She's over here," he said to someone I couldn't see. "I found her."

I could feel my face brighten. That was quick! Beckett? Mad-Eye? Rose? Rescued. We could get back to our own version of normal.

I heard some more rustling coming from several different directions and then a person was standing in front of me. Expecting the dark, camouflage colors that the Alliance wore, I was confused when a body clad all in white emerged, contrasting sharply with the darkening woods around me. I didn't recognize the face of the person, which didn't bother me at first because it felt like I saw someone new every day in Headquarters. At first, I thought that the newbie was just a fan of white. But then I remembered the day before as I had looked back at the Strung with the Compound bearing down on them.

It suddenly clicked that the person in front of me was no member of the Alliance. This was someone from the Compound. But why would Alistair be with someone from the Compound? I looked at him, searching his face for answers, but the statuesque features that I had once appreciated seemed nothing but cold marble. I started to back away from them, not sure where to run, but I bumped into something. I turned around and was face-to-face with another white-clad figure. My eyes darted in every direction. They had formed a circle around me. I was in full panic mode. My heart was a bass drum in my chest again, my breathing pattern was elevated, and I couldn't put together a single coherent thought. I looked around the circle for the weakest link. Standing still for a minute, I tried to make myself look like I was about to surrender, and then I bolted towards the smallest person.

But they were too fast. Three of them had grabbed me before I even reached the poor petite woman, also in white. I began to scream, for Beckett, for anyone to help. They wrestled me to the ground. I felt a sharp pinch in my arm.

I vaguely remember hearing someone say through the fog, "It's okay, Eloise. You're going home now."

And then everything went black.

When I woke up, I was disoriented. It took a minute for my eyes to regain focus and take in my surroundings. My brain was still expecting to see the walls of the annex, but instead there were four clinical-looking white walls surrounding me. I was on my back in a bed with starched white sheets. There was nothing else in the room, not even a window. The door was shut. I knew better than to hope that it was unlocked, but my instinct was once again to escape. I sat up quickly in bed and a wave of nausea rolled over me. My vision went spotty and black for a moment and then recovered just as quickly. Sudden movements were out of the question. That was going to make a swift getaway virtually impossible.

Tentatively, I stood up. Once I knew that I had my balance and there was no fear of keeling over, I walked the few steps to the door. The room was actually slightly bigger than the annex, but since it lacked any homey touches, it felt more claustrophobic.

I turned the metal knob and was surprised when it clicked open and the door swung in towards me. *That was way too easy*, I thought to myself. I peeked into the hallway and saw no one. It wasn't possible that they would leave me unattended when they knew I wanted to escape. Then again, how *would* I know how to get out of the Compound, so what was there to worry about? The only way I knew of was by helicopter through a broken window, and I wasn't so sure that anyone would be able to swoop in and save me this time. Nevertheless, I had to try to get out of there, wherever 'there' was. For all I knew, I wasn't even in the

Compound. Maybe they had taken me to a completely different secret facility until they figured out what to do with me.

I had a choice to either go left or right down the white hallway outside of my room. For some reason, left made me think of an exit. I tiptoed down the hallway, stopping every few feet to listen for human noise. It was as if the place was devoid of all sound except for my heavy breathing as I nervously crept down the hallway. I began to pass other open doors, but the rooms were completely empty, not even a bed to fill any space. It reminded me uncannily of the physics wing where my parents worked, except those rooms had been full of scientists, equipment, experimental matter. A violent and frightening thought occurred to me. Would they have done away with all of the physicists after they figured out Mildred and Barnum couldn't be trusted? Had they sent me here first to teach me a lesson about what happens when someone betrays the Compound? I walked faster, desperate to find some sort of answer. If this was the reaction they were hoping to create, they were getting just what they wanted.

At the end of the hallway was a metal door – of course, painted white – with a single panel of window. I pushed through it so quickly I didn't stop to look through the window to see what was beyond the door before I entered. It opened into a room shaped like a hexagon, with a door on each side. One of them was propped slightly open and light was coming through. I crept quietly towards it and peered in through the crack. I could see two people sitting in high-backed leather swivel chairs, and the backs of their heads looked like Mildred and Barnum.

"Mom! Dad!" I said as I burst through the door without a another thought.

The two people turned around, both peering over the tops of their glasses. Neither face belonged to my beloved parents. Before I could register anything else, someone else in the room cleared her throat.

"Hello, Eloise. I see you've woken up."

I turned to my right and saw Eleanora Blake standing there, with her bob looking freshly cut. I hadn't noticed her right away, probably because dressed in white from head to toe, she blended in with the walls. I turned to run back the way I had come – I didn't know where to, but away from her – but two beefy looking men were standing in my way.

"Now, now, dear. There's no need to make a scene. There's nowhere for you to run. And besides, why would you want to? You're home," said Eleanora with a voice like satin and poison.

Alistair stood next to her.

"You bastard!" I yelled and lunged for him. The two men grabbed my arms and prevented me from launching my attack.

Eleanora turned to Al. "You've done well, thank you. Now you see that she is safe. You may go."

I struggled against the grip of the men as he passed by and left with a satisfied smile. When the door closed, I was released and Eleanora stood staring at me.

"What are you going to do with him?" I asked.

"Nothing. He will return to the Open and continue the life that he already had," she replied.

"You're lying."

"I'm not. Alistair came to us willingly with information about you. That is why we had a few close calls before we were actually able to secure you."

"Why would he do that?" I asked, the sting of betrayal still smarting.

"That, perhaps, is a question that you should ask him. But since our young, pathetic friend is being escorted out, I will tell you. Alistair craved to be a leader, but he did not possess the charisma or the intelligence no matter how hard he tried to rise up above your Beckett. When you arrived in the Open, he saw you as an opportunity, a stepping stool if you will, to become something more. When you denied him, he decided that he had had enough of living in the Open. So he sought out my soldiers and leaked information of your whereabouts in hopes that he would find a new life in the Compound. But of course that would never do, so we are bringing him back to where he came from. He will resume the life he already had, unharmed, except for maybe his ego once again."

Her account of Alistair seemed accurate when I thought about his behavior. The conversation left a bitter taste in my mouth.

"So, this is the Compound?" I asked, changing the subject.

"Naturally. Where else would we be?" she said rhetorically and clicked her heels a few steps in my direction. Immediately, I backed up into my muscular new friends. Eleanora rolled her eyes dramatically and put a hand on her hip. She gestured towards a chair. "Please, have a seat."

I stood firmly in place.

"I insist," she smiled hostilely through gritted teeth. When I still didn't move, she gestured towards the two men who reached to grab me by the arms.

Without delay, I stomped on the foot of the one on the left, causing him to lean slightly forward, just enough so that I could make sharp contact with his nose with my elbow. Not expecting it, the full force of my insignificant arm connected with his face, and blood started pouring out of his nose. I tried to take advantage of his moment of weakness and work on the other one, but I had lost the element of surprise. And unlike Beckett, he didn't seem to care much that he was injured. He grabbed my arm more forcefully, and with the help of the second man, forced me into the seat.

Eleanora clicked a few buttons on a control panel that had appeared, and metal straps fastened on my arms, which were resting on the chair, and around my calves.

"Merely a precaution," Eleanora purred. "Everyone else, you may leave now."

The brawny men, the man and woman who had been sitting in the swivel chairs, and another woman who had been busy on a computer all left the room. It was just me and Eleanora.

"We need to have a little chat, girl to girl," she continued. "You see, Eloise, you've put me in quite a difficult predicament here. Or at least your friends have. I assume that you are now aware of your position in this community?"

I stared at her, tight-lipped.

"Please, don't make this any more time-consuming than it needs to be. I have an appointment in the spa sector at noon," she said. When I still didn't answer, she added hastily, "I also have your parents readily available, and if you cooperate you may see them."

I was sure she could see the flicker of interest cross my face. I would never be good at hiding my emotions.

"Yes," I answered reluctantly.

"The question is, dear, just how much of it was the truth. I'm sure you've been told whatever suited the initiative of – what do they call themselves now?- the Alliance. Ah, such a cute little name. But I can also be sure that most of it has been exaggerated. Why don't you give me a little summary of what you've learned so that we can all be on the same page?"

I clenched my jaw. I didn't want to tell her anything, but I also needed to know that my parents were okay. I wanted to see them, hear their voices....just to know that they were alive.

"I lived another life in the past as a physicist and experimented with time travel. The results were catastrophic, which in turn resulted in the building of the Compound. My infant self was extracted from the past and sent here in an attempt to undo all that had been done by traveling," I said curtly.

"Well done," Eleanora clapped gleefully, as if I were a toddler that required praise for putting toys away. "I'm quite surprised that there were no negative inserts about the Compound."

"Well, you know, I figured discussing how evil it is to keep secrets about the real world from the rest of the community, to keep them boxed in and oblivious, wouldn't really help the conversation....*dear*."

She tried to disguise her sneer with an actual smile, but apparently Eleanora wasn't very good at hiding her feelings either.

"You're more cynical than I remember. Has the Open made you sarcastic or has it just escaped me all this time?"

I sighed and went to cross my arms, but then remembered I wasn't able, so instead I just looked away from her. I might have been restrained, but she was testing my patience.

"Very well, that's neither here nor there. The truth is, Eloise, I want to be friends. If we work together we can accomplish great things. I know we've gotten off to a rocky start, but I'm sure that if we discuss everything together, we can arrive at a mutual conclusion."

"That conclusion being me taking part in time traveling again," I said sourly.

"Yes, that is a means to a very important end, but you seem to already have your mind made up. Tell me why so I can try to change it."

I rolled my tongue around my mouth and bit my lip, stalling. Did I stand to lose anything by telling the truth?

"I've seen what it looks like out there. The cemeteries, the empty homes, the Strung with their broken minds. I've even been able to glimpse into the past and witness some beautiful and horrible things. People died because of the choices I made. The world was thrown into chaos because of the choices I made. I don't want to be a part of that again. We have to stop repeating history. It never works out. Never," I said.

"What if I could guarantee you that history wouldn't repeat itself? What if you would only do good with your actions? Wouldn't it be worth it to save lives or to at least change them for the better? We've studied this branch of physics in much more depth now than you ever had before. We have more knowledge about the worm holes and the appropriate travel measures to proceed with. There is a much smaller margin of error now. It's safe, Eloise."

"How could you guarantee that history wouldn't repeat itself?" I scoffed. "And in all of this new research you've been doing, you've clearly been sending Stringers on travels since there's a population of Strung living out there. What about them? You think it's just okay to discard them like garbage? These are *human beings* we are talking about. How many lives have you destroyed for the sake of your experiments?"

I could feel the heat rising in my ears, my voice getting louder. I felt more passionately about stopping time travel than I thought. Did that mean that I wholly agreed with Beckett?

"The Strung are a tragic group, no doubt," Eleanora said as she actually tried to look convincingly saddened by it. "But those people were not forced to travel. They chose to. Those members of our community were volunteers. They knew the consequences going into it. We even had them sign nondisclosure agreements that listed the possible side effects in detail. I can show them to you if you want proof. And if you've seen them, you know they are unpredictable. I can't endanger the general population by welcoming them back into the Compound once they're Strung. It's part of the agreement, and they know that."

That put a new perspective on things. That many people were really willing to risk their entire lives for the sake of gaining some kind of information through time traveling? Were they thrill seekers who thought it was all a game and had 'not me' mentalities about becoming Strung? Or were they truly zealous about scientific discovery? If people were signing up to be Stringers, I couldn't blame anyone for the result. A conscious choice is a conscious choice. It might not be one that I would make, but those people were entitled to making their own decisions about their own fates.

"What is the purpose of traveling at this point? You have a perfect, secure little life inside the walls of the Compound. This community is completely self-sufficient. The horrors of the past are over. For the most part, the Open appears to be safe. Why can't you focus your energies on making connections with other communities? Time traveling doesn't have to be the answer," I insisted.

"Ah, but that's where you fall short, dea- Eloise," said Eleanora, catching herself before using her condescending pet name. "The Compound has existed for as long as it has and that is a miracle in itself. You protected us with this structure for many years and I think it's safe to say that we are all grateful for that. But we are outgrowing our space here. Our people continue to reproduce, causing the population to rise, and eventually this place we call home will become too small. We cannot hide behind these walls forever, but we also cannot predict what lies ahead. Continuing to time travel when necessary ensures the safety of all of us, in the Compound and in the Open. Humans are very unpredictable, Eloise. They cannot be trusted. I fear that if we do not travel, history *will* repeat itself eventually, not the other way around."

For the first time since I had met her, Eleanora sounded genuine. I was starting to understand her perspective, though I wasn't sure that I necessarily agreed with it. I believed that she really felt continuing time travel would be a way to assure that wrongs would be righted. In her mind, she was planning for the future of a community that she felt a duty to protect. That was more than I could say for Old Eloise, who initially made decisions driven by a selfish desire to obtain some sort of glory.

"How did you know I was the Harp?" I asked. Who would think to single out a sixteen year old girl out of all the people who lived in the Compound? Had they conducted some secret blood test on me during my regularly scheduled physical that I didn't know about? "Do you test everyone for their ability to travel?"

Eleanora smiled, warmly. She seemed more at ease with me cooperating. "Well, yes, of course. It is one of the initial tests we run when babies are born, along with all of the other genetic abnormalities that we look for. But you, Eloise, were a different story. You see, right now we are in a section of the Compound that most people don't even know exist. There is a very short list of people who are allowed down here due to more sensitive subjects and documents that we cannot just make privy to everyone. This, too, was a part of your own design. I must say, you were a very thorough person, because you even kept a file on yourself. As Head of the Council, I have access to that information. I've known about you from the moment Barnum and Mildred mysteriously brought you home after a travel. I probably know more about you than you know about yourself, truthfully. I presume you left the document for yourself, or perhaps it was a careless error, but nonetheless it has proved valuable information."

"If you've known about it all this time, why didn't you do anything about it?" I was truly engaged, curious about why this woman had kept such a secret if she had intended me to travel from the very beginning. Why did she let me parents carry on with their façade if she knew it was just a masquerade?

"You were just a child, Eloise. You're still just a child as far as I'm concerned. I wanted to tell you when the time was right so that you would be able to make an informed decision as an adult. You needed to grow up first, to make your own choices. I didn't anticipate things turning out this way, with me having to defend myself and my beliefs instead of sharing them with you over a cup of tea. But these are the cards that we have been dealt, and so we need to learn to trust each other. I'm still not asking you to travel right now. I want you to return to your studies, to learn how to be yourself. You cannot be expected to be the Eloise that you once were. You are not her. You cannot be her. But I want you to be on my side, to give yourself time to grow and understand. I know that you *would* eventually understand. We don't need to be enemies," she concluded.

Freshly confused, I didn't know what to make of this new information. I had walked into the room with Eleanora as a villain, and now she seemed much less intimidating or dangerous. The fact that she had allowed me to live my life like a normal person without telling me about my gruesome past spoke to me about her character. But what if I "grew up" and decided that I still didn't want anything to do with time traveling? What would happen then?

"What if I don't want to?" I asked.

Eleanora shrugged, which momentarily struck me as slightly comical as she was always so prim and proper. "I hadn't really anticipated that as being a problem. I've always thought that once you knew the truth, or once you understood the way that we have made time travel work now, you wouldn't have any objection."

The two of us sat in a stalemate of silence. I knew Eleanora was waiting for me to agree to be her golden girl, but I couldn't commit to something that I knew nothing about. And what if she was lying to me about everything? What if they were just going to keep me locked away in the Compound for the rest of my life? What would it be like to never know the freedom of the Open again? To feel the natural wind in my hair instead of one produced by climate control? What if I decided not to travel? Would they force me to anyway? I believed that Eleanora thought she was acting for the good of the people, but I also believed that she would do just about anything to get her way.

Moments kept passing without either one of us saying anything. Finally, Eleanora pressed a button and said into the air, "Bring in the boy. And rooms one and two as well."

She said nothing else to me. Eleanora just stared at the door, waiting for someone to walk in.

I heard the door click, but being strapped down I couldn't turn around to look and see who it was. Whoever it was did not want to cooperate. Sneakers squeaked on the waxed floors, like they were being dragged instead of taking steps. Musclemen one and two from earlier dragged the figure in front of me, still holding him solidly on each side.

"Beckett!" I exclaimed with relief. I had had no idea if he had survived the ambush. There was what looked like a muzzle for humans on his mouth.

"You can remove the silencer," Eleanora instructed the one with gauze up his nose. The man appeared to type a code into the blank space on the front, and then removed the silencer gingerly, as if he was afraid Beckett would bite. He probably had already tried.

"Is that your work?" he gestured with his head towards the gauze. I smirked and nodded. "Don't worry, dude, I've been there before. It'll heal."

It continued to amaze me how he could switch modes so easily. He had been a bit of an old soul version of himself with me lately, but when he talked like that, he could easily pass for a first-time teenager.

"Eloise, the boy – the man? It's really difficult to know what to call him- anyway, *Beckett* can stay if you want him to. There's one promise I make if you will return to your classes and your life here," Eleanora said.

Beckett and I looked at each other. I knew that there was no way he would agree to that, not even for me. Or if he did, he would sabotage the Compound at the first chance he got. He'd have the Alliance attempting a complete takeover. But besides that, I didn't know that I wanted to commit to something like that. Beckett and I had a history, but while his flame was freshly ignited, I wasn't sure if I even had a spark. How could I face dragging Beckett into a life in the Compound when I wasn't even sure that I could even offer myself to him the way that he would have wanted? I couldn't ask him to give up everything that he knew and believed in for something that was so unsure.

The door clicked again and I heard two sets of feet shuffle in. My parents appeared in front of me, whole and alive.

I smiled at them, unsure of what to say. Now that I knew they weren't actually my parents, was I supposed to call them Mildred and Barnum? Nothing would change the love that I felt, but maybe they considered me a burden after everything that had happened in the past few weeks. After the dream I had, I wondered if they had regretted going through all of the trouble of bringing me from the past.

"Eloise," my dad – Barnum – said to me, smiling. Mom had tears in her eyes, tears of joy, it appeared. Their expressions betrayed that their love had not faltered either.

"Hi. Are you okay?" was all I could manage.

"We're just fine, sweetheart," my mom sniffled.

"Just as I promised," Eleanora butted in. "And though their actions could be considered treason, I will allow them to stay in the Compound as well if you choose to stay. If not, they will have to go before a jury and their fate will be decided for them. I am not trying to bully you, Eloise, but I want you to be aware of the possible consequences of your actions. We have rules in the Compound and we will stick to them."

"But you've known all this time that I wasn't….who they said I was!" I couldn't say that I wasn't their real daughter, not aloud. The sting would hurt both them and me. "Doesn't that make you a party to their supposed crime?"

"Nice try, Eloise, but no," she said, back to being an ice queen.

"Eloise, don't listen to her," Beckett said. "Whatever she's told you, you have to assume it's a lie. She's going to make you do whatever she wants, no matter what. You don't want to stay here. You'll be trapped here forever."

"We're on your side, no matter what you decide," Dad said.

My heart ached, the three of them standing before me, waiting for me to make a decision. No matter who I had been or how old I had been before, I was a teenager. I couldn't decide the rest of my life, just like that. Neither option sounded like it would make me completely happy. My experiences in the Open had given me new insight, but I needed more than a couple of weeks or a couple of minutes to make that kind of choice.

"You're asking a lot from me right now," I admitted. "All of you. Mom, Dad, I could never imagine anything bad happening to you because of me. I couldn't live with that. Beckett, you were right when you said you saved me. The truth was, though, that you didn't save me from the Compound. You saved me from myself. All of this happened because of me. And Eleanora, you're not a very easy person to like or to trust. And maybe that was out of your control, but I can't tell you that I'm going to want to travel in ten years from now if I stay. I'm still figuring out who I am, just like you said I should. And right now, I don't want anything to do with any of it. I just want to be myself. I don't want to have that kind of responsibility, not now, maybe not ever. I can't give any of you the answer that you want. I'm sorry."

My parents nodded at me. Beckett looked crestfallen. But Eleanora looked contemplative.

"Eloise, I respect what you have said and I agree that this is a lot to ask you to do right now, in this moment," she finally said.

I breathed a sigh of relief. She wasn't evil after all. And maybe there was no easy decision for anyone. Eleanora was doing what she thought best by continuing her research and experimentation with time travel. Beckett was doing what he thought best by trying to stop the time traveling completely, and my parents had done what they thought was best by agreeing to bring me to the Compound as a baby. The world wasn't black and white. There was no clean-cut line between good and evil. People were just people, making decisions and trying not to mess things up.

Eleanora sat with her hands clasped prayer-like under her chin like the first day that I had met her, deep in thought. She looked from me, to my parents, to Beckett, as if she was trying to decide what to do with all of us. I assumed she would let my parents and I go back to our apartment and continue on with our lives, and she would allow me to ask questions and take the time to make a decision when I got older. Beckett would go back to the Open and be their leader, their protector, and do what he did best. Maybe he would come and visit me sometimes. Maybe this would even create new ties between the Compound and the Open.

"I respect what you have said, Eloise, but I'm afraid it's just not the answer that I was hoping for," Eleanora sighed and continued. "I was really hoping to avoid this, but unfortunately I don't think that you will be able to truly understand without it."

My stomach was suddenly in knots. What was she talking about?

Beckett began to struggle against the musclemen. "What are you saying?"

Eleanora pressed a button and the mousy woman who had been working on the computer came back in.

Then she looked me dead in the eye and said, "Send her back."

I had enough time to see Beckett pale in horror before the woman typed something into her computer, and my chair glided swiftly backwards and then to the right. A glass casing came out of the ceiling and sealed me shut, away from the others.

My parents were crying.

I could see Beckett trying with all his might to injure the bodybuilders and his muffled screams came just audibly through the glass as his face turned violent shades of red. "NO! NOOOOOOO! NO, DON'T YOU DO IT! DON'T YOU SEND HER! I'll KILL YOU! NO! NO! I'LL FIND YOU ELOISE! I'll FIND YOU! DON'T YOU PUSH THAT BUTTON! I SWEAR, DON'T YOU PUSH THAT BUTTON!"

Eleanora and I made eye contact one more time as I realized exactly what she had meant. Her lips were drawn in a tight line, and she did not look satisfied, as I had expected her to.

There was a high-pitched whirring noise, a flash of light, and then nothing.

I could feel my body, but I couldn't see. My world was completely enveloped in darkness. I was moving- I had to be- even though it felt like I was still sitting in the chair.

I tried not to be afraid of the unknown that I would undoubtedly soon be facing alone.

Back. I was going back to the past.

Acknowledgements

Wow! What an amazing journey the last year has been. I have experienced such support and encouragement from family, friends, and strangers alike. I would like to give an enormous thank you to everyone who has been involved in this process. Writing has been a lifelong dream and goal, and it has been so exciting to see my work come alive. To be able to share it with you all has been such a gift.

Mom, Nonni, Auntie Jen, Auntie Karen, Ashley and Maryellen: thank you all for your continuous love and support as I have worked on this second novel. You know that I could never do this without you.

Danny: thank you for riding the storm that is my writing, for being patient (in your own way) and giving me the space to create. I know that it is not always easy to come home to me when I am being a mad scientist at the laptop.

My sister, Maddie: your enthusiasm for my work is endless, and though I may not always show it, I know how lucky I am to have you on my team.

Stef: the most underappreciated makeup artist in the world. Thank you for your assistance in making this cover so unbelievably amazing. You truly have a gift for making people feel beautiful. Thank you for being such a great, patient friend.

Pat: thank you for having championed my writing for the past year. From an event in my honor, to an article on GoLocal, and all of the conversations in between. I appreciate the support immensely and look forward to returning the favor!

And finally, to all of the wonderful humans on this planet who stay peaceful when others are being reckless. Eventually good will triumph over evil.

About the Author

BRIANA SASSO teaches sixth grade in Worcester, Massachusetts, where she lives. She enjoys crafting, DIY projects, reading (especially about history), food, traveling, and spending time with family and friends. This is her second novel.

An excerpt from the author's first novel,

Elisabetta

Nonna

I was born in 1934 in Bisceglie, Italy, a poor fishing village right at the top of the heel of the boot. Though I didn't know it growing up, it was a place untouched by time, unblemished by the technology and luxuries that were in full swing in the States. Electricity and indoor plumbing didn't exist there yet. Roads were dirt. The stucco and brick buildings had been built so closely together that you couldn't imagine trying to fit a regular-sized car in between them down the cobblestone. There were still large, metal rings attached to all of the buildings to tie up the horses. Bicycles leaned up against sides of buildings and there were always people walking about. We were behind the times, but we still had a sense of community, a sense of belonging to one another.

Hugging the shoreline, the town thrived on its business from the port. Almost all of the men who didn't own a business were fishermen, relying on the ocean to keep their families fed. Every morning the men left early. Three, four, five in the morning. And they wouldn't come back until five or six at night, all the boats lining up in the harbor like little soldiers reporting for duty. The men always smelled like fish. We only bathed once, maybe twice, a week and they never could wash the stench away. I know because my father was a fisherman

We lived in a second floor, one room apartment in the oldest part of town. The building looked sturdy enough from the outside, but the stucco peeled and it always looked like it was leaning in towards the street. The ivy that crept up the walls looked like arms trying to stop it from crumbling. The apartment itself had no electricity, no running water. There were eight of us living in the one room that we used as a kitchen, bedroom, and living area. My parents, my five brothers and sisters, myself. When it was warm, we went outside when the sun came up and we didn't come back until the sun went down. When it was cold, we either still went outside or we drove each other crazy and our mother, too.

In the summertime, we would run around the streets of Bisceglie with all of the other children, playing in the piazza or going to the beach. There was no sand like the beaches you are used to. Instead, smooth white rocks packed on top of each other. We didn't have extra blankets to lie on, so our small bodies got used to the hot rocks against our skin. It wasn't easy to run or jump or play, so we always had skinned knees and bruises from tripping on the rocks. Still, the beach was a second home, a kingdom we could call our own all the warm months of the year. The men were busy working, and the women were busy taking care of the smaller children or the cleaning, so we older children were left to roam.

Bisceglie held a lot of history, always having been a busy hub for trade. Children used to be warned to stay away from the port, away from the pirates that might steal them away to a foreign land, never to be seen again. At one point, it was probably true. The buildings nearer the port still had holes from cannons being blasted into them. They were never repaired. People just continued to live there with gaping holes, a scar that was a reminder of just how long the buildings had been standing. And all that they could survive through.

It was a hot summer day, and a hot summer day in Bisceglie was like being on the equator. Unless you stayed in the ocean all day, there was no relief from the sweltering heat and humidity. The girls all wore the lightest of cotton dresses, and the boys left their shirts at home. Everyone walked barefoot. You had to save your shoes for the wet and the cold so they wouldn't get ruined too quickly. Plus, your feet just sweat when they were enclosed. The heat had stolen our energy, and we were all just wandering the streets at a snail's pace, too hot and too tired to chase after one another. It was a day when you would have to run across the beach to the ocean, or the rocks would burn sores onto your feet. That did happen sometimes.

I remember the distinct feeling of hair stuck to my face and neck. I kept trying to swipe it back into the rest of my hair, but living on the ocean meant there was always a breeze. It didn't cool you down, but it did make sure your hair matted to the sweat on your face. Normally the girls would walk the streets arm in arm, but today sticky skin against sticky skin was just too uncomfortable. I was walking next to my friend, Valentina, when I heard my name being shouted from somewhere in town. Everyone knew everyone else's kids, so it didn't even mean it was my own mother. And the women had voices so loud you could hear them call from far away. Maybe even from across the world.

That summer I was eleven years old, the oldest child in my family. The older I got, the more my mother would call me home early to help with some chore or another. Sometimes I didn't even get to go out. My mother said any real woman knew how to take care of a house, and it was about time I really learned. She said she had let me be a child for too long, and now I was becoming a lazy pig.

I almost ignored the yells for my name. I would pay for it later, but at least I would have the day to relax in the unrelenting sun with my friends. Too dutiful for my own good, I said ciao to Valentina and turned around back towards our little apartment. I took my time, somewhat because of the heat, somewhat because of my lack of desire to go home. A woman's voice kept yelling my name, but getting louder with each step I took in her direction.

"Elisabetta! Elisabetta, andiamo! Basta!" she shouted.

Yes, I'm coming, I'm hurrying, I thought to myself, irritated.

When I got to our street, I saw that my upstairs neighbor, Signora Sacco, was yelling from her balcony. After she spotted me, she said a few rude words about how slow and lazy I was, as was the custom for women to do for each other. It was as if insulting each other's children was proving what a good friend you were. Then she met me in my apartment.

When I opened the door, the air in the apartment was thick and heavy. We didn't have many windows to let any air in, not that there was much difference outside. But it was harder to breathe in the apartment, the walls trapping and storing the heat like it was making a collection. Signora Sacco waited, standing by one of the two beds we had, which was strangely occupied by my mother. The only time my mother was ever in bed was at night, and I wasn't even sure she was in it long then.

"Cosa di sbagliato?" I asked her. What was wrong with Mama?

She told me that Mama had collapsed, probably from the heat. Signora Sacco had found her on the floor when she came to get her for their daily trip to the outdoor market. She had helped her into bed and put a cold cloth on her forehead.

Mama lay in the bed with her eyes closed, face streaked in sweat. She was stripped down to her undergarments, something a modest woman never did during the daytime. The slip clung to her thin body like a second skin. When she was lying there, I could see the wrinkles in her face and where her skin had become a little looser from having babies. She was only thirty-two, but she was no longer vibrant and young. Time was not treating her kindly.

I wasn't really sure what I was supposed to be able to do for her. I thought she could just take a nap. Did Signora Sacco want me to sit there and watch her the whole time? I might as well still be outside, out of her space to let her rest. For sure, that's what she would've wanted.

Signora Sacco told me I had to go with her to the market to get food for tonight's dinner, and then cook it since Mama needed to stay in bed and rest. I knew better than to grumble about it, so I went along with her. She picked out the items I would need to make a simple sauce and some vegetables to go with the pasta.

"Anche un idiota puo cucinare questo," she told me. Even an idiot could cook this, meaning even I could cook it.

I carried the food back home and up the stairs, and I got the sauce cooking right away. The best sauce always simmered all day long. Then, I took the bucket for the water down to the well a couple of streets away and carried it back. It seemed to get heavier with each step. I had to stop a couple of times along the way because it was just too hot to be carrying a bucket of water.

By the time I got back upstairs to our apartment, Mama was awake and thirsty. It was a good thing I had gone to get water, because she would have never made it down to the well that day. Her voice sounded weak. It was as if the woman I had left earlier that morning had suddenly wilted away. Mama sounded as if she had been in bed for days, or maybe even weeks.

I got her a cup of water and tilted it to her lips slowly so that she could drink. A few minutes later, she fell back to sleep again.

I cooked dinner, and eventually Papa and everyone else came home, all surprised to see Mama in this condition. She had woken up a few more times, each time asking only for a drink of water before slipping back into her slumber.

I took care of cleaning up everyone's plates, sweeping the floor, preparing the little ones for bed. Papa went out to the tavern to drink limencello with his friends. I was already asleep by the time he got home and still asleep when he left for the boat.

When I woke up the next morning, Mama was still in bed. I shook her gently to wake her, to ask her if she had felt better. She opened her eyes and said something to me that I couldn't understand, her voice was too soft. I could tell she was frustrated with me when I asked her to repeat what she said. Finally she lifted up the sheet a little, a confused look falling upon her face. I pulled it back all the way to reveal that she had soiled herself.

At that moment, I remember feeling fear take me over from head to toe. In my eleven years of life, I didn't remember Mama ever being sick. She was always a strong, reliable fixture, unwavering in her ability to boss me around and scold me. Now she lay in her own urine and watery feces, and I was the only one who could help her. And I didn't know how. Maybe she was right. I had been a child too long. I instantly began to regret all the days I had spent lying on the beach and splashing in the ocean instead of learning how to be a woman.

"E bene, Mama," I said, trying to reassure her that it would be okay. She seemed like a child, weak and helpless.

I tried to get my thoughts together, to think of what to do first. I had to get her cleaned and the sheets cleaned, which meant several long trips to the well carrying buckets in the stifling heat. I was pretty sure that it was the only set of sheets that we had, so I would have to clean Mama and then put her back on an empty mattress while I cleaned the sheets.

I also had to wake up the other children and get them fed and out of the door so that I could do what I needed to do. I thought about going upstairs to enlist the help of Signora Sacco, but I knew that Mama would be mortified if anyone else saw her in this state.

I decided to pull the sheet back up over Mama so that the children wouldn't see, though the smell was starting to give her away. After waking everyone, I fed them quickly and shooed them out the door, telling them that Mama just wasn't feeling well and to leave her alone. Before he got away, I grabbed my oldest brother Giuseppe's arm, telling him that he needed to help me carry the buckets of water. It would be faster if I didn't have to do it myself.

He tried to shrug me off and tried to get away, but I boxed his ear as I had seen Mama do so many times and told him that Mama said he had to help. Reluctantly, he grabbed two of the buckets and I the other two, and we walked to the well to gather the water. As soon as we had carried them back to the house, I decided that it would have to be enough and I let him go outside with the others.

After dragging the tub next to Mama's bed, I warmed up the buckets of water on the stove and dumped them in, hoping it wouldn't be too hot. I stuck a foot in to test it. The water was warm, but not scalding. It would probably stay warm all day, as the heat hadn't lessened any overnight.

Mama was weak. She could barely hold herself up, and as she was much taller than me and heavier, I struggled trying to hold up her weight. I undressed her, trying to avoid the soiled parts of the garments. With much effort, I got her into the tub, but she swayed as she sat in the water, seemingly too dizzy to stay in one spot. I was worried that she would tip over in the water, but I had to get the dirty sheets off of the bed so that I would be able to put her back in it after.

The mattress was wet in places where the urine and diarrhea had soaked through the sheet. I puffed out a breath trying to blow the stray hairs out of my eyes. What could I use to clean the mattress?

I took an old moppine and a bar of soap and scrubbed the best I could, hoping the odor would at least be removed. Then I scrubbed at it with a dry towel, soaking up some of the moisture. It was the best I could do. With yet another cloth I tried to wash Mama, holding her up with my left arm and lathering her with my right.

When I was sure that I had at least washed where she used the bathroom on herself, I managed to stand her up and throw a towel on her. She sat swaying on the edge of the bed as I tried to get clean undergarments out of the one dresser we owned. I dressed her, and she kissed me on the cheek, her breath hot and stinking of sick and rot. Then, she leaned her head down and vomited all over my feet.

I was at least thankful that she managed to keep it off of herself now that she was clean.

Though the water was now murky and filthy, I stuck my feet in and washed them off. It was disgusting and I felt dirtier than ever before, but my job wasn't done, and I couldn't go walking around stinking like vomit.

I got Mama a drink of clean water from a separate jug that I had put aside and lay her back down. She fell asleep almost instantly. I needed to get more water to clean the sheets and Mama's clothes, but now I was on my own and the tub was full of water that I needed to get rid of. Thinking I would die myself if I had to carry the dirty water down in buckets and then carry clean water back up without my brother, I did the one thing that I could do.

There were two windows in our apartment. As they were both already wide open trying to let in any relief of a breeze, I stuck my head out and looked up and down our street. I didn't see anyone in sight. It took me a few minutes, but I pushed the tub over to the window, managing not to slosh the water all over the floor.

Luckily, the window was almost exactly level with the height of the tub. Using every ounce of strength that I had, I tipped the tub up towards the window, spilling the dirty water all over the street below. I heard it splashing against the cobblestone and hoped that no one would decide to walk by at that moment. I got almost every drop out, and collapsed on the floor, heaving with the effort it took to lift the tub. Again, I tried to brush the hair off of my sticky face and planned my next move.

I really didn't want to take two long trips to the well and back, carrying heavy buckets of water in hellish temperatures. Instead, I came up with the idea of carrying everything to the ocean to wash it there. I could go away from where I knew all of my friends and siblings would be and take the linens to the water, instead of the water to the linens. It seemed like the easiest solution, but then I thought of the salt that would cling to the sheets. There was no other real option except to carry those god awful buckets of water back and forth.

After taking a nice long drink of water, I grabbed the handles of two of the buckets and made my way to the well. I hauled up the water and rested before my trek back. It was only a few streets away, but it seemed like miles. I had to stop a few times to catch my breath and rest my arms; they felt like they were stretching with the weight of the buckets. I carried them upstairs and checked on Mama. She was still sleeping, her mouth hanging open, her breaths seeming ragged.

Resolving that there was nothing I could do for her at the moment, I set the two full buckets down and picked up two empty buckets. I made small talk with the other women at the well. They asked why I was getting the water, and I told them that Mama wasn't feeling well. They asked if there was anything they could do to help, as was traditional in our community. I told them no and struggled back to the apartment once again.

I was exhausted. I felt like I was baking both from the outside in and the inside out. It was still before noon and I was ready for bed, but I had so much to do still. I decided right then and there that being a woman was awful, terrible.

When I got the last two buckets upstairs, Mama had vomited again. I felt discouraged, but this time it was contained to her pillow. I took it away from her and put Papa's under her head, praying that she would stop spewing the contents of her stomach for just a while more.

I dumped all four of the buckets into the tub once again without bothering to warm them. It would take up valuable time and energy that I did not have to spend waiting. Plus, the water from the well wasn't cool, but it felt refreshing on my arms as I washed because it was cooler than the air around me.

Scrubbing at the sheets and Mama's underclothes, I hummed to myself. It was too quiet, the sounds of the town seeming distant and otherworldly. I got most of the stains out. It probably wasn't as good of a job as Mama would have done, but at least they were cleaner than before. I hung all the linens out to dry on the line that hung outside our second window. Then I check the street for activity, and dumped the water out of the window again. The water from the first time had long since dried in the sun.

Around eleven, there was a knock on the door and then Signora Sacco walked in. Knocks were more like a warning than an announcement at that time. It was to let you know the person was going to walk in, not to ask for permission. She saw that Mama was still in bed and asked me about her condition. I told her that I thought she was worse, leaving out the specific details about the bed. Signora Sacco, eyeing the tub in the middle of the room and the laundry on the line, probably deduced the situation without me telling her. She offered to go to the butcher and market for me so that I could stay by Mama's side and care for her.

I was truly thankful, as I didn't think I could walk carrying anything more that day. Signora Sacco left with the money that I had given her, and I pulled a chair over to Mama's bedside. I felt her forehead with the back of my hand. It felt like I could cook something on her face. She looked almost lifeless except for the rise and fall of her chest. I decided to hold an empty bucket in my lap, just in case Mama started throwing up again. I didn't know how she had anything left to get out. She hadn't eaten in almost two days, and she drank little when she was awake.

We sat like that all day, only interrupted by Signora Sacco coming back with the ingredients for the meal I would cook and my daydreaming about what my friends were doing at the beach. Mama got sick a couple more times; I managed somehow to catch it in the bucket, preventing any more washing for the time being. When she woke up, I made her use the bedpan. Everything came out liquid. She drank more water with me encouraging her to take in more than she actually wanted to. Then, she went back to sleep.

Later that afternoon, Papa and the kids came home, only the kids seeming concerned about Mama being sick. I cooked the meat and vegetables and served it to my family, checking on Mama in between. Before Papa went to the tavern, I saw him go over to Mama and brush a piece of hair away from her face and kiss her on the forehead. It was one of the rare instances that I had ever seen my father show my mother affection, but then he ended up leaving anyway. When I put the kids to bed, they all said goodnight to Mama even though she wasn't awake to hear them.

I tried to stay up as late in the night as I could to take care of her, but I was exhausted from the events of the day combined with the unrelenting heat. Eventually, I gave in and went to sleep with the kids on the other side of the room. I collapsed and fell into a very deep sleep.

When I awoke in the morning, the first thing I did was check on Mama. I knew from the moment I stood up and began to creep towards her bed that something wasn't right. She was too still, too stiff. Her chest didn't go up and down. When I got closer, I saw that there was a line of congealed vomit that trailed out of the corner of her mouth. Her mouth held a pool of it, too.

Mama had choked on her own vomit in the middle of the night, either after Papa had left for the boat, or he was too drunk to hear her choke when he was next to her. I remember my hand going to my own mouth, running over to the bucket to vomit myself. I was shaking and crying quietly. The other children were still sleeping, and I was alone with my dead mother, not knowing what to do next.

Mama was right. I had been a child for too long, and now I didn't know how to be the woman of the house.

Made in the USA
Middletown, DE
18 May 2015